LAKE OF HEAVEN

AsiaWorld

Series Editor: Mark Selden

This series charts the frontiers of Asia in global perspective. Central to its concerns are Asian interactions—political, economic, social, cultural, and historical—that are transnational and global, that cross and redefine borders and networks, including those of nation, region, ethnicity, gender, technology, and demography. It looks to multiple methodologies to chart the dynamics of a region that has been the home to major civilizations and is central to global processes of war, peace, and development in the new millennium.

Titles in the Series

LAKE OF HEAVEN

*An original translation of the Japanese
novel by Ishimure Michiko*

TRANSLATED BY
BRUCE ALLEN

LEXINGTON BOOKS

A division of
ROWMAN & LITTLEFIELD PUBLISHERS, INC.
Lanham • Boulder • New York • Toronto • Plymouth, UK

LEXINGTON BOOKS

A division of Rowman & Littlefield Publishers, Inc.
A wholly owned subsidary of The Rowman & Littlefield Publishing Group, Inc.
4501 Forbes Boulevard, Suite 200
Lanham, MD 20706

Estover Road
Plymouth PL6 7PY
United Kingdom

British Library Cataloguing in Publication Information Available

Library of Congress Cataloging-in-Publication Data
Ishimure, Michiko, 1927–
    [Tenko. English]
    Lake of heaven : an original translation of the Japanese novel / by Ishimure
Michiko ; translated by Bruce Allen.
        p. cm.
    ISBN-13: 978-0-7391-2462-8 (cloth : alk. paper)
    ISBN-10: 0-7391-2462-5 (cloth : alk. paper)
    ISBN-13: 978-0-7391-2463-5 (pbk. : alk. paper)
    ISBN-10: 0-7391-2463-3 (pbk. : alk. paper)
    ISBN-13: 978-0-7391-3137-4 (electronic)
    ISBN-10: 0-7391-3137-0 (electronic)
    [etc.]
    I. Allen, Bruce, 1949- II. Title.
    PL853.S535T4613 2008
    895.6'35—dc22   2008029546

Printed in the United States of America

♾™ The paper used in this publication meets the minimum requirements of
American National Standard for Information Sciences—Permanence of Paper
for Printed Library Materials, ANSI/NISO Z39.48–1992.

CONTENTS

TRANSLATOR'S INTRODUCTION

I shimure Michiko[1] was born in 1927 on Amakusa Island off the coast of Kyushu, the southernmost of the four main Japanese islands. At the age of three months she moved with her family across the bay of the Shiranui Sea to the small nearby city of Minamata on Kyushu, where she spent her childhood and much of her adult life. Her father worked as a stonemason and she and her family lived in close contact with fishermen and farmers. Ishimure grew up in a closely knit community, steeped in traditional customs and culture. She loved to explore and play in the fields and hills and to listen to and take part in the local stories, songs, dances, and festivals. Ishimure's childhood presented her with two strongly contrasting realities. One was the beauty and wonder of the natural world. The Minamata of her childhood was dominated by green mountains, forests, fields, and farms and the beautiful coast of the Shiranui Sea. The other reality was the growing presence of industrial society. Minamata gradually evolved from a traditional fishing-farming area to an industrial city, centered around the operations of the Chisso Corporation, which produced fertilizers and a range of electrochemical products. Chisso prospered and become a leading *zaibatsu* conglomerate;

at its peak it ranked as the third largest manufacturer in Japan.[2] Proud to be part of the industrial-technological process of modernization, for a long time most Minamata residents were unaware of, or overlooked, the adverse effects that the industrial process was inflicting on their culture and environment. But by the 1960s it became undeniably clear that something had gone gravely wrong with their human and natural environment. Ishimure was one of the first to notice the warning signs, to investigate, and to speak out about the problems. Her investigative work led to the exposing of what has been called "the single worst long-term, man-made industrial disaster in history."[3] The organic mercury-laden waste products released into the Minamata bay by the factory had poisoned the sea and all who ate from it.

These contrasting experiences of beauty and sorrow in the face of natural and man-made environments provided the raw materials that inspired Ishimure's work as a writer and as an activist for environmental and social causes. They shaped her commitment as a writer of place; one who has remained steadfastly devoted to recording and re-telling the local stories of the people of her home area as they have struggled against the degradation of their natural environment and the interrelated degradation of their community and culture.

Ishimure initially became well known following the publication of her documentary novel *Paradise in the Sea of Sorrow: Our Minamata Disease* (1972),[4] noted for its activist impact as well as the beauty of its literary style. The work's title highlights the contrast between the former abundance and the later destruction of the natural and human environments around Minamata. *Paradise in the Sea of Sorrow* served as a wake-up call to the world regarding the dangers of industrial pollution. The work quickly became a bestseller and has now gone through more than thirty reprintings. Due to its tremendous impact, Ishimure is widely regarded as a founder of the environmental movement in Japan and she has been called the "Rachel Carson of Japan." Since completing this work, Ishimure has published over forty volumes in a wide range of genres, including several novels, works of historical and documentary fiction, autobiographical memoirs, children's books, essay collections, poetry, and a Noh drama. A scholarly seventeen-volume collection of her complete works is now in publication. Ishimure has been awarded numerous literary prizes internationally and in her own country, including the prestigious Asahi Prize in 2002.

Ishimure has described herself as "just a housewife," and speaks of preferring to avoid the public limelight and involvement in big city literary and social movements. Despite her wishes for a simpler, more private life, however, the tragic events of Minamata pushed her into accepting the role of a leading activist in the struggle to gain recognition, reconciliation, and recovery for the Minamata victims. She was a founding member of several leading activist groups in the 1950s and 1960s, including the Citizens' Council for Minamata Disease, the Minamata Disease Research Group, and the Shiranui Sea Interdisciplinary Research Association. She has continued to be a leading figure in the ongoing struggle to settle the political, social, and spiritual problems surrounding the Minamata Disease problem; a process that has now continued for more than fifty years since the first public recognition of the disease.

Although Ishimure became identified as an environmental writer early in her career and her work clearly suggests the need for political and economic change, her wider concern has been for revitalizing human culture and community life by drawing on the rich local traditions of stories, dances, music, ceremonies, and spirituality. The starting point in this process, she suggests, is the developing of a deeper awareness of the natural world. This awareness can effect a change of spirit such that we may learn to live in closer harmony with our environment—used in the widest sense of the word. This concern for human culture, and its connection to the natural environment, is a central concern of her novel *Lake of Heaven* (1997).[5]

Lake of Heaven is a work of fiction, but it is firmly rooted in Ishimure's conversations with real people from the mountains of Kyushu who became victims of environmental and cultural disruption when their village was sunk in the process of dam construction. The theme of environmental destruction and the related questions of how to restore what has been lost in the process of modernization connects this work to themes and narrative methods Ishimure employed in *Paradise in the Sea of Sorrow*. In *Lake of Heaven*, however, her focus is more directly on the world of storytelling, myths, songs, and local culture. Never opting for merely romantic, nostalgic accounts of past history, Ishimure grounds her imagination in the bitter realities of class conflict, exploitation, and human greed. Yet her attention to the redemptive power of dreams and culture provides hope for a possible restoring of culture and environment.

Lake of Heaven may be roughly classified as a novel, yet its narrative style and poetic imagination are based in a mythopoetic imagination steeped in the world of Noh drama and local tales of the supernatural rooted in traditional Shinto and Buddhist lore. Yet Ishimure's tales do not remain focused only on the world of the rural past. The narrative often leaps to considerations of contemporary urban life and to the complexities that arise as we try to reconcile the frictions between traditional and modern, and rural and urban identities. Ishimure narrates the stories in *Lake of Heaven* with a circular conception of time in which the episodes are recursive, sometimes fragmentary, but ultimately interwoven. This narrative style often involves a quality of multi-dimensionality regarding people, places, and times. These elements are allowed to overlap and suggest new connections. Gary Snyder has described *Lake of Heaven* as "a remarkable text of mythopoetic quality—with a Noh flavor—that presents much of the ancient lore of Japan and the lore of the spirit world—and is in a way a kind of myth-drama, not a novel." The story becomes a parable for the larger world "in which all of our old cultures and all of our old villages are becoming buried, sunken, and lost under the rising waters of the dams of industrialization and globalization."[6]

Ishimure is a storyteller at heart and *Lake of Heaven* represents her ongoing attempt to revive the spirit of storytelling in modern culture. Fundamental to this attempt is her hope to bring about a renewed attention to the "world of sounds" and, with this, to the *kotodama*—a traditional Japanese literary term that translates literally as "word spirit." Ishimure suggests that the common language of people in traditional cultures once possessed a far greater sensitivity to this world of sounds and *kotodama*. Thus she gives great attention to the local dialect of the villagers in her stories and the way their language shapes their connections to and awareness of the world. This awareness is not an intellectually generated, but a culturally transmitted one; one which is in need of continual creative renewal.

As a supporting step toward reviving language and culture she insists that we need to notice the subtle signs (*kehai*) of nature that are all about us in our daily lives—even in the city. These signs are readily available, but most of us have lost the ability to notice them. She shows how this loss of sensitivity becomes a fundamental cause of our loss of respect for the environment and, in turn, precedes our political social and economic problems. By providing both a hard look at the destructive tendencies of modern society and a vision of the possibilities for a revival of culture, Ishimure gives readers a realistic and poetically inspired lens through which to view our future.

Several years ago when I visited Ishimure-san in Kyushu we talked about her life with stories. She admitted that the power of her stories to change society is, "quite frankly, very slight" in the face of the tough realities we face. Yet she maintained an ultimate faith in the necessity of telling and creating new stories. Her admission that this power often seems slight, forcefully reminded me of a haiku by Kobayashi Issa, written after the death of his infant daughter:

This world of dew
is but the world of dew
and yet . . . and yet . . .

It is this eternal "and yet . . ." which represents the ongoing hope that very slight things, stories, and dreams may continue to sustain and change the world.

More recently, I joined Ishimure-san and a group of her friends on an early summer trip to the countryside. We were hosted by a local potter who lives in an old traditionally built home at the foot of the Kyushu Mountains. As we talked over dinner we shared our own stories and spoke of the affairs of the world. Then we got up for a walk outside, into the gathering darkness, along a deep streambed cut into a ravine. Fireflies appeared and flashed their light trails across the black ravine. Overhead, a comet glowed in a deep indigo sky. The place, people, and talk suggested the revitalization of communities and the natural world. At the end of the evening, we climbed into taxies and headed back to our lives in the city. Yet the memory remains. The power of stories and dreams remains elusive and endangered . . . and yet . . . and yet . . .

NOTES

1. Ishimure's name is written in Japanese order, with surname first, followed by the given name.

2. Timothy S. George, *Minamata: Pollution and the Struggle for Democracy in Postwar Japan*. Cambridge: Harvard University Press, 2001, p. 17.

3. Ibid.

4. *Paradise in the Sea of Sorrow* is available in English, translated by Livia Monnet, Ann Arbor: Center for Japanese Studies, University of Michigan, 2003. The original Japanese edition, *Kugai Jodo: Waga Minamata-byo,* was published by Kodansha, Tokyo, 1972.

5. The original Japanese edition of *Lake of Heaven (Tenko)* was published by Mainichi Shimbun Sha, Tokyo, 1997.

6. Personal communication.

ACKNOWLEDGMENTS

This translation is the result of a community of support, starting with that of Ishimure Michiko. Major reader-advisor-supporters included Yumi, Mark, and Kyoko Selden, Gary Snyder, Yuki Masami, Noda Kenichi, Yuko and Naomi Aihara, Miura Shoko, Livia Monnet, Karen Colligan-Taylor, Akamine Reiko, and Yamashiro Shin. The translation project was initiated by a request from the US and Japanese branches of the Association for the Study of Literature and Environment (ASLE) at the international symposium held in Hawaii in 1996. Among the ASLE members who helped support the project are Scott Slovic, Noda Kenichi, Yamazato Katsunori, and Ikuta Shogo. Members of the Ishimure study group in Kumamoto, including Iwaoka Nakamasa, Watanabe Kyoji, and Yamamoto Tetsuro provided local community support. Juntendo University generously provided research funding assistance. Lexington Books made the publication possible. My wife, Mitsue, has been my overall supporter in all aspects of the project. To all these people and groups, and to others not mentioned who have helped, I express my deep gratitude. This translation is dedicated to my parents, Barbara and Henry.

①

BIRDS LEAVING

Ohina wiped on the front of her kimono the early season persimmon she had just picked up, and bit into it. It was still bitter, as she'd suspected.

Some of her teeth were still strong. A hint of sweetness trickled down the back of her throat as she munched on the unripe fruit and swallowed. Probably it would have been ripe in another few days. For a moment she hesitated. If she went ahead and ate the whole thing it might give her indigestion. And so, remembering that she still had one more left, she tossed the persimmon into the thicket of grass.

As she bent over, the other persimmon rolled out of the fold in her kimono. She reached for the fruit and placed it within her sleeve so it wouldn't slip out this time. From what she'd seen, it looked like there wouldn't be many fallen persimmons this year. She tilted her hat back and looked up at the treetops. Since she had to squint, it was hard to tell how much fruit was up there.

Three days ago a typhoon had blown through. Judging from all the broken branches that lay scattered about in the bushes, she could imagine how strong the winds must have been. So, she thought, it looks like a lot of persimmons must have rolled down to the bottom of Utazaka Hill. Ohina gazed for a while at the surface of the lake and then muttered to herself.

"Where that red dragonfly just disappeared is where the old straw sandal shop used to be."

After typhoons, persimmons used to be set out in front of that sandal shop, ripening on trays. Some would still be green, while others showed some color of ripening.

"They get those Utazaka persimmons for free, you know," the villagers would note.

It was said that the Utazaka persimmon tree had stood there for six hundred years. At the time of the O-bon festival the fruit sweetened up. It was such a huge tree that not many people were able to climb it. When the season came Ohina's eldest son, Yukihito, would be called by the children. No one could blame them for taking the fruit since it came from the village's common ground. But people warned that if you fell from the tree you could lose your life. Even though its limbs were big, their connections to the trunk were brittle, and even if you hooked a leg over a branch and hung on, the branch could snap and break. Yukihito would cling to the trunk holding on with one hand and with the other hand using a pole he'd pry off the persimmons. He managed to drop the fruit into the thicket of grass in such a way that few were bruised and he never injured himself, even once.

On mornings after a typhoon the early comers could easily pick up twenty or more fallen persimmons from the broken branches strewn about. The area where they fell was so wide that some might roll all the way down the hill as far as the front of the Kannon statue. But now the statue too lies submerged beneath the water.

Utazaka Hill could easily be seen from everywhere in the village. And since everything that entered the town—whether for good or for bad—came by way of Utazaka, the villagers were in the habit of looking up to it from time to time during the day from their fields and mountain huts. When traveling entertainers came into town their arrival was soon known to all. The performers too were aware of this, and so when they reached this hill they would start dancing and playing on their samisens and hand drums as they came down into the village. And at times when the villagers sent off soldiers, people would walk along, plucking at a samisen as they went. When Ohina's husband Tetsutaro had sent her a letter from the battlefront she had asked the postman to read it for her:

This world is so incredibly huge. Unless you see it for yourself you can never imagine it.

For a short while he had looked around at this world he had written about. Yet this man who had crossed over the mountain pass was never to make it home again. And Yukihito too had crossed the mountain path, never to return.

For Ohina, Utazaka had become the passageway to the lost village. When she had come here three years ago, even though the mugwort and bamboo had grown up above the height of the old stone pillar of the travelers' guardian deity, she'd still been able to see the place. But this year she was just barely able to locate it. The area had become so overgrown with kudzu vines that she couldn't easily find the old stone figures. She was glad she'd brought along her sickle. She had bought the sickle a long time ago at the old straw sandal shop. After moving down to the outskirts of the town she hardly used it any more. There were no tools in the house her daughter Omomo had built and when Ohina had left the old village about the only thing she had taken with her was the sickle. Ohina knew better than to mention to her daughter that their house had only one window in it.

"At least it doesn't leak when it rains, and we've got three tatami mats, so even if Yukihito comes back we'll still have one mat each to sleep on," was the way Omomo spoke of it.

But even if it was just a cheap little plywood shack, as long as they weren't chased away, it was theirs. Since it was on a riverbank, they didn't have to pay rent for the land. The sickle was always hanging from the wall of the shack. Omomo, who had hardly even been able to attend school, had managed to build this little place above the river just outside of town. But there were times when Ohina would come back after trying to sell her *hyakumeigan*—the traditional "hundred lives tablet" medicine she made from poison snakes—and find that Omomo had locked the door from the inside and wouldn't appear.

Still sleeping, Ohina would think to herself, but she couldn't really say much about it.

"Would you bring me the sickle? The sickle. It's hanging on the wall."

Saying this in a voice louder than usual, Ohina went around to the window that faced the river. She made tapping sounds beneath it. The shutter opened and with a thud the sickle dropped.

"Some driftwood's washed up. I'll go and bundle it up."

With just the sickle she could go to the river and cut kindling and kudzu vines and make them into bundles. In barley and rice harvesting time she could go out and earn a living. And with her woman's hands she could catch poison snakes. Ohina was said to be an expert at catching snakes, and yet she was still unable to earn enough to pay back the money Omomo had borrowed. Back when the old village was sunk to build the dam, the relocation settlement money had disappeared with Ohina's eldest son Yukihito.

"We're so deep in debt we can't even celebrate O-bon or the New Year's festival. You can send my regards to Father at his grave."

It was these words from her daughter that had hurt Ohina the most. When Omomo saw the reaction on her mother's face it must have made her think a bit, for this year she said to her mother, "I can't go myself, but since it's been three years, I'll buy some lanterns for the O-bon festival. If you hang them from a branch on Utazaka Hill they'll be visible from the bottom of the lake."

In any case, she had bought three small red lanterns, of the sort children might have, to take to the graves.

"The wind at the top of the hill is strong, but with this hat you should be all right."

And saying this, Omomo had given her mother a hat she'd picked up somewhere, along with the lanterns.

"Well—it looks like you've bought me a dancer's hat. The hat's not bad, but with this red chin cord, won't it make me look too young?"

"It'll be all right. Father was young when he died, wasn't he?"

Omomo had said this without cracking a smile. When Ohina realized she'd forgotten the sickle she went back to the house and found herself locked out again. She guessed there must be someone else in there with her and told herself this was probably because Omomo worked nights, but still it left her with a bad feeling. She opened the pack she'd carried on her back. Inside were some brown sugar O-bon cakes, some incense, and the paper lanterns with candles. When Omomo was a child, Ohina had always bought her one of these grave lanterns and let her take it with her when they went to visit the grave. One year Omomo had asked, "Where's Father's grave?"

"Over there, at the bottom of the lake."

Omomo gazed into the water for a while and then looked up with a puzzled expression.

Thinking back on this, she wondered if Omomo thought these children's lanterns were the ones to be used for O-bon. In any case, they were the very cheapest of lanterns.

Ohina wondered what branch to hang them from. It had to be one she could reach, but lanterns in mid-day without burning candles just didn't seem right and fretting about it left her tired out. Her waist and ankles felt strained and since they were starting to throb she lay down on the top of a bundle of grass she had cut. Soon she fell into a dream. At the bottom of the dammed-up lake the petals of a weeping cherry tree were swirling about wildly—like in one of those miniature water-filled globes. And then night fell on the bottom of the lake.

"You must have come from Oki no Miya, the Palace of the Sea. It must be a very long way from here."

When Ohina said this, the weeping cherry just stood there and shook its countless branches, setting loose a flurry of petals all around.

"It must be painful, not being able to say anything."

Ohina started to speak again, but she too became sad and looked as if she was on the verge of tears. Then, distinctly she heard the voice of Omomo ask,

"How can I get to Oki no Miya? I can't find the way through the thick concrete of the dam. Come, show me."

At that point her breast heaved and she woke up. Her hands, legs, back, and all her muscles hurt. Beside her was a *sarusuberi* tree, its branches smooth and slippery. Still hazy from sleep, Ohina blinked her eyes open. Grabbing on to a branch and pulling herself up she muttered, "I wish this water would dry up. If it were gone I could see the original pathways."

At the bottom of the lake, the large rounded shape of a hill was dimly visible. Along it some big pagoda trees, chestnut trees, and hemlocks were standing in the water, all bared of their leaves.

Why was it that in my dream I saw that weeping cherry tree with its petals swirling about in the water? It wasn't one of those scene-in-a-bottle toys they used to sell to children at the nighttime stands in town. That ancient weeping cherry from Oki no Miya had become the tree whose petals were swirling about in the water. If possible, Ohina wished she could have shown the townspeople the old cherry she had just seen—but she had just heard Omomo say that the road to Oki no Miya had become lost.

No doubt even now that sacred old cherry tree still exists in the world of Amazoko Village, but it must have come on hard times since it was sunk to the bottom of the lake. Every year the villagers used to watch it blossom. But just now, I was the only one who saw it—alone, without a witness. It looks like the spirit of this cherry tree has come to depend on me, showing itself in the water like it's squeezing its body and spirit together and trying to say something.

The little *sarusuberi* tree shook when Ohina grabbed it to pull herself up. It looked as if thin petals were fluttering gently toward her from the tips of the branches, carried along by the river breeze blowing up from the base of the dam. She was overcome with a strange unfathomable sorrow mixed with anger. It left her feeling as if her hair was standing up and streaming wildly in the wind—if someone should see me now they'd probably run away in fright, taking me for an avenging ghost or some such creature. Her hands trembling, Ohina stroked her breast to calm herself. Then, clutching at a branch of the tree, she sat down and soon drifted off into sleep again.

The next thing she knew, she was crawling along the shore of the lake and sniffing at the mirrored surface of the water. The water had a hard taste. You couldn't call it the taste of fresh water. Neither the land of the mountains, nor the roots of the trees, nor the water, nor the sunken village had been properly mixed yet. But it was no use fretting about this now; she had come to visit the grave. Remembering this, her first thought was to pour some water on the gravestone. And so, with both hands she stroked the water of the lake and reached toward the bottom. Respectfully, she repeated this motion three times.

Gazing into the depths of the water, she saw a mound of earth from the mountains gathering up and spreading out, supporting a thicket of wild grapes. Visions of piles of rotting leaves with white fungus glared out at her like successive images cast upon a screen in the back of her eyelids. The smells of mushrooms filled her nose. Wild young monkeys pranced about on piles of decaying leaves and dirt. Without a sound, they danced nimbly about the *saseppo* and *tabi* trees and bit into the small fruit from the trees, staring into Ohina's eyes from time to time.

Their eyes looked innocent to Ohina, as if they were drunk on liquor. How lovely. She realized she was being revived, little by little. From deep in her heart a sinking voice called out.

For the weeping cherry of Amazoko to return to life, these water jugs must dry up completely once, and the ground must become dry and smooth. And the birds must carry seeds and drop them there. And the gentle rains of the most ancient of times must fall like the rains of the Tanabata festival on even the people who cannot hear the voices of the rains. And the buds of grasses and trees must push their way out like the first sprouts that came into the world.

As she listened to this inner voice, Ohina saw her own face sinking into the depths of the water along with the fallen leaves. How strange. She hadn't seen herself in a mirror in ages. Now, with the red cord tied on her hat, it seemed rather embarrassing.

Years ago when I was young there was a night I danced with a hat like this covering my face. It was in a garden, after a funeral. I danced barefoot with all my heart to the voices of the men as they sang. After funerals families would put out five different kinds of liquor and, little by little, they'd serve it to the dancers. There was wild grape wine and chestnut sake, and *kuma shochu*, and the red peach wine that's made in the rainy season. And there was apricot wine too. "Those are wines for the deceased—so drink it little by little." And so, drinking like that, it was as if the body had slipped away from itself and become spirit, and as if this world and the world beyond had become one. And the lanterns were so beautiful. Where has all of this gone now?

Ohina tried waving her sleeve in the motion of the dance. A small leaf of bush clover fluttered down on her white O-bon *yukata* robe.

In the water it looked as if a red newt were slowly waving its body about. An illusion of the eyes, it was actually her chinstrap, moving as she talked to herself. For a moment Ohina felt as if she were crawling toward the bottom of the water where Amazoko lay. The vision of the red newt was already leading Ohina on.

At the back of the old Silk Estate there was a stream that flowed from a well. Ohina had been about sixteen years old when she was first employed in the service of that household. She had no mirror of her own. When she washed rice she would use the water as a mirror in combing her hair. A newt was always there, showing its red belly, crawling slowly along the wall and walking through the water. One afternoon while she was putting up her hair there had appeared, reflected from behind, the face of Masahito, the eldest son of the household. Startled, she turned around and when she saw his long legs there so close to her she had dropped the comb from her hand and it fell into the water. With his legs straddled over her, Masahito had picked up the comb floating in the stream and wiped it off on the knee of his pants.

"Sorry, I'm sorry. Did I surprise you? Could I have some water?" he asked, and then handed the comb back.

If he'd needed water, there was a dipper on the edge of the well right behind him. Anyone could drink from it at any time. And after all, it was the well at Masahito's own home, wasn't it? Why then, just at that time, did he ask me to give him some water? He was four years older than I and was going to school off in Kumamoto, so he only got back at times such as when the peach trees were in blossom, or during the O-bon Festival. Probably that time they met had been during his spring vacation. His pants had been black. That was long, long ago.

"Excuse me ma'am. Hello . . ."

To Ohina's surprise, a voice called out to her from behind. She had been so absorbed in her thoughts while gazing into the water that when she tried to rise she cried out "ouch!" from the pain in her knees and paused halfway, bent over. A young man was standing there holding some pinks and *jorobana* flowers. He was wearing a straw hat and carrying something on his back.

"Sorry. I guess I surprised you."

It was a young voice. In the backlighting it was hard to make out the face. The young man took off his hat, lowered his head, and wiped off the sweat with a handkerchief.

"Hey—you startled me."

Ohina cut her words short and scrutinized him carefully. Then, after a pause, she asked in a husky voice, "Could it possibly be? No, it couldn't. And yet . . . Masahito? Why yes, it's Masahito after all."

The young man's face expressed surprise, yet he smiled with pleasure.

"Excuse me ma'am, Masahito was my grandfather. I'm his grandson."

Ohina caught her breath.

"Masahito—your grandfather? . . . But yes, your voice is similar too."

Ohina had been standing in the water when she said this, but then she got out, reached out a hand, and looked for a tree to hold on to. The young man pointed toward the lake and asked, "Are you from this village? Did you know Masahito?"

A strong smell of grasses filled the air. Perhaps stopping some train of thought, Ohina gave her head a shake.

"When I saw you there it looked as if some pilgrim was drowning herself in the lake. I was worried. I've been watching you for a while."

Ohina now noticed the flowers for O-bon he was holding.

"Did you, by chance, come to visit a grave yourself?"

"Yes. Today is the sixteenth. I finally made it here."

When it had been decided that the village was to be flooded in order to make a dam, there had been three families who hadn't been able to dig up their graves and move them. Ohina was a widow and she had known that her family had no savings. When they received the relocation compensation payment from the government, the money was swindled from her eldest son Yukihito by a certain merchant who often came to the village, and so she'd ended up without even a new address to move to. When the other villagers heard that she couldn't even afford to move the graves they had sighed with regret, but they too had no money to spare.

And there were a number of rumors about what had happened to the Silk Estate. One story had it that the relatives of Masahito's stepmother had split up the settlement money amongst themselves. Another was that Masahito had sunk all of his fortune into investments in Osaka and when this had failed he had tried to break up the old estate of 300 years standing and sell it off to the people in town who had some money but had been unable to find buyers.

"Masahito's grandson! *Yume no gotaru!*—it's like a dream!" exclaimed Ohina.

Gotaru, gotaru, as Grandfather used to say too, he thought. Remembering, the young man rather endearingly laughed aloud.

"Ah—just like Masahito!"

The young man could see Ohina's mouth moving, but he couldn't make out what she was saying.

He felt as if he were looking at one of those women from the old days he'd seen in the illustrations in old novels—a woman wearing a hat, looking off into the distance—and yet she was just an old country woman.

I thought she was about to drown herself, but I guess I was jumping to conclusions—he thought to himself.

A crimson column of dragonflies, looking as if it had been sucked out into the middle of the lake, floated back into sight and drifted between the two people like shimmering water. Kneeling, Ohina grabbed a thin branch of the *sarusuberi* tree, raised her heavy eyelids, and looked up at the young man. Then, her eyes suddenly lit up, she spoke.

"So Masahito too has come back to Utazaka."

"Masahito's my grandfather—my *grandfather*."

Since he was speaking to an older person, he repeated the same words slowly.

"Ah, your grandfather . . . So you made it here on the sixteenth day of O-bon. Good things always come in by way of Utazaka Hill."

The young man had begun to think this old woman was somewhat strange, but he recalled having heard of Utazaka. His grandfather had spoken of it from time to time.

"Now it's at the bottom of the lake, but if you look down from the top of Utazaka Hill you can see the weeping cherry tree of Oki no Miya. You'll never find a cherry like that in Tokyo. When it's in full blossom, even if there's no moon, its flowers are still bright. It's the marker of the village. Poor way-farers often used to come here as a place to die. Beneath that cherry there's a spring-fed stream that's good for sending off dead souls. It was a village where beggars and down-and-out folks often came. You could say those folks were also guests of the village."

Fondly, Masahiko's grandfather had told him stories of how the village children had gotten on with those poor visitors. Likely his grandfather too had hoped to return in his last years to this "village where beggars often come."

"So this is Utazaka Hill?"

"Right. The slope of Utazaka runs from here down into the water. And from where you're standing now, look, behind you there's a big persimmon tree, isn't there? The fruit is already ripening."

Saying this, Ohina rummaged about in the sleeve of her kimono.

"Hmm, I picked one up and put it in here a while ago— where could it have gone? Did it roll down the hill? I bet it would have been a sweet one too."

Muttering pitifully to herself, she glanced at the young man. The bottom of her *yukata* sleeve was wet. A while back when she had been reaching into the water and gotten her sleeves soaked he had mistaken her for someone trying to drown herself in the lake. Perhaps looking for the persimmon she had dropped, Ohina stared for a while at the bottom of the water. Then, perhaps remembering what she had been asked, she shook the branch of the *sarusuberi* tree covered with red flowers. Finally, she pointed with a finger of her free hand.

"From below where you're standing now the hill continues on down into the water. You see?—all the way down there. And can you see how, in the deep part, there's a bent-over tree, and how the slope also bends there? That sunken roadway is where Utazaka begins. You haven't forgotten, have you? Well, you haven't been back for a long while. It's changed a lot, don't you think? It's been many years since it was flooded."

The young man didn't quite know what to think, being asked if he had forgotten the road to the village. He'd come here looking for the place called Utazaka and had met this old woman who seemed to be from the old village. So as not to be mistaken for his grandfather, he said his name.

"Ah, excuse me ma'am."

"Yes?"

"My name is Masahiko."

"What?—Masahiko? You mean to tell me you're not Masahito?"

"No, I'm not Masahito. I'm his grandson, *Masahiko*."

"Masahiko, is it? Well, you shouldn't try to deceive people about names. That guy who ran off with the compensation money, he used a fake name."

Masahiko guessed that this settlement money probably referred to money given out when the town was flooded. He had heard that his grandfather had also had a long, difficult time about it. But that was long before he was born.

"Since the old times they've always said you have to be careful about Utazaka. All sorts of creatures are there to bewitch you. And where did you say you come from?"

"I'm from Tokyo. Tokyo."

"Hmm. You look just like Masahito. Maybe you're one of those black badgers from Jogahara—taking me for a lone woman up here."

"Please ma'am."

"Ah, that's right, Jogahara is also on the bottom of the lake now. You must have been lonely and wanted to see some humans again. Up from the bottom of the lake."

"Up from the bottom of the lake? Me—a black badger?"

The two stared at each other for a while. Then, his eyes expressing delight, Masahiko looked up and tossed the pinks and *jorobana* flowers into the air. The wildflowers, like golden grains of millet, scattered their pollen in the air, painting an arc across the surface of the water as they fell.

"Well all right then—let's suppose I *am* a badger from Jogahara, then what're you going to do?"

Quietly, Ohina drew the paper bag of O-bon sweets toward her and groped about with her hand, searching for the sickle. A while ago, after she had cut and cleared the bramble thicket she had hung the sickle on the *toge* tree—but just where it was she'd put it, she couldn't quite recall. Her face took on a puzzled expression—like that of a monkey separated from its band.

"You know, I've heard of Jogahara. My grandfather told me that in summer it used to be filled with day lilies in bloom. If you don't mind, could I ask how you know Masahito?"

"How? Well, I used to be in service at the old estate. And Masahiko, is he getting along well?"

"My grandfather . . . well, actually, he died. It was last year, after the O-bon festival."

Ohina raised her hand that had been searching through the grass. She reached for the sky as if trying to grasp for a time that had vanished.

"So then, it's as I thought. I suspected I'd never get to see him again. It's just as I expected."

The hat tipped forward, hiding her face. Behind her the leaves of a dense thicket of kudzu vines were trembling along with the motion of her hat.

Masahiko stood there for a moment, dumbfounded, watching the old woman, a stranger, who had dropped down overcome in the thicket of grass. He'd met her at the top of the mountain by the lake and while they had barely exchanged names, all of a sudden she had confounded him by calling him a badger. After all this was the real countryside—in the midst of a living folk tale. But to think that the old woman would suddenly begin to weep. He found himself at a loss.

When Masahiko had finally reached the old roadway along Utazaka that formed the entrance to Amazoko—the village his grandfather had so often spoken of—he found a lake spread out about a dam, just as it had been described. Someone had already arrived. It had appeared to be a woman. Wearing a white robe and a hat, she was standing at the water's edge, staring downward. At first, seen from a distance, it had looked as if she might be a water bird, a part of the landscape, with the pale green lake silently reflecting the shadows of the surrounding mountains. Masahiko had heard that the villages of Amazoko and Tsukikage had both been flooded.

He had noticed some small schools of fish swimming about.

"Look—the fish out there," he'd called out.

When he thought about it, he realized it shouldn't be so unusual to see fish. He wondered if the *yamame* and other fish ever swam down to the lower currents around the base of the dam. On the bottom, where shadows of fish were moving about, he could still see the land's surface all covered with still-standing trees, and the stone walls of the terraced hillside farm plots, and the faint traces of their pathways. It looked like the remains of a village.

"So the sunken village has become the home of the fish," Masahiko muttered to himself again.

A strange sort of image had filled his mind: *If I were to look upward from the pathways along the edges of the fields that now lie at the bottom of the lake, the fish would be swimming up in the sky along with the dragonflies. I'd be like a sea ray, swimming along the mountainside.*

The feeling was as if he had been suddenly upended from his normal position of standing on the ground and left hanging upside down with his thoughts all reeling about. He wondered if the spirits—the spirits of those who had been unwillingly taken from this village—weren't also in such a state.

A heaviness filled his heart, leaving him somewhat ill at ease. And then—just when he had started wishing someone else were there—a woman wearing a hat of the sort seen only in historical dramas had appeared, bent over and advancing into the water. Without thinking, he had called out.

After a closer look, he had realized that she wasn't a young girl. And it had seemed just as well, for it would have been a bit too much if, on his way to see the village at the bottom of the lake, he had just happened to chance upon a young girl. Instead, it had turned out to be an old woman, the likes of which he'd never seen in Tokyo. Nonetheless, it had left him with a certain sense of premonition.

"I really don't know anything at all about my grandfather's village, or about the, er, old estate. You say you were employed in the service of my family. Well . . . thank you."

Masahiko felt he wasn't coming up with quite the right words, but seeing Ohina in such a state he thought he should try to say something to console her.

"After all, that was before I was born. Before I was either shadow or shape."

The words "either shadow or shape" seemed to soothe Ohina a bit, and her heaving began to subside.

Masahiko continued, "But these days, isn't it a bit too formal to say *in service*? May I ask how old you were then?"

"From sixteen to twenty-one."

"I see. And your name is—?"

"Ohina."

"Ohina-san . . . The village of Amazoko must be near here, isn't it?"

While he was pointing with his finger in questioning her, Ohina pressed her reddening eyes, and nodded.

"I've heard there's a graveyard. Do you know in which direction?"

He couldn't bring himself to ask her where the old household had been. He was afraid that he would be assaulted by an unexpected wave of emotion.

Her finger trembling, she pointed in the direction of the opposite bank. Masahiko rubbed his eyes—it looked as if the trees along the bottom were swaying. There couldn't have been any wind blowing them at the bottom of the lake. It seemed it must have been he himself who was shaking. It was as if the time that had been stolen away was now rising up from the bottom of the lake and entwining itself around these two people. Leaves of pampas grass not yet come into seed were faintly rubbing against each other.

"There. Over there. There's no bridge, so we can't get there."

"A bridge? . . . Wouldn't it be hard to have a bridge with such a large dam?"

"No, no, I don't mean a bridge like that."

Ohina lifted her hat and shook her head firmly. She held back her running nose with her sleeve and fretted.

"In the r—river. There was a bridge over the river. But since the bridge was taken out there's been no way to get there."

"So you're saying there used to be a bridge over a river? Whereabouts was it—that river? Do you remember?"

With her back bent over and looking infirm, Ohina grabbed on to the *sarusuberi* tree and pulled herself upright.

"There's a ginkgo tree. Over there. It was the tree of the gods. The ginkgo tree is still there, watching over the graves. Can you see the graves of your family beneath it? I haven't been able to see them since they were flooded by the lake. All I can see is the ginkgo. I always leave some incense for them up here. That's no ordinary tree. It's so big that even six adults with their hands joined couldn't reach around it. Now it's all bent over. That sacred tree has grown old in the depths of the water. And I've grown old as well."

And in saying this, Ohina bent over too.

"In the spring it was the weeping cherry of Oki no Miya. In autumn it was the great ginkgo of Kodenbara. These were the trees of the gods, and the trees that were the markers of Amazoko village. It won't be long now before the leaves change colors. When that tree in the middle of the valley changed color, people realized how special the village was. You won't find a ginkgo like that anywhere else. From here on Utazaka Hill you could get a good view of it, all lit up in yellow. And when it turned completely yellow and its leaves swirled around through the center of the valley it was the most wonderful sight in the entire world. When the sun went down and the world darkened all around, all that remained was the silent dancing of the great ginkgo of Kodenbara. There was one time I happened to meet Masahito by the graves beneath that ginkgo tree . . ."

Ohina bit her lip, stared into the bottom of the lake, and then fell into a silence. Her disheveled hair was sticking out from beneath her hat. Her hair was black. Omomo had spoken to her about this before Ohina set out to climb up here.

"If you're going to visit the graves for O-bon, why don't you dye your hair? You never know who you're going to run into from the old village."

If you look too old you get depressed, so you better make yourself a little younger, Omomo always said. No doubt that was why Omomo had gone to the trouble of buying her a hat with a red cord.

Back when she had been drinking the water at the lake, her chin had gotten wet and the red cord had tightened up on her and begun to itch. She had tied the cord tightly to keep the hat from blowing off, but now the tightness made it uncomfortable to speak. Realizing that her fingers were trembling, she untied the cord and wiped the sweat from her hair. It made the top of her head refreshingly cooler. And for some reason, when she took off the hat, suddenly she felt closer to this young man who had called himself the grandson of Masahito.

It seemed the sky had grown wider. Ohina looked to Masahiko with deep modesty and bowed formally. The young man's eyes expressed affection as he looked at her. And as if breathing a sigh of relief he took off the cloth bag he had been carrying on his back and placed it on the grass. *My goodness, that must be a* biwa *lute*—thought Ohina when she saw the bag.

Stretched along the bottom of the lake was a village roadway that appeared like a long scratch. No doubt even now the river was still flowing alongside that roadway. Ohina had said you couldn't get to the graveyard unless you crossed over the river. But he thought that if he were to go down the cliff on the opposite bank the graveyard might be nearby. He imagined there would be a steep cliff. It looked as if the dam was surrounded by mountains. The lake was much larger than he had imagined.

All the places his grandfather had told him about—the Hall of Kannon, the monkey seat rock, and Oki no Miya shrine—he wondered where they were now, submerged in the lake. Only the trees were still visible at the bottom, indicating the remains of the village. Masahiko was overcome with sadness. He had never expected such emotion.

His grandfather had said to him, "We can't get to the graves of our ancestors any more. They're at the bottom of the lake now. When I die, I want you to scatter the ashes of my bones on the water around the dam." That would mean for him to scatter the ashes on this lake, which had now become the sky above the village. The ashes would then settle and land on the ground of the village, or on the graveyard, and they would look up at the sky of the water's surface. Could ashes become spirit? Facing the ashes of the bones he'd carried on his back, he called out—

"Grandfather, I have a feeling some strange things are going to happen."

On his back he had also carried the *biwa* that had been his grandfather's favorite. At his grandfather's old home there had been a number of very old mulberry trees. The mulberries had led to its being named the Silk Estate. Before the village was flooded, his grandfather had ordered a craftsman from Fukuoka to make him a *biwa* using the wood from one of those mulberry trees. "You can't find top quality mulberry wood like this any more," the maker had said, "It'll give you a superb tone." A *biwa* player himself, he had been very pleased about it.

Masahiko had made a stop in Fukuoka to get new strings and had put them in his rucksack along with the container that held the bone ashes. Cutting through a valley of rice, its ears starting to form, he then climbed the mountain path toward Utazaka, passing through bush clover just coming into bud and through countless day lilies in full bloom. The thought of scattering the ashes on the lake hadn't been disagreeable.

The old household, with all its traditions and its tales of the countryside, had sunk beneath the water. Masahiko, who shared that family blood too, although he was a young man from Tokyo, had come to make his farewell. As a parting ceremony he had planned to scatter his grandfather's ashes on the deserted lake at the beginning of autumn, with the sun going down. The idea of playing something on the *biwa* to remember his grandfather had pleased him.

His grandfather had often played a selection he'd learned somewhere from the *Tale of the Heike*. Though it was a rather ordinary sort of piece, now that his grandfather was gone it remained in his ears as the most treasured of sounds.

He had been entertaining a thought for a while—why don't I play something for him? I have an idea for a piece I'd like to work up for a concert. Before I go back I'll try to finish this one piece for him, here on the banks of the lake around Yukari Dam; the dam that was so fateful for his life—but although this was the sort of trip he had imagined, all kinds of unanticipated thoughts were starting to well up inside him.

As he watched, thinking there was a stirring half way up the mountainside, all at once the trees started to bare the undersides of their leaves—the winds are at play!

This was his first time to see mountains sway in such a manner. From time to time the surface of the water heaved and rose up like a living being as the feet of the wind buffeted the wide expanse of the lake. Along the shore with the waving of reeds and grasses a fragrance rose, whether from the smell of the water or of the mountains. Masahiko took a fresh look around, wondering at the kind of place where his grandfather had grown up.

All the frenzied noises of the city had ceased in him—all the frantic grating sounds of automobiles, the screeching of brakes and the jarring noises of the opening and slamming of shutters that had been so deeply imbedded in the marrow of his bones. The ceaseless digging and filling and the tearing down of things had gone. What sort of world was that? Could it be I've somehow been carried away like a rocket, using the energy from the clamor of the giant city, and given a soft landing here?

All about his body lingering reverberations of air currents were still whispering faintly. Perhaps, he thought, my grandfather Masahito's strange words and ways have given me the thrust to get here.

In his later years Masahito was said to have become a rather reserved and strange old man. One afternoon the woman at the public bath had mentioned to Masahiko casually, "Don't you think your grandfather has gotten a bit weak up here?"

The elderly woman had pointed to her head with a sympathetic smile. "Since he's old it's understandable but, you know, he doesn't wear his kimono properly, and he whispers in my ear. He rambles on about how we have to disband the Imperial Guards. Once he asked me, glaring at me as he stood in front of the mirror, 'What d'you think of the Imperial Guards?'"

His family too had begun to wonder if he might not be getting a bit senile, but this behavior at the bath house had been a sign that from then on there could be no telling what sort of problems he might cause for those around him. But in spite of the fact that they had a Western style bathtub in their house—where Masahiko's mother could bathe in soap bubbles as she liked—Grandfather and the men in the family still liked to go to the public bath.

Finally, when it had come to having Masahito put into a mental institution in the suburbs, in the car as they were taking him there Masahiko had clearly seen the extent of his grandfather's condition. As soon as they got onto the Route 7 Expressway, Masahito had obviously begun to get frightened.

"Masahiko—the tanks! You hear them, don't you—the ground's rumbling? It's a whole corps of tanks. The enemy fleet's filling the bay off beyond Kanagawa. The capital will be completely surrounded! You hear it don't you Masahiko?"

His eyes filled with despair, Masahito had pointed ahead and thrust his body forward on the car seat. But after a moment he sealed his lips and just looked sadly at Masahiko.

"Grandfather, I know it's an awful noise, but it's just the normal sound of cars. I can imagine it's like the sound of tanks though."

"It must be the old days he's thinking of. He keeps going on about an enemy fleet."

Masahiko's elder brother had said this facing straight ahead as he drove the car. The shape of his neck and ears bore a strong resemblance to that of his grandfather.

"Damn it, we're trapped. Right in the midst of the enemy. Twenty or thirty ranks of 'em—you can't even count them. Don't you see them? There's no way we can break through. We're in for it now."

In a low, covered voice, as if disclosing an important secret order, Masahito had spoken to the two of them.

"We're jammed in here with the enemy tanks. We'll just have to go on like this. It's our only hope to escape—right?"

There was no way to answer.

His grandfather had been right; the reverberations of the vehicles all about were pounding and rocking the axis of the earth. And that was just from the cars alone. And as a result, the world was left trembling and dashed about. It seemed that in whichever direction he turned there was no way to escape the tremors of the land. He realized that what his grandfather, in his struggling thoughts, had called the "enemy" had been the overwhelming force that was steadily engulfing people everywhere. No doubt his grandfather's thinking had been right about that. Just how many cars, he wondered, were there running about the city now? To his grandfather they all must have been enemies.

Masahiko's brother's wife had been sitting in the front passenger's seat of the cramped four-seater car. Grandfather's commitment to the mental institution had been decided by just one word from this woman.

When they had gotten onto the expressway, the *kin-kon-kin-kon . . .* warning sound from the car's speedometer started up. Whenever the car went over 100 km per hour the thing went off and it always made Masahiko nervous. He sank into a fear of being trapped in a car he couldn't stop—caught in a senseless competition for speed, like a racer just barely escaping from the edge of death but never able to fully resign himself to it; that was what cars did when they sped along the expressway. Music blasting away, randomly switching channels one after another, they charged on ahead.

Suddenly his grandfather had cried out in a pathetic voice, "Masahiko! The string of the *biwa*—it's snapped. I'm done for. Just shove me in!"

"You shouldn't scare us like that, Grandfather," Masahiko's brother had snapped disgustedly.

A distinct vision of the white sedan that had just passed them raced through Masahiko's mind. Unable to make the turn, it slammed into a guardrail. And then into the flaming wreck, one after another, the cars behind crashed into it. The sky was blue.

"There it goes—blowing itself up!" muttered his grandfather.

Each time they put him into the car Masahiko had heard his grandfather bark out the order; *"Shove me in!"* And under the blue sky, cars were going over a shining white guardrail and slamming down on top of each other, one after another. Up on a cliff by the sea, above a town lined with shops, every day without fail somewhere on the Japanese islands cars were blowing themselves up like that, and then other new cars were taking their places.

"Japanese islands—just go blow yourselves up! Go on, go blast yourselves to bits—you hear me? The *biwa* string of Moonshadow Village."

It was while saying those words that Masahito had breathed his last breath in a room of a mental institution.

That "*biwa* string of Moonshadow Village"—what had it meant?

Perhaps what had been coming back to Masahito's thoughts were the atrocities of the war in Okinawa. His thoughts must have been related to the shelling from the battleships and tanks and all the fighting he'd been through. He had lost his right hand and been sent back out into the winter's fighting with his arm amputated at the elbow. He had put in long hours of work for the army as a noncommissioned officer. But more than military affairs he had loved literature, and more even than writing he had loved music. Once, in reminiscing, he had spoken of how he wished he had gone into the navy since they had a musical band. Ever since the war, until the time his strange behavior began, he had avoided speaking of his experiences on the battlefield. But there could be no doubt that those thoughts had continued to weigh heavily on his heart.

For some reason or other, he had taken a great liking to the big old gingko tree that stood near Nakano Station in Tokyo. When it turned yellow he would go there with a broom in hand, as if driven by a rush of passion, and sweep up the leaves and heap them about the roots of the tree. The commuters and shoppers who rushed past him must have taken this old man for some kind of street sweeper. His odd ways had already started back then when he stood beneath that big old ginkgo tree with his sad wan smile.

With the wind blowing from the lakeside and swathing him in the fragrance of the mountains, Masahiko was carried back to thoughts of his grandfather standing under the ginkgo tree.

So *that* must have been where it came from—the ginkgo at the bottom of the lake. And that must have been what Grandfather was seeing. The ginkgo must have marked the road to his distant hometown that now lay sunken at the bottom of the lake. That solitary ginkgo that stood exposed to all the exhaust fumes near the train station—it must have been the dimly visible entrance that Masahito had found to a roadway of return; a passageway connecting him to the hometown from which he had been cut off. Each year, from the time the leaves started to change color until they lay completely scattered, an exchange of messages took place between this old man who had been cast adrift from the mountains of Kyushu and that ancient ginkgo that had stood in Nakano since the times when the area had still been called Musashino.

That must have been what Ohina had been referring to a while back when she was on the verge of tears. Somehow her feelings—when she mentioned that there was a graveyard on the far bank at the bottom of the lake and that a big old guardian-spirit ginkgo tree was standing there—these feelings must have been bound up with her thoughts for his grandfather who had stood alone beneath the ginkgo tree. She had been talking of how they should go to look at the ginkgo since it would be changing colors about now. But the water was a muddied, murky green and such things could not be seen.

Ohina sat down on the grass and started spreading out a *furoshiki* cloth patterned in an arabesque design.

With her hat off, Ohina's hair seemed a bit too dark for the age one might have guessed her to be from seeing her face. She was dividing the contents of her bundle and laying them out on the grass. There were three toy-like lanterns, some candles, a bunch of incense sticks, a bag of sweets, and something wrapped in newspaper.

Looking about and noticing some butterbur leaves nearby she got up, picked some, and laid out several of the large round leaves on the grass. From within the newspaper wrapping she took out a large rice ball generously sprinkled with sesame seeds. Masahiko was famished. Slowly, Ohina laid the rice ball on the butterbur leaf and then looked up at Masahiko.

"Won't you have some? It's a country-style rice ball."

To Masahiko's surprise, when she smiled her face took on a look of innocence.

"I'm sorry I can't fix you tea here, in a place like this."

With a pained look she pointed to the lake in front of her and said, "I suppose you could drink that water. If you could get to the bottom there's a good well with delicious water."

Masahiko bit into the sesame rice ball.

"Amazing—it's so heavy! Do people here always eat rice balls like this?"

"This one here's actually a pretty small one. When the men go off into the mountains we make bigger ones."

He worked it down his throat and then stood up to get some water.

The sun's rays played about the tops of the trees. Looking closely at the thick stands of andromeda trees you could see they were composed of closely packed layers of leaves. Delicate rays of sunlight were cast among the leaves and absorbed, one by one, until the entire surface of the trees became wrapped in dense black shadows. The surface of the lake reflected the mountains, composed of patchworks of these trees, mixed in with groves of cedars and stands of various other trees. Ponderous shafts of light and shade shimmered about and enveloped the two people.

Masahiko noticed how the motions of his body—whether munching on a rice ball, or stooping over to drink water, or sitting down on the grass—all harmonized completely with the feeling of the mountains. It felt as if the lingering traces of the tormenting sounds that had been lodged so deeply in his brain were being summoned, one by one, and taken in ever so carefully by the murmurings of the trees. As he shook a drop of water from the palm of his hand the thought struck him—this is silence; the silence that shelters light. Quietly he turned toward Ohina.

Her face expressing the look of a woman who preserves the bloodlines of all the mothers of the ancient past, Ohina held up a small unlighted red lantern, as if to make some sort of signal.

Beyond the tops of the mountains Masahiko could see the edge of a still-higher range. That must be the ancient sacred seat of the Kyushu Mountains. Before starting his trip he had studied a map of these mountains and kept it in mind.

"Ohina-san—the highest mountain over there, what's its name?"

In the midst of opening a folded paper lantern, Ohina held up her hand to shield herself against the glare.

"What, that one over there? There are so many. I suppose it must be Kunimi Peak."

Masahiko hadn't really expected an exact answer. Deep within he felt the quivering of a chord, one with a secret timbre that had never sounded before. It was an absolute sound, one that had never inhabited his body until now. Masahiko's mother had worried that he, her second son, might be taking after his grandfather in his abnormal sensitivity to sounds. Masahiko and his grandfather had often talked about such things.

"Masahiko, you know there's a forest of andromeda trees up there in the mountains."

"You mean the kind for bonsai—the ones with the beautiful flowers like lilies of the valley?"

"No, no. Not such little ones. I'm talking about great big ones."

"Andromeda trees can grow big?"

"The ones in the mountains grow huge. They can grow as big as a house."

"That's hard to imagine."

"When the sun goes down, if you're surrounded by them in a forest they call out in voices—all the leaves and buds of the andromeda."

"What's it sound like?"

"Well, it's a sort of whispering, murmuring sound. It's subtle and it gives you a nice feeling."

"A nice feeling? So the trees act as a sensitive instrument when they move with the wind? And the buds become wind chimes when the andromeda forest sways in the evening?"

The sounds of trains and long-distance trucks would interrupt these conversations that had gone on between grandfather and grandson like the confiding of secrets. The grimy polluted air sank into the little potted andromeda tree that had been placed in the tiny city garden just as a decoration. Even though his grandfather carefully sprayed it with mist, the grime wouldn't come off. After his grandfather's death, with no one to water it, the tree too had withered and died. Masahiko had even forgotten about that, but now, facing the big forests of andromeda trees on the opposite shore, the pitiful sight of that potted tree was brought back to him.

For how long had those andromeda trees stood there? Had his grandfather walked this area when he was young? He'd spoken of how, when the sun went down along the mountaintops, the andromeda trees would give off faint murmuring tones. But much as he strained his ears to hear, those sounds did not come to Masahiko.

He had heard that there used to be a bridge over the river that flowed along the bottom of the lake. On the other side of the bridge was his grandfather's house, known as the Silk Estate, and the village graveyard. In this bowl-shaped stretch of land had been the village called Amazoko. There was a well by the house that flowed with the purest water. He'd often heard his grandfather talk about a well.

Everyone in the village had drunk from that well—the postman, the cowherds, the children, the beggars, the festival go-ers, the soldiers. All had loved it. Masahito had said, "Before I die I want to drink the water from the well by our house."

Things Masahiko had listened to casually now welled up from the recesses of his memory and took hold of him. Water was memory. He had a feeling that these memories were being conducted through his two legs from the bottom of the lake. At first the memories seemed something like the faint flashes of distant lightning but suddenly, to his surprise, a shock was sent to his chest, as if it might send him reeling. It was a sharp, sweet, delicious shock that penetrated the depths of his body. It touched a string that had never sounded until this moment. More than an actual note it was like the sounding of the mysterious, yet it called out faintly. It was similar to the lowest tremors of the *biwa*. Standing barefoot in the water, alone and facing a world in which he had no place, Masahiko felt he had finally found a narrow foothold.

He was struck by the thought of how he had come here for escape from the helter-skelter, clangorous, end-of-the-century world. He hoped that after scattering his grandfather's ashes and looking into this lake with its sunken village that seemed to hold such meaning he might receive some inspiration for a new piece of music and then return home. He wondered—was it only my grandfather who was calling me?

And inspiration for a new piece of music—what is that?

But even before that, I need to restore my ears. It seems they've been mostly destroyed.

What could have been the very first musical tone ever heard by a human ear? Imagine, for example, that it was the sound of an original flute, and that someone noticed it and gave it a name. Think how sensitive that eardrum must have been. Perhaps it was when a sound struck a highly sensitive eardrum and for the first time someone thought of it as coming from an instrument and called it by a name. All the senses must have been struck together within the ear and in great surprise. Back when there was neither form nor word for "flute" or for "whistle" there must have been some person who placed the blade of a supple reed to the lips and produced a faint sound. And then, after blowing and concentrating on trying to create that sound again, the person must have realized that the human body, together with voice, was itself an instrument of music.

Back in the time when the true soul of language still existed, the human voice and the sounds of things must have been bound together far more closely than they are today. They must have existed in mystical relationship to the structure of the world. Something that has now come to take on an existence similar to that of a musical conductor must have once possessed a far greater power, extending to the farthest reaches of the craggy mountains and to the depths of the swirling high seas. And if so, the ones who first performed the incantations in those early times must have possessed eyes with which to decipher the world, and an incredibly refined sense of hearing. Could it be that the reverberations of those beginnings still linger about the bottom of the lake around the spring of Amazoko?

The first time Masahiko noticed that his ears had become blocked up and damaged was at the national theater, where he'd gone to hear a recital of early Chinese *tonko* music played on an ancient flute called the *hichiriki*. It had come as a shock to him, always having thought of himself as so in touch with the rational sound systems of modern music, and then hearing the gentle sounds of that ancient music, sounds that were so completely different. And now those hazy, cosmic sounds that came from the borders of the world seemed to drift back into his ears.

Standing in the water and feeling as if he he'd been called out to through some sort of song or verse, Masahiko turned to look back.

The old woman was standing on the top of a rock, surrounded by ferns and bamboo grass. By the side of the rock was an old *sakaki* tree, although Masahiko didn't know its name. Shading her head with some ferns she'd picked, Ohina looked as if she were wearing a crown. The sun in back of Masahiko must have been blinding her eyes.

"Look—over there," Ohina said, standing with some ferns held in her extended arm.

"At the bottom of Utazaka Hill you can see the *yusu no hikari* tree—the tree of light." Gently she intoned the words *yusu no hikari*, as if singing. He gazed into the depths of the water. How many decades of accumulation had it taken to cover the old Utazaka Hill to the point where all that could be seen now was slime and rotting leaves? Masahiko knew nothing about a tree of light.

"I've never heard of a tree of light."

"Oh come on. You must be able to see it. It's the guiding tree."

Masahiko had never held such a conversation before. He sensed he was being drawn into something strange, but on hearing the calm tone of Ohina's voice with its rising intonations he felt more as if he were being called out to in song. Behind Ohina and above the wooded mountainside was a waning day moon. So the east must be over there. In the direction of the moon. For Masahiko, seeing both the sun and moon in the vast unobstructed sky that stretched from east to west evoked a pastoral mood. He had never seen such things in the Tokyo sky.

"The guiding tree, where does it point to?"

"It marks the beginning of the village of Amazoko."

He felt a rush of excitement. Although this old woman may be full of strange ideas, I get the feeling she's casting a sort of spell, as if we're in an old mystical tale, just on the border of reality and unreality. It seems she's going to be my guide as I carry Grandfather's bones to this world I have to enter. Her fern sunshade looks like a crown. It's like the opening of an old musical drama.

"From the entrance, where does it point?"

"To the big ginkgo tree I was just telling you about."

"You mean to the graveyard?"

"It's the guardian tree of the graveyard. You must be able to see it, can't you? . . . If you're Masahito. It's golden. I can always see it."

There she goes mistaking me for my grandfather again. I hate having to correct her each time. But—what if I were to let myself be my grandfather in his younger days? And then Masahiko realized—well all right, so now I've entered. Thanks to this woman I've been guided to the old times of this lost village. When I was listening for the voices of the trees I had the feeling it came from the silence at the bottom of the lake, but those sounds must have been the first chantings of the mountains. It seems the fallen leaves of dead trees have formed little currents on the bottom of the lake. Masahiko felt an impulse to lay his body on the surface of the water.

Then Ohina spoke.

"You won't be able to get across like that—swimming upside down."

"Swimming upside down?"

As he raised his head and repeated her words, Ohina crouched down and attempted to light a cigarette.

"Even if you enter the water upside down you can't swim to the other side."

And then, stamping out her cigarette, she twisted her legs back around in an uncomfortable-looking manner and stood up, grasping onto the trunk of a *sakaki* tree. After a few moments, knitting her brows, she gazed into the depths of the water. Tremors shook the tops of the branches of the *sakaki* tree that Ohina had used in pulling herself up. As they danced about, the pale red leaves of vines that hung all about the tree looked as if they were inscribing the lines of a musical score in search of the subtle sounds of secret notes.

The *sakaki* was a special tree used in offerings at Shinto rituals and at the altars placed in people's homes for the gods. When they went into the mountains to gather firewood they never cut the tree thoughtlessly. And strangely enough, even on rocky mountainsides where it was especially difficult for trees to grow, this tree alone thrived and sheltered the rocks. As yet, Masahiko knew nothing of Ohina's doings in such places.

"Won't you step over there?"

Ohina pointed with her finger.

"There's a special seat over there."

Masahiko looked at the extensive root system of an andromeda tree he had seen earlier. It was as wide as a small building. The bushes had been cut back around one spot and there was a space where a person could sit and relax.

An old andromeda tree with a backrest set into it—now that's something, he thought. He went over and tried it out. His back settled into a deep cushion of thick leaves. They felt thick, fleshy, and somehow orderly in arrangement. The abundance of andromeda leaves cradled Masahiko's body comfortably. The soil beneath him felt warm.

Masahiko felt he'd made his way into a world of the senses completely different from anything he had ever known before. This place, it seemed, was his point of entrance. It was filled with subtle yet distinct signs. There was a gentle breath from the world of plants; one that was entirely different from the nerve-splitting, chaotic, discordant sounds of the city that had held sway over him until now. Though complex in the extreme, it flowed together in an ordered and cosmic manner. Above the land and below, the gentle breath of the plant world was calling back and forth from the depths of the andromeda tree, which was like an entire forest in itself.

A vision, a memory, flashed through Masahiko's mind; a
fleeting, hushed moment in a Nakano alleyway. A cramped little park. The breathing of the bewildering city and all it meant.
It had caught his eye when he was leaving Tokyo, in the tiny
park near the police station. Just a glimpse of some old men
slurping down instant noodles from styrofoam cups.

Perhaps they had made an appointment to meet at noontime under the sparse shade of the trees. Even if it was only to
eat instant noodles, at least the men had met to have lunch together. From hearing their conversation he hadn't been able to
catch anything about their pasts. But he felt a bit relieved that
at least they hadn't been alone. On other days, in this same
place, seeing sights like a lonely old woman eating instant noodles by herself had left him with a gnawing feeling of uneasiness for the rest of the day.

Even when one of the right-wing groups' loudspeaker-
mounted trucks pulled up blasting away military-patriotic
songs at ear-splitting volume, the expressions on those three
men had hardly changed. Pricked with anxiety, Masahiko had
reflected; all of us who consume these unnatural synthetic
chemical things—like we're some sort of bacteria—can we survive in the midst of all this din and discord we've grown so accustomed to in the city?

For that matter, the sound of sound itself has come close to
becoming a lethal weapon. And all those vehicles, suited up in
steel armor and trampling across the earth—the trains, the
long-distance trucks, and the regular passenger cars—they're
all weapons for a blood bath. It's been attacking me through
my ears. That time I heard the sounds of the *tonko* instruments
was when I noticed it. And also the time when I heard Grandfather shouting, "Shove me in!"—back when he was starting to
lose his mind—it struck me then too. It's like he said; we're being surrounded by an overwhelming enemy invasion.

The faces of the people at the recital that night, and there were quite a few of my generation too, they seemed gentle and filled with a sense of grace. What was that?

Perhaps that brief time allowed a respite for people who are so caught up in the brutal humdrum of the city—like a time in a hospice. Perhaps it granted them a sacred moment in a hospice run by the self, carried out in the face of death, which may call on us at any time, unexpectedly. The people's faces seemed quiet and filled with an acceptance of the fleeting nature of life.

As the faces of the audience he'd seen reflected in the lake faded, he thought he smelled hints of autumn in the air. Along the shore several long stalks of *susuki* grass were swaying in the breeze. Their tasseled ears had just broken through, still giving off a moistened-looking luster. It was still too early for the autumn foliage.

Seven or eight wild geese flew over the lake, all in a line. He also heard other birds exchanging calls all over the waterfront. It seemed the birds had adapted themselves to this artificial lake. And with its surface quietly reflecting the clouds and shadows of the mountains, the scenery looked quite natural. If you didn't think of the sunken village that lay below it, this might be just an ordinary mountain town that had passed through the ages without a change.

Still holding on to the trunk of the *sakaki* tree, Ohina watched the young man attentively. She noticed his eyes growing heavier, as if he were about to nod off into a dream.

And then as he glanced in her direction, suddenly Ohina repeated her previous question as if reading from some invisible script.

"Why don't you speak to the *yusu* tree, the tree of light, at the bottom of Utazaka Hill?"

"Speak to the *yusu* tree? It's not that I mind trying, but I've never even seen one."

Ohina scrutinized Masahiko carefully.

"What—never seen a *yusu* tree? You're not telling me that, are you?"

She seemed to be saying that in order to meet the people of the sunken village he would have to meet with trees he'd never seen before and ask them the way. He thought; this woman Ohina has been talking about trees. Her words are different from any I've heard before. She has a sort of world of her own, and because of it her words sound like they're newly born.

Ohina waved her hands in front of her face several times as if brushing away spider webs. Then she opened her palm and glanced into it as if looking at some trifling thing. She reached to the back of her hair, as if feeling about for something, and mumbled.

"That time—you picked a shiny leaf from a young *yusu* tree and put it in my hair as an ornament, didn't you?"

Masahiko couldn't hear her words very well.

"You mean you've forgotten? Well, that goes to show how the city has stolen your soul. And now you've even forgotten the way home."

Masahiko was moved by her words. One time his grandfather had gone out and not returned home for three days. When he was finally led back he had said,

"My soul's been stolen. I went looking for it but I couldn't find it anywhere."

After all their worrying about this faltering old man, his family might have felt relieved to hear these touching words. But immediately his mother had looked up at him and said in a low voice, "Masahiko, this is no laughing matter you know—you're the one who's most like your grandfather. Someday you could end up in a mental hospital too. This business about his soul going off somewhere. If the both of you turn out strange you'll cast shame on the family name."

Cast shame on the family name? Perhaps in part her words had simply reflected the confusion of the times, but his mother took inordinate pride in the fact that her father had been in the diplomatic corps and she had spent her early childhood in Switzerland.

"My husband comes from Kyushu. You must know of the Aso family, don't you? Well, it's a very old family and it's said to have been very close to the Emperor. His family is in the direct line of descent. Historians have verified all of this, you know."

She could go on talking like this with ease. Just hearing such words from his mother soured his feelings. Not only in his mind, but throughout his entire body he'd felt he needed to get away.

"Don't you think you've been acting rather neurotic lately? Locking yourself up in your room alone like that and talking to someone. Are you really composing songs in there?"

To tell the truth, he really had been talking to people. Sometimes it might be with an unknown girl who appeared in a dream. Or it might be with an old man with an inquiring eye who lived in the old ways. Short fragments of songs seemed to be coming to him. He felt that to some degree it was possible to write down as images the memories of the dreams that appeared, but the sounds that came to him lingered for a short while only and then were lost.

The space between reality and the world beyond—a world that includes dreams—was always separated by an invisible curtain. It wasn't that the two worlds were divided absolutely, for essentially they were deeply connected. But like Siamese twins that have been pulled apart, dreams and reality were left confused about each other.

Perhaps the spirit passes over to the other side and then in its absence another self, a terribly empty one, appears. From the outside—whether it's from my schooling or because of my mother's efforts to give me such a modern upbringing—my self has become like an empty room from which the interior has fled. Perhaps that's how my grandfather lost track of his soul too.

And that was what Ohina, a survivor of the sunken village, had been getting at.

"So you've forgotten? So the city has stolen your soul, has it?"

In this old woman who had appeared to him so unexpectedly there seemed to be no split between words and spirit. Suddenly he felt warmth toward her welling up within himself.

"About that soul—I've brought Masahito's soul here with me, since he wanted to drink the water from the family well."

Ohina was sunk in thought for several moments. Then she released her hands from the trunk of the *sakaki* tree and, with a painful-looking movement, got down from the rock. The white *tabi* coverings on her feet had become damp. The tips of the *sakaki* leaves swayed, scattering the blue of the sky to and fro. Two green butterflies fluttered up amidst the bushes and then vanished from sight on the surface of the lake as if they had been inhaled by the water. Ohina picked another butterbur leaf, folded and fashioned it into a dipper, and then bent over to draw water.

"Here, have some water from the old well. It may help your soul return, Masahito."

Water was dripping down from the butterbur leaf. It's like a ceremony. It's as if the souls of both Grandfather and my own self are returning within me. The water had a hard taste. Lowering her eyes, the old woman drank the rest of the water. When she let the leaf fall into the bushes by the side, immediately it shone like a mirror. Everything conveyed a sense of reverence.

"Ohina, I'm sorry I don't know about the *yusu* tree. But that weeping cherry at the bottom of Utazaka—I've heard about that. I'd like to know where it is. I've heard that on moonlit nights it floats up and becomes the guiding marker to the village."

"The weeping cherry . . ."

With a sigh, she concentrated her gaze and pointed with her finger.

"It's at the bottom of the flood-gates of that dam."

She spoke with a sunken voice. He hadn't expected it would be in that spot.

"Masahito."

Her voice straining, Ohina called out his grandfather's name again.

"That cherry tree sacrificed itself for the people. In the old days, it used to be the tree that showed the way to Amazoko, but now it's become a sacrifice. Now it's in pitch dark."

"The cherry, a sacrifice?"

"Well, it's pitch black down there in the valley of Amazoko now. Heaven fell, and it dropped down here."

"Was the cherry tree cut down before the village was flooded?"

"It was cut, but that was on a hazy moonlit spring night, when the cherries were in full bloom. The cherry tree was in full bloom in a water globe."

A weeping cherry, blossoming in a water globe? Darkness gathered over the depths of the water on a pale moonlit night. At the bottom of the lake the sound of running water could be heard. Grandfather had often spoken of it. Over the old Moon-shadow Bridge made of vines had passed one-legged people, one-eyed people, and people who looked like they were from good old families but had fallen along the wayside. They all looked toward this village. The waters of this well provided solace during their last moments. The people of the village had carefully laid the dead to rest.

At nightfall the village had grown silent and there had been only the sound of a little water wheel pounding quietly husking rice, but it had told of the presence of people living there. When spring came and all kinds of flowers started to bloom the red flowers of the quince and the mountain camellias were still in blossom. And at noontime the lowing of cows had sent peaceful echoes through the village.

"Can't you hear it—the sound of the water?"

Masahiko glanced at Ohina absent-mindedly.

The sunlight was cast at an acute angle. Ohina fixed her gaze on the bottom of the dam.

"In the spring, just when the flowers were at their peak . . . the old cast-off shells of the red crabs and the petals of the *ko-gome* cherries floated up around this valley. Year by year the crabs have been growing thinner. Now it's nearing the fifteenth night of O-bon. When they pass over Moonshadow Bridge their shells must be getting thinner too. Those crabs, they miss people, and these days not many of the newly dead pass by any more."

He had heard stories from his grandfather about red crabs passing over Moonshadow Bridge.

At the bottom of Utazaka Hill, if you walked just a bit farther, there had been a wooden bridge over the Isara River and below it had been a pool. In daytime horses and ox-drawn carts passed over it, and at nighttime bridal processions lit up with numerous lanterns crossed it. Over the years, the stories of these events had gradually worked their way into fables. But at nighttime it could be frightening. The villagers' stories about the nighttime were colored with tales of foxes and wild boars walking over the bridge with their children. But also, at times, there were the "People from Long Ago," standing there for some reason.

Deep in the night, under the light of a full moon when no one was passing over the bridge, red crabs would form row upon row and march forward like one giant shadow. The villagers could make out the sounds of the little crab feet—like the swaying of water plants—amidst the sounds about the stream.

"The red crabs are making their procession, following the river god and walking down to the sea. Do you suppose any newly dead have arrived already?"

"Here, give this as an offering!" one of the elderly women would call out—and saying this she would draw the young wives and children together and do an incantation. She would chew on raw sweet potato or buckwheat grains and then spit them out onto the openings of the wells by the houses and on the irrigation gates of the nearby rice fields. The crabs grabbed onto these bits with one claw or carried them in their mouths and then went on their way along the travelers' path. Unless this was done, in the still of the night after all the villagers were asleep, if a dying wayfarer should cross over the bridge and lie down under the weeping cherry tree, the procession of crabs would come upon that person. Without fail they would pick away at the newly cold body with their claws and take away something as a souvenir for the sea gods.

"And if this happened, even if the people held a memorial service for the dead person, people's dreams would be cursed throughout the village, so they always put out bits of potato and buckwheat beforehand."

In the old days all the women, both young and old, used to gather at Masahito's place. There were stories of how, when they discussed the river festival—and this was a ceremony for women only—they would tell the men to go off and take care of warming the *sake*. Masahiko had heard these stories from his grandfather.

"Do the crabs always take the same route?"

Masahiko felt embarrassed at having asked such a silly question. Ohina replied, glancing down on the surface of the water.

"The crabs have all sorts of routes, but the one by the cherry tree is the most painful."

She glanced over at Masahiko, the red of her eyes flashing as if in rebuke.

"These days the shrunken flow of the Isara River pours out from the mouth of the dam. When it's the right season the cherry petals flow from the bottom of the river. Not the ordinary kind, but cherry petals that look like they're mixed with blood. From early evening throughout the night. You must know that tree well, don't you Masahito? When it was cut down, blood gushed from its wounds. We all saw it. That tree sacrificed its life for us. It fell without crying out. It was the people who cried out and wailed, all choked up with tears. The story must have reached you in Tokyo, didn't it?

"Whenever I go to that embankment, it seems all of a sudden I run off or scramble up the embankment. I don't know why it happens, but it leaves me with a strange feeling. My daughter Omomo tells me I'm crazy. She says it's hard to look at me running about on that embankment with my chest bared. She says I'm crazy."

"The embankment?"

"When the dam was finished it was given a name. When the bottom of Utazaka Hill was flooded and the people were left with no way to go or come from their former village they just stood around and stared into the water. In springtime the petals of quince and *kogome* cherries passed under the spillway and flowed into the Isara River. Even if people did slip away and were no longer there the season of flowers came to the bottom of the water.

"Tonight's the sixteenth night of O-bon. Along the banks of the upper Isara River the young ears of pampas grass must be damp and glossy and shining softly in the light. Why do I feel this chilling sensation tugging at my neck? I wish I could fly away along that river."

For a moment it seemed to Masahiko as if Ohina was the transformation of a fox. Above the point where the Isara River flowed from the bottom of the dam a fox was jumping about, its blue eyes flashing with light. It was coiling an invisible rope. All of a sudden it pitched the coil toward Masahiko. As he felt the thin rope tighten around his chest it seemed he could see the darkly lit river in Ohina's eyes.

"In my dreams I see . . ."

The words slipped from Masahiko's mouth unexpectedly. These were precisely the words his grandfather Masahito had mumbled, about the time he started wandering. "What did you say just now?"—Masahiko had asked him. His grandfather had replied quietly;

"In my dreams I see only Amazoko."

Masahito had said this as if he bore a responsibility to speak about it to someone. At the time he said that, the sad feeling must have sunk into the depths of Masahiko's mind. And so it seemed as if—with Ohina's saying, "I wish I could fly away along the gentle shining Isara River,"—a bubble had floated up from the bottom of the lake, and with it his grandfather's words had sprung from Masahiko's mouth.

Soon the eyes of Ohina, who had been eying the young man skeptically, filled with a gentle radiance. And then, as if uttering a password, she repeated his words.

"In my dreams I see only Amazoko."

They both stared at each other in surprise. Feeling as if his body were swaying toward the lake, Masahiko stuck out his leg to brace himself. He joked, "I guess I'll run about the banks of the dam too. It looks like I'm going to fly—and not just in my dreams."

For the first time, Ohina laughed.

And then, from the shade of the andromeda tree on the slope behind them, a young woman's voice was heard.

"Mother, where are you? Mother?"

"Omomo? Omomo. Here, over here."

Ohina turned around and looked at Masahiko as if seeking his agreement.

"What's this now? You said you weren't coming, but here you are sneaking up on us from behind."

Flagging from fatigue as she approached, Omomo sat down on the grass.

"It sure was some climb up here. And it's just like I thought. I figured I'd find you up here on Utazaka."

The woman, wearing a blue wide-brimmed hat that covered her rounded face and perspiring with beads of sweat strung across her forehead, gazed suspiciously at Masahiko. Perhaps sensing the friendly relationship between her mother and the young man, she bowed to Masahiko. Her long hair, gathered in back, was swaying from under her hat. She must have hurried in climbing since her shoulders were heaving beneath her T-shirt as she breathed heavily.

"How's that for intuition—finding you right away like this?"

"Oh come on, you were up here three years ago."

"Well, is that so? Not even a word of thanks? I thought you might be lonely up here all by yourself. And I knew you'd planned to light the lanterns. I thought about what could happen if a forest fire started, so I hustled in getting up here. Not a bad job of looking after my mother, I'd say—don't you think?"

Masahiko cracked a smile and Omomo added, just loud enough to be heard, "That's the truth, you know.

"Like I figured. So are you going to stay up here over night? You looked so serious when you said O-bon was going to be different this year. Up on the top of the mountain at the beginning of O-bon—what's the deal? You had me worried, you know, so I pushed it all the way up here."

Ohina thought Omomo's increasingly brusque manner of speaking stemmed from the influence of the young man from the city. It wasn't as if she herself didn't have any memories of that sort of thing. She remembered her younger days when she was working at a spinning mill and had been called out to by some of the young townspeople, and how she'd made a point of talking back to them in her rough mountain dialect to give them a shock, and how it had brought her some small satisfaction. But now her daughter had taken on that same trait—and to a far greater extent than she had done it in her own youth.

Omomo called out sharply.

"Look, the last time I came up here you could see the graves and the ginkgo tree at the bottom of the lake . . . Now you can't see anything at all."

And then all of a sudden her voice fell into words spoken to herself.

"It's all covered with green slime.

"Yes, it's clouded up. With this man . . ."

Ohina thrust out her jaw a bit.

"I was telling him a lot about the river in the old days, but I don't know if he understands or not. His soul hasn't come back."

"Oh come on Mother, don't be ridiculous. How could someone who's just come from the city to the mountains for the first time possibly understand?"

Masahiko was at a loss to respond. With her back to him, Omomo spoke, as if she'd just found something she'd been searching for.

"I've been thinking; this guy here—seems I've seen him somewhere before."

"Well perhaps so, but Omomo, you don't know him."

Ohina stared at Omomo as if her daughter were starting to flirt.

The smooth outline of the skin on Omomo's neck leading down to her shoulders looked particularly fresh and young.

And what seemed even more likely to lead to trouble was the clearly visible outline of her breasts. These days young girls and married women alike were wearing T-shirts that looked like hardly anything more than underwear. Omomo liked to be noticed, and today she was wearing a canna flower-colored shirt that showed her breasts to advantage. In the old days no doubt it would have been regarded as seductive.

When Ohina had stopped by the house Omomo hadn't opened the door. When she called out, Omomo had dropped the sickle out of the window, but afterward she must have felt bad about it and then followed her mother.

"You know, I think I've seen you somewhere."

Masahiko was also taking a good look at her. There was a certain resemblance in her cheeks to the rounded features of an *okame* mask, though it wasn't particularly evident. Her slightly upturned nose had a charming look and her unaffected rural dialect lent a pastoral touch.

"Ah, now I remember—that old brown photo of Mother's. He looks a lot like the guy with the student's cap."

Ohina grew flustered and waved both her hands.

"That was someone from way back—the dead grandfather of this person here."

Does she really understand who I am? She keeps on mistaking me for him.

"He's come all the way from Tokyo to scatter the ashes of his grandfather's bones."

"Come to scatter bones? Then his family must be from Amazoko. All the way from Tokyo—that's pretty good."

Omomo took off her blue hat, wiped away the sweat, set her big rucksack on the grass and bowed.

"Come all alone for a funeral, you say? Mother, is there any saying we could offer for condolence?"

Now seeming to be looking for a way to help, Omomo glanced at her mother and spoke nervously.

"Mother and I are from this village so you could let us offer some words of condolence for him and we could carry out some of the rites."

Masahiko hadn't expected such a thing.

"No, that's OK. I just came to scatter my grandfather's bones. We already had the funeral. It's just that . . ."

He tried to say that he just wanted to do it by himself, quietly, yet now it had become difficult to express this.

"Omomo, don't press him. He must have his reasons."

"I suppose so, but I don't know anything about them."

"He's the heir to the old Silk Estate of Amazoko. I used to work there when I was young."

"Please, you're suggesting too much about me. There's no estate to inherit any more. And I'm only the second son."

"How did the two of you meet?"

"It was a dream. I had a dream—a true dream." Ohina spoke as if she were an oracle delivering her words.

"A dream . . . really?"

"If it hadn't been for my dream I doubt we ever would have met."

"It's like I'm being held captive by a fox," Masahiko muttered to himself.

Masahiko didn't mention that a while back he'd thought Ohina might be the incarnation of a fox.

"On the night of the thirteenth I had a dream. In the moonlight, at the edge of Moonshadow Bridge, I was bending over and looking down on a procession of red crabs pattering their way along. 'Where are all of you off to,' I asked them.

"Then a baby red crab called out, 'I'm being taken by my mother to Oki no Miya.' "Oki no Miya—that must be far away. What are you going to do there?" I asked again. The baby crab crept up to my ear and said, 'We're going to receive lives. We're all going to receive lives.'"

"And then to my surprise a person came and pointed with his finger. The leaves of the ginkgo tree were fluttering above the Isara River. And then from below, Masahito, dressed as a soldier and wearing a white sash, walked this way, beckoning with his hand. I could see his face smiling clearly. And then I woke up with a happy feeling. The ginkgo leaves were dancing about and the moon was rising."

Omomo broke in, "My mother believes her dreams tell the truth."

"Well—if dreams aren't the truth then what is? This world's made up of a skin of lies. And you too—you often lie to me. And I too, I hide from others the things I can't talk about. If this world of lies weren't just a temporary one do you think we could go on living? And all that's happened—what with your running into debt, and my making medicines too—unless I tell myself these things are all just moments in a bad dream, I couldn't go on living. And all that's happened about your father's grave, and about Masahito's estate too, it's too much to believe. Whatever trouble humans can get into, it ends up happening. And the fire that night too."

Ohina's pupils began to narrow and with both hands she yanked at her breast and jerked her knees. Omomo stood up quickly and grabbed her mother by the obi wrapped about her kimono.

"Come on, Mother—you just met this guy, so what are you saying? This isn't the embankment."

"The embankment—Ahh."

As if embarrassed, Ohina glanced toward her daughter's face and started to grumble.

"Well, I have a pain in my back here."

"Maybe so. Say, why don't we have our O-bon right here and go to greet the souls of the dead. From next year I may not be able to make it here again. Ah—that reminds me, I brought some somen noodles and a pot. It's the somen that father liked so much, and I also brought some O-bon dumplings."

Seeing Omomo take an aluminum pot and a ladle from the rucksack, Ohina's expression turned to amazement.

"My goodness, you even brought a pot—though we don't have a stove."

"So why don't we fix up a fireplace? All we need is three stones. We've got water here. And look—I brought some shiitake mushrooms, and fried tofu, and some flavoring for the broth."

Masahiko was fascinated watching the preparations for the ceremony being laid out in front of him. Though the fireplace was just roughly put together with materials at hand, somehow the sense of its being made of essential things of life captured his attention deeply.

Is this, he wondered, what the relation between a mother and daughter is really about? In Tokyo he had never experienced such exchanges between his mother and himself.

He'd been thinking of going down to the village at the base of the mountain to look for lodging. But as he became involved in the tasks of gathering firewood and making a ceremonial altar, feeling as if it were natural to do such things, the thought of searching for a place to stay soon vanished.

Ohina and Omomo's movements were striking.

A pleasant *swish-swoosh* sound rose up as Ohina cut away the stalks of pampas grass from their roots. With a regular flowing motion her left hand grasped and bundled the supple leaves and gently arranged them on the ground. In no time at all the thicket of pampas grass was transformed into a freshly laid-out reed carpet and the clearing took on the look of an open-air teahouse.

Ohina stretched her back and, nodding her head, looked around at the branches swaying in the strong wind.

"We'll need some good posts. Let's see if we can round up some." Omomo was on her feet in an instant and set off to look for branches. Ohina then cut up the gathered branches, wielding the sickle skillfully with her practiced hand. From the bushes she pulled out a rock about the size of a baby's head and then called out to Masahiko.

"Say, excuse me but I need to put up this post—could you lend a hand? I'll hold it straight and could you just pound it into the ground for me?"

He held the branch, about the thickness of a clothesline pole, over the spot on the ground she indicated and stuck it into the earth.

"We're making a hut for tonight."

Holding the rock in his hand he hesitated in the presence of these energetic women.

"It's not going to work if you hold it that way. Look, you have to do it like this."

Ohina thrust the point of the pole firmly into the ground. She had Masahiko hold it in place for her and pounded it in with both hands grasping the rock. It sunk about six inches into the ground.

Then with Ohina urging him on, her lips pursed tightly, he tried to pound with the rock, but the still-living tree had an unexpected elasticity that resisted his efforts. The mountain topsoil was soft and deep.

Once the four posts were in place the roof took shape rapidly. She cut and pulled vines from the undergrowth, stamped on them, chewed them, tore them apart, and fashioned them into a kind of rope. Ohina explained as she worked that kudzu and wisteria vines make something stronger than regular rope. He supposed she must have taken him for a weakling.

For the roof she carefully placed the freshly cut pampas grass and dwarf bamboo. The walls were constructed in a similar fashion, and by the time the sun began to sink beneath the mountaintops the hut was completed. Upon entering and looking into this hut filled with the fragrance of fresh grass he got an impression of what the very first houses made by humans must have been like.

It was just one long room with an opening on one side that apparently served as the doorway. The women were gazing up at the sky. The sunlight was growing dimmer and in the orange-tinted sky the evening star appeared.

Ohina gathered some branches and stones and set up an informal ceremonial altar in the back of the hut. On it, as an offering, she placed the sweets and dumplings, along with the persimmons she'd picked up on her way up Utazaka Hill. She hung the two small paper lanterns at the entryway and at the side of the altar to welcome the souls of the dead.

"You can place the ashes here too."

And so he placed on the stone altar the ashes kept in the unglazed urn he'd carried on his back in his rucksack.

"It's not going to rain is it, Mother?"

"No, it's not going to rain. The first star's beautiful, isn't it?"

"Shall we light the lanterns soon?"

"Before that, let's have the O-bon somen noodles. You must be starving."

Hearing these words, Masahiko's stomach cried out. Already for some time he had been wondering what kind of noodles they might cook up here.

The women pushed three rocks near the water into a U-shape to make a simple fireplace. There was an unlimited supply of firewood. Smoke turned to red flames and soon the noodles were dropped into the steaming pot. Somen takes hardly any time to cook and if you add a little flavoring broth and seasoning you can fix up a "beggars' stew" in no time.

"When you're busy, it can't be beat."

Then Omomo picked some butterbur and heaped some of the slender noodles from the boiling pot onto their large round leaves.

"This is for the mountain god. This is for the Buddha. And this is for Masahiko's grandfather and our father as well. Makes a decent offering, don't you think?"

Next she divided the noodles and dished out portions for the three people into some light plastic bowls.

Slurping down the clear hot noodles brought back a powerfully nostalgic taste.

"What, doesn't our simple fare suit you?" Ohina asked him with deep concern.

"No, I love it—is this what you call 'simple fare?'"

Ohina and Omomo looked at each other and laughed.

"Well, it'll have to do. This is the sort of makeshift meal we fix when we're in a hurry. Sorry."

"Oh, I see. Anyhow, it tastes great."

As soon as he said this Omomo cut in with a rough voice.

"You must be hungry because you've been working . . . But myself, I don't really go for this sort of soppy noodles."

"What's this nonsense?—after you lugged all these things up here yourself."

"OK. Actually I was thinking I'd rather have instant ramen, but since it's O-bon I decided I should make somen. The thought of making the broth and fixing all the ingredients for somen and then lugging up the bowls, the bamboo noodle racks and the pails and all—it gave me a headache. So in the end I decided on beggars' stew."

Omomo's voice seemed to carry a scornful tone. Perhaps her pride had been wounded by serving such a plain meal to a guest. She added,

"You know Mother, in the shops in town now they're calling this sort of thing 'new style' noodles."

"Well, it's fine with me."

Masahiko was amused at hearing the argument going on between mother and daughter.

A while ago, back before they had put up the hut and while Masahiko was pacing about by the water and wondering where he should scatter the bones, Ohina had called to him.

"I think we should do it after we've offered a prayer together."

To this, Omomo had added rather brusquely, "I doubt the fish will eat the bones while it's still light."

His grandfather had told him to feed his bones to the fish. But, he wondered if it were done at night, would the fish eat the bones? Just when he had started to get tired of holding the urn of ashes they made the decision to scatter the bones at night.

"It seems appropriate that since he was from Utazaka you're leaving his ashes there too."

Ohina said this after she lit the lanterns. Already Utazaka Hill had grown dark.

"It would help if we had a boat when we scatter the ashes."

"If we had one we could put this lantern on it. Shall we make one now? A reed boat?"

"Even if we take the bones on a boat, the currents in the water around the dam flow only on the bottom. I'm afraid the bones won't be carried anywhere by the currents and they won't reach the Western Paradise of Amida."

"What direction is the Paradise of the West, Mother?"

"It's beyond where the river flows—in the direction of Oki no Miya, isn't it?"

A bit surprised at being asked to agree, Masahiko responded,

"Actually, I've never thought about such things."

"Really? Not even once? And you came back here to scatter your grandfather's bones?"

The two women looked at the young man as if they were regarding a strange creature.

As he finished his noodles, Masahiko's attention was caught by the chopsticks that had been made out of mountain azaleas. He placed them in the palm of his hand and laid them on top of the bowl.

A while ago, when he had been sent to look for wood for making chopsticks, just as he was reaching for a small tree with red leaves, Omomo had yelled at him—"Hey! Don't do that!"—and jumped over and given Masahiko's hand a hard smack. The shriek penetrated his skull. Again, Omomo snapped at her mother.

"This guy here, it seems he doesn't know anything at all. And he's supposed to have graduated from some university, isn't he?"

"OK, OK, but you don't have to shout and startle us like that."

In saying this Ohina blinked her eyes and looked toward Masahiko in bewilderment.

"If you use poison sumac for chopsticks your whole mouth will swell up."

Just the thought of it made Masahiko feel itchy. This was his first experience eating something using the branches of trees. Come to think of it, it figured—the first tree he'd been about to touch turned out to be poison sumac. He'd heard that these trees could make you itch, but he'd never seen the real thing. And here in the mountains he hadn't known that these were the first trees to turn color. Even so, they had such an inviting fresh red color.

The word "university" had stung. He felt Omomo had been keeping her eyes on him. As he held his chopsticks he became conscious of how his fingers were so much smoother than those of the women. The air in the narrow hut grew a bit denser and Ohina began to move about making rustling sounds.

"Well, it's getting dark. Shall we light the lanterns?"

With the lanterns lit, the altar in the thatched grass hut looked as if it contained implements for some sort of sorcery. The women brought out their prayer beads and lit incense. There was a sound of pouring liquor and the aroma filled his nose.

"So let's offer a prayer. Here's an offering of *shochu* as well."

The *shochu* was poured into *sake* cups so small they looked as if they'd been made for children playing house. After the prayers were finished she instructed him to drink.

"If you don't drink this you won't be able to greet the souls of the dead."

Taking this as a part of the ceremony he drank it down quickly but he gagged on the overpowering fragrance.

The women exclaimed together.

"What, is this your first time?"

Along the darkening waterfront the sounds of birds' wings and voices were audible, but as the moon swelled these sounds grew harder to hear. Whenever the three moved about the hut they stirred up the smell of the grasses that lay spread about them.

Though Masahiko had intended to drink only one cup it was passed around again and again. Something brown in color that looked somewhat like cheese was placed on wide dwarf bamboo leaves. They called it "miso-pickled tofu." It tasted great.

"So everyone, here we are at our O-bon feast. The souls of the dead should be pleased."

"Well, if it's to please the souls of the dead, I guess I can do anything."

Feeling the sudden effects of the *shochu*, Masahiko continued in this manner.

"First we have to do this! This!"

Suddenly he stood up, holding the container of bones.

"You're right. We need to scatter the ashes."

Omomo went first in line, taking the lanterns and heading down toward the water.

"Which way is it to Utazaka, Mother? It's dark."

"If we head toward the persimmon tree we should be able to find it. It's a big tree."

The two women looked around. The water wasn't very cold. The light of the lanterns spread out about their feet. Then Omomo called out.

"Say, look over there—it looks like some lanterns moving along. About five of them."

"What? Which way? I don't see anything."

"Over there. Now and then you can just see them flickering. Where do you suppose those souls could be from?"

"You must have drunk too much, Omomo. I can't see anything."

"Someone besides us must have come for O-bon."

"Well then who could it be? I haven't heard that any families were planning to come up here for O-bon. I don't know of anyone who's died in the past year so there shouldn't be much reason for it."

Masahiko felt the waves lapping comfortably against his feet. Perhaps someone was coming to Utazaka.

"Look! Again—the lights."

Ohina remained silent for a while, probably searching for the lights.

"Which way are they?"

Omomo held out her arm but Masahiko had no sense of where it was in the old village she was pointing to.

"Omomo, your teacher used to say your eyesight was pretty bad from astigmatism. I heard you used to paint four or five moons. Don't you think it could just be the reflections of our lights jumping around over there?"

"You mean like a mirage? But it seems I see lights here and there," Masahiko added.

"You must be drunk on the *shochu*."

"Maybe so. But what if I get even more drunk?"

"Before you're completely gone we need to scatter the ashes of the bones. This must be Utazaka, right here. Omomo, lend me a hand will you?"

Without speaking, the women with their red lanterns walked slowly toward Masahiko. He removed the lid of the urn. His hands were shaking and the lid dropped into the water.

"It's okay. It's okay. No need to pick it up. Soon we're going to scatter what's inside."

In the faint light of the lamps, the ashes appeared blackish. Suddenly Ohina's voice became choked with tears and she held out both of her hands.

"Please—the bones. Won't you let me scatter the bones?"

Masahiko had no reason to refuse. He nodded and held out the white urn, tipped it, and spilled some ashes into her hands. Bending over, she chanted *Namandabu, Namandabu . . .* but she choked on her tears and tried to hold the ashes to her breast. She must have spilled them, as she was brushing her chest repeatedly. "What happened, Mother? Spilling the bones like that."

"What shall I do? The moon—the moon over the lake—it carried me away."

"Whatever you say, you've spilled them now so what are you going to do?"

"It's all right. Don't worry about it. We were going to scatter them anyway. As long as it's over Amazoko, any place is all right."

Holding the urn with one hand, Masahiko felt he must have looked like the old character Hanasaka in the fable; the one who scattered the ashes that made the trees blossom. As he poured the ashes they felt gritty to the touch.

I will never forget this texture as long as I live. Grandfather, you often said your dreams were filled with Amazoko. Now I'm standing at the entrance to dreams. It feels good, Grandfather. Two women are beside me. You know Ohina, don't you . . .? I can't tell whether she was beautiful once.

With these words, tears began to well up in Masahiko's eyes.

Ohina is covered in ashes. Her sobbing is turning to heavy tears. Perhaps this is what happens at good memorial services.

Her voice choked with tears, Ohina tugged at Masahiko's shirt.

"Don't go out any farther. Omomo, you have to help me. You mustn't drown yourself. We don't want to have to do a funeral for you tomorrow."

"Don't worry about me. I can swim all right."

"You don't want to have to swim here now, in the dark and cold."

"I'm not going swimming. They're gone. The ashes."

Masahiko had a strange sense of a gap existing between his feelings and his actions. Decisively, he hurled the empty urn into the dark water. There was a splash. Then he turned around and saw Ohina with her back to him, standing in her underwear and washing out her kimono.

"What are you doing, Mother?"

"I've spilled Masahito's ashes all over myself. I'm sending them home."

The moonlight quavered about the water. Ohina's body was dimly lit as she walked out of the water carrying her wrung-out clothing. Slowly, Omomo returned to the water's edge carrying a change of white clothing she had gotten for her mother from the hut, shaking out the clothes in the air as she went. The scene looked as if large birds were touching down and arranging their feathers. Silence returned.

The women entered the hut. They gathered the *sake* vessels and silently handed out the cups.

"Omomo, why don't you try singing the songs for O-bon?"

There was no response. Ohina tilted her head.

"Somehow, tonight it seems the feeling has slipped away. It seems we can't make it back to Amazoko, no matter how much we look for the entrance."

"Even here at Utazaka?"

"Even at Utazaka. I wonder why."

"If we can't get there . . . why don't we call it up—call Amazoko to come to us?"

"Oh . . ."

Surprised, Ohina let out a sigh. Then she replied,

"You're right. We need to summon it. Call it up from the bottom of the lake."

I guess that's what it means to be taught by your own child, thought Ohina. And at that time a vision from back in the old days—of Oai-sama wearing her distinctive white headdress that reminded one of a bride—passed before Ohina's eyes.

That's exactly what I was thinking; the idea struck Ohina. In the times of drought it seemed I was being called out to by someone from the depths of the water. Surely it must have been Oai-sama. And even if it wasn't her, haven't I seen visions of Oai-sama any number of times passing along the pathways at the bottom of the lake with her head covered in white? She walked through the deserted village with her cane in her hand, supporting her hunched back and with her head tilted to the side. Certainly Oai-sama wouldn't have gone anywhere else.

She must still be watching over the village now at the bottom of the lake and stripped of its houses and people.

And so that was why Omomo had said, *Why don't we call it up—call Amazoko to come to us.* If they summoned Oai-sama, the sunken village would appear.

Whether in fair weather or foul, Oai-sama had never gone out without a white towel done up about her head. Whether she was in the tea fields or the mulberry groves, in the shade of the school playground or the outhouse, or in the alleyway at the back door of the house of a newborn child, there was never a day when Oai-sama's white hood was not seen.

"Oai-sama, how are you today?"

"Where are you going today, Oai-sama?"

There wasn't a child who, in coming upon that bent old back of hers, didn't call out to Oai-sama from behind and receive her nod of acknowledgment before passing by. Every one of them had been helped into the world by this old midwife. They might forget even their schoolteachers, but not one of them ever forgot Oai-sama. And now everyone from that village was gone.

Already thirty years had passed since the dam had been filled and the village was left submerged on the bottom. In the beginning, wanting to check on the sunken village, Ohina had trudged up there through the bushes, all the while worrying about snakes under foot. It had been hard to suppress the desire to go and be near the area around the dam.

Along the stream, where some washing stones had been placed, there had been a small double-arched stone bridge where they had set up a water wheel for hulling rice. Near it there was a sandalwood tree that spread its branches as if it were gazing upward. The stream meandered gently through the valley and, in a place where there were lots of the flat washing stones, the sandalwood tree had stood like a huge umbrella. After the autumnal equinox the tree began to turn color. And after the hoarfrost dusted the valley a few times, countless little bell-shaped, dark peony-colored flowers would come out. When you passed beneath it to wash out the offertory rice bowls the water would be faintly steeped in red and the stream took on the appearance of a shimmering mandala laid out in cloth upon the surface of the water.

And there by the stream at the autumnal equinox the soul of a stillborn baby would come to Ohina; a soul unknown to Omomo. When Ohina was washing her bowls and gazing on the surface of the stream it looked as if the water was dyed in the colors of five different clouds. All of a sudden she would break out in tears. Had the baby lived, it would have known only hardships. It was for the best that it had become a spirit of the water. This is what Oai-sama had done, taking it to the other world. A cloud of spray covered Ohina's face. She wiped her eyes on the sleeve of her cooking apron.

As they did their washing together at this same place, with the spray from the stream dancing about them, the women would say;

"How good it feels; everything floats away."

The reddened color of the water would play about and reflect off the faces of the women.

"Yes, everything floats away."

With her forehead sparkling in beads of water, Ohina also would say that. The women were always bustling about at the washing place. Had it all been just a dream? That day when the village was flooded and the people all stood about the dam with their hands folded—the sight of it flitted in and out and mixed with Ohina's thoughts. Words, like those in a song, drifted from her mouth.

"The fate of this world and the fate of that world are not separate."

Those had been the words Oai-sama had sung in her mourning song for departed children. Ohina could hear her voice calling out and floating up from the depths of the lake.

Yaa
Hôre yaa
Sixteenth night of O-bon
Flowers of the moon
Scattering, scattering
Night of flowers

At some point Omomo climbed up on the rock and sat down. She sang just two verses, as if listening to a voice from the depths of the lake.

Yaa
Hôre yaa
Five-colored clouds
In the moonlight

Had Omomo forgotten the words to the song, or was she adjusting her voice? She sang no further. Slowly, in a low-pitched voice, Ohina took over.

Five-colored clouds
In the moonlight
Just barely visible
In the mirror of the water

The far side of the lake was not particularly dark. Hearing this unfathomable, otherworldly singing sent a shiver down Masahiko's spine that left him clenching his fists. These were melodies and words of a sort he had never heard before. Could

they be from those old dreamlike *imayô* songs that have become incomprehensible to people today?

Yaa
Hôre yaa
The far side of the waters
Embraces

The darkness
In the distant world

The voices had a powerful effect on the human soul.

It seemed to Masahiko that what lay beyond in the water
was something that was gazing upward from the depths of the
lake. He noticed how the blackened mountains lay gathered
upon each other. He thought; those mountains, they're about
to go to sleep holding innumerable lives in their breasts. We
exist in the midst of such an enormous breathing. I felt this
when I lay against the andromeda tree at noontime and heard
the sound of the sap in that giant tree circulating all around
me.

The moon had climbed high and the sky was filled with
stars. The darkness in the sky beyond the waters was something that could not be expressed in the words of astronomy.
Until now Masahiko had never realized that the spirit of a song
could affect him so deeply; that it could relate a tale with such
passion. What sort of song was this? It was entirely different
from the kind of songs performed on a stage where the audience is expected to applaud.

A while back when Ohina complained that she couldn't get
back to the sunken village, hadn't Omomo replied, "*If we can't
get there, why don't we call up Amazoko?*" That really struck me.

Call up? How could a person do such a thing? Masahiko couldn't help feeling that they had intended to cast some sort of sorcerer's spell. Mere skill alone could not have brought forth this voice, filled with the strength of supplication, rising up and piercing through the hard night skies. The *miko* shrine maidens in the old times must have sung like this woman. She must have intended her song as an invocation. And even if a part of her inspiration may have come simply from wanting to sing a country song for this city boy from Tokyo, her spirit was by no means explained by that alone. Her singing was supported by some overwhelming sense of yearning.

Omomo stood on a rock in the moonlight. Her straw hat looked black. It was the one Ohina had worn at midday. She was swaying her body gently. Ohina thought; *Could it be? Is Omomo going to dance?* It had been ages since the two of them had performed the O-bon dance.

So Omomo may prove to be a true daughter of Amazoko after all . . . The people in town have been saying all kinds of things about her. I've had to put up with it, shutting my eyes and ears, knowing the time would come when her good nature would show through. And look, now she's telling us what none of those folks who stood up there on the banks of the dam could have thought of—"*Call up Amazoko.*"

I'll leave the best part of the song for you . . . And as Ohina was thinking these things, slowly, softly she summoned her daughter's voice with her song. Yes, thought Ohina, we'll call it up—the two of us. Let's call up the village of Amazoko, and take along the spirit of Masahito, even.

Behind Ohina's eyelids, floating up from the soil of the village below, countless bubbles spread out and broke open on the surface. Back at the time when the water was let in to flood the village, for two or three days or more, tiny mud-colored bubbles had risen up to engulf the trunks of all the trees in the village. They crept up to the surface of the water and remained there for a while before breaking. The sandalwood trees disappeared, and so did the elm trees at the bank of the Isara River, along with the great old ginkgo trees at the graveyard, and the pagoda trees. And the tea fields on the slopes along the mountains also cast up countless bubbles when they were flooded. Muddy-colored bubbles were blown away on the wind, sometimes sticking together and sometimes being pulled apart and disappearing. The old women had watched, holding back tears with the edges of their sleeves and calling out, "Souls—those are souls!"

Three years had passed. Five years had passed, and still the trees remained with their roots spread out on the bottom of the water. It looked almost as if they were still alive now. Ohina thought to herself; In those days my legs were still strong. My eyes could still see far.

Since the time the Isara River had started to flow from below the dam and the place came to be known as the Otachidote Embankment the people of the village had begun to scatter and leave. The remains of the old houses at the bottom of the lake had also disintegrated and been lost. And yet—Ohina thought to herself—the graves are still there. And the spirits sheltered among the trees—they must still be there. And the guardian spirits of the estate and of the farmlands too. And the gods of the rocks and wells too—they wouldn't have gone far. And the ancient guardian spirits of the village, just like the weeping cherry—they wouldn't want to go off somewhere else. It's as if I've become one with those guardian sprits who are now at the bottom of the water.

Among those who now and then still came up to the embankment to look over the area around the dam there were, besides Ohina, four or five old women who had belonged to neither the opposing nor the supporting factions but had hesitated without taking a decisive stand. When they happened to meet at the embankment they felt at a loss for words, embarrassed.

"Ah, so here we are again."

When they met, they would nod and exchange greetings. Somehow, in the manner of the old days, their hands would fall into the accustomed motions of reaching down to the roadside to pick up fallen branches for firewood. But even as they started, their motions would slow.

"With gas-heated baths today we don't need firewood anymore. But the gas can sometimes be cut off can't it? I don't suppose the young people will want it, but I'll just make up a small bundle and take it with me."

And so, although it wasn't really the sort of thing to take home, the old women would sit on their bundles of sticks, and as they gazed at the bottom of the water they would reminisce fondly about Oai-sama.

With one hand at her back and the other clutching a hemlock cane Oai-sama would stand with her patchwork cloth bag. Everyone knew what it held; some *jintan* lozenges, coins, cut tobacco, roasted *kusagina* shrimp, and pills. In her younger days she'd carried a fine leather bag filled with all the equipment of a midwife.

In good weather or bad she appeared always with a towel wrapped about her head, and even from a distance people knew it was she. When she was working at pulling out weeds in the tea fields she would use an old towel. If she were going to the temple she would wear a brand new one. Whenever the women of the village had any old towels that could be used for head coverings they would say with a bit of embarrassment, "This is a bride's headdress for Oai-sama."

The occasions when the village women carried parasols had been special days such as weddings or town festivals, or when a young woman who had moved to the city returned for a visit. Walking down Utazaka Hill in one's finest clothes and carrying a parasol had given the feeling of walking down the stage of a theater. And the sound of a silk hem brushing against the feet was so very different from that of cotton. The rustle of silk sent a smooth feeling all the way up from the bottom of the feet to the nape of the neck. Those who were working in the fields and tilling the ground would stand up to look. Those gathering brush would drop their work. Seeing a parasol appear like some enormous flower coming down Utazaka Hill was a sight that never failed to capture people's eyes. *I wonder whose daughter that is coming home.* Thinking about this while doing some routine work brought pleasure, and a young woman's homecoming was a welcome sight.

Before nightfall everyone would know whose daughter had returned. And whether she were coming back for the O-bon festivities, or for a wedding, or if it was because of an illness, when she walked down Utazaka Hill she would pluck up her spirits and walk along in the spirit of a flower. For the old folks, just seeing the appearance of the girl and catching the expression on her face had given them enough to imagine the prospects for her family in the future.

If a girl happened to meet Oai-sama at the foot of the bridge it was good luck.

"Oh—*baachan*, Oai-sama, how are you getting along?"

Oai-sama would raise her towel-covered head, blink her eyes and figure out which family's girl it was. She knew the distinctive features of the faces of all the families in the village. To her the girl would be the very image of some old childhood friend. It brought her a comforting feeling, as if someone had returned from the past. Even the voice would call out in the same way. And when she heard it, the wrinkles around Oai-sama's eyes would break into a smile.

"Oh my goodness, what a fine young lady you've become."

"Ah, you still remember me. I was just thinking we might meet at this bridge. And it turned out I was right—we *did* meet here."

"Yes, yes indeed. And you have such a nice flowered parasol. And have you gotten rid of those nasty old *kan* bugs—the old jealousy bugs—yet?"

"Obaachan, they don't bother me any more. Your 'mountain shrimp' did the trick."

Bursting out in laughter, the girl's voice would be sucked up into the flow of the current beneath the bridge.

Whenever there was an outbreak of the *kan* bugs among the village children it was usually Oai-sama who took care of them. When the children were two or three years old or so and a new brother or sister was born, the symptoms of the *kan* bugs would invariably show up. The children would grow jealous of the newborn baby and in their fits of rage they'd do things like putting a cat on its belly, or covering its face with a cushion, and at night they'd cry out even more than the baby. At those times the parents would call on Oai-sama to cast her spell on them.

"Who is it? Who has the *kan* bugs now?"

And then she would remove the towel from her head and wipe around the back of the children's head and neck, and then, leading them on, she would exclaim,

"Aha—here they are! Here! They're right here—those nasty old *kan* bugs! Look—one, two—three of them!"

And as she counted them in her palm, right before their eyes she would lay out some *kusagina* bugs.

"Look here. Look what I found! It was going after this child! I'll just eat this bug right up."

"Umm-mm— . . . Dee—licious. How wonderful. Mountain shrimp. What a treat. Just open your mouth and try one."

And so the child who had been sulking and crying would be taken in by the movements of Oai-sama's hands and mouth and by the longish shape of the insect that looked like a burned silkworm and had a fragrant smell. As if charmed by magic, the child would open its mouth partway. And before it could close it again, in a flash Oai-sama popped the bug right into the child's mouth and kept the child from spitting it out.

"Like this—just keep on chewing on it."

Oai-sama would show how it was done by making the motions with her own mouth.

"Ummmm. Such a wonderful taste, don't you think? Mountain shrimp. Weren't they delicious? And now those *kan* bugs are dead. All gone. So now you won't have to bother about the baby any more."

That mysterious sensation, with the smell of the *kusagina* bugs and their crispy, crunchy feeling on the tongue, was such that the young children never forgot it. The spell worked perfectly. Seeing the babies, who were just learning to move their own hands and feet, the children felt as if those slithering white insects were coming right from their own necks, and it gave them their first experience of such mysterious, frightful things.

These insects, which have a fragrant odor when roasted, live on the *kusagina* bush and crawl about in a house made of sawdust. When problems with the jealousy bugs appeared among the children Oai-sama would take some of these insects and roast them on skewers. People let the children eat them because they were said to be good for curing the problem. And if they had Oai-sama's spell on them they worked wonders in curing jealousy. And they worked not only for children, but for curing beriberi in grown-ups as well.

Ohina had been taught the methods of preparing such traditional medicines and remedies by Oai-sama, and even today she earned a living from making them.

It was these images of Oai-sama that came back and floated about in Ohina's mind when she was told by Omomo to call up the village from the bottom of the lake. For the past year she had been hounded by a feeling that she was being called out to by Oai-sama. And when she realized it, it seemed as if the air around her were being ripped apart, as if it were water.

The three hanging lanterns all went dark. Their candles had burned out.

The lake was flooded in tones of silver. And from the grasses all about the dense bushes the earth called out in the voices of insects. The moon above the water had shifted farther into the direction of the graveyard.

"The fireflies are settling down for the night, but look—over there—there are still a few left. And there too."

At Ohina's prompting, when Masahiko turned around he could see faint lights flickering on and off, playing about in the low thickets.

"It's so soon after Masahito's bones have come back, but . . . tonight's the sixteenth night of O-bon."

Suddenly the tone of Ohina's voice dropped and became like the voices of the insects on the ground. He couldn't make out the expression on her face.

"I saw them in my dream—three lanterns. It's good we brought them."

"At least we were able to make it here this year for O-bon. Even if it's only for one night."

As Omomo spoke, she maintained the tone of her song from before. Even Masahiko realized that this night, being the sixteenth night of O-bon, was the night of the sending-off of the souls of the dead. Ohina and Omomo seemed sorry that they could spend only one night in welcoming Masahito's soul.

"I too am glad I could come here for O-bon. Tokyo is no place for the souls of the dead to return to. I think I'm starting to understand Grandfather's feelings a little better."

Masahiko's words came from his heart. When he was still alive his grandfather must have dearly wished to return here. In this place it seemed that a primordial presence linked day with night, moving from the mountainside through the forest and extending into the pulse of the water. It seemed to him as if the roaring, screeching nightfall in Tokyo was all an illusion. In such a place do things like sunsets really exist?

For people who hardly even notice whether the sun goes down over the tops of the ranks of skyscrapers, from where does the impulse come to scratch away at the gasping surface of the earth? Doesn't it seem that some giant invisible hand is reaching out and grasping the outer skin of these crowded islands—or rather, taking the real skin from beneath their surface—and turning it inside out? And the cars; isn't it as if they've all been placed on a mosaic grid of one of those models of a city at an architectural exposition, and as if the giant hand has suddenly pulled the earth's skin inside out with them on it?

The people riding on top of this surface make no effort to be aware of the fate of the body. Driven on by anxiety as if being chased toward some unseen cliff, they scurry about in cars and trains and hardly take notice of the brutal excavators flailing their arms about in the night skies. Cut off from their hearts they pass along in a flurry, trying not to notice that those machines are shoveling away the very earth that once nursed them into being.

It's the sensitive but nihilistic young who lead the way, rushing on toward that dark edge. Instinctively they realize they're the pied pipers of the end of the century. Pipers claiming allegiance to no country, they blow with all their might. Raising a

colored fog to cheer them on, and decked out in artificial flowers and laser beams, they wail and call out.

Ah—that tree
in our dream
Will that shining white magnolia
bloom for us?

It seems such a short trip—
just like our lives
Just one leap and
we'll slip through that casket
decorated in flowers
You, my love, before me
look back and wave to me
with your tender smile

That's the sort of thing they sing, preening about in fashion.

Masahiko saw an enormous casket floating on the dark surface of the water, decorated about its edges with flowers. The
casket was like a hole. Gradually its borders changed colors,
and then suddenly it took on the appearance of a roulette
wheel. Amber-colored beams of light flashed into the center
from all directions and then faded out. From time to time faint
green-colored, flame-like shapes gathered together and then
scattered, pulling and pushing cars and young people coming
in from outside the casket. For some reason Masahiko took
these flickering green flame-like things to be spirits of the
earth. Neither balls of fire nor drops of water, they seemed to
be the undulating colors of life itself.

Masahiko had never imagined such things before. Perhaps it
was Ohina's earlier voice, sounding as if it lay hidden in the

earth that had started him thinking this way. From both Ohina and Omomo who were nearby, and from his grandfather beneath the ginkgo tree, he had received a strong sense that they were all staring together into the scene appearing and disappearing on the surface of the lake. He heard a voice.

You seeds who fall to the earth to bear seeds. You are seeds of yet other seeds. Your embryos have melted away.

And yet, knowing your body is the earth, you who already know that you are offered as sacrifices, you come back to life through songs.

These hidden songs are the pathways for approaching the gods.

The voice was an echo of a sound that crept up though the heavy water. Crouching down in front of the ginkgo tree, his grandfather Masahito was bending a thin finger.

"There goes one. And another—now it's two. And still they're coming—there's a third one . . . And they're still so fresh and young. But it can't be helped."

I wonder if there are sounds under the water where that casket is floating. And then, in the time between when I left and I arrived here, could there have been some sort of sound? Didn't I hear something?

I can't recall it well now. Perhaps there was an invisible cave at the roots of the ginkgo tree that stood in front of Nakano station where my grandfather often passed the time. Grandfather's spirit must have called out from there and urged me on, and so I came here. I got on a plane, but it seems that somewhere along the way there was the haunting voice of a crying baby. As long as the crying continued I felt so uneasy. It was as if the voice was calling out a warning that we were going to crash. Inside the airplane everything was silent. It seemed there was no one else on the plane, other than the baby. Could the scream have originated from the feelings I experienced way back when I was still in the womb, worrying about being born? Could what happened to me in coming here from the cave by the ginkgo tree in Nakano be a memory of time travel?

Was this an illusion? Something like a faint flame of water was rising up from the lake.

This was the village in the valley. It seemed that for Ohina, who had continued to watch over it, her old hometown had never died. It was as if Ohina and Omomo regarded this artificial lake, constructed with the latest engineering technology, as but a transparent cocoon that contained sleeping within it the chrysalis and silkworm of the village of old.

It must be thirty-five years now since the village was flooded. But the things sleeping at the bottom of the lake must be much older than that. These two people believe it's like a chrysalis that's going to break through a cocoon, and that these things will one day appear again from the bottom of the lake. The name of the village, "Amazoko"—"the bottom of heaven"—shows it's had a deep meaning from the beginning.

From all he'd heard from his grandfather's stories, Masahiko wished he could pull together the scattered images of the village at the time it was flooded and had crumbled and been sealed off beneath the waters. But how could he, with his city upbringing, expect such things to reappear when he'd never been to the village even once? All that appeared in his imagination now were the muddy-colored bubbles of water.

He drew a breath. It seemed strange how quickly he'd been taken in by all the things of his grandfather's village. And it seemed it had been his good fortune to escape so easily. It was not as if he'd made any conscious attempt to escape, but following the voice of his grandfather, with whom he'd gotten along so well, and then in coming here, he had come to think of the bloated, cracking city of Tokyo as a giant cancer cell. It seemed as if, by coincidence, he had just slipped away and landed here.

He heard the reverberations of a voice coming from the far-off forest, crossing over the waters.

"What's that sound?" he asked.

In a low voice, Ohina explained.

"Ah, that. It's a *kozo* bird."

"An owl—it's an owl," added Omomo.

So *that's* a *kozo*? Those regal birds live here in this forest? Perhaps it's here that what we call "voice" originates. And perhaps that's why the voices of Ohina and Omomo are so different from those of other people.

Masahiko was drawn into the depths of his inner being. He felt as if he had shed the supposedly rational patchwork covering of the civilization of concrete and had been left as a soft, naked nerve, lying quivering and nestled among the blades of grass about his feet, dissolved in the midst of the evening dew.

It seemed that the essential meaning of the world must be held in something like the flowering of moss on a rock somewhere in this sunken village. It must be something like the way human thought overflowed and became voice for the first time.

In the time since he'd met these two people it was as if, in just a brief instant, in the wink of an eye, meaning had taken on a new existence. He thought back on the time when the mountains had stood out most vividly, just before sunset. The madder-red sky overflowed with scents of the most exquisite herbs, and the beginnings and final moments of the earth seemed to be vibrating in lingering tones, spreading out to eternity. When he thought of this, almost for the first time, Masahiko had a feeling of wanting to pray. In this place, except for the dam, there was not a single straight line of expressionless man-made things.

As Masahiko watched, the phantom-like image of the flower-lined casket floating on the dark surface of the water became superimposed with the transparent cocoon that Ohina and Omomo had seen, and then the image faded away. It occurred to him that all material phenomena in the world must be layered, connected, and bound up, embracing life. This noon Omomo had pointed to the ground and taught him about the dwarf grasses that were just staring to come into color. As if he himself were grass, he began to realize that he was becoming able to hear clearly for the first time.

Again, the voice of the *kozo* bird drifted past. It was a voice filled with hints and suggestiveness. Muting the sounds of their footsteps, the two women went back into the grass hut and lit the little children's lanterns again. A faint trace of the incense drifted about. A while back Ohina had spoken of the last fireflies of the night, but probably the voices of most of the other insects had faded out as well. He didn't know their names but he could hear that, amidst the little plants and the bamboo thicket about the lake, the night was filled with the muffled tones and secret voices of birds preening themselves.

The sounds of the night winds seemed to ripple over the mountains and enter into the heart of the forest in the way the roar of the ocean can also be heard faintly from far, far away.

And as he heard this sound, suddenly from a short distance the clear tone of a bell rang out. It was like the sound of a bell used at a Buddhist altar. Probably it had been brought here for this night. The tone was uncommonly lovely and mysterious.

Like the rumble of the ocean, like the sound of distant waves, the sound drifted faintly and slowly in. Then, with a quiet *chirin* sound, the bell rang once again. Its beautiful reverberations were mixed with waves. On the top of the rock, Omomo stood up slowly.

Yaa,
Hôre yaa
Sixteenth night of O-bon
Flowers of the moon
Scattering, Scattering,
Flowers of night

Masahiko's entire body became an ear. The song conveyed the feeling of the low voice he'd heard before. But what was this voice? It was like a strangely colored sort of string. It drew in something invisible, and then in an instant it seemed to release. Where had she disappeared to, that light-hearted country girl he'd seen in the daytime?

Yaa
Hôre yaa

This time it was Ohina. Her voice sounded deeply. Perhaps those sounds that had seemed like insect voices a while back had come from her warming up for singing.

Stay
Just one night
Lingering farewell
Shadow on the water

Masahiko lowered his head and gazed out on the surface of the lake, seeing what appeared to be a dark rising flame of water. A profound grief, the sort that would make a person straighten right up, rose from the depths of the lake. What sort of face was it that rose up before Ohina in her thoughts? He felt pained at knowing nothing about the ways of the people from this village tucked away in the mountains.

His grandfather had sometimes talked about how the people of Amazoko were so good-looking.

Yaa,
Hôre yaa
This village
Shadow of heaven
Snows bedded down
Rise up

Become a person
It is destined
Distant light of
Oki no Miya

In the travelers'
Lodging
Flowers trail down
Along the heart

Ohina and Omomo took turns singing. With the bell sounding slowly between the verses the melody conveyed the feelings of a *shomyo* song of parting, or of an old *kudoku* song of wooing. As Masahiko listened to the two voices he tried to follow the tones of the invisible strings, but it was a melody like a rainbow in a moonlit night, arching across the mountainsides. The distant forest captured it and reverberated in a deep chord. It seemed as if the sounds were aware of their own positions and they were flying away in the birth of a new song.

Ohina's voice had a supple, penetrating quality which she concentrated and directed toward the bottom of the lake.

Then her song changed into a sort of epic tale.

This time it was mixed with the tones of heavy dried wood. Masahiko recalled having heard this sound before. At his grandfather's funeral, the Amida sutra had been read to the accompaniment of the pleasant sharp rap of wooden clappers. Ohina and Omomo had brought a pair here with them. These clappers were known as *ongi*, "sound trees."

The old tales tell of a traveler who came and left. People kept the seeds of a flower secretly and let them grow in Oki no Miya.

One of the verses of this tale served as a kind of historical record of the village of Amazoko. As Masahiko listened and entered into the story it seemed as if the villagers and the souls of the dead were even more strongly present than when they had lived in this world.

So is this the way things are? It seems the dead become better souls by returning on O-bon.

Had the passage of time since the sinking of the village made it possible to think such things? But then, despite the fact that in the old times the pathways to the world beyond had all been open, it seemed that until now, for him, they had all been closed.

When did he fall asleep? From the bottom of the lake a flame was rising up.

He had seen flowers in the water before. But a fire in the water; this was a first. In the distance a bell sounded softly. It was not the bell of a fire alarm; rather, it was like the bell that had accompanied the song he had heard—*Flowers of the moon, Scattering, Scattering.*

Villagers appeared, circling around a house going up in flames. It was quite a large building. Both men and women were lit up in the colors of flames with their loose hair blowing about in the night sky. An old man who was staring into the flames with his arms folded spoke to Masahiko.

"It's quite a sight when things come to an end. The bell tonight, it has a good sound."

It was a face from the past that he'd known well, and yet he couldn't recall it. From what era could this person have come? A little girl appeared, glancing downward and then lifting her face. It seemed he had known this girl too in the past. Cradling something like a doll, she spoke as if seeking agreement.

"I guess I have to let this go too."

Held in front of her was a terribly soiled doll made of cloth, missing its eyes and nose. The doll might have been in the original image of the ones known as *amagatsu*. Masahiko was captivated by the innocence of the girl's voice. Appearing to be the kind of person who notices everything, the girl made him feel as if he were some sort of ceremonial attendant following along behind. She looked about five or six years in age. She was wearing a kimono in the red colors of a peony and an obi that shone with a silver color. The obi was embroidered in blue and gold stitching with designs of dragons and flowers.

The little girl passed through the openings among the trees, wending her way through the densely growing leaves, lit up by the light of the fire. The place was called the Otachidote Embankment. Coming to an abrupt stop and then facing the other direction she exclaimed,

"The flowers of the moon. The flowers of the moon."

After saying this, the colors of the fire in the night scene faded away and countless butterfly-like objects fluttered about. Taking a closer look he realized that they were gingko leaves, falling from above the graveyard. The course of the Isara River extended far up into the dark valley.

The little girl raised her sleeve again, shook it, and called out.

"Oki no Miya. Oki no Miya."

What was it she was trying to say? He wanted her to turn around so he could find out, but in silence she went down to the river, heading in the direction of its source. Was there something up there in the upper reaches of the Isara River? Yet it seemed to Masahiko that Oki no Miya should be *down-stream*, in the direction of the sea. The colors of her obi, tied in back and hanging down, swayed and trailed off into the misty reaches of the river as if in an illusion. With its muted silver tones the sheen of the fabric made it appear so close that he might even touch it if he reached out. If he were to pull on the obi she would be turned around toward him—yet he feared that doing anything like touching it or speaking out might make it all vanish.

Behind her was a valley with toppled trees all piled up. In one giant fallen tree that faced this way there was an opening of a cave. The girl was standing in front of it and it seemed as if she were waiting for something. Feeling afraid—for what reason he couldn't understand—Masahiko stopped short. What should he do? Should he follow along into the opening? And then once again in the distance the bell began to ring plaintively. Its striking sounded more like a temple bell than the one he'd heard before. He heard a voice singing that filled the valley. The voice sounded like Omomo's.

It's near the striking
Of seven now
Flowers are turning colors
In the sunken village

The sadness, sweetness and beauty of the voice filled his chest. Then, suddenly, the moonlit night landscape became alive with color and throughout the valley the varied threads of the streams and waterways appeared in daytime colors. In the stands of trees the colored leaves shook and rustled. The smells were of deep mountains and water. In the midst of his dream, Masahiko thought;

This smell, it's something I've known from ages back, from back before I was born. Yet how could I have gone back? I must have been too closed in. I came here naïve, straight from the city. And then as he was looking ahead, as he'd feared, the girl disappeared into the opening of that great fallen tree. In the dark depths of the cave faint lights were moving about.

Coming closer and straining his eyes it looked as if, in the spaces between the rank ferns and their beard-like roots, snails were scurrying about in surprise all over the place, in little bands. Masahiko was held in astonishment. A city inside a tree in the valley? A swarming city of snails? What's going on here? Why did I come here? I can't remember. Do I have to pass through the opening in this tree in order to get further up-stream? I can't do it—I'm not the god *Okuninushi-no-mikoto* am I? It's a snake's den in there. It would be like entering a room filled with centipedes. If it were just one snail in there I could hold it in my hand as I go along and it would probably just feel a bit ticklish. But this tunnel must be filled with tens of thousands of snails.

But wait a minute—if you look at how each moving spot is shining faintly, perhaps this cave is like the inside of that air-plane. Perhaps it's like a time-tunnel of life. It seems as if my being drawn along, following after the swaying silver-colored obi of that girl, has carried me into this world of ferns and snails.

Still, there's something creepy about all this living stuff. He hesitated as to whether to continue on through the cave or to turn back. At one point, thinking he couldn't get through, he feared he'd be turned into one of those striped snails. It seemed he might never be able to return to himself and he would have to spend the rest of his life in this cave. But then, amidst the dark ferns, one by one, pale yellow flowers similar to little orchids began to open. Thinking the girl was beckoning him to look at them, he found himself gasping—and then he woke up. The smells of grass and trees filled his nose. When he got up he realized he'd been sleeping alone on a bed of reeds.

Little by little, he recalled the events of the previous day. Before he fell asleep he'd heard the faint reverberations of a bell. He'd heard Ohina and Omomo's voices fading out and sinking into the depths of the lake while three small red lanterns swayed along the surface of the water. Had that also been a dream? He shook his head in thought; Certainly we did make this grass hut. He remembered the preparations step by step. Certainly the three of us made it and then we scattered grandfather's ashes. But where could Ohina and Omomo have gone?

He sat up straight and looked about. At his bedside was a rock. Two country-style *dango* dumplings had been placed on top of it. Could this be part of some sort of spell? Leaves, apparently recently arranged, had been placed in a circle around them. Ah, that's right, we made a stone altar and placed on it some candles, incense, and implements for celebrating O-bon. The fragrance of incense lingered in the air. He looked about the area around the stone and saw matches and the burned remains of incense.

It hadn't been just a dream. Masahiko felt relieved. If those burned out traces about the rock altar hadn't been there I'd think I was going crazy. What a day this has been. And yet isn't it possible that I'm still in a dream, even now? He emerged from the hut and as he gazed at the lake he fell into thought.

Numerous birds of some sort were flying over the lake. Mist remained on the tops of the trees and grasses, and the air was clear and pure. Watching the shapes of the birds grow smaller as they flew off into the distance he was filled with a strongly affectionate memory of the two women. Where could they have gone? Faint traces of their songs from the night before remained in his ears.

Why didn't they wake me? I must have lost track of what happened after they had me drink that *shochu*—I'm not used to it. I suppose they left the dumplings for me, thinking I'd be getting hungry. They must have put them here and then gone. He was gripped by a feeling that almost made him want to stamp his feet and cry, but then he broke into a slight smile. What's happening?

It seems my connection to those two women comes just from the fact that my grandfather was also from Amazoko. They didn't have any responsibility to take me around and wake me up to all of this. And as for Ohina's strange reaction to me—the way she seemed a bit out of it—that must have been because she mistook me for Grandfather in his younger days. Anyhow, I must have a hangover. Even though they went to the trouble of making these dumplings I don't feel like eating. I hadn't planned to meet these two women. Now that I've scattered Grandfather's ashes, and while the scent of these old mountains is still with me, I want to try putting my feelings from last night into music before they fade away.

Masahiko picked up the bag for the *biwa* he'd carried with him and checked inside it to make sure he hadn't lost the spare strings. As he groped around, searching through the bag, he felt the aching in his head. Since yesterday when I met Ohina I've been wondering if I could express on the *biwa* the sounds I've heard here—the sounds of the sap flowing through the roots of the andromeda tree and those skittering, whispering, warbling tones of the voices in the mists that came from the far reaches of the earth. They're subtle, faint sounds; ones that don't exist in the Western musical scales. Yes, that's it! That thick, soft string of the *biwa* will bring out that sound! I must remember it now—all that happened yesterday from noon until late into the night.

The feeling of inspiration that's been shut off within me—suddenly it's been called from the depths of this moonlit lake. It appeared along with the spirits from the old village, on the roadway that unites that world and this one. It must have been drawn out from the far reaches of those old tales. Certainly Ohina said she knew from her dream that Masahito would return. Perhaps it's just coincidence, but perhaps I was being waited for too.

Before him lay the town that had been sealed off at the bottom of the lake. Probably he would have to search there if he were to understand the reasons his grandfather had become so strange. Ohina and Omomo had said to call up the sunken village—but was such a thing possible? Masahiko looked about, feeling as if he were chasing lingering traces of incense. On the top branches of a persimmon tree on Utazaka Hill, faintly colored fruits were shining in the sun. A shrike called out sharply, *kiri! kiri!* He couldn't see any place where he could tell that the landscape had actually changed, yet he couldn't help feeling that something had been altered. He felt brimming with energy. He realized that everything about him was breathing—the grasses, the trees, the light, and the shadows too.

Where was the entrance—the entrance to that world of the night before?

It was everywhere. A storyteller within was telling Masahiko that anything his eyes touched upon, whether in light or in shadow, has meaning. It's Ohina and Omomo who've taught me this and who've led me through the entrance to that world; to the village of the scattered flowers of the moon on the bottom of the lake. He reached for the neck of his *biwa* and whispered,

"*Isara-maru.* You too have heard voices from that other world."

Isara-maru was the name of the *biwa* his grandfather had left him. "That's the thing that brought your grandfather such pleasure. If you need it, why don't you just take it?"—is what his mother had said at the time it had become his. Did the *biwa*'s name come from the name of the river in his family's hometown?

"We'll go back to last night's story. From here on you and I will become as one body."

Slowly, he got up and stood by the water to wash his face.

It seemed as if a voice was calling from far off. He stared into the distance as he wiped his neck with a towel. Unmistakably, on the opposite bank of the lake there were five or six people moving about and climbing onto some logs floating in the lake. Then, clearly he heard them cry out over and over again, "*Helloo . . . ! Helloo . . . !*" He felt he was being called out to. And in calling back to them in reply, "*Helloo . . . !*" Masahiko found himself being led onward and walking around the banks of the lake. From a closer look he could see that two men near the shore were standing on a log raft and pulling up on something that appeared to be extremely heavy and difficult to remove, working in cooperation with the other people on the shore.

Suddenly he gasped. That couldn't be Ohina, or Omomo, could it? The people cast somewhat suspicious glances at this unknown young person, but their attention was focused more on the man on the raft who was struggling to keep his balance as he grabbed onto the obi of a body that had been in the water. As the other man poled the log raft toward the shore the people waiting there, calling out to each other, splashed their way into the water and pulled up the body.

The body they lifted from the water belonged to a girl who was wrapped in a twisted, indigo-colored kimono and whose silver-toned obi had come untied. Her body was covered with long weeds from the lake.

"Any breath?" one person asked.

"Nothing."

An older person pulled down the hem of the kimono from where it had ridden up above her waist, so as to cover the lower part of her body that had become exposed. Masahiko was shaken by the sight.

"So this is how it's ended for her. Oai-sama will be weeping over there in the other world. *Namandabu. Namandabu . . .*"

"Look, that's the same material, isn't it? The same material that was covering the mirror."

"I think I've seen it before—in the *komorido* meditation hall. Was that an obi?"

The image of the obi, tangled up with the body that had been dragged up from the bottom of the lake, remained vividly impressed in his mind. He recalled already having seen a dark silver cloth. Masahiko doubted his eyes. The cloth here was deeply stained with mud and waterweeds, but he remembered having seen the designs of grasses and flowers embroidered in blues and golds. This was the obi of the little girl he saw in the dream he had just before waking.

"If this were still the Isara River she wouldn't have died."

"It's because of the dam. If this were the old Isara River she'd never have thought of jumping. But now it's grown so deep."

"Looks like she came back to die above the old village."

Masahiko imagined the people must be from Amazoko. Among the men, an older one stared at Masahiko and inquired in a quiet voice,

"You look so similar—may I ask, are you by any chance related to the family of the old Silk Estate?"

Not again, thought Masahiko. He told them briefly about how he had come to scatter his grandfather's ashes and had then joined Ohina and Omomo in the O-bon ceremony. The men expressed their regrets at how Masahito hadn't met with good fortune and had ended up dying in Tokyo. They spoke of how sad it must have been for Masahito to ask his grandson to scatter his ashes about the dam. After commending him on what he'd done they regarded him closely again.

"Looks just like him, doesn't he."

The men regarded him with affection. For a moment the matter of the drowned person was forgotten.

"It was fate. Last night—one night," said one person.

Nodding their heads, the men began discussing what to do with the body and then they chose a person to go and call the police. They debated about how they should proceed in carrying the body down to the village. While the men were cutting straight saplings to make a stretcher, Masahiko heard someone say, "This too, somehow, is fate." He was given the duty of shooing away the flies that were swarming about the body.

"Quite some obi this is. What a woman."

"So it looks like the last caretaker of Oki no Miya has gone.

"Her mother died beneath the cherry tree and she was raised by Oai-sama. But what a fate to die like this."

"Let's take her back to the temple and then we can discuss what to do."

This was the sort of conversation Masahiko overheard. Since meeting Ohina he'd heard of Oki no Miya any number of times. He asked one of the men about the place. The man replied, "Well, it's sort of difficult to explain, but . . ."

Now there is just one small stone marker along the banks of the Isara River. You can't see Oki no Miya from there. Those red crabs that used to go up and down the Isara River have gone back to the main branch of the Aka River. Down by the river mouth, through the thickets of reeds you can see Oki no Miya, far off in the distance.

2

OKI NO MIYA

Masahiko felt something welling up within. A something that had never been there before. A something like the mist of life.

Strange; ever since the age he he'd started to take notice of things he had wondered about where he had come from. He had watched all sorts of TV science programs, like "The Birth of Life" and such, but even if they explained the general outlines of the origins of life they never helped him get at the basic question, Why I am here? Entirely different from the sort of things on those shows, his wonder at the fact that life has a voice and a presence was something that continually ran through his consciousness. Why, for example, did humans begin to sing?

Around the time he entered elementary school, Masahiko had seen a measuring worm crawling along the branch of a cherry tree near his house. The worm was probably about the length of his little finger. The pale yellow-bellied insect arched its entire body upward and then extended it as it made its way forward. But when it reached the end of a branch it stretched its neck around as if thinking, and then after a while turned its limbless upper body about in the air, considering which direction to take.

Realizing there was no path forward, it deftly turned its upper body back around in the direction from which it had come.

Masahiko could recall feeling himself become almost like the measuring worm, tensing and then relaxing. The inch-worm had stood there on the tip of the branch with its neck held up, deep in thought. The May breezes rustled through the green leaves and reddening cherry fruit. It had seemed to the young Masahiko that the inchworm was listening to the sounds of the universe and thinking about the meaning of the fact that there are things in the world that cannot be measured.

At that time I think I felt great respect for that insect, entrusting itself to the waves of the May sunlight. When I entered high school I wrote my first piece of music. It was a short piece for cello called *Satsuki*—"May." I put this image into the notes.

It was in a forest. Through the leaves the stirring of a gentle wind was blowing a narrow pathway in and out of sight, again and again. A determined, philosophically minded little insect was out for a walk (this part was associated with Grandfather Masahito). The insect had dedicated itself to the task of going about the world and taking measurements with the length of its own body so as to determine in a rough sort of way what kind of place the world was. That there should prove to be any great difference among the kinds of trees in the forest, or among their ages, or among the colors of their trunks and leaves, and that each would give off its own smell, was something it had not imagined, but measurement was its responsibility and so it did not shirk the task.

The time its thoughts were most deeply affected was when the insect realized that its road came to an end. It was there, at the time when all things come to an end, that the grace of heaven lay. That time, with the wind and sunlight playing about gently on the back of its neck, was when, in an instant, the eternity of existence came to dwell in its tiny body. The forest spread out wide as the insect gazed out onto it and then returned back into its midst.

It would be easy to misinterpret his piece as a rather contrived, theoretical sort of thing but actually he'd intended it to be whimsical, where the truth lay hidden in the play of the wind and leaves.

What now recalled to his mind that still-unperformed first piece for cello was his finding, right here in front of him, an inchworm lying on the branch of a fallen tree. Compared with the ones he was familiar with in Tokyo this one was greener. Suddenly, thinking of how the insects up in the mountains must be even more different, he returned to reality. In front of him lay the body of the drowned girl. Trying as much as possible not to look at the dead person, he held some fern leaves in his hand and swatted away the flies that were settling on the body.

"You too, you've had your own misfortunes."

One of the men engaged in making the stretcher spoke in a consoling manner. Masahiko was somewhat at a loss as to how he might reply but his attention was caught by the color of the dead girl's obi. Perhaps the sunken village that Ohina and Omomo had spoken of calling out to had already started to take form. As they continued their work, the men talked about the girl who had died. Without particularly trying to listen, Masahiko overheard various things about her.

The name of the dead woman, it seems, was Sayuri. She had served at the shrine of Oki no Miya. Back when the droughts had come, the people in the village had gathered around the place where the Isara River joins the main branch of the Aka River and, with their thoughts directed toward the distant Oki no Miya Shrine, they had prayed for rain. Originally, it seemed, there had been a great shrine there facing the distant ocean, but at some time it had been washed away in a flood. On the spot where it had once stood was a small stone marker inscribed with illegible small characters. Before Oai-sama died she had brought up her foster child Sayuri to become a *miko* shrine maiden and had set up a temporary shrine there, but with the building of the dam it too had been sent to the bottom of the waters. And so now, with the death of Sayuri, the traces of Oki no Miya Shrine had completely disappeared.

Oai-sama's hands had first bathed many of the villagers at the time of their birth. But before she gave up her work as a midwife, Oai-sama had said as she delivered the child of a dying woman who had fallen beneath the weeping cherry tree,

"For ages I've been taking care of other peoples' babies, but I too would like to have a child of my own."

And so it had happened that Oai-sama came to bring up the child of the woman who had died beneath the weeping cherry tree.

That had confirmed the villagers' thoughts of Oai-sama being a different, special sort of person. But when they learned that the baby girl was born unable to speak they had said among themselves, "Somehow that child must be blessed in the thoughts of the gods." When Sayuri turned seven, Oai-sama had dressed her in a white figured satin kimono with a scarlet *hakama* outer skirt and presented her with a flowered fan—the sign of a *miko*. It was the fan she had once received from the head priest of Ontake Shrine. They had walked up and down the slopes of the village in the valley, presenting their greetings to every household.

"Thanks to you all, from today Sayuri will become a *miko*. She will serve Oki no Miya Shrine and will have the responsibility of keeping the oceans and the mountains joined through the courses of the water. We ask your kind favor."

"My goodness, have you ever seen anyone so beautiful? That clothing suits you so well. It's so lovely. What a pity you can't speak."

This was how the people of the village had congratulated her when they saw Sayuri bow innocently to them.

"She may not be able to recite the Shinto prayers, but she can perform the dances. Whenever you have the need, please ask her to dance."

And so Sayuri had soon taken up her responsibilities. Whenever the villagers sent her an invitation—whether for a gathering of girls at the festival for the twenty-third night of the moon, or for the river festival, or for any of the festivals for the mountain gods at the little shrines on even the smallest of hills—Sayuri would come and dance with a bell attached to a long tassel. Although there was a male priest, since he was old and it was troublesome for him to go out, she didn't have to worry about interfering with his affairs. When Oai-sama thought of the future of her adopted child who was unable to speak, it wasn't so much that she was afraid she would starve, but she worried about how Sayuri would make her way in the world after she was gone. With this in mind, Oai-sama had tried hard to make Sayuri a part of the life of the village as soon as possible.

In this village although the rebuilding of houses was rare, the rebuilding of cow barns was a common occurrence. At such times Sayuri would be called on for the groundbreaking ceremonies. It was said that when Sayuri danced with the bell in her hand the cows showed tenderness in their eyes and voices. The cows and horses had all been fond of this girl.

Sayuri was born to a woman who died by the wayside and whose identity was unknown. As long as she was together with Oai-sama the village would help take care of her. But Oai-sama must have been especially worried about how, after her death,

Sayuri would get along. Oai-sama had once said with a very serious face,

"Sayuri is no ordinary child. I believe she's a princess of Oki
no Miya."

Since she couldn't speak it was unlikely that Sayuri would be
taken as a bride. Yet even when Oai-sama thought of Sayuri in
comparison to herself—a woman who had gone through life
without marrying—she worried about the fact that Sayuri was so
beautiful and about the way that, for all she couldn't speak, she
might become too affectionate and attached to people. And so
perhaps it was in order to protect Sayuri from being taken advantage of that Oai-sama had decided to regard her as one who
possessed the qualities of a god. After she stopped working as a
midwife she accompanied Sayuri to all her working engage-
ments. On the streets they looked like an ordinary mother and
daughter, but when they entered into a ceremony Oai-sama
would change completely and act as one who was carrying out
the duties of attending a goddess. And in laying out the individual ceremonial dining tables she would give Sayuri the seat of
honor. Naturally, the villagers had followed her lead.

The oldest-looking man stepped back from the stretcher,
now apparently complete. He rubbed his hands, smelling of
the green branches. And then, in a low voice, he spoke.

"All things change, they say—but to turn out like this . . .
Back in the old days, the magnolia flowers were in bloom. Under the flowers by the big house, Sayuri—she must have been
about nine or ten then—what a beautiful girl she was. She
would dance among the cows, ringing her bell as she moved. It
was such a peaceful sight. The cows must have understood too;
their voices became different."

Seeing the back of the leg of the dead girl, Masahiko began
to feel dizzy. Green water plants clung to a swollen, wrinkled

body that showed no traces of having once belonged to a beautiful young woman. One of the elders picked some bunches of gentians and, without speaking, placed them around the body, its hair still wet.

"Whereabouts was that magnolia tree?"

When Masahiko asked this, the men, with plaintive expressions, stood up together and pointed toward a place at the bottom of the lake. He was also told that the house where the magnolia flowers bloomed had been the main building of the old Silk Estate. Masahiko slightly regretted having asked. For even if they told him, he wondered if he could understand. Even if he tried to find out how the sunken village had looked in the old days, how could he, who had never even looked into the eye of a cow, possibly understand?

In the summer of the fourth year after Sayuri became a *miko*, a drought had come—one such as had never been experienced before. Oai-sama had thought, now the time has come for Sayuri to perform the ceremony. Oai-sama had vowed that if they should get through the drought safely she would put up a building that anyone who saw would recognize as the shrine of Oki no Miya. She would do this both for Sayuri and for the village.

The time had come to have everyone realize that this girl was serving the gods. When she appeared in front of them for the ceremony, if she were to perform as she had until now— even with her graceful movements, her way of sounding the bell, and her dancing—she would still be unable to call forth the rains.

Above all, Oai-sama had wondered how to teach this daughter who could not hear to realize that she herself was the one who stood between the gods and the people. The purification rite and the fasting had to be performed together at the Isara River. From the time she retired from midwifery

she had become able to concentrate on these things. This was
the way this determined old woman had decided to spend the
remainder of her life. She hadn't made any promise, yet these
were the final respects she paid to the woman who had collapsed under that cherry tree. She couldn't help feeling pity
about it. She wondered whose child Sayuri really was. And for
what reason had she been born beneath that cherry tree?

The fields of upland rice had gradually stopped producing
seeds and remained with barren ears. Countless cracks spread
across the land. Frogs lay belly-up and dried out. Eventually
the villagers had climbed up to Ontake Peak and gathered together by the side of the memorial stone for Oki no Miya and
begged for water.

After a prayer dance that expressed everyone's urgent
hopes, the people had taken bamboo containers and filled
them with water by dipping them in the bottom of the shallow
Isara River. This was for carrying up to the top of Ontake
Peak, the point closest to heaven, and pouring onto the source
of the watershed in order to call out to the dragon god of the
waterfalls.

Looking out and seeing the empty-eared rice plants and the
dried up waterways did not ease the people's worries. With rice
so scarce, the villagers had to gather all sorts of wild grains,
buckwheat, maize, beans, and chestnuts. For these people the
waterways that wound through the villages were not simply
channels of runoff water; they were the waterways of the gods
of the mountains and seas that carried the basis of all life. And
so the old villagers had listened carefully for any signs of the little gods in the mountains and they were well acquainted with
their comings and goings. And it was also in such a way that
they had looked upon the slightest efforts of Sayuri.

Night and day the gods looked down on the network of waterways, wells, and rice paddies, checking to see that the water

was flowing properly and making sure that none got clogged with litter and became shut off. An indication might come from something like the appearance of a snake at the roots of a reed bamboo, or a rain frog in the top branches of a *tabu* tree. The villagers all turned out to take care of things like conducting the memorial services for the dead insects of the fields, and helping with the *mogura uchi* work when they beat away the moles; and they had to pay attention to the eyes of the gods, making sure they didn't overlook anything. It was in such a way that there came to be instilled in the villagers a sensitivity to these capillaries of the earth, and a caring to ensure that the system always flowed properly. Should these lifelines of countless waterways that ran all the way from Oki no Miya to the source of the Isara River on Ontake Peak dry up, the life of the village would be cut off.

"It was in a place where there was deep fog." Prompted by some thought that seemed to bear no relevance to what was going on, another of the men who'd been attending the dead body began to talk.

"The fog had really settled in thick. It made for good tea. Somehow it made the smell of tea from anywhere else no good.

"Yeah, the taste of the tea sure was different. But how did I get started on tea? When was it? The path from Ontake Notch was all fogged in. I thought I was lost so I sat down on a rock to wait for it to clear.

"Then from out of the midst of the fog, shadows of a lot of people, ten to twenty of them it must have been, passed by without a sound. As I sat there, someone went right by me. Without thinking, I stood up and walked alongside. I suppose I was worried I might be lost. But in any case I found myself walking along with forty, maybe fifty of them who'd appeared out of the fog. I wondered whether they might be the mountain folk. They were short in height. After a while, when we got to the river, the shadows disappeared as if they'd sunk into the water. And then the fog lifted and it cleared. When I looked around, it was a familiar landscape but I realized I'd walked quite a way. I wondered what they must have thought of me."

"Well, as for me, you know, I've seen four or five foxes jump out in the fog. I could tell they were foxes by the shadows of their tails. And when the rain lifted you could hear the rush of water sounding through the valley."

"You never know what you'll meet back there in the mountains."

"Right. One time that old lady Okume went looking for catnip and didn't get back for three days."

"Yeah, she went off into the mountains to gather things—but there was no telling where. Maybe into the Kazura Valley, where it's all covered with vines. People warned her she might have been eaten up by a big snake. The old women in her family would have cried and been all broken up. There've been stories from way back about the big snakes in that Kazura Valley, with all its vines."

"We went in with sickles and axes, making a big fuss in searching for her."

"Right—and that was the time we saw the curtain of butterflies."

"Yeah, I remember it. At first I thought it might be a covering of *katsura* leaves stuck to each other, but that too would have been strange. It turned out to be thousands of butterfly wings. It was so beautiful looking through the sheet of wings floating like that and moving with a slight fluttering motion. I'd hardly ever seen that kind of butterfly before. They were azure-blue butterflies, covering a little hill and floating almost motionlessly. Looking at them from a little way off, it seemed like the curtain of a theater had dropped across the space between the hills. Just little butterflies, but there were thousands of them. When I looked at them one by one they trembled a bit but didn't fly away. And then as I watched they floated off into the mountains and disappeared, as if carried off in a fog. It was really enchanting. No one knows the names of those butterflies.

"Old Okume was just sitting there resting by the roots beneath that curtain of butterflies."

"Right—and finding her there, it doubled our surprise. It was a bewitching kind of scene. Made us think it might be some kind of huge snake lying there under the curtain that had just disappeared. We all wondered—is that really Okumesan? It left us speechless."

"Finding her alone up there, it must have been pretty frightening."

"Sure it was frightening. But then, as if nothing had happened, old Okume started to talk, 'Hey, what are you all doing up here?' and we felt the tension break."

"I've been working flat out since yesterday. It's been nothing but work and I'm beat. After lunch I fell into a deep sleep. I slept soundly for the first time in ages, and then in a dream I saw everyone up there on top of Ontake Peak. The dream told the truth. So good of you all to come."

"After all we'd been through we were exhausted and it almost made us laugh to hear her say, 'Hey—I'm starving, doesn't anyone have something to eat?' It sort of brought us back to our senses."

"What was she working for?"

"Wild mountain grapes and mushrooms. Loads and loads of them. So many she couldn't carry them by herself."

It seemed to Masahiko that, except for the dead body, the mood was like that at any ordinary break time among mountain workers. He found all of these stories deeply moving.

The fragrance of the kudzu flowers they had used in building the grass hut the day before had grown stronger.

In order to carry the dead body of Sayuri down the mountain the men had cut fresh trees and tied them together with kudzu vines in the same fashion. The bunches of red-violet kudzu flowers that yesterday had still been buds had now begun to open all at once in the shape of inverted wisteria blossoms. Omomo had told Masahiko that these were the kudzu's flowers. As he looked closer he realized that there were flowers all over the area around the dam. Each time the wide leaves and flower stems were cut they released a fragrance. Masahiko thought; if it weren't for the smell of Sayuri's body lying in the grass I'd be completely wrapped in the fragrance of the mountains.

What was this good smell? As he looked between his feet at the fresh autumn soil, taking in its rich aroma of fungi, he became absorbed in thought. He'd never really looked carefully at soil before. Images came to mind of things like scooping up garden soil and putting it into a test tube, adding water, shaking it and examining it for bacteria. Or of squishy mud oozing out of the cracks in the pavement at a construction site. Where, he wondered, had his grandfather bought that yellow-colored soil for his potted plants? Those twisted, bent over pine and *nanten* plants had been watered and grown up and taken on their dwarfed shapes. But after the old man died they'd mostly withered and died. No one in the family had paid much attention to his grandfather's spirit.

It seemed to Masahiko that the soil in the city had become enfeebled. The village of Amazoko had been flooded by the dam and a girl named Sayuri now lay dead in front of him. And yet from hearing the talk of the men it seemed as though in the area around here the earth was still venting a mist that

issued from the depths far below. It appeared that even now
the inhabitants of Amazoko were coming and going amidst
things that appeared and disappeared in the mountain mists.
Masahiko was captivated by the talk of shadows that flitted
about in the mountain mists. It was a living story that existed
beyond the realm of what's called intelligence. He thought
back on the *kanpachi* cloud of smog above Tokyo. What was
that about, he wondered. The name had been coined by city
people, in reference to the clouds of exhaust that hovered
above the Kanpachi Highway.

Masahiko wanted to shoo away every last fly when any tried
to land on Sayuri. He held a tree branch ready. The men had
gathered and picked up the scattered kudzu flowers and laid
them alongside Sayuri's body, beside a pillow of bellflowers.

"There's a bit of a smell—you think it'll be all right?" he
asked.

One of the old men who were looking on answered, "It'll be
OK. We don't have any incense, so the kudzu flowers will have
to do."

While the men were taking a break, one who had gone down
to get the police and a doctor from the clinic returned with
some new people from the village. To his surprise, Ohina was
among them.

"Thanks for helping out."

She nodded her regards to Masahiko as if he were one of the
regulars from the village. And then, with an expression of intense grief, Ohina knelt down beside the pillow by the dead
body.

"Sayuri, so this is what you've come to."

As she said this Ohina reached out to touch the shoulder,
but the policeman quickly held her back.

"You're not allowed to touch it. The body's involved in an investigation, you know."

The discussions about how to move the body continued.

"At least we need to inform the people from Amazoko who are still living near here. We all owe her so much."

"As for those who are far away, well, I suppose it can't be helped."

"What kind of a fate is this—coming here and dying?"

"Her mother who died beneath the cherry tree, where do you suppose she was from?"

"I've heard she was from the Mimigawa River. Sayuri from Mimigawa—her mother said that just before she died by the roadway. I'm sure I heard that. Isn't that right Ohina?"

It was well known among the people of Amazoko that Ohina had been especially close to Sayuri and her foster mother.

"I've heard of the Mimigawa too. But why do you suppose she crossed over the mountains to come to Amazoko, rather than going down the river by way of Hyuga?"

Ohina fell silent after asking this.

"So we've lost one more from Amazoko."

"She couldn't speak, but what do you suppose she saw in this world?"

The stretcher carriers had been decided upon and now they took turns in carrying the body down. As they began to walk, one of them said in lowered voice, "That was quite some fire last night."

The person who heard this replied, as if he couldn't help talking about it, "It burned completely to the ground. Jimpei was burned badly. The prefecture police came and are investigating it."

"Looks like arson, don't you think?"

"Sh- - - ."

The man who said "arson" glanced back to make sure the local policeman wasn't lurking somewhere in the shadows of the thicket and then replied, "I've heard that this dead one here could have done it."

"What the hell are you saying that for?"

The man in front glanced back reprovingly.

The group fell silent. They took rests where the footing along the path was bad and at last they made their way to the temple at the base of the mountain. Somehow, word had been passed along and a surprisingly large number of people— young and old, men and women—had gathered for a wake.

"I'd thought it was going to be a pretty lonely wake, but with all these folks it should bring some peace to both the dead one and her parents."

After reciting a sutra for the dead, the stooped-over elderly priest joined his palms together. The villagers' thoughts were drawn back to the times before thoughts had even occurred to them of things happening like the village being flooded for a dam. They remembered the woman who died beneath the cherry tree. At that time too this elderly priest had recited a sutra at the request of Oai-sama, who had taken care of the dead. No doubt the villagers' words "her parents" had been addressed to both the parent who had given birth to her and the one who had raised her.

Masahiko felt awkward at finding himself in such a place. He wondered if Ohina and the men had explained about him, since the villagers were looking at him with particular affection. He wondered if his grandfather too had ever been in such a situation in the past. As he glanced at the fence around the *o-mido* hall where the statue of the Buddha was placed he was surprised at what he found. Among the rows of black-painted wooden markers he found one with the name of his grandfather written on it. The names were arranged in order of the amounts of donations, stating how much money had been given over the generations. As his grandfather had been the largest donor, his name was written in bold strokes of gold. Suddenly aware that his own presence at the wake held a special significance, Masahiko felt nervous and self-conscious.

CHAPTER 2

It seemed that those markers somehow linked him to his unknown ancestors and to his fate in connection with things of the past. But also, he couldn't help seeing them as small markers pointing the way to the village that had disappeared. Somewhere in Masahiko's consciousness—still uneasy about the atmosphere at this wake in the mountain village—a wooden marker separated from the temple wall and began to float about as if it were a piece of the remainders of the houses floating on the water about the dam.

"Whew! Sayuri sure was heavy."

People were taken by surprise and fell silent. Suddenly Masahiko recalled placing her on the stretcher. The thick coldness of her upper arms; he would never forget that, all his life. He had helped cover the newly made stretcher with reeds. He had helped lay flowers on the body. But then he had just stood there, expecting that it would be the villagers who would lay the body on the stretcher.

He'd heard a voice call out, "Could you lift that arm for me?"

Even after the doctor forced out the water from her stomach it had seemed that Sayuri's body was still swollen with water. And although the men caught glimpses of the autopsy, they had tried to occupy themselves by smoking or doing small chores like bundling up the stray branches. Before long, however, they ended up sitting down and staring at the surface of the lake. The hushed voices of the policeman and the doctor were faintly audible. From time to time the surface of the lake shone with lights.

It had seemed as if the men's thoughts were being sucked up and carried off into the depths of the water. The village at the bottom of the lake held connections for each one of them. What sort of world, and what sort of compressed time lay sunken beneath that stagnating green water? Something that looked like a string moved through the water. It turned out to be a small snake. They all had seen it, but it disappeared without anyone mentioning it. Had the snake been crossing over to the other side? Where could that valley of *kazura* vines be now; the one with the big snakes they'd been talking about a while ago? It must lie at the bottom of the dam.

A man with a dark beard had stood up as if to urge the others on.

"Well, we'd better be getting back before it gets dark."

"Right, before it gets dark," someone else had repeated, and then the bearded man bowed in front of the pillow.

"Sayuri, everyone's here now, so let's get you down to the temple . . ."

The man had bowed his head and folded his hands in prayer for a moment. Then calling out once more, he had taken the body from its position on its side and lifted it up by placing one hand behind the shoulders and the other on the back of the neck. Taking this as a signal, the other men lifted the body and placed it onto the stretcher of woven branches and grasses. Ohina had cried out, her voice all choked up, "Cover it up. Cover it with kudzu flowers."

Then the policeman had said, "The doctor's fixed things up a bit so the body won't smell, at least until you get it down there, so everyone just try to hold out a little while longer."

The mountain path had been narrow, adding to the difficulties of carrying the body along. At points along the way where the path widened the stretcher-bearers took turns in relieving each other. Masahiko had been the youngest among them.

"Lucky we met you here. This should be a good funeral."

"We don't have any young folks with us, so you really helped out. It worked out well."

He hadn't minded at all being talked to this way by the men, but this was the first time in his life he'd done such heavy labor.

The day before, in helping build the grass hut, he'd also done something previously unimaginable. Today's work had been a continuation. Starting with his meeting Ohina, and continuing with these people, it had all seemed to happen in a rush of fate. But now, after going without any lunch, he felt almost dizzy. Arriving at the temple he was thanked by women he'd never met before.

"My goodness. Coming all the way from Tokyo—and the grandson of the family of the old estate, and helping out with carrying the body."

Being greeted like this by the old women had been a bit hard to take but now Omomo was among the women setting out the small individual dining tables and he noticed her looking his way from time to time. Since she was busy she couldn't come over, yet Masahiko felt relieved. He was surprised to find himself wanting to tell this girl he'd just met the day before about how he'd worked during the past day. *Shochu* liquor was passed around and gradually things got under way in the living quarters of the temple and the mood grew more lively.

Women came in carrying sake glasses and asked, soliciting agreement, "Isn't this a fine wake—so festive and all?"

Masahiko had never imagined feeling festive at a time when a dead person was present. Wouldn't his grandfather also have wished to meet his death in a place such as this? Grandfather Masahito's funeral had been just a formal ceremony; with a set schedule, according to orders spoken by funeral directors' gloomy voices, and hurried along by the crowd behind him. Would they ever have given such a warm send-off to a drowned person who was involved in a police investigation? Even though he'd heard that she had no relatives other than the parent who had raised her, the people of Amazoko were talking of their deep ties to her.

He dimly recalled what Omomo had said to her mother the night before facing the dark surface of the lake; *If we can't get our feelings through to Amazoko, why don't we call it up?*

Now, as time had passed those words came back to Masahiko's ears with deeper meaning. Could it be that these people here were the people they had called out to?

The policeman's face had grown quite ruddy, but recalling his duty he began questioning the man who had brought the drinking cups.

"So tell me now—who was it that saw Sayuri last?"

After getting the policeman to take a cup, the man being questioned replied, "Well this is really something now, isn't it? I see you can't forget your job even now."

"So the last person to see Sayuri was . . ?"

"All right, all right, I heard you already—so you want to know who was the last person Sayuri was seen by."

"Well, who was it?"

"Plenty saw her—people who went to watch the fire. Who was it that saw her the most? Well, it must have been Tamayo."

"Who's Tamayo?"

"Tamayo—she lives near Jimpei."

"Ah, you mean that kid who doesn't like going to school."

"Right. Tamayo. The one who hates school. But even if she doesn't like school, none of the adults can beat her at gathering catnip."

"So what was this Tamayo saying?"

"All last night she was watching Sayuri. From start to finish."

"Is that so?"

"Tamayo sleepwalks—but you must know about that already. It was a moonlit night. She was walking along the Otachidote Embankment. And then across from her, like a doll in the *joruri* puppet theater, Sayuri approached. Tamayo said she looked like the *teradehime* princess. Sayuri's face was all white, like a *teradehime* in those performances that come to town from time to time—you know them don't you?—Well OK, even if you don't, it's no matter. Anyhow, it seems she was walking along like some *joruri* doll. Tamayo may not like school but she loves *joruri* so she remembered a lot from it and she copied it. So she bowed, and in the moonlit night she must have gotten caught up in the spirit of it and walked along, imitating the samisen music with her voice.

"Then she arrived at Jimpei's stable. Sayuri loved horses and cows, and they were fond of her too. For a while she patted and stroked the horse and rubbed her head against it. The horse sighed. It wasn't fully grown yet. When she was younger Sayuri danced at the groundbreaking ceremony for the stable. From then on the horses grew attached to her.

"I don't know what she could have been thinking, but she led the horse out of the stable, and then along the way she tied it to a willow tree. Tamayo must've thought it strange and followed along behind. Whatever Sayuri was thinking of, she left the horse there and turned back. With the horse there all alone, Tamayo wondered what to do. She looked around toward the horse, and then toward Sayuri, and then approached the horse and spoke to it.

"While Tamayo was doing this she noticed the fire starting up beyond the reed thicket on the embankment. She ran. The fire was in Jimpei's direction. She paced back and forth, wondering what to do with the horse. While this was going on Sayuri came back, still walking along slowly, just as before. Even in the daytime she looked like a woman at the peak of her beauty in her forties. But all made up in red and white she looked just like a *teradehime* princess. On her head she was wearing something like a crown made of ornamental hairpins.

"Sparks and flames shot up. Tamayo stood watching the fire and Sayuri drew near the horse and then started to dance, holding her bell and her fan in her hands. Then the horse nodded its head and started off along with her in the direction of Otachidote. Tamayo—even if she was a sleepwalker—she knew that the path led only into the lake. She said that even in daytime it was scary there, but it was especially bad at night. She'd heard the stories about the cut-down weeping cherry tree at the bottom of the dam and she said the place frightened her.

"For us too, it's no good going there at night.

"I don't know if Sayuri knew about all that—about how the mother who gave birth to her died under that weeping cherry tree. But in any case, when it was cut down the broken tree and all the remains were like blood. One of the men who helped cut it down died in an accident soon afterwards.

"But even if she didn't know about those things, that dam had all kinds of associations with her mother. Why d'you suppose she took the horse from that house on the night of the fire and went to the lake? All those folks who ran over to Otachidote to watch the fire—they may not know as much about it as Tamayo, but plenty of 'em saw it.

"They say it was like a scene at the theater. The fire bright red, silver obi trailing, rouge on her lips. Someone was riding a horse. You couldn't see it clearly, but there was something on the horse.

"The next day the horse returned. The stable and the house were burned to the ground. Well that's how Tamayo tells it, anyway. She must be about ten years old now, I'd guess."

To the people gathered for the wake the events of the fire the night before and those of Sayuri's drowning seemed like strands of one entwined story.

The villagers were used to seeing Sayuri with her face powdered. But going out in the middle of the night of the fire, not even for prayer—and with her face painted pure white and with her bells and leading a horse—what could that have been about?

Tamayo had arrived at the scene of the fire before the embers cooled. She claimed, "Sayuri came and took Jimpei's horse. That was when the fire started." Because Tamayo told that story to everyone, some people had felt they should question Sayuri about what happened when the fire started and so several of them went looking for her. They checked the prayer hall attached to her house, but Sayuri hadn't been there. They realized that since she couldn't speak, even if they found her they probably wouldn't learn much from questioning her, but still they might discover something. Jimpei, who had been caught in the fire, almost died of the burns. And the horse really had gone off. Perhaps what Tamayo said might have been true.

Tamayo had walked about telling her story to the exhausted people who'd been up all night on account of the fire and then had returned to see the burned ruins. Even those who on first hearing had considered it to be just a child's tale were now beginning to take it more seriously and were getting more concerned. Jimpei's wife had been completely shaken by it all and was restlessly glancing around in confusion, hardly able to recognize the people in front of her.

"The fire balls of the *inugami* dog spirits, they came and danced about and set the fire," was what Jimpei's wife had whispered in the ears of the people who came to see her injured husband. And when they asked what happened to the horse she replied, "They came to take it from Amazoko. Those *inugami*, they've been after our family's horses for the past three hundred years now. And they picked up Jimpei with their whirling balls of fire and just carried him off—right into the middle of the fire."

Telling this story the wife gazed at her listeners with eyes that looked like sunken pits. Many thought to themselves—ah, Jimpei, he's already beyond help. At the same time they recalled old memories of the *inugami* spirits.

Jimpei had been a leader of the pro-dam faction.

"I was the only one who really faced the Construction Ministry and the prefecture officials and talked to them directly," he'd boasted. And before the compensation money allotments were decided he had gone around in the night calling on the families to whom he imagined the payments were going to be small.

"You know, I have a lot of pull with the prefecture officials, so I can get you special treatment. But don't go letting on about this to the other families."

This was the sort of thing he was said to have talked about on his walks and visits.

The old women had spoken in hushed voices with concern about what would happen to the shrines of the *inugami* spirits and to the resting places of Oki no Miya if they were sunken by the waters of the dam. Since they hadn't been able to bring up the subject of the shrines at the village meetings, whenever they happened to meet this big shot in the street they spoke to him about it, despite their hesitancy, but he just screwed up his mouth and dismissed them with a wave of his hand.

"What's all this fuss about shrines for *inugami* spirits? It's just this sort of superstition that the modernization this dam represents is aimed at doing away with. The people at the National Construction Ministry and the prefecture offices, they won't put up with listening to such old-fashioned nonsense. There are too many folks around here who just don't seem to get it. In this day and age those things are just eyesores. Just sink them. Just sink 'em I tell you. If you sink things like that it'll clean the place up. Look, it's not even worth calling this a problem. Can't you see I'm too busy for this sort of thing?"

This talk had troubled the old women even more, but they hadn't had the strength to push the matter. These things, however, must have weighed heavily in the thoughts of Jimpei's wife. And so it must have come about that the *inugami* spirits who had been threatening for three hundred years had appeared in the fire, right before her eyes.

This topic had been making the rounds among the people at the wake as they got comfortably inebriated. The liveliest group had formed around the old woman Oshizu, nicknamed "the trumpet of the treetops." She was one of those who, whenever they had time, went up to Otachidote to look at the bottom of the lake.

"Seems a long time's gone by without much trouble, with us just worrying and staring into the water. But now, after all, it's happened. After thirty years already."

"Yeah, I guess it's really been thirty years . . . You heard about what happened, didn't you?"

"Well, I heard plenty of things, but the biggest shock was seeing Jimpei's wife there in tears and all, crawling about on all fours, just howling away like that. I tell you, it really shook me up."

"It must've been too much for her to take, what with the house, the stable, and everything else completely burned, and not being able to help her husband, and Sayuri taking away the horse and all."

The horse had gotten back on its own. It made its way back alone from the dam, feeding on grass along the way. It must have been surprised to find the stable in ashes. With no stable to stay in, it had walked about the neighborhood and made its way to Sayuri's house, poking its nose inside to look around, until someone tied it temporarily to a magnolia tree.

"Wasn't the horse injured?"

"Everyone checked to see if it was hurt. If the *inugami* had come and ridden the horse with Jimpei, you can be sure it would've been hurt."

"It doesn't seem like much happened to it."

"Yes, but even if you can't see anything, that doesn't mean nothing happened. The horse—with its caretaker gone and its stable gone—I can hardly imagine it got off completely unscathed."

"Now hold it a minute. It was Sayuri who led the horse out, wasn't it?"

"Well, that's just the point."

Among the men and women involved in the discussion it seemed the one at the center was Oshizu.

"Here's the way I see it," she exclaimed decisively. "When they flooded the place they didn't carry out any of the proper rites or follow any of the customs. And I don't mean just for the shrines of the *inugami* spirits, but also for Oki no Miya Shrine, and for the wells of all the houses too. They went about it without a thought, as if it was all right to just let the water rush in. And the worms and the birds' nests—just think how many other things there were that had houses there too. The birds and the butterflies too, all swooping down and dancing about, all crazy-like. How can anyone take that as nothing at all?

"When they started letting the water in, just about the time it began flooding Sosuke's clover fields, incredible numbers of caterpillars and crickets rose up from the ground, bubbling up all over the place. Everyone gasped when they saw it. With them all floating about on the top of the water like that—it choked us up to watch it. Even now I can't forget the sight. And just think of how—when people way back first built that field—how they took so much care, holding observances for the insects and everything.

"On a hill in the cemetery there was a stone pagoda with words written on it, *Memorial for the souls of the ten thousand beings*. And when it said it was for the souls of 'beings,' that didn't mean just the humans. That stone marker on the hill was dedicated to the souls of *all* beings—and not just the birds and insects either; it was also for the souls of the things we can't see with our eyes. Our ancestors put it there out of thanks for all the creatures and beings that helped protect their village.

"These past years it's been eating at my heart. And now the water in the dam has gotten so low, especially with last year's drought. I think the village I was born in is still living, but it's melting down into the banks of the old river at the bottom. And now, just when I was thinking something might rise up from the bottom, it looks like the *inugami* spirits have showed up. The visiting places of Oki no Miya Shrine are all buried under the mud so you can't even see their remains. If the streams of water down there get blocked, the life of the mountains above will be destroyed as well. There's still something bad to come—you can count on that. You can imagine how Sayuri must've gotten that way, can't you, Ohina?"

Ohina, who had just brought in a tea tray, sat down quietly beside Oshizu. Sayuri—the *miko* shrine attendant who'd taken over the duties of looking after Oki no Miya, knowing how much her mother Oai-san had done to care for the visiting places of the shrine—was now dead. To Ohina, who had thought of Oai-sama as her spiritual parent, Sayuri had been like a daughter. Ohina not only had dragged her aching legs to make two round trips to the dam since yesterday, but Sayuri's death affected her so much that she was quite unsteady on her feet.

Picking up on Oshizu's words from where she'd left off, Ohina began speaking in a husky low voice. Masahiko strained his ears to listen. It was a voice like that of the ground bugs he'd heard late last night after he scattered the ashes of his grandfather's bones. Compared to Oshizu's voice, which tended to fly right out into people's faces, Ohina's more covered voice drew them in to listen.

"There are waterways that run from the mountains to the seas, passing through all places and lands. But if we in this village with the name Amazoko abandon Oki no Miya Shrine, the resting place of the dragon god, it will affect the waterways in all the other places too. When we ask for rain, where will the dragon god stop to rest on his travels from the ocean? From old times this has been the route he's taken. He stops to rest by Oki no Miya, then he climbs up to Ontake Peak, and then he calls on the clouds. If the water didn't pass through there it would mean taking away the pathways that connect the sea, the mountains, and the sky.

"From way back before the time the dam was finished I've been thinking how important the village's name Amazoko is. Amazoko means the 'bottom, or base of heaven.' This place was the base of heaven. And what does the word 'base' mean? Doesn't it mean the foundation of this world of ours, with all its untold and unfinished works? Why, even an old hag like myself, I'm grateful to be here. Amazoko—the base of heaven— this is the place where the foundations of the world have been entrusted. It's a fine name.

"If the waterways become clogged up at the resting places where the gods stop on their travels back and forth between the mountains and the seas then it will amount to cutting off their ladder to heaven, won't it?"

Suddenly Ohina's voice became choked with tears.

"Last year during the drought I went with Sayuri and we climbed down to take a look around the bottom of the lake where the land resurfaced. Looking for Oki no Miya, I also wanted to show her about the weeping cherry tree that was cut down there."

Ohina sobbed for a moment and all the other people around her began to feel their own tears welling up. Everyone knew the story of how Sayuri's mother had died beneath that cherry tree.

"We searched all over for the tree, but it was all covered with mud. The mud had covered it over about six feet or so. A surveyor went there and that's what he told us. There was no way we could have found it. It must still be there somewhere on the bottom of the water, all covered with mud.

"If that drought had hung on a little while longer there's no telling what might have appeared. You know what sort of person Sayuri was, so when she couldn't find the remains of either Oki no Miya or the cherry tree she seemed terribly dejected. And so after that in the evenings she took to making up her face in white, like she'd done at prayer times, carrying her bell and walking around the banks of the dam.

"Last night, who knows what she was trying to call out for, or where she planned to go with that horse she was so fond of. Myself, I was up there with Omomo and we were with the grandson of the old estate to scatter Masahito's ashes. It seemed there was something strange floating about on the far bank. At that time, I wonder, was Sayuri already dead, or was she still alive? I couldn't hear any sounds of a horse."

It was Tamayo the sleepwalker and several other people who'd been out walking along the embankment who had seen Sayuri, lit up by the flames of the fire. They remembered how she looked leading the horse—how she seemed so different from others. People had said that her mother, who died beneath the cherry tree that now lay at the bottom of the dam, was born in the neighboring town of Oku Hyuga, along the Mimigawa River. A few of those who were listening to Ohina's story wondered if Sayuri might not have been directly related to the *inugami* spirits. But no one had spoken of it openly.

When Sayuri went to the village meetings she had always left her face natural, without any make up. Whether she understood the discussions that went on there or not, she never seemed to mind carrying out the job of serving tea, as if it were her own appointed role. And even if she had passed the age of forty, the graceful sight of her shoulders and the nape of her neck caught everyone's attention. When the men amused each other and told jokes the women kept an eye on what they were up to. The women often met in the house with the attached prayer hall that Oai-sama had built after the village was flooded and there they listened to lectures about Kannon and held festivals for the moon. Perhaps this had been partly out of concern for Sayuri, whose mother had died and who had been left alone.

Oshizu had been watching the young man from Tokyo who was related to the old Silk Estate. Since he hadn't turned toward her she devised a pretext and carried a small tapered cup and a *sake* decanter with a thin neck shaped like a crane. With a gentle look she nudged her way in alongside him.

"So you've come back here for O-bon, have you? And you even did a memorial ceremony out by the lake. That's very kind of you. I imagine you must have been quite surprised."

Never having even spoken to this old woman who had just edged her way in to sit by him, Masahiko wasn't sure how to deal with the situation.

"Well, yes, I guess so."

Blinking his eyes as if startled, he broke into an embarrassed laugh. He realized he'd gotten a bit drunk.

With people continually saying things such as "you must have been so surprised," and "it must have been some kind of fate," it seemed that no matter what they said now he wouldn't be able to take it in.

"Well, it look's like this guy's drunk his fill already."

Oshizu, showing disappointment, urged the *shochu* on the others and helped herself to it as well. The stewed vegetables known as *otoki* that were served at the wake tasted particularly good. In Tokyo there wasn't anything like this. Having been initiated into drinking *shochu* the night before, he had accepted the drinks poured for him by the bearded man seated next to him. Omomo carried in a huge plate heaped with the stewed vegetables and bowed politely. She appeared to be working particularly hard.

"You must be pretty hungry."

"Ah, thanks for yesterday."

He didn't know where to begin his reply, as there were so many things that had happened to him. While Omomo moved about as she took care of the guests, it seemed she was keeping her attention on Masahiko. But when she sat down right in front of him, he found that the intimacy of the night before somehow fled and he felt himself just sitting there stiffly, as if they were meeting for the first time. He thought; I've been wanting to say something to her when she comes, and yet now my body is shaking.

Probably the apparent change in her appearance from the day before was due to her being dressed in a simple white dress, instead of the red T-shirt she'd worn then. Since they were taking part in a wake it was only natural to dress more formally, yet it seemed a little surprising to find this rather wild-spirited woman looking so neat and proper.

Omomo was gazing rather blankly at the large plate of food she had brought in. But then, as if suddenly snapping back into attention, she reached with her chopsticks and dished out some big triangular pieces of fried and boiled tofu.

"All right, here you are. Could you just pass your plate over this way for me please."

Though a bit formal, still her voice retained that soft quality he had heard yesterday. *Now that's the voice I wanted to hear.* For the first time Masahiko felt relieved. Just at that moment a man's voice called out beside him.

"Hey there Omomo—looks like you're serving the best of the cooking to our young gentleman!"

Omomo immediately changed her tone of voice and replied.

"This is food for the vigil tonight. So Goro, how about some tofu for you too. Here you go."

"Well, I suppose if you're twisting my arm, I must. OK then, all right."

"Say Omomo, it's been ages. How about a little something for me too?"

"All right. All right. Here's some *konyaku* for you."

"Well, now how about that? Looks like she still remembers. She gave me my favorite."

It must have been on account of her talk with these men that Masahiko's impression of Omomo had changed from that of the day before. Her quick-witted way of dealing with these old men aroused a new interest in him. But just when it seemed he might get a chance to talk with her, now with this sort of conversation going on he couldn't easily get started. Perhaps this sort of atmosphere was what the priest had been talking about when he spoke of wakes as being festive occasions.

Raising his glass from time to time the older man on the left nodded his head, following along with Ohina's story. This was the one called Chiyomatsu, who had been giving the directions about what to do with Sayuri's body back in the daytime by the bush-covered banks of the dam.

At that time he had called out to Masahiko. "Say, could you by any chance be related to the family of the old Silk Estate? You look so similar. Do you mind my asking?"

In this place too the old man seemed a bit reserved, yet when he sat down next to him without saying a word for some reason Masahiko felt relieved. While the conversation was loosening up it seemed that a group of quiet elders had been gathering around this slightly built old man. Perhaps it was a group of the most senior of the men. Masahiko hadn't noticed it, but he'd been given the seat of honor as he was the guest who had come from the farthest distance. Sliding on her knees, Ohina made her way over and bowed deeply to the elders. Old Chiyomatsu spoke to Ohina in a deeply consoling tone of voice.

"Thank you for saying that. Sayuri's death has been hard on us all. Amazoko is a village that has a special responsibility. I share the same feelings toward it as you."

Ohina glanced intently at the old man and, her eyes suddenly welling up in tears, broke out into a smile. What a gentle expression, Masahiko thought.

"Thank you so much Chiyomatsu. I felt so sad, my words just spilled out from my heart."

"Well I think all of us feel pretty much that way too. You spoke for us all."

The row of elders nodded their heads together in agreement.

"I've been talking about the things we've been taught for a long time."

Together the elders nodded and then a man in his fifties at the end of the line began to speak.

"Ohina, you're our bridge between this world and that world. Even after we die we depend on your help. But who's going to go first—that's something we can't know."

"That's the truth. We can never know who's going first."

From another group a woman's voice could be heard; "Even tonight or tomorrow morning we might find another messenger of the dead." It seemed to Masahiko that people were speaking of Jimpei as if he were already dead.

Chiyomatsu added, "You know, all day long today, I don't know why but for some reason it seems I keep recalling that time we went up Mt. Ontake."

"Ah, that time—it's the same for me too."

The quiet group of elders seemed to be warming up to talk.

"Oai-sama and Sayuri really showed their strength that time, didn't they."

"That time they did the ceremonies and prayed for rain, that was quite a dry spell we went through."

Ohina's eyes were narrowing into a half-open state, as if she had suddenly recalled something.

"Yes, that time. Oai-sama poured her whole life into it. She fasted and transferred her soul completely to Sayuri; I know what they did. And Sayuri, even if she couldn't speak, she understood completely what was going on and how Oai-sama poured her entire being into it. The two of them, together they performed the *misogi* purification rites at Isara River. But now that Isara River, it's down there too at the bottom of the dam."

Suddenly Ohina's words sank into silence. Everyone's thoughts must have been wandering around the bottom of the dam. They seemed to be hearing the sounds of water. It was a soft murmuring sound that emanated from the smallest of the streams of water all about Amazoko. The silence flowed on. Masahiko recalled a scene from the twilight of the previous night. A verse of song came back to life in his ears.

Yaa
Hôre yaa
Sixteenth night of O-bon
Flowers of the moon
Scattering, scattering
The evening of flowers

Through the open sliding door he gazed at the empty garden. A moon was perched between the trees. Whatever kind of trees they were, their black branches were all woven into the sky. Last night was the sixteenth night of O-bon. Ohina had said that the banks of the Isara River, where Oai-sama had performed the *misogi* rites to pray for water, had been mostly "melted away." Even for Masahiko, who had never seen what the old village had looked like, this state of affairs seemed wrong. Ohina's voice crept into his ears.

"Oai-sama once talked about how it was a strange drought and how it might have been a sign of something bad to come. That was still long before all the talk of the dam started. She spoke of how, of late, the children she'd given birth to didn't seem to come back very much. And even when they did, she could no longer see the black pupils in their eyes seated stably. She wondered what had happened. It seemed their souls had been stolen. Their faces seemed to have become different from those of the villagers. It was as if they'd washed off all the dust of the countryside with the water of the city and become sophisticated. She didn't feel good about it at all. 'I wonder,' she had said, 'do they really think it's so wonderful to become a city person?'"

"And it's not just in Amazoko. Even in the villages way off in the back reaches of the mountains, the people who go off to the cities don't come back. And then the fields and mountains go untended and wild and nonhumans come in. Sometimes new people like those Kishu charcoal makers come in and stir things up for a while, but they don't stay."

"Right. And Oai-sama used to talk about that 'French Mountain' over there, and all the noise they kicked up from the engines of their motorcycles running up and down the mountainsides. That was back in the days before we had motorcycles here."

"Yeah, right. I heard all about it—back at the end of the Meiji days, it was—and how that French outfit bought up the mountain."

"Right—that's the mountain where they had the riots. I heard stories about that too. They put in some sort of French lumber mill at the foot of the mountain and it made such a racket, no one could stand it. That stuff was what led to all the landslides and forest fires. And it never got any better after that. The gods of the mountains must not have been able to stand it. Even the local people rarely climbed such a far-off mountain."

"Sure, those mountain gods mustn't have been able to stand it. Red-roofed cars, blue-roofed cars, all lined up. The windows all shiny. Glass windows. And bringing in all those machines, it was like some sort of witchcraft, magic. And suddenly cutting down all those trees of the gods, one after another. Just cutting and toppling them over like that. And then running those motorcycles around all over the place. The mountain was screaming with the ruckus everywhere. And then the big floods hit."

"It went on all through the mountains—even way off in the areas where the *yamabushi* monks who passed through the back reaches of the forests did their practices—back where not even an ax had ever been brought in before. That was back even before they put in the railroad."

"And then the sightseers started coming in with their picnic lunches. I heard about it from old Keisuke who's dead now. At the end of those troubles the landslides came and washed everything away. That foreign project flowered in vain. Keisuke heard all about it from his friends among the charcoal workers."

Ohina spoke up to resume her story.

"Oai-sama talked about those things too. She said, 'The city is a flower that blossoms in vain, and that French Mountain was the start of it all. One time some of the villagers went to see what was going on and it couldn't be stopped. But when they got back home they realized that right here in Amazoko we have all the five grains, and that our souls are at peace here, and for that reason we should maintain the village without changing it.

"We have the mountains for gathering firewood and making charcoal, and buckwheat and millet to harvest, and mushrooms to gather too. As long as we in Amazoko live by relying on ourselves we can maintain the things we've enjoyed through the ages. And for this reason, Oki no Miya, the place the waterways meet, is essential—what do you think Ohina? Those people who go off to the city and eat only white rice— do you think they remember the tastes of all the grains of Amazoko? That white rice is no good for their bodies. When they run off and become city folks they lose the ability to hear the voices of the gods.

"'Amazoko doesn't even have many rice fields, so we've gotten by on millet and other grains and grasses. And actually that's better. Our babies are strong and healthy. I've been a midwife and delivered babies here so I know these things. And if that girl was born beneath the weeping cherry, then she's a child of Amazoko. I've done my best to bring up Sayuri,'—that was what Oai-sama told me."

Ohina's voice choked up.

"I can't help feeling I've failed Oai-sama. Sayuri-san—tying on that obi . . . that obi was her only connection to her hometown on the Mimigawa River. And now, she's dead. I . . ."

Hanging her head in dejection, Ohina reached out with her hand. Coiling the ends of her hair that fell in limp strings on her thin shoulders, she let out a deep sigh. Seeing Ohina looking that way, the elders fell into silence.

Hearing Ohina say the words, "tying on that obi," right in front of him, Masahiko was taken aback. He felt something riffling about in his mind, like some sort of air turbulence. He felt that in the present circumstances he couldn't just come out and say that this was the same obi he'd seen in his dream this morning when he saw the back of that girl. The obi that was wrapped about Sayuri's dead body when she was raised out of the water had been stained with a smoky dark color of water. He hadn't realized that the material was an authentic piece of the finest *shuchin* silk, but from seeing its refined, subdued luster he could tell that it was a fabric of great elegance and refinement.

But then, what of that dream he'd woken to this morning? It couldn't have been—and yet . . . It seemed things were getting stranger and stranger. He wanted to ask Ohina what she thought about it, but surrounded by the glances of the elders, and with Ohina looking so dejected now, he didn't feel he could bring up the story of his dream here. Perhaps feeling concerned about this mood, Oshizu got up again and drew closer, sliding on her knees.

"It looks like I'm going to have to look after that boy."

Holding a glass in hand she remarked,

"This is a beautiful liquor here. It's really delicious. They say it's made from mountain peaches and strawberries. We only serve it to special guests."

He was beginning to feel like trying a bit of this liquor now—the one he'd been turning down. Perhaps if he got a little drunk on it he'd be able to continue that dream. The glass he was poured held the fragrance of the fruit of mountain trees, and as he drank it seeped down deep through his entire body.

"All right, that's the spirit now—drink up! Say, let's have another round here."

The men were used to Oshizu's manner of entertaining guests. In an instant the tense atmosphere seemed to lighten up and then someone spoke up to change the topic of conversation.

"You remember that time Ohina offered the prayer song to the Buddha in thanks for the rains? We all danced together."

"That's right. Oai-sama asked for it."

"We asked too. That was no ordinary happening that year."

"That year we lost a lot of people. Three died."

"When it gets too hot or too cold we lose a lot."

"Right. That year just at O-bon, all through the night, starting from the houses of the dead, we went around from house to house doing the *nembutsu* dance for Amida Buddha to console their souls."

"Old Kirihito-san the song leader—how many years has he been gone now?—he had a great voice and he accompanied Ohina's songs so well. He used to sing all through the night. And he danced too, with all his soul."

"Right, right. The people in his group said his dancing that time was like he'd gone off into a dream land and was dancing in a place somewhere off beyond this world."

"Today we hardly ever offer prayers for rain and now the water at the bottom of the dam's gotten all mucked up. That can't be a good sign, that sort of thing."

Could the people of Amazoko really see the water at the bottom of the dam? Come to think of it, this morning when Masahiko looked at the bottom of the dam it appeared agitated and he had thought this was because of Sayuri's obi.

"You came from Tokyo for Sayuri's night attendance."

Hearing Oshizu say this, he wondered if her mention of a "night attendance" referred to the wake. The words struck him as coming from a distant age.

"It's a shame none of us attended Masahito's funeral. What with Tokyo being so huge and all, even Ohina didn't go."

With her eyes cast downward and her head bowed down showing the back of her neck, Ohina made no reply. Masahiko looked on the silent Ohina with fondness. His family hadn't even sent a funeral announcement to the old village his grandfather had long ago turned his back on. No one here had even been told of it. Looking about, he wondered where Omomo was. Perhaps in the kitchen, washing dishes or something. She must have been looking after Oshizu and the other elders.

"We thought no one from your family would ever come back, but now with the village sunk at the bottom it seems you've come after all."

So old women get drunk too, he mused. Masahiko stared at Oshizu. Suddenly, right in front of him, she raised one of her elbows above the opening in the sleeve of her kimono with a gesture that looked just like that of a praying mantis. Then she opened her mouth and let out a laugh.

"All right—now it looks like he's put some color back into his face. Looks just like Masahito when he was young—don't you think, Ohina?"

But Ohina wasn't there. She had gotten up quickly and left. People were now moving in closer and slapping each other on the back. The *sake* vessel with the crane-shaped neck lay on the *tatami*. Someone's foot had caught on it and knocked it over. This sort of scene was waving about in Masahiko's eyes.

Masahiko looked up at the walls and ceiling. It appeared to be a very old temple. Its construction was different from that of the ordinary houses of the villagers. He tried to recall something. Yes—there had been a name marker, with golden characters written on black lacquer—certainly there had.

The words read;

For the recitation, in perpetuity, of sutras for our ancestors— the sum of 20,000 yen. Mikihiko Aso. Amazoko Village.

Mikihiko was the name of his great-great grandfather. Certainly he had never thought he would find the name Mikihiko in a temple such as this. It had been written before the flooding of the village. Sixty years before, or maybe seventy. How much had 20,000 yen meant at that time? It conveyed both an air of ostentatiousness and a sense of emptiness.

The name marker had become detached from the wall and appeared to be drifting about. Could it be that this place was already at the bottom of the water?

A deep voice called out to him, and then he was clapped on the shoulder. "Well now, our young Tokyo gentleman—you really put in a day's work, didn't you. Don't you feel better now, after some of our special wine?"

It was the bearded man, the one who'd spoken the words to the dead body—"Sayuri, everyone's here now. So let's get you down to the temple,"—back when they had carried the stretcher from the banks of the dam.

"Since you've taken the trouble to come here and spend this night with us, you have to register yourself as a member of the Amazoko Citizens' Council—*Masahiko-shan*."

The man's face had turned bright red, and the grave expression he'd shown earlier in the day now looked friendly. It was the first time Masahiko had ever been addressed with the intimate form "Masahiko-*shan*." The feeling it gave him was not at all bad.

"Is there such a thing as the Amazoko Citizens' Council?"

"I just made it up now. Why, up in Tokyo you have citizens' councils, don't you? What I've made here isn't something way off in Tokyo. It's at the bottom of the water. The Citizens' Council of Amazoko, at the bottom of the water. Pretty good name, don't you think? And for you, making it here all the way from Tokyo, I hereby designate you Original Founder Number Two. How's that?"

"Me—a founder?"

"Come on, don't talk like a fool. You're already drunk on Oshizu's seven-flavored wine?"

The bearded man laughed with his whole body shaking.

"Come on now, drink up. You have all the qualifications of a founder. Wasn't it your family who was the first to run off from the town of its birth? The very oldest family. Isn't it always the ones who've left their hometowns—the ones who've lost their birthplaces—who start up these associations? So you must have better credentials than anyone else."

"But I . . ."

"Come on, talk some sense, won't you? That slow—yeah that slow way of talking of yours, I kind of like it. Sure, you have all the credentials you need for a Citizen of the Depths."

"Well, I do have a feeling the waters at the base of the dam are swaying around."

Masahiko woke to a cool breeze that covered his body like a stream of flowing water

"Ah, you're awake?"

The reserved-sounding voice came from a woman he didn't know.

"Excuse me, the door was open."

He sat up. The woman bowed and left the room.

He shook his head and thought. Where am I? Who was that woman? The room was so bright. Beyond the corridor flowers were swaying. Those are cosmos—even I know cosmos. Beyond the garden was a high hedge. Ah, that's the same tree as the one at the Philosophy Hall in Nakano. But this isn't a house in Nakano. He began to recall the events of the previous night. Ah, that's right—I carried a body from the lake. This is the temple—there's incense in the air.

The sharp shriek of a bird sounded. Masahiko didn't recognize it as the call of a shrike. A yellow cat jumped up lightly onto the porch. It stared at Masahiko, stretched out, raised its head and then lay down—an amazingly long-bodied cat. Again the cosmos swayed about. It seemed both the cat and he himself had been sleeping there for ages. While sleeping it had seemed that a voice from a sutra had been flowing in and out of his dreams, time and time again.

"Why don't you go with us to the place the bodies are cremated?"

A pleasantly familiar voice had filled his ears again. It was the voice of the bearded man. Masahiko was clapped on the back by a big hand.

"These days we put fuel oil on them, so they burn a lot faster than in the old days."

He remembered replying that he would go. Would he really go—to the place where they burned bodies?

From the previous day sometimes it had seemed as if he had crawled into the center of an enormous tree. He felt as if his blood had been assimilated into the sap of the tree and it was flowing through the tree from the trunk to the tips of its leaves. He could feel its roots searching out the little trickles of water. The smell of the rocks and stones filled his nose.

He got up, gathering some of the bedding about him. Suddenly he felt his breathing constrict. He stamped his foot and then shook out the bedding and folded it up.

"Pardon me, I've woken you so early. Shall I put away your bedding? Oh my . . ."

It was the same woman he'd seen before. I can't remember coming to this room last night. I guess I must have been drunk. I wonder how I got into this room to sleep. The cat raised its head, gave an annoyed blink and then went back to sleep.

"Ah, excuse me, your lunch is ready. You can wash your face here."

The woman returned and pointed.

"Your *biwa* is over there."

The instrument had been placed standing up in the *tokonoma*.

"Do you play the *biwa?*"

"Well, yes," he replied vaguely.

She seemed older than Omomo. Her skin shone. Now he re-membered—this was the young wife at the temple. Back when he helped carry Sayuri's body and came to the temple, this was the woman who had seen the *biwa* on his back and held out her hand and then withdrawn it.

"Carrying something like that on your back, along with the dead body—that must have been quite difficult."

"Well not really. Along the way, Ohina carried it for me."

Suddenly the woman's face grew suspicious. He avoided go-ing into the matter further. He was starved to the point it felt he was about to faint.

"This persimmon is from Ohina."

On a tray, some salted *umeboshi* plums, a cup of green tea, and a peeled persimmon had been placed.

"Ohina said these are good for hangovers. They're supposed to help you get over it. They're the first of the season. Her daughter brought them here."

He tried to rouse himself, but his head was still reeling.

"It looks like you overdid it a bit. But with everyone making you drink like that it's not surprising. Here, have some tea, and some *umeboshi* too."

She waited for him to finish drinking the tea before asking,

"Is Ohina a friend of yours? And Omomo-chan?"

He answered that they had known his grandfather. He didn't mention that he hadn't known them until two days ago. He recalled the scene of Utazaka Hill, with the sky and the branches of the persimmon.

"Ah, that persimmon . . . probably it's still not quite ripe. It might be a bit sour," she added, drawing in her breath. "The per-simmon may be all right, but for a hangover *umeboshi* are best."

The warmth of the thick futon had been so pleasant but now, suddenly, he felt pulled back into reality. It seemed the woman was a bit put out by the fact that the persimmon had been brought by Ohina and Omomo.

"Please, why don't you try some?"

He took an *umeboshi* and put it in his mouth. This seemed to put the woman into a better mood and she stood up with a smile.

"Your lunch is ready over there."

Perhaps because he'd eaten the salty *umeboshi* plum first, when he bit into the crisp, not quite ripe persimmon it tasted delicious.

Moving into the large room set up with individual *ozen* tables, he found there was food on one table only. Women were busy cleaning up. He must have slept a long time.

"Momo-chan—why don't you fix something to eat for that fellow from the old Silk Estate," called out one of the women.

From the kitchen Omomo called back, "You must be tired from all your work yesterday," and then she came out wearing a white apron and knelt on the floor.

Unaccustomed to such a greeting from Omomo, as it sounded like that of a country housewife, Masahiko cleared his throat uneasily. Feeling like a young kid who doesn't know the ways of the world, he realized the women were straining their ears and listening.

"Please eat as much as you can."

He was surprised by the bowl that was given to him. It was piled with so much rice he wondered what the women might be up to. Noticing his perplexed look, the women broke out into laughter.

"My goodness, I haven't seen anything like this in ages. It's a feast for a Buddha of old. I guess it must be a surprise for this young man from Tokyo."

Omomo also broke out into a laugh.

"You're right. It certainly is a feast fit for a Buddha. Not a bad farewell dinner for Sayuri, I'd say."

Masahiko raised and lowered the black lacquered bowl as if it were quite heavy and then he slowly picked up his chopsticks. The women approved of his manners. Setting out the various dishes of cooked and pickled foods they remarked, "Oh my, Momo-chan."

Outside in the yard straw mats had been set out and men were busy with various tasks. Some were cutting out shapes of horses and flowers from white paper. Others were stripping the green coating off lengths of bamboo. Still others were sawing planks. And as he watched, a fresh wood coffin was constructed right before his eyes.

"There were several generations of Mikihikos, but anyone who saw their funerals will tell you they sent the dead off in coffins they made themselves. At the time of the funeral of the last of the Mikihikos I was still only nineteen, but I sure learned a lot from the old people about how to do a funeral."

The elder Chiyomatsu, seated on the veranda watching how the work was proceeding, spoke to them from time to time. Masahiko had been watching the men's activities with only mild interest, but when he heard the talk about Mikihiko's coffin he was pulled back to attention.

All the men and women had their own tasks and it appeared they were fully enjoying their work. All sorts of talk went on, but Masahiko couldn't catch more than a fraction of it.

"In the old days, half the men went off to dig the graves, but now that the graveyard's at the bottom of the lake the work of grave digging has fallen off. Nowadays the bodies are cremated so it's gotten easier, but the dead must think our compassion has grown weak.

"I'm with you there," another elder broke in. "In those days when we carried the coffin and laid it into the opening in the ground it always seemed there was something special about the weight. It's hard to explain. Even though it was a dead body it felt like it had the weight of a person. When we laid people's bodies into the grave I felt they'd fulfilled their roles in this world. I felt I too had played a small part in it. But what with burning the bodies these days, and using oil, and the sound and all—well, it just doesn't sit right."

Even amidst the conversations, when one of the elders said something the others strained their ears so as not to miss anything. And the mention of the unpleasant sounds of the crematory brought an immediate reaction from old Oshizu-san who came over, still eating and holding a rice scoop.

"That burning sound really gets to me too. There's not even enough time for a farewell. It just isn't right."

"She's right," another woman added quickly, "After dressing it up so nice in robes for sending it along, and then with that sound of burning oil, it just doesn't give a decent send-off for the dead."

Other than the elders, the only one not involved in the work was Masahiko. Sitting on the verandah, he looked at the palms of his hands. They were an unblemished white. His fingernails were long and slightly soiled. He hid his hands behind his back and for a while there was silence.

Could it be that everyone was hearing the sounds of the burning oil at the time of their own deaths? The sounds from the crematory were not right for the dead of Amazoko. When Amazoko people were laid out in robes of white it was only proper that they should pass over Moonshadow Bridge by Otachidote Embankment, and over the Isara River, and then head off into the mountain mists. No doubt this was what the old men and women must have been thinking. To be disposed of in an oil-fired oven, at the flick of a switch—even if the body had already become a soul—it just wasn't right.

"In the old days," Chiyomatsu began, "when a person died, everyone took special care in preparing the way for the soul's journey over the bridge. They helped send the person along as it crossed over on its way."

Oshizu spoke in a voice almost panting, "We had them wear white leggings on their feet and coverings on their hands, and we had them take dumplings for the deceased, and a coin purse. We checked to make sure nothing had been overlooked: Were all the children there? Had all the lanterns been prepared?—we told the children to be sure to take them all. Had the children eaten the dumplings?—if they didn't chew the dumplings they'd be taken along with the dead person.

One by one the women began to speak out.

"That's right. When a dead person left, sometimes a child might be taken along with it too. That's why we checked for marks of flour around the children's mouths, to make sure they'd eaten the dumplings."

Chiyomatsu broke into the discussion again.

"All the children stood at the front with the lanterns and the young people's group held a banner for the departed. That was the kind of procession they made to send off the departed souls."

"That was the procession for the day of the soul's departure. The children carried lanterns and pounded out rice to make Omaimo-sama's dumplings and they spread pebbles they'd gathered at the Isara River around the building at the cemetery."

"Yes, and in Amazoko even after a death there was a road for going out and a road to return by."

"And they spread the message of the dead—'We're sending off Sayuri. Tonight is her wake. Even the crows, and the cows and horses, and the dogs and cats know it's the day of her passing. Their voices are different.'"

"The crows and dogs went too and returned over Moon-shadow Bridge."

"I wonder if the water's still flowing there now."

"The water where?"

"What do you mean 'where?'—under Moonshadow Bridge, of course."

"Ah, the Isara River. Now everything's down there at the bottom of the lake."

"It's strange, but if you look to the bottom the lost world seems to come back to life."

"Certainly there's a world that did exist."

"There are still signs of it here and there."

"The branches of the ginkgo trees and horse chestnuts are swaying in circles and reaching out with their sinewy hands. They're signaling and calling us from the depths of the lake."

"Yes. They're calling us. Back that time when the water dried up I went and looked and it really surprised me, what I saw. The big ginkgo was bending over and raising its skinny arms from its side."

"When you think of it, in the old days in Amazoko we had everything we needed."

"That's right. From *miso* to *sake* to everything we needed for the festivals, we could get them all at the straw sandal shop."

"The only things we couldn't get there were salt and fish from the ocean."

"And we didn't have gambling either."

"Once the dam construction started, the gambling came in."

"Yeah, at that little shack. I heard they'd just been let out of jail and they brought the gambling with them. That's how I heard it got started."

"That guy Santaro. He was the first to start up the gambling."

"Yeah, he's the one who comes to mind as the guy who started it."

"I wonder where he is now."

"Followed the older ones who taught him their tricks—how to screw folks out of their money."

"That's where most of the compensation money went."

Suddenly the talk fell into silence as the people were caught up in thinking back on the rumors about that swindler who had made off with the fortunes of the old estate.

A woman in her fifties made her way into the midst of the group.

"It looks like Sayuri may be the last to get a proper funeral like this."

"If Sayuri's the last one then it looks like the rest of us are headed for that oil incinerator. We won't even be able to have our little chat with the old king of the underworld."

At this everyone laughed and brightened up.

"Hey, let's knock off thinking like this. Everything that happens is a sort of practice. If you've gone through training for hell once, what happens afterwards is easy."

The bearded man spoke with a serious intensity.

The younger priest's wife came in after Omomo and started preparing tea.

"Well, it looks like things are starting to liven up. Here, have some tea, won't you? The priest said that when you're finished making the lanterns we can head off for the cremation."

"All right, all right. We'll be finished soon. This bearded guy here knows all the stories about hell. Seems he's proud of it."

The priest's wife watched the man as she handed out the teacups.

"Yeah, I guess I know about it pretty well by now—I've been there and back a few times."

Everyone knew the story of how this fellow had gotten drunk on *shochu* and walked along the top of the dam construction site and fallen. Even though he'd hit an iron construction rod and gotten skewered all the way through his body from his rear end to his neck, he'd been saved by good fate. They all regarded it as a stroke of special luck.

"Myself, I don't take any particular pride in it. It was just that one time. It was the first time in my life I was in the papers. They didn't mention anything about the iron rod though. People came from all over to see me after they read about it."

Everyone could imitate that tone of voice of his, and whenever they'd had enough of his telling this story someone would mimic and tease him.

"On and on about your getting into the papers—don't you think we've heard enough of it already? You were about to land in the obituary column."

Everyone had been prepared for Kappei to launch into that old story again today, but somehow it didn't come up. Always at the close of his story he used to tell of how Sayuri had come—"dressed as a shrine maiden, beautiful as a wisteria flower"—and prayed for his recovery. He believed it was owing to her care that he had been called back from the depths of hell and so he always spoke of her as his Kannon, his savior.

About the time the sutra reading for the departure of the procession from the temple came to an end, it began to cloud over. Looking up, people pointed to the sky and wondered.

"I guess we should be able to make it back before it starts to rain."

"Compared to carrying her down the mountain, taking her to be cremated should be easier. So let's get moving."

But as the body turned out to be heavier than expected they added extra carriers to help out. And still others, the children and the women, joined the procession carrying lanterns and incense.

Before they started off, Chiyomatsu gave a greeting.

"Well, it seems that with Sayuri this may be the last funeral like this. Every one of our families is indebted to her. It may be hard on you who carry the coffin, but let's get started. These days funerals have become such stiff city-style affairs and the body of the departed is whisked away in a hearse so quickly we hardly even have a chance to take a decent last look."

The women all nodded as they stood in place. Since it had been agreed that it wouldn't do for Masahiko to be dressed in the same clothes he'd arrived in, he was given the elderly priest's formal kimono and a robe with the family crest. It seemed that the others who wore robes with family crests were the leading men. There were five or six of them. On seeing Masahiko changed from wearing a T-shirt to a formal kimono, the women made quite a stir. One of the elderly women gasped, "Oh my goodness. It looks just like he's come back."

Ohina was also among them, but she held her breath as she looked on and gently wiped her brow. The procession began to move forward. Along the paths among the fields the grasses and heavy-laden ears of rice were swaying. Slowly the group moved along, following the pace of the women and children.

"All the fields are ripe and full."

"Such beautiful fields."

"In the old days Sayuri prayed and danced here for the rains so many times."

With eyes narrowed as he gazed at the colors of the rice, and his voice choked with tears, one of the men said, "If she could see these beautiful fields now she'd be so happy—but she's gone."

"Her soul may still be nearby, so she may be watching the fields now."

Dressed in mourning clothes and wearing white *tabi* socks, the women were walking along the grassy path, stepping with graceful movements that differed from the way they walked when they were working. The soft gentle earth felt different from when they worked the fields. With each step, they felt from the soles of their feet that they were walking along a special path.

"This is a quite a funeral, Sayuri. Everyone has turned out to send you off."

With her chin partly hidden in the collar of her kimono, Oshizu spoke out softly, "Yes, it really is a wonderful funeral. It looks like the funerals from now on are going to seem pretty lacking in spirit."

"I'm glad I could come."

"Yes, it's for times like this that we make these mourning clothes."

The women complimented each other on their clothing. A cool breeze rose up, ruffling the hems of their kimonos. With their hems held up the women revealed legs of uncommon elegance.

"Ohina, what have you been up to these days?"

Called out to from behind, Ohina turned around. It was the younger priest's wife.

"What have I been up to? My usual work. Why?"

"Ah, catching snakes. Have you been getting many?"

Ohina's eyes blinked as if she were trying to pull herself back into the conversation. She replied, "Hardly any."

"They say most people can't catch any at all."

Oshizu rebuked her; "Tsunako-san, this is no time to talk about that, at a funeral. We've all had enough already."

"I didn't mean anything special. I was just asking."

"Well then don't go asking needless questions. There are times for bringing up things, and times it's not called for."

The younger priest's wife waved her fan back and forth and turned aside. A heavy fragrance wafted from her fan. Oshizu, making a slight gesture of fanning herself with her handkerchief, stepped up beside Ohina.

"Thanks for all your help from yesterday."

"Oh, you're welcome. It was no trouble."

"That obi—do you know what happened to it?"

"Well, I thought we should put it in with the coffin, but on second thought I kept it."

"Seems it might have been better to have put it in with her, doesn't it? I couldn't decide either. It would really bother me to have it left behind."

"I thought we could take care of it at any time, so I left it hanging on the *sal* tree. I thought someone would think of it."

"It's probably because of that obi that I can't forget the time she prayed for rain."

"Were you there too, Oshizu?"

"Certainly I was there. Why even now I can still see it. But where's that *sal* tree—the one the obi was left hanging on?"

Oshizu's tone of voice dropped suddenly. Tsunako had stopped waving her fan but now she started up again, as if nothing had happened.

"It was on a tree near Sayuri's prayer hall."

"Well, I hope so."

The old woman nodded twice. At the temple also there was a *sal* tree with a trunk that glistened. Oshizu's words implied that if the obi had been left at the temple, Ohina probably would be reprimanded.

The night before, the leading women had washed and prepared Sayuri's body for the funeral. They cleaned and purified it, dressed it in white robes, and prepared it for its journey.

"Ohina-san, please," one of them had said as the comb was passed and Ohina was brushing out Sayuri's long hair. Normally when the women met they were talkative, but this time they all had been silent.

"She looks so different . . ."

"All her color and luster are gone," Oshizu remarked sorrowfully.

With brusque movements the women combed out her hair and poured hot water on it. Sayuri's hair moved along with the water and became slightly tangled in the mat made of rough bamboo straw.

"If you just look at her hair it still looks like she's alive."

With a sigh someone said, "She was a shrine maiden. No perms or hairdos for her. Such beautiful hair."

After the men had set out the straw mats and erected a circular enclosure in the yard in back of the temple they hadn't looked at the area where the women were washing and preparing the body. At a quick glance, Masahiko had been able to see smoke from the incense and steam rising upward from the circle, but he couldn't hear much of the conversation going on within.

He heard someone call out, "Salt, salt," and then the women covered their hands with the smoke of the incense and came out from the enclosure. The last ones to emerge were Ohina and Omomo, but since Omomo was carrying the obi in her arms Masahiko's eyes were fixed on it. The mother and daughter had nodded about something and then, after they separated, Ohina watched her daughter as she walked away.

When the funeral procession began, Masahiko took a position that was neither too close nor too far away, such that he could watch Ohina and Omomo. Omomo walked with her head cast down, following her mother. Off and on Masahiko caught bits of the conversation as it floated in and out of his hearing. Oshizu's voice had possessed dignity when she said, "Don't ask needless questions." He had heard the temple woman remark in an overly ingenuous voice that sounded out of place, "Catching poisonous snakes!" He felt he was beginning to understand the feelings of the villagers.

Omomo, wearing a black mourning dress, looked thinner
than she had the night before. Before leaving, when he was
given the "dinner for the departed" that included that huge
serving of rice, Ohina had been laughing with the women in
the kitchen in an easygoing mood. From the day before all
sorts of unexpected things had been happening, and especially
after approaching Sayuri's dead body and thinking of it in connection with his dream at dawn it seemed his body had been
calling out from within. He wished he could talk about these
things with Ohina and Omomo but the chance hadn't seemed
to arise. The Omomo who laughed so gaily as she served the
bowls of rice had seemed a completely different person from
the woman who had sung in the moonlight the night before.
In the morning, with his hangover, he had never expected to
hear such a carefree laughing voice. The word "beatitude"
came to mind.

But as for this "different person"—what sort of person was
that woman of the previous night? For the most part she had
seemed like a normal girl brought up in the countryside. He
had the feeling that this woman might be found anywhere.
And yet it also seemed that he hadn't really established any
clear image of how she looked. From behind, the shape of her
head and shoulders looked so healthy. Where had she gotten
such a divine singing voice?

They came into the midst of a dense field filled with a
strong fragrance. As he was wondering where the smell came
from, Omomo spoke in a soft voice.

"Ah, the rice flowers. The rice plants are in blossom now.
Don't they smell good? Look how their pollen is blowing all
about."

He turned his head back and forth to look on both sides of
the road. The surface of the rice fields lay smoothed and ca-
ressed by the wind. A soft sighing sound rose and it looked as

if a dazzling white powder was wafting up from the densely growing ears of rice and spreading out across the entire field.

When Masahiko had first heard Omomo mention the flowers of rice plants he had imagined them as being shaped something like those of the Chinese milk vetch and having yellow petals. But now, hearing that they gave off a powder, and actually seeing this powder blowing all about, the fragrance struck him with an overpowering presence.

Once again he heard the voices of Ohina and Oshizu.

"What do you think we should do about the obi?"

"You think we should ask the men about it?"

"They'll just say, 'Why didn't you put the obi in the coffin?'"

"That won't do. Do you think we should ask the people at the temple?"

In mid-sentence, old Oshizu glanced over in Tsunako's direction.

"If we ask them, they'll just tell us to burn it."

"I suppose you're right."

"But if we burn it, we'll have nothing left to remember Oai-sama by."

"Here's what I think. I told Omomo we should wash it a bit and hang it in the *sal* tree."

"It's not the sort of thing you can just wash out easily. It needs to be sent to a specialist for cleaning . . . It's the only thing we have left from Oki no Miya."

Did Oshizu think so too? After Oai-sama's death Oki no Miya had been flooded, along with the village. The waterways that Oai-sama had cared so much about now lay stopped up at the bottom of the dam. It had seemed that Sayuri's function would come to an end with the flooding of the village after the dam was completed, but there had been enough requests for her to help with things such as horses' digestions and problems with the gods of the cooking stoves and such, and so she had remained quite busy after all.

The house that Oai-sama had left for her, along with the prayer hall she built that time after they prayed for the rains, had all been sunk. The villagers had felt sorry for her since she couldn't speak and she couldn't do things like negotiating for compensation money. So they gathered up discarded materials and lumber, and people who had free time had helped build a small makeshift prayer sanctuary. Sayuri had moved in there, taking only the minimum of implements needed for worship and the sacred Shinto mirror, but it had become the place where the women held their monthly ceremonies of worship and observances for the moon and the river. That light blue obi had been used as the covering cloth for the sacred mirror and it had provided the only decoration in the little building that served as a shrine.

She had put on that obi before she died—but what was it she'd been thinking of? Ohina's eyebrows were furrowed. In washing the body for the burial, first they had needed to untie the obi. Having soaked up the water, the *shuchin* silk had become rather difficult to get undone. In fact, this was not the first time Ohina had touched that obi.

While Oai-sama was still alive there had been a year with a long severe drought. Ohina and Omomo, who had no other relatives they could rely on, had thought of Oai-sama as both a parent and an elder sister. And in earning their living by gathering medicinal plants they had also relied on her knowledge of medicine in countless ways. When Sayuri finally came to take on the responsibilities of a shrine maiden and was about to perform the rain prayer rites, Oai-sama had come to visit them. She carried with her a large pair of tailor's scissors and was deep in thought. In front of her she held a large piece of material.

Realizing that Oai-sama had come for some matter quite different from the usual, Ohina had given her a rather hushed greeting and then looked at her face and at her hands that held the scissors and then gazed at the beautiful material she spread out.

"I'm thinking of cutting this."

At the time, Sayuri still had long hair. Ohina had watched as Sayuri tilted her neck and looked up to her mother as if to ask her something. What a beautiful girl—just like a princess— Ohina had thought.

"This ceremony for the rains is going to be very difficult. It's been such a long drought it doesn't look like it's going to be easy to get the rain to fall. I'm thinking of taking this piece of brocade that's been covering the mirror and making it into *hakama* pants for a formal kimono. Or I'll make an obi for her and let her dance, dressed in a white kimono, with this as the obi."

"Yes, it's such beautiful material. No one has an obi of such material."

"It's true. No one has anything like it. Actually it belonged to this child's mother."

"What? The woman who died beneath the cherry tree?"

"That's right. It was hers."

"Well, it's certainly a treasure."

"Yes, it's this girl's treasure. The woman held on to it all along her way and it wasn't stolen."

"I can see it wasn't stolen, but how did the woman make her way to the place beneath the cherry tree?"

"I wish I knew. Just after she gave birth she died. She was wearing the obi over a comforter around her belly. She must have been a well-loved child. It seems she must have come from quite a high class family—this really is quite some fabric. But there was no time to ask her about it."

"I wonder where she was from."

"Well, I couldn't hear her very clearly, but I heard her say something about the Mimigawa River. That much I heard clearly. The rest I could hardly make out."

"The Mimigawa—that's off in Hyuga, isn't it?"

"Could there be other places called Mimigawa? The Mimigawa River in Hyuga—I'm thinking that someday I'll save up the money and take Sayuri with me and search along the Mimigawa. It's a strange sounding name, the Mimigawa—the 'Ear River.' I have a feeling that if we take this material along with us we'll find out something. What do you think Sayuri?"

Nodding, Sayuri had looked at the two women attentively as if wondering what was going on. They were nodding. As it turned out, the material was never made into *hakama* but it became the obi.

The day of the ceremony for the rains had been like a coming-of-age rite for her. It wouldn't do if Sayuri made a mistake, so when Ohina was asked to help she had rushed over to assist Oai-sama. While they were tying on the obi for a trial Ohina had stared in wonder. In the simple new white robe with the slightly narrow obi tied around it and hanging down in back, Sayuri cut a figure of the utmost dignity and elegance.

"My goodness, she's so beautiful. It's such a pity she can't speak."

The words had just slipped out without thinking as Ohina glanced up but she couldn't forget what Oai-sama said in reply.

"By the grace of her not being able to speak, until now she has lived in purity without being harmed, but I worry about what might happen to her when I'm no longer here."

That day not only the elder men and the younger ones still in their prime, but also the leaders of the group of women had climbed Mt. Ontake together. Since Sayuri was going to carry out the prayer ceremony it had been necessary to have some other women assist her. At the well by the old mansion they filled containers made of fresh bamboo with water for the ceremony and carried them on their backs along with rice balls. The strong young ones took turns in carrying the heavier loads.

Although the springs had almost dried up in many areas during the long drought, at Masahito's place cool water still continued to gush out. In all seasons throughout the year the women took newly made Shinto paper strips to bless the rivers. But on this special morning they offered holy *sake* to the gods and then drank it in reverence before setting off.

Sayuri went to the spring wearing new white cotton skirt-like *mompe* trousers. Ohina knew that for several days Oai-sama had been working late into the night in order to sew the outfit. Ohina had been asked to help Sayuri purify her body with that water and to help her dress for the dance when they arrived at the source of the Isara River.

"I wish I could climb up there with you too, but my knees are in no shape for it, so I'm asking you. Her hair should be bound tightly with white paper from behind so it stands up high, and her white robe should hang out at the hem and her obi should be tied in a *Yoshihisa* knot.

"This time it's going to be different from the way she usually dances in *hakama*. She'll be calling to the gods of Mt. Ontake, so she shouldn't be thinking of herself as a person. I've told Sayuri she should dance like a divine being. She should change her white *tabi* socks too and prepare herself in the most dignified manner. Even if there are thickets of grass and brush, she shouldn't lose her balance. I've prepared some mats to make an area for the gods. They're rolled up and I've asked the men to carry them."

As Ohina watched the ears of rice waving back and forth, all her thoughts were carried back to that time and to the intense looks and words of Oai-sama.

It had been in the first dim light of dawn. At the sight of Sayuri's white robe, people had exclaimed,

"My goodness—this is like a scene from an old drama!"

"She looks so wonderful."

"All right, so let's get ourselves into the spirit too."

And at the sight of Sayuri their spirits had risen. When they reached the third valley they could see the sun breaking out across the parched rice fields. They all sighed as they spoke.

"It doesn't look good. All the fields are in the same state."

"But it's strange. Compared to the land below, up in the mountains there's more moisture. The colors of the grass and trees are different. They're thicker and greener."

"Maybe you're right. When you get up higher and look around, the world below looks pale."

"I'd thought the mountains would be dried out too, but the air's got some moisture."

"Yeah, but look over there—over by the erosion dam above Kazura Valley. The valley's all withered and drying up."

"Hmm, it looks like the trees have all faded and dried out."

"It's a bad sign if the Kazura Valley's gone dry."

"Yeah, and this is the first time the water from Kazura has stopped flowing into our fields."

"The erosion dam, that reminds me—the road the forestry department put in runs up there."

"From below you can't see it, but when you get up higher you can. Looks like things are in bad shape."

"Let's go take a look. It's only a couple hundred yards off— really pretty close."

And so some of them had decided to go and they headed up the slope of Kazura Valley.

"In the mountains there's still a little water. The grass and trees smell different."

And then, just as someone had said, when they got onto the narrow forestry road the vegetation grew thicker and was covered with dew that moistened their bodies, and all around there was actually the fragrance of a summer morning in the mountains.

Someone mentioned in a pained voice, "I wish this dew would turn to rain."

Walking along between the trees, pushing their way through a thicket of ferns and then going up a rocky slope, they could see the valley below them.

"Look—the sacred tree, it's dying."

For a while no one had spoken.

Even now Ohina could not forget what she'd seen that time. Actually, she had known already that the great *katsura*, the Japanese Judas tree, had died. It would have been better if everyone had noticed it then. Afterwards, little by little, unfortunate events started occurring. Or rather, perhaps everyone had already been dimly aware of it.

"It doesn't look good," was what they had muttered at the time.

With no water in the valley, the dried moss clung fast to the stones around the rocky river bed. It had seemed that if the moss could just get a little water it would turn green and swell up before their eyes. The men went down, cutting back the bamboo bushes as they went. They could be seen poking up among the rocks along the riverbed. Those at the top looked down intently. After a while one of the men waved his hand, signaling that there was no water. Everyone stared at each other.

At the time people entered the mountain to develop it, Kazura Valley had been a sacred water source. The valley had also been a place where wild *wasabi* horseradish grew, and in the gathering season the local people would take only the leaves and stems, breaking them off with their hands and taking great care to leave the roots unharmed. Had the watershed gone dry?

"Kazura Valley's dying," someone had said.

The morning mountain breeze rustled as they crossed the valley which no longer carried the sound of water. They listened for a while to the sound of the breeze. The dew from the leaves lightly moistened the necks and cheeks of many.

"If only it would rain," one had said.

"If the rains would fall the valley would return to its old self."

As they spoke, they looked up at the sky and then gazed over the valley.

"If it would rain the water would come back."

The feeling for the rain ceremony grew more intense. Still craning their necks, they had returned to the road.

Kazura Valley was above the place where the Amazoko Dam was later built. Ohina went there only rarely. The *katsura* tree that had been spoken of as the tree of the gods had withered away so much that it had become scarcely recognizable. Just the stump and roots barely remained. The valley never revived, and only the older people knew that *wasabi* had once grown there.

In climbing they had spoken of their resolve not to go back down until they got it to rain, but when they discovered more water coming out from the river source than they had expected they felt their energy revive.

"All right then, let's pour out some of the water we brought. Sayuri, would you start, please?"

The bamboo water containers were handed to Sayuri. The people of Amazoko believed that the god of the waterfall who lived in the headwaters was coming. Sayuri leaned toward the source with an opened fresh bamboo container.

The men had hung a curtain about a thicket of shrubs and the women helped Sayuri change her clothes. Ohina assisted in wiping her body and dressing her in simple white wear. Standing on the mats that had been spread out they tied Sayuri's obi. Her waist was still slender. They wound it about her twice and as they pulled it tight from behind Sayuri bent backwards slightly, staggered, and turned her head to signal it was too tight. The silk fabric was neither stiff nor pliant but pleasant to touch. It brought back thoughts of Sayuri's mother who had worn it around her waist when she was carrying the baby in her womb. What kind of woman had she been? She had brought a child into the world and then died beneath the cherry tree.

"Sayuri, you're going to put yourself into the dance completely, for the sake of both of your mothers."

As she said this Ohina had stroked Sayuri's back. Then she sang a sacred song to help her dancing. This had also been the fervent request of Oai-sama. Ohina had often seen Sayuri's dancing, but this time her dance had the quality of a butterfly as it begins to spread its wings in the shadow of a tree, making the air about it soften and breathe with life. Ohina thought such dancing could not be surpassed. When Sayuri looked up to the sky and started to ring the little bell it felt as if the exquisite sound emerged from the whole of creation, whirling about and pressing close. Those who watched were completely caught up in it. They had the feeling of a cool freshness rising up and passing along. Some, without knowing why, looked up to the sky with tears in their eyes, feeling they could barely hold their bodies still.

On the top of the mountain at the height of summer, every time Sayuri turned softly in her white gown with the material of her obi hanging below slightly, the obi caught the colors of the sun and reflected them on the people. Her expression took on a serene look, as if she had become spirit. Ohina imagined that Oai-sama must be fasting and praying and looking up at the mountain.

It had probably been about three o'clock. The second invocation of prayers finished without any signs. And then, when the third reading came to an end and everyone's exhausted eyes had grown dizzy, up in the sky around the summer sun that shone on the mountains, a black cloud appeared. Sayuri's appearance became that of a Miko shrine maiden and she almost collapsed. The women rushed to her, gave her some water to drink and wiped the sweat from her mouth and neck. Lightning flashed all around and suddenly it grew dark.

The people on the mountain gathered around Sayuri and she began the dance. It felt as if Ohina's singing voice had become one with the spirits of all of them and circled about amidst the mountain peaks.

In the midst of the downpour they helped her change her clothing so they could go back down the mountain. They remembered how, all around the exhausted Sayuri, there were lovely little pink *nadeshiko* flowers standing in the pelting rain. Her soaking wet obi had been hard to untie, but with several people working on it, finally it was undone.

Last night when they were washing the body it had brought back so clearly the scene from that former time. Sayuri had moved her body so flexibly in the rain. But now, after being submerged in the water and becoming a corpse, although her body had been nicely shaped for a woman of around forty, she'd become all puffed up, expressionless, and pitiful looking.

The year she summoned the rains, the harvest was so meager that they just barely survived, but in the following year the rice plants were completely covered with flowers. Sayuri could sometimes be seen along the edges of the rice fields bending over to pick ears of rice and decorate her hair, moving with a smile. Although she didn't work in the fields, there was no doubt about the significance of what she had accomplished by performing the ceremony on the mountaintop.

Nor was it just the rice that had flourished. The plums and apricots and wild peaches were uncommonly laden with fruit, as if draped in chains, such that it astonished everyone. As if to make up for the previous year, not only the plums and apricots, but the camellias as well had stretched themselves to their limits in bearing fruit and flowers. It was often said that this was thanks to Sayuri, and the people had taken a new faith in her as a Miko shrine maiden.

Ohina raised her head and looked ahead at the coffin. The trees in the grove surrounding the cremation place quavered and the clouds moved about mysteriously.

"Don't you think we should get going? It looks like we're in for some rain."

With one hand raised, Kappei, the bearded one, called out in a hearty voice and directed the procession. The hems of the women's kimonos fluttered about and it looked like it was going to pour.

Omomo mused, "It seems Sayuri was a spirit of the waters . . . Yes, a spirit of the waters."

Sayuri's mother had come from the Mimigawa River area and given birth to her beneath the weeping cherry tree. Oai-sama, who'd taken her in, had been the guardian spirit of the waterways. Perhaps it was just as Omomo had said.

Kappei came by and fixed his eye on Oshizu.

"Say there Oshizu, how about if I carry you on my back?"

"What's this nonsense? You think I'm so old I need you to carry me? Have you forgotten I used to change your diapers until you were five or six?"

"Nah, I just meant I wanted to do a little something for you."

He glanced at Masahiko amiably. Dressed in the formal *hakama* and a summer robe, Kappei was drenched in sweat and he wiped himself with a towel.

"Oh, so here he is, our young gentleman from the old Silk Estate."

Kappei was apparently in fine spirits. From the side, Oshizu called out, "Well, I wouldn't mind getting a ride on the back of the young gentleman from the old Silk Estate."

All around, people broke out into laughter.

"You've got me there Oshizu. I see you still have your fancy for younger men."

"Well, I'm still eighteen at heart."

Chuckling to themselves, the women hurried along the path through the fields, covering their heads with one sleeve of their kimonos and glancing up at the sky.

"It's starting to rain. Let's hurry. Masahiko, won't you take Oshizu's hand and help her?"

The procession hurried along. Someone called out,

"This would make Sayuri happy. Let it rain. Let it snow. Let the waters fall!"

As it grew darker, the green of the fields deepened, as if they were illuminated by lamplight. Masahiko felt that the single file of the procession was somehow wrapped in a kind of pure light.

Just as the group gathered under the eaves of the crematory, a clap of thunder sounded and the rain began to pour. Normally, just the family of the departed would have remained, but as Sayuri didn't even have any distant family members and as the rain didn't let up, the whole group stayed until the burning was finished.

And so in that place, amidst what seemed as if it might have been just loose talk and jesting, Masahiko was inducted into the Amazoko Citizens' Council. The one who brought up the subject was the same bearded man, Kappei Yamashina. Having been told only the night before he'd been named a founding member—amidst all the revelries going on at the time of the wake—Masahiko thought it might have happened just as a sort of joke.

Oshizu asked in a droll voice feigning ignorance, "Say there Kappei, tell us, what are you going to do at those citizens' committee meetings of yours?"

"What are we going to do? Well that's what we're going to decide now."

"Come on, don't tell us you haven't even decided anything yet."

"Well, actually there's one thing I *have* decided."

"Kappei, it sounds like you've been bragging too much and trying to build up your stock again."

Kappei looked a bit annoyed. The elders took pleasure in listening to what was going on and observed the proceedings as they relaxed and occupied themselves smoking their pipes.

"Actually, what I'm thinking of is rebuilding Moonshadow Bridge."

Suddenly the elders' hands, which had been busily engaged in refilling the pipes, came to a stop.

"Moonshadow Bridge? But that's . . . it's at the bottom of the dam."

"Well, for now it's at the bottom, but . . ."

"You're not planning on rebuilding it at the bottom of the lake are you?"

"Well, we used to talk about rebuilding it, way back when."

Oshizu looked toward the group, her face expressing the thought—there he goes, carrying on with his crazy talk again.

"But that was years ago—before the dam was built."

"Right, that was before the dam."

"It was back when you were still just a little kid."

Kappei looked down with a sheepish grin, as if he'd just been told something incredibly pleasing.

Masahiko had never seen a man with such a charming smile.

"Yeah, I sure was a wild monkey of a kid."

3

MOONSHADOW
BRIDGE

With his thick eyebrows bobbing up and down, Kappei had taken on the look of a somewhat absent-minded bear. Then suddenly he stopped this motion, leaving his eyebrows set in a straight line. He blinked hard and opened his mouth, leaving it gaping wide open. Everyone wondered if he was about to cry.

For a while no words came from his mouth. Sayuri had been Kappei's savior, his Kannon-sama. It brought tears to the eyes of some of the women to see him look this way, trembling as if he were about to fall and his mouth just opening and closing. This was the same man who was known as "Porcupine," the one who since the previous day had carried the dead body and helped with the preparations for the wake and led the procession with such energy.

"I . . ." With a facial expression so crumpled that, strangely, it almost looked as if he were about to laugh, Kappei wiped his face with a hand towel.

"Yeah, I was a wild monkey—and I saw Moonshadow Bridge fall in."

Suddenly everyone remembered: that time in the Year of the Horse when the waters broke through. Kappei's father had gone to rescue an elementary school boy from the next village who had tried to cross the bridge. While Kappei's father was carrying the child back in his arms the bridge had collapsed and they both had been washed away. The fire brigade found his *happi* work coat some ten kilometers down the river where it had been caught in an eddy behind a boulder, but the two bodies were never found. At that time Chiyomatsu, who'd been working for the fire department, had been piling sand bags around the foot of the bridge. He looked up and saw that little monkey of a boy Kappei climbing a big nettle tree along the riverbank, swaying in the torrential rain. The boy had been looking down on the river and for some reason he was playing with something like a lasso.

"Who's that kid?"

Just as this voice called out, Kappei's father ran out to the middle of the bridge that was shaking with the waves of the river. Probably he hadn't noticed his own child on the top of the nettle tree.

He dashed out to save the boy from the neighboring town. The boy had been staggering along, his umbrella blown away. Just at the moment he grabbed the boy in his arms, that part of the bridge broke off, as if it had melted away. It all happened in the blink of an eye. People still speak of it as the flood of the Year of the Horse. Kappei could never forget that scene, even in his sleep. What in the world had possessed him to climb that tree that day, as if to catch a glimpse of his father? That old nettle tree had remained standing on the banks by Moonshadow Bridge until the dam flooded it. After that day of the muddy floodwaters, even though it had been severely scooped out around its roots, when the waters cleared the tree had thrived like a great water plant. The fine hairs of its swaying roots harbored fish, such as eels and catfish. A great round tree-shelter, year after year it added healthy new leaves.

After Kappei's father's funeral, the adults had asked him about it in low voices.

"What ever made you climb that tree at a time like that and coil that rope? You could've been washed away and drowned."

The boy had cast his eyes downward with a dejected expression and said nothing. He came to be thought of as a somewhat eccentric child. At the time of the flood his intention had been to try to catch a serow as it was crossing the river. From the stories about the countries of the world he'd been told by the medicine vendor who came once a year from Toyama, he'd heard that the antlers of a certain deer from the distant mountains of China were used to make a medicine. He'd been told that it was so expensive it would set your eyes on fire if you heard its price. There was no chance that ordinary folks could get it, even if they had a fatal illness.

"Well, it's something that royalty and aristocrats take. But folks like us—we might get to take a look at it, but it's not something we can ever have. At most we might get some bear stomach medicine."

He had also heard that cows sometimes got washed away in times of flood but that wild boars and deer were good at crossing rivers. His mother had often been laid up in bed because of the "road of blood," such that she was unable to get out and take part in public affairs.

Many times it had been Kappei's job to tell people, "I'm sorry, but my mother isn't feeling well now so she won't be able to attend tomorrow's meeting."

"Onami-san isn't feeling well. It must be the 'road of blood' again," was what the women would always say. For Kappei, it had been hard to bear this talk.

"That time I was trying to catch a serow to get its horns."

Only one time did he let out the reason he couldn't say anything when he was questioned about it by the adults. The time he fell from the dam construction site and Sayuri visited him and said a prayer for him all the men had thought there was little chance he'd survive. He was told that he'd been gored through his rear end by a steel rod and there was little hope he'd live. When they cut off the steel rod with a blowtorch he was still in convulsions and everyone said it looked like he was gone for sure.

Sayuri, along with Oai-sama, had come to see him and had brought some apricots. The fruit, flecked with dots of crimson, were more beautiful than any in pictures. It seemed their special tartness worked an effect on his body. Truly Sayuri was nothing less than a Kannon-sama.

Kappei had a wife and children, but any number of times he'd had to shake his head, trying to drive out the futile dream of how it might be to take care of Sayuri as an older wife—if, that was, he didn't already have a wife and children.

When he got better he went to them to express his thanks. When Oai-sama saw Kappei bowing his head and folding his hands she waved her hands saying, "I delivered you when you were born, so I have to see you through your whole life. It was just a little help. For you to recover from such a bad injury it must have been your dead father who helped you out the most. You'd better go pay a visit to his grave, don't you think?"

Being spoken to in this way, the words had just slipped from his mouth.

"That time when I climbed the tree—I was looking for a serow crossing the river . . . When Father was washed away I couldn't do anything to help."

Oai-sama, seemingly surprised, had said "Ah, that time," and gazed at Kappei's head for a while.

"A serow? Why was that?"

"For the horns. I wanted to use them as medicine for my mother."

"Ah—deer horns."

She heaved a big sigh and looked at Sayuri as if she were gazing into her own heart. Oai-sama had great affection for the two of them.

"I clearly remember the words I heard when you were born. Your father came running to meet me, carrying a bamboo dipper. When I asked him what he was doing with the dipper he answered with a concerned look, 'I have to get some hot water to fill the wash basin. The water hasn't boiled yet. Hurry—the baby's coming.' He grabbed my hand and pulled me along. Without even putting on my apron I ran to Moonshadow Bridge. You had a good head of black hair and a strong body."

As soon as Kappei heard the words "Moonshadow Bridge," the sight of his father being swept away returned and his eyes started to well up with tears. The village gong had been sounding and the mountains and the land were being shaken by the torrential rains. Adults were running about and screaming out loud. The fields and forests were hidden by a rain that looked like smoke. The village had taken on a completely different appearance from usual.

"Don't you go outside!" his father had yelled sternly as he pulled on his fire brigade coat and ran out of the house into the downpour. Kappei had followed after—making sure he stayed out of sight, hiding behind the pomegranate tree of the water god.

Around that time, Kappei had made a lasso and amused himself in the shed by playing imaginary games of catching boars and badgers. Often, families of boars and badgers would cross over Moonshadow Bridge. If a lone young boar came along it was easy to catch, but when the boars were out with their parents they charged along and it could be dangerous. If you caught a young badger and all went well you could bring it up with the dogs and cats. Probably Kappei's hunting instincts had already been shaped during his earlier days when he'd played Tarzan swinging across the ravines on the wild wisteria vines, but these instincts were really called into play that day when he saw his father go off. Certainly there had been a connection to the serow's horn. But what really spurred him on had been a vaguer instinct.

He had taken pride in being the best at tree climbing. The adults were working with all their might piling up sandbags. He too had wanted to do something to help out. Seeing the muddy waters swirling about, he had gone out full of youthful enthusiasm to Moonshadow Bridge to take a look. He brought along his rope. Would a serow come? There was one with horns he'd seen at sunset standing at the top of the cliff above Kazura Valley. The waves of the river were striking at the girders of the bridge.

In his dreams he sometimes saw the scene of his father going after the child from the next village, as if the picture were being replayed from a movie in slow motion. He had been caught up in the excitement of the moment. Stepping firmly on the branches of the nettle tree he had thought of being swept away in the raging current of muddy red water. He had also felt he might be hung upside down, suspended from a cord from the sky.

When the adults yelled at him so sternly and he turned briefly toward them he caught sight of his father running. And then, in an instant, the bridge had given way, carried away by the swirling red torrent. The rope had fallen from his hands.

Thoughts of the story of that time still tugged at his mind. It was hard for him to explain his feelings about running out after his father. Didn't it seem too unbelievable, even for a child, to say it was because he was hoping to catch a serow crossing the river in the midst of a flood? And even more so, to say he was trying to get the horns to make medicine? Wasn't it really because he'd been so caught up in wanting to be out among the adults and see what was happening with the flood?

The men of the fire brigade had gathered about the foot of the tree with angry looks. They motioned him to get down on their shoulders and five or six of them grabbed his legs. What had he really intended to do with the lasso that time? Had he really planned to try to catch a serow?

In times when it looked like there would be flooding, the normally outgoing man known as "Porcupine" would become silent. He would still go about his duties in checking on the water, but his face looked troubled. Often he would find *okera* bugs swimming about. Bending over to see, he'd place them in the palm of his hand and take a good look. In times of floods these insects would appear along the edges of the rice fields. Probably when the holes they lived in became flooded they would swim away to escape. As they swam they moved their heads about with such vigor. He thought of how he himself at that time had been like one of those insects.

At the time when the water was first let into the dam, these same *okera* bugs had been mixed in along with all the other insects of the mountains, covering the surface of the water. Along with the other villagers, he had often gone to stare in amazement at the town as it was submerged by the water. Oaisama and Sayuri had been among those who watched.

What had once been mountain forests, terraced gardens, and pathways along the hillside were gradually turned into the banks of a lake. Countless insects floated about on those banks. That day when Kappei bent over to look, he saw the tops of the trees in the bottom of the water. He saw the trees of Osubo-san's woods and the enormous Japanese bread tree as well as the fateful big nettle tree on the deep banks of the river. He imagined that his footprints still remained on that prominent tree. He had scooped up some *okera* bugs into his hand from the grasses by the river where they grew and showed them to Sayuri, who stood by his side.

The *okera* squirmed about for a while in the palm of Kappei's hand until, as if surprised, they moved their heads and tails about busily and dropped onto the grass with a thud. With the squirmy sensation lingering in his hand, Kappei had felt there was something loveable about those little insects. A smile flickered on Sayuri's face. He noticed her comparing him with the insects in his hand. Kappei had been touched by her gentleness.

Meetings had been held frequently about the matter of re-pairing the bridge. His mother Onami and his grandmother, who was still living at the time, took turns in attending the meetings. A system was set up whereby each household was to be assessed for its "fair share" of contribution.

"Since Kappei's still a child and his father's gone, couldn't we be exempt from the assessment?"

After the meetings, his mother and grandmother would al-ways sit by the fire, feeling lonely and hanging their heads. The villagers who came to the first O-bon ceremony after his father's death had talked of the subject.

"At least if it's a stone bridge it won't be washed away."

Since his father had lost his life in attempting to rescue someone his household was granted an exemption from the payments for the new bridge. The one who had proposed building a stone bridge was the elder Chiyomatsu. But in the end, as it turned out, the plan had never been realized.

The reasons given were: not enough stonemasons, and prob-ably not enough money. Escorting his mother, Kappei had been present at that meeting. The idea of a stone bridge had left a strong impression on him.

At the age of fifteen or sixteen he had gone to work in the mountains and he had been a laborer here and there and so he had begun to gain some experience out in the world. When he saw the magnificent stone double-arched bridge known as the "Spectacle Bridge" in the Mt. Aso highlands, it made a deep impression on him.

Why was it that listening to the fire that burned Sayuri's body had brought back to mind those childhood scenes?

It was not as if he'd been thinking constantly for all these years of Moonshadow Bridge and its connection to his father's death. And the Isara River and the big old nettle tree that lay submerged beneath the waters of the dam—along with the meeting that night and the horns of the serow—they were all phantom visions. He shook his head as if in disbelief.

He was recalling his childhood days. The faces of the old ones who had sometimes scolded him and sometimes given him affection—they all came back clearly. The smiling face of the toothless old man with the cane who climbed up to the fields to pick for them those bright red tomatoes that ripened in the scorching summer sun. The beads of sweat running down old Rokusuke who chased him with a pole when he'd climbed one of his pear trees to steal fruit. The young girls returning from the city, the beggars and the performers who came and went along Utazaka Hill. Lead on by some unknown prompting, Kappei talked on and on.

"I think we should rebuild Moonshadow Bridge."

Oshizu was quick to tease Kappei about this, and here and there a laugh broke out among the group, but soon afterwards they fell into silence. When the rain let up a bit, the sound of the burning body became particularly noticeable. Suddenly, cutting through this mood Ohina said,

"Last night I dreamed of a bridge."

Everyone knew that Ohina sometimes had dreams that told of some truth.

"It wasn't a dream of the bridge that washed away, it was a dream of that old rope suspension bridge that was Moonshadow Bridge way back when."

Kappei didn't know about the days of a hanging rope bridge. Chiyomatsu pursed his lips, drew a puff of smoke and laid his pipe on top of the table. Even in this age of cigarettes the old man would simply cut them up and transfer the tobacco to his little pipe to smoke.

Masahiko found it somehow touching to see how country folks treated tobacco. He had no idea how the people who'd been separated from Amazoko Village had lived most of their lives, but he could see that they still got together from time to time at funerals and exchanged news. He realized that he wasn't beyond being overpowered by a person like Oshizu, but he also wondered if he wasn't being drawn in and charmed by all of them. With this thought in mind he cracked a wry smile.

The world was more profound than what he'd read about in the books he had on his desk. Somehow it seemed that just seeing Kappei's grin was enough to soften his heart. A while back Omomo had whispered to her mother, "Sayuri was a spirit of the water." But, he wondered, what is *my* spirit? Among these people it seems death is not the cessation of everything.

They say our generation is one of deprivation and loss, and that we take nihilism as a fashion. But it seems these people of Amazoko, who've lost their village, have resurrected the real meaning of existence.

The windblown rain didn't let up. The spray striking against the eaves created a fog that crept inside the room through the cracks in the entryway.

Everyone drew their chairs together and huddled around the furnace in the crematory. In front of it was a large concrete stand on which Sayuri's coffin had been placed. A brief sutra was read and the final words of parting were said. After the cremation was finished the remains would be placed on the stand again and the bones would be removed with tongs.

"Looks like we're in for it now. That rain's really pouring down out there."

Several people hung around the window and peered outside. The crematory was set back in the woods on a gentle slope that opened out onto the plain of fields through which the funeral procession had passed. The rice plants, just ripening and turning color, were bent and shaken by the winds that blasted down from the hilltops. In front of the crematory the winds whipped against the roots of the trees, forming sudden updrafts that blew the rain back upwards again.

"We can't go back in weather like this."

"Well, it should stop in a while."

As the sounds of the rainstorm periodically swelled and then diminished, the talk among the group lulled and then resumed along with it. The flames charged the air with sounds. Trying to remove the encrusted dregs from his pipe, Chiyomatsu knocked its bowl against the swollen joint of his middle finger. His movement seemed strange to Masahiko. After striking the pipe several times there was still some fire left in the ashes he had removed. Unperturbed, the old man calmly held the live coals in his hand and then after a while rolled them into a lump and dropped it by his foot, where he finally stamped it out with his sandal. His *hakama* was open, showing his feet, which in their white *tabi* socks looked like those of a classic *joruri* doll.

Glancing down on the spent ashes the old man bit into his pipe, making sucking noises in the bowl. Taking it from his mouth and blinking rapidly he called out.

"Ohina-san."

Ohina, who had been absorbed in listening to the sounds of the burner, raised her head and spoke. "A long time ago, Moon-shadow Bridge, it was a rope suspension bridge."

Several people nodded their heads.

"Well, last night in my dream I saw that suspension bridge."

With the driving rain pelting down still harder people were worrying about getting back. Masahiko noticed expressions of relief settle over their faces as they listened to Ohina talk.

"Back in the days of the old suspension bridge there was Oak Mountain on the far side."

Chairs squeaked as the group drew closer and people murmured in agreement that there had been an Oak Mountain over there.

"There aren't many of us left now who can remember that suspension bridge."

Hearing this, Chiyomatsu urged Ohina to continue.

"What sort of dream was it?"

"What sort? Just a dream."

"Your dreams often turn out true."

"Not really. Most of them don't mean much at all. In my dream I couldn't get across the bridge."

"Well, in the end that bridge broke and fell in. That's how it ended up."

"Right, it collapsed finally, and with those people on it."

"Those people?"

"Yes, those people. In my dream."

"There was a pilgrim with a child, wasn't there?"

"Yes—my dream was about what happened after that."

To the listeners it felt as if their eyes were being turned inward to search for something. Then Oshizu broke in.

"That time when the suspension bridge broke I went to take a look too. I was still young and it was in the fall. Part of the bridge had given way and was hanging down. And then for some reason, on the far bank a group of monkeys was playing about at the entrance to the bridge; taking turns entering it, climbing up and down the severed part and looking around. It was something no humans could have done.

"They romped about on the dangling section, playing with it like a toy, as if it were laden with grapes.

"The monkeys were on the far bank and the people were on the near side and they were both watching each other.

"For the monkeys, even if the bridge fell in it was no problem. They could go back and forth across the valley without any trouble at all.

"For the humans to cross, they'd have to take off their clothing. In summer you could do it, but . . ." Apparently sensing the need to work the conversation back to the main topic, Oshizu stopped herself and turned to ask Ohina in a formal tone of voice, "And then what happened in your dream?"

"Well, I was on the near side of the bridge and I started singing that song.

> The going is all right
> But we know not the return
> In the middle of the bridge
> Don't look back
> Throw in a rice cake
> If you haven't got a rice cake
> Throw in a hairpin
> If you haven't got that either
> Throw in a baby
> If you haven't got a baby
> Then throw yourself in

"In the old days we used to sing that song when we were rocking infants and playing with them. Crossing over a rope suspension bridge probably wasn't the best time for singing a song like that, but in my dream that's what came out. I sang it with all my heart. And as I sang, the leaves in the valley turned to the red colors of fall. It was so beautiful. It was a brocade pattern, different from any foliage I'd ever seen before. And then—the fallen suspension bridge slowly came back to life, rising up and extending itself back across to the near side. I wondered what on earth could be going on. That suspension bridge was the guardian spirit of Amazoko. It was the guardian of that flooded stalactite cavern.

"That suspension bridge was made of vines cut from the violet wisteria that hung from the big oak trees and of the white wisteria that hung from the cassia trees by the prayer rock on Mt. Ontake. I immediately started singing a soothing song. The landscape was so incredibly beautiful. The area about my feet turned completely black. I felt as if I were about to be sucked away into it, so I sang out. A blaze of color flashed from the ripened persimmon tree on Utazaka Hill and I thought to myself—that must be someone's life passing on.

In the evening
When the wind fills the valley
I miss someone
In the mist
A single ripe persimmon
A single remaining life

"Suddenly, the bridge of wisteria vines extended itself to the near side. The fog thickened and thinned, again and again. And while this was happening the ripened persimmon tree I'd just seen disappeared—even though just a moment ago it had been a brilliant vermilion red. It was gone. Whose life could it have been that went out, I wondered. Suddenly it had vanished.

"It seemed that someone from another place had come to Amazoko. Perhaps it might have been a wandering *yamabushi* mountain priest. Or it might have been an itinerant blind woman musician. Hadn't there been any sound? If it had been an experienced blind musician, before crossing the bridge she'd have played a piece on the *biwa* and sung a song to let people know she wasn't someone suspicious. Or if it had been a *yamabushi* mountain priest, he'd have given a blast on his conch shell to announce his passing through. I tried to listen for a sound. It seemed it must have been a traveler who'd met misfortune along the way. When the light of the persimmon tree went out amidst the fog I imagined it must have been for someone who'd become an offering. And so this happened because I sang that song.

"Right in front of my eyes I saw proof that the severed bridge had come back to life. There really was such a being, the Lord Guardian of the stalactite cavern. In the past, it had lived in the belly of the mountains. Sometimes it came and went about, and it might get hungry. In the daytime it let the monkeys play about and it let the people pass through. And in the middle of the night it let the creatures of the dark pass by too. But in the evenings, the fog rolled in, and at those times it couldn't be helped if on occasion someone who passed by along with the crabs might become an offering to the guardian spirit of the bridge.

"On foggy nights when it had the chance, the Guardian would cross over the suspension bridge, slip into the village, and look down from the top of Utazaka Hill. And the people who looked at Moonshadow Bridge were branded with the mark of plum petals. The guardian of the rope bridge would leave a mark that showed they belonged to Amazoko Village. I've seen the marks myself.

"And when Masahito-sama left the village, I went to see him off. I watched him turn back to look from the other side of

Moonshadow Bridge. In my dream it was a moonlit night and the fog had rolled in. Masahiko-san, I went to see your grandfather off. There *was* a mark of plum petals on his neck—wasn't there?"

Masahiko was confused. Suddenly he recalled images of his grandfather's figure from behind—watering the trees in the garden, or when he was being taken to the mental hospital, or sitting beneath the ginkgo tree, or doing other such things—but he never had a chance to notice whether or not he had such a mark. It didn't seem that Ohina was expecting an answer from him.

"Moonshadow Bridge was the guardian of the stalactite cavern of the drowned village of Amazoko. That was the guardian spirit of Amazoko."

Excited expressions lit up people's faces and hushed voices rose up here and there.

"I too cross that bridge in my dreams."

"I forget it in the daytime, but when I sleep I return in my dreams."

"Me too. When I dream it's always about Amazoko."

The voices were soft but clear. Their sounds were lovely. Masahiko thought; this is the first time I've ever heard such voices.

The man tending the furnace opened the door of the crematory room, wiped away his sweat and took a look at what was going on in the waiting room. He nodded his head as if indicating that he well understood what was happening. Then he walked over to the window to look out at the rain.

Her eyes still fixed on this man, Oshizu appeared to be sunk deeply in thought as she spoke.

"Everyone's talking of how they forget the sunken village during the daytime, but when they sleep at night they remember it. Now, because of Ohina's dream, it's coming back to me. The women stop by my place and they've told the story.

"A long time ago, on a rainy, windy day there was a pilgrim carrying a baby on her back who'd come to cross the suspension bridge. In crossing, she slipped and fell in. According to another person who happened to arrive there about the same time, the bridge was swaying about on that day. After considering whether or not he should try to cross he decided it was no day to take chances. Just as he was turning back, he saw the pilgrim starting to cross from the opposite side. Thinking it was too dangerous to try to cross with a baby, he looked on nervously. And then, just as he'd feared, he saw her foot slip. She flailed about for a moment as if she were swimming. He called out, but in an instant she fell. He ran to the town to tell the people and everyone rushed to the riverbank and looked but they couldn't find the mother or child. Before long, however, they located the body of the mother. But there was no baby. The person who told them about it said it was definitely a young woman on a pilgrimage and that she'd been carrying a baby on her back, and so they searched for a baby. But had she really been carrying a baby? Or had it been a trick of the eyes? And it seemed that in the time it would take to search, the baby would probably already be carried out to Oki no Miya. While they were talking of abandoning the search, the storm let up a bit and they turned back, saying it's about time to build a new bridge.

"An energetic fellow took the lead and the others followed along behind. Then he came back, shifting about awkwardly, so everyone assumed the rope bridge had fallen, as they'd feared. Then the man spoke out, gesturing with his hands and feet.

"'There's a baby—I saw it! Over there!'

"'A baby? Are you sure? Where was it?'

"Everyone said how wonderful it was that he'd found the baby. The man sank to the ground, sat and pointed toward the bridge.

"'At the entrance to the bridge—the guardian spirit, he made a basket cradle and he was looking after the baby.'

"'A basket? How could a basket have gotten there?'"

As the questioning continued they began to understand. What the man was saying was that, amidst the wind and rain, the guardian of the stalactite cave—who sometimes took on the form of a wisteria vine bridge—had appeared. There he'd shown his true nature by coiling himself around the entrance to the bridge, and in that coil he'd carefully placed the baby and was rocking it. So according to his story, it seemed that the baby had been put in a cradle and was being taken care of.

"'The baby looked like it was in good sprits. It was clapping its hands and sucking its fingers. Really, it's true. You have to go and see. And there was also a strange grating sound. The guardian god's scales were opening and closing as it chased away flies. Its scales were making a grating, rubbing sound.'

"As he went on like this the people were greatly surprised and they all went to look. By the roots of a big cedar tree at the entrance to the bridge, a lovely baby was sleeping. They couldn't see any guardian spirit. All that was there was a nice cradle made of *susuki* reeds and dwarf bamboo leaves. But when they looked over on the other side, the rope coils of the bridge appeared to be flapping about, like a skin being cast off by a giant serpent or dragon."

One person who had been listening closely to Oshizu's story spoke out in a reserved voice.

"Well, in recent years it's mostly stayed back inside the stalactite cavern and hardly comes out. But sometimes people coming and going along Utazaka catch a glimpse of it. A few have even seen its tail."

"And by any chance, was that baby Oai-sama?"

The atmosphere grew more intimate. Everyone could recall that story. Ohina turned her head slowly and looked at Masahiko.

"Your grandfather Masahito's grandmother lived to be over a hundred years old, and in her old age she took in that baby and raised it. She named her Ai, so she came to be called Oai-sama. She said it was a child who had been entrusted to her by the Lord of Amazoko. She gave it her best care in bringing it up."

Masahiko had thought this was just going to be the telling of Ohina's dream of the night before, but the story became so interwoven with the stories of Chiyomatsu and Oshizu that he had no idea where the dream had merged with the others' stories.

It was said that the stalactite cave now lay at the bottom of the dammed-up lake. Judging from photographs, it seemed the stalactite cave wasn't a very comforting place. The cavern twisted its way along, issuing from deep within the belly of the mountain. From its roof hung countless limestone stalactites, in the shapes of icicles and breasts. From them, drops of underground water slowly dripped down. Flowing through the cave was a river that made a faint sound. Could there have been any fish in it? It is thought that even today, deep down in the earth some of the original forms of life are still alive. But for Masahiko, born and raised in the city, this thought gave him an uneasy feeling.

How did the first humans who entered that cavern feel—going in there alone, without even having lights? It was not hard to imagine how people could have thought that in such a cave there must be a guardian spirit who inhabited it and governed the mountains and water. It seemed the old people who gathered for Sayuri's funeral procession still believed in the protective god of Amazoko Village, even if they didn't actually see its form. They spoke of how, from time to time, it would emerge from its dwelling place, change its body into the shape of a wisteria vine bridge and come down into the village and place the mark of plum blossom petals on the backs of the villagers' necks as a birthmark. Masahiko could hardly believe it, but he found himself wanting to touch the back of his own neck with his hand.

Piecing together the threads of the stories so far, it seemed that both Sayuri and Oai, who had brought her up, had come from other villages. According to the stories he'd heard over the past few days from Ohina and the other villagers, this woman Oai, who had been a midwife, was also thought of as a person who had assumed a sort of divine nature. She had come into the village as a baby, entrusted to it by the patron spirit of Amazoko. Masahito's grandmother—in other words Masahiko's great-great-grandmother—had taken her in. Thus her role in looking after babies had come to her from birth, leading to her becoming a midwife; the work she'd carried out faithfully throughout her long life. As for her relationship to Sayuri, the newborn baby of a wayfarer who died as she was passing through the village, everyone imagined that Oai-sama regarded her as her own child. And now Sayuri, who had taken over Oai-sama's duties, was dead.

"The bones haven't cooled completely yet, but with weather like this . . ."

The attendant opened the partition door and removed Sayuri's still-warm bones from the hearth. Everyone got up together. No one spoke as a wave of heat spread out around the platform.

"Here are the tongs. Would the closest family member remove the bones please?" The attendant spoke in a low voice, probably trying to avoid sounding too business-like.

Everyone glanced at each other uneasily and no one came forward to pick up the large chop stick-like implements. Not only was there no closest relative, there wasn't even a single blood relative among them. The voices of Chiyomatsu and Ohina could be heard, expressing hesitation. Then there was a request for the woman from the temple. Being called upon as the woman of the temple, the young woman waved her hand in refusal.

"Oh I really couldn't. I have almost no relationship with the deceased. The funeral was another matter, but this, I . . ."

With a chuckle, Oshizu remarked, "Funerals are business matters too, you know," and then for moment there was silence.

"Well in that case . . ."

Chiyomatsu picked up the implements and continued, "I'm not a relative, but seeing as I'm the oldest here, I suppose . . ."

The worker continued, "Would you start with the leg bones please, and place them in the urn in a sitting position. The two legs first, and then the shins, the kneecaps, and the thighbones. They've burned very cleanly, I see. She was still young. For forty-two or so, these bones are quite beautiful. Here are the hipbones. They're a bit heavy, so would someone with strong hands pick them up please? Isn't there anyone who will lend a hand . . ? Well then, it looks like I'll have to do it myself. There's a knack to it."

The attendant seemed particularly concerned that the just-cremated bones be placed into the urn in precisely the correct fashion. Following his instructions, silently, they carefully picked up the bones and placed them into the urn.

"Hmm, now where's the Adam's apple?"

He raked through the bones, among the ashes, with the tongs.

"Do women have Adam's apples too?" someone asked.

"Well, they're not so noticeable, but they have them. But I can't seem to find it here. Seems it's missing. The body burned well. These bones are very cleanly done. Sometimes the bones get all blackened."

Oshizu looked at Kappei across from her, trying to avoid touching the tools. His expression seemed different from before. His big eyes were blinking and it seemed as if his body had shrunk, as if he'd bottled himself up in a transparent jar.

It seemed to Oshizu that her dream of the night before had proven true. Last night Kappei had appeared in the moonlit valley, transformed into a crab. He'd been naked, like a crab that's just shed its shell. Did that show the form that he was born into, or did it point to the form he would take in the world to come? In any case, seeing Kappei, who was normally so manly, in the moonlight on the banks of the Isara River looking thin from having shed his shell—that had been quite a surprise. Whatever wish could this shedding of the shell have been expressing? In the midst of her dream Oshizu had thought for a while and then spoken.

"It can't be helped. Since you've shed your whole shell, right down to the tips of your claws and eyeballs, you'll have to go on with that soft body and crawl your way through the valley below Moonshadow Bridge and make it to the village of Amazoko."

"Is that Oshizu's voice?" Kappei the crab asked, his voice shuddering.

"Look, I've just shed the covering over my eyes and so my eyes are still watery. Even if you tell me to go to Amazoko, my eyes haven't formed properly yet."

"Is that so? Your eyes are still watery and unformed? Well, there are times it's better to have no eyes at all. It can help get you along in the world by not seeing things that are better not seen."

Telling him to come a bit closer, Oshizu reached out and placed her palm on Kappei the crab. Then with her fingertips she stroked the horns on the right and left sides, where his eyes stuck out.

"Look here! They've melted away on both the right and the left. You don't need eyes any more!"

She spoke with a gentle voice and released the crab into the water. Kappei the crab skittered upstream along the Isara River at the bottom of the lake. It appeared to require quite an effort to go upstream since the force of the river was powerful.

"I'm counting on you—with your water-eyes. Look, behind you everyone's following. Go back to the sunken village. If you were still in human form you wouldn't be able to get there. But as a crab, now you can go."

Oshizu had leaned over, calling out as she watched. The crab Kappei, with all the others following along after him, had pushed on forward, flopping along and thrashing through the water plants that stuck to them, time after time, making their way upward along the water pathways of Amazoko.

Oshizu had begun relating the tale of last night's dream to the silent crowd when all the bones had been taken out. A while back everyone had spoken of how they seemed to forget about dreams during the daytime, but when they slipped into bed they could return to Amazoko in their dreams and meet with the people of long ago once again.

"At the bottom of the river there were water plants. In their midst was a beautiful white plum tree, still in blossom, swaying gently in the water. You can't get to the bottom of the lake in human form. Thanks to Kappei's changing into a crab he was able to go there. That's the way I get back to Amazoko too."

For a while everyone's talk was about the dream.

"Your grandmother, has she been showing up in your dreams these days?"

"Well, not in mine, but she's been in yours, hasn't she? And she didn't have any bad things to say, did she?"

"Yes, it was a good dream all right. Over by Koushin's place I was carrying the washing and your grandmother brought some pomegranates. She took them out of her bag and they had a nice color. She gave me some and told me, 'These fruits will give you a long life. Take some to your mother.'"

"Oh, they were from that pomegranate tree, were they? That old tree by the washing place was a real old one. It had such beautiful fruit. It was grandmother's joy to take them to people who weren't feeling well. So she went to see you, did she?"

"The pomegranate tree and the washing place are both at the bottom of the lake now."

"But it's good you had that sort of dream. My grandmother used to shout at folks, and even in dreams I imagine her voice gets pretty loud. But if you had that kind of dream, she must be all right. It's good to hear."

"It certainly was a nice dream. Her voice was just the same as when she was alive. It was good to see her in such spirits."

"It sure brings back old times. Now it's only in dreams that we can see those people."

In their dreams they saw visions of people digging clams, and building the stone walls about Amemiya Shrine, and passing through the valley of vines carrying firewood on their backs, and gathering mushrooms. And the women were filling bags with the fruit of the silvervine that covered the valley.

"And between my dreams too they're working. And there's no pain and they're happy. And when I wake up I'm not sad. It's strange; even though I can't really go back to Amazoko I go there in dreams. I want to go back again."

"There's a song from way back called "the path of dreams.""

It was Chiyomatsu who brought the conversation to a conclusion. Oshizu nodded; it was owing to Chiyomatsu's advanced years that he had such composure. There could be no doubt that Kappei's appearing in the dream in the form of a crab and shedding his shell had signified that he had some role to carry out. And that crab—there in the valley of Moonshadow Bridge, back in the old days when it had been a hanging bridge of vines—its trembling must have been on account of Kappei's carrying the souls of all those who wanted to return to Amazoko. And if one were to follow the course of the river along the valley that passed beneath the bridge of hanging vines, wouldn't it be possible to walk on the pathway into the village that had been closed off by the dam?

Kappei, who had returned to life after falling from the dam construction site, possessed the power to carry people's souls. Hadn't he also been serving as the guardian spirit of both Oai and Sayuri? Oshizu believed it was her praying from the bottom of her heart that had caused him to appear as a crab. And if Kappei took on the form of a crab, she believed he could travel to where the guardian of the cave lived. Everyone, she thought, has been asking how to get back to the village at the bottom of the lake—but haven't Kappei and Ohina and I found pathways already?

Oshizu's eyes met those of Ohina, seated beside Kappei. Ohina nodded. A woman like her understood such things. It was Ohina who had first made a point of bringing up the talk of the dreams at this place. She glanced up at Kappei once again. Water appeared to be flowing in the midst of his eyes. "It's because I stroked him with my finger in my dream that this big man's eyes have now become like the eyes of a trembling crab. Go on, go on, with those eyes." Urging him on, she gazed at the storm outside.

When Ohina began telling the stories of her dreams, Masahito also started to feel that he was in a place where people returned in dreams. It wasn't only these two old women and Chiyomatsu—it seemed that the others too returned to the village at the bottom of the lake and met with all the people there. It seemed there was no border between their times of waking and those of dreaming. They could travel freely between both.

That's right, he thought; when grandfather was spending his time around the ginkgo at Nakano Station he must have been looking for a passageway back to this kind of world. Even right by that station where the trains and people passed by ceaselessly there was an entrance to the village beneath the lake.

"What about these bones?" Chiyomatsu asked. He looked around, holding the container he'd been handed by the attendant. Omomo turned around with a surprised expression. The look in her eyes, peering into the urn of ashes, seemed to Masahiko so very gentle. To old Chiyomatsu, likely it held a deeper meaning. He looked at Omomo and asked,

"Will you carry them?"

"If you think it's all right."

"Yes, you're the best one to do it."

The ones who had handled the tongs looked on in silence at the faces of Omomo and the woman from the temple.

"We'll leave them at the temple for a time. Omomo will carry them and I'll go with her."

The squeaking door blew open with a strong gust of wind and then quickly slammed shut again with a bang.

The gust that had blown into the room brushed about the floor. As it passed over the stand it blew up a dark, smoke-like puff of the remaining ashes of Sayuri. All together, everyone gasped.

"It looks like this isn't going to let up. It'll be getting dark. Are we going to go out and get soaked?"

"Even if we get wet, let's go. It can't be helped."

"What about our mourning wear?" one of the women asked.

"That's right, our mourning clothes. We have another funeral coming soon."

"I wonder if they'll dry out by then."

And at that they all remembered that there was one more person who had died. The funeral of Jimpei, the village assembly member who had died in the horse stable fire, had been delayed on account of the autopsy performed on his body. Suddenly an agitated, uneasy feeling came over them.

"We'll be busy, so let's get back soon."

"Right. We can't just wait around here until morning for the storm to pass."

When the urn was handed to Omomo everyone stood up together.

"Well let's get moving, even if we're going to get drenched."

And so, talking as they went, they set out into the midst of the wind and rain. Women and men alike hiked up the hems of their robes, tying them with towels and cloths. Several in front got caught by the wind as they set out along the path through the rice fields. Those same rice plants that had looked so lush when the group passed through earlier in the day were now being tossed and flailed about by the wind. Kappei and Masahiko held back the door, which looked as if it were about to be blown away. The women made their way out. Last among them was Oshizu. Before going out she looked up at Kappei and whispered, "It's thanks to you that we know the way to Amazoko."

Kappei smiled back at her. When she left, Oshizu tied up the black train of her kimono. Showing beneath her white undergarments, surprisingly, was the sight of a bright red sash. As she walked briskly behind the others, her thin old legs kicked up the red cloth. Omomo, holding the urn of ashes in her arms, turned about, faced the rear and took a step back. Her hair blew up and played about her face. Then she turned again and headed off once more. For some reason, Masahiko was startled by the sight of her.

All about the rice fields, scarecrows made of the feathers of dead crows were being tossed about by the wind as if they were dancing. Seeing the people in their drenched black kimonos walking amidst the feathers of the dead crows flailing all about, Masahiko had the feeling of being caught up in a medieval world of sorcerers and magic.

An opening appeared in the rain clouds. For a brief moment the sun broke through and lit up the rice fields in bright green. And then in an instant it grew dark again. Kappei muttered, "Looks like the rice is going to be spoiled again this year. And it had been ripening so nicely."

Masahiko was at a loss as to how to reply to such talk.

"Do you grow rice?"

"Well, I don't have any fields myself but when we get these storms I worry about how the rice is doing."

Another gust of wind, one that seemed it might blow the door down, blasted away. As the two of them held back the door, Masahiko remembered something. Back when they had come through the fields, Ohina had remarked as she looked at the rice, "If Sayuri were still alive she'd have been so happy to see the colors of this rice."

It seemed that Kappei too must have been thinking of Sayuri in this way.

"Masahiko, this isn't just any old wind, you know."

As the two of them held the door shut they realized that the attendant was there on the inside, waiting.

"This one looks different from the usual storms. I think you'd better take care in getting home," said the voice from within.

Kappei called out in a big voice, "You okay in there?" and knocked on the door in a solicitous manner.

"If this place is damaged, everything will come to an end."

"All right then, but Chikazawa-san, Chikazawa-san."

With something apparently on his mind, Kappei knocked harder on the door this time and called to the attendant.

"Sorry, but I forgot something. There's something important I forgot. Could you let me in for just a minute?"

He turned and looked at Masahiko.

"Could you wait just a moment? Just hold the door so it doesn't blow off. I'll be back soon."

Apologizing again, he entered with a hushed silence and placed his hands carefully on a small box covered with a white handkerchief.

"These last ashes of Sayuri . . . It's just too much."

His lips pursed in silence, he glanced around uneasily. But then, spotting a nylon wrapping sheet covered with polka dots, fluttering in the wind where it had caught on a branch, he carefully wrapped it around the small white box to protect it from getting wet. Then Masahiko noticed Kappei, bent over, clutching the grass with one hand and breathing heavily into the ground. The wide shoulders of his heavy kimono were blown back, flapping in the wind.

It had only been the day before that Masahiko had met this warm-hearted man when he came upon the dead body of Sayuri near the dam. Kappei stood up, seemingly having forgotten about Masahiko, and started to walk off into the rain. Masahiko followed, noticing the splotches of mud covering Kappei's formal *hakama* leggings.

When they arrived at the temple a young, cool-eyed priest was waiting for them. He invited Masahiko into the room with his family. He told them he was succeeding to the position as the main priest here and that he had just returned from *Honzan*, the head temple, where he had completed his training.

In the priests' quarters, the people who had returned from the crematory were changing out of their wet mourning clothes. Exchanging greetings while they looked up at the condition of the sky, they seemed to be preparing to leave for home. Judging from their familiar manner in saying their good-byes, it seemed that this temple was used not only for funerals, but that it was also a place where the people of the old village of Amazoko, who were normally separated, met for important discussions. This was evident from their friendly, relaxed voices. From the younger priest's greeting, it seemed that he had already been told about Masahiko.

"You've come a long way to get back here. I hear you spread your grandfather's ashes by yourself. I'm sorry I couldn't say a prayer with you."

Not knowing how to reply, Masahiko lowered his head in confusion.

The elderly priest, seeing him in this state, opened an old hand-stitched book and showed it to him. On it, in bold black ink characters was written, "Record of Contributors to the Rebuilding of Joko Temple." It was dated the third month of the twelfth year of Meiji.

"The temple was burned down during the Seinan War. This is the record book from the time when the contributions were made for the rebuilding. There were donations from many people, but if you look here you can see that the name of your great-great-grandfather, 'Aso Mikihiko,' is written at the head of the list.

"All the wood used in the temple—for the pillars of the hall of the Buddha, for the beams and rafters, the carved panels on the transom, the flooring in the inner sanctuary, the stairways, and elsewhere—it all came from the forests of the Aso family. That was about ten years into the Meiji Era. All the details are recorded here. If you take a look you can see for yourself. It was such excellent wood. These days, no matter how hard you look, you won't find anything like it. Fortunately, when Ama-zoko was flooded, the temple was outside the flood zone so it escaped destruction. Now people from other villages continue to come here to worship the Buddha.

"I heard from Ohina and the others about your return.

"The dam was built during Masahito's time here and after it was finished he went off to Tokyo. Once in a while some word of him reached us back here, but since he stopped contacting us we hesitated to try reaching him. So the other day when we heard the rumor that you had come and spread his ashes by the dam, well it really was quite a sad surprise.

"It seems your coming here and what happened to Sayuri had some fated connection. If you take things back to their roots, Oai-sama, who brought up Sayuri, was connected to your family. In any case, the past has returned and now a grandson has returned to this temple that's remained here in memory of the Aso family.

"It's weighed heavily on us, thinking we couldn't do any-thing, but now at last the day has come when we can offer prayers for him.

"You've made quite a trip coming here. Since there's noth-ing left of the old Silk Estate or of the land around it the only thing that remains is this temple. We've been waiting and hop-ing we might be able to perform the funeral rites for him as soon as you returned from the crematorium."

From the side, his plumpish wife added, "For ages now it's been said that the rebuilding of the temple was made pos-sible by the Aso family. We have always hoped we would be able to meet the relatives. We greatly appreciate your coming.

"And both last night at the wake and this morning too, all the old people have been saying they feel as if Masahito has come back to life and the old days have returned. We're all happy about it.

"We don't quite know what to think about what happened to Sayuri-san, but Oai-san, who brought her up, said she was connected to the old estate of your family. It's said that your great grandmother Nazuna—no, she must've been your great-great-grandmother—she brought up Oai-san. It's an old, old story but it's said that the baby Oai was not the child of a human, but of the Lord of Amazoko."

The elderly priest interrupted abruptly.

"Now don't start nonsense like that. How could she be anything but a human's child? This sort of thing is the way women are always causing trouble."

"I really have no idea whose child Oai was or where she came from. I still wonder about it. And Sayuri-san too; she was the orphaned child of a woman who fell by the roadside."

"Well that's just what this temple is for. The Aso family took care of the child in place of us. We're the ones who were taught the Providence of the Buddha. Now we can carry out a small act in return."

The young priest, who had been nodding with the sleeves of his kimono folded across his body as he listened to the stories of his parents, now relaxed his arms and expressed a smile of relief.

"As you've heard, you are most welcome to stay here as long you need to. And your *biwa*, I've been wondering about that. Do you play it?"

When Masahiko told them of his grandfather's having a *biwa* made from the mulberry tree of the old estate, the family of the priest, including the young wife who was waiting behind them, gasped all at once.

"But I know almost nothing about the old estate."

At that, from the back of the room, the elder priest's plump wife called out in a faint voice and reached out with one hand as if holding on to something.

"Ah yes, there were a lot of mulberry trees around there. It was called the Silk Estate. And there was a very nice spring there too. When I first came here as a young bride I visited the house. I was given some mulberries and I drank the water there too. There was one big mulberry tree there by the well. Was the *biwa* you brought with you possibly made from that mulberry tree?"

Masahiko, feeling as if he'd been asked by the family to show it to them, stood up. As he walked along the finely built porch—thinking of how it probably was made of wood taken from the mountains at the time when Mikihiko lived—he recalled something about his grandfather Masahito and about the house in Nakano.

He had been a man of few words. But although his words had been few, now they came back to life in Masahiko's ears with deep resonance. It struck him how his grandfather had belonged to the same world as the people who had been telling their stories back at the crematorium. His grandfather's attempting to return to the village that had been taken from him was similar to these people's way of returning in dreams with a clarity of feeling exceeding even what they had felt in the days past. No one else in his family had noticed that.

It seemed that his old lost village must have been separated from the rest of the world and remained as a pure unmixed stratum of the older world.

At the time the girl they called Oai was a baby it had been feared that she might not be the child of a human. According the dreams of Oshizu and Ohina, the guardian spirit of the village, who was said to be able to change into the form of a giant snake, had transformed his body into the Moonshadow hanging bridge. He had dropped a woman pilgrim who had been carrying a baby into the ravine, and then he had made himself into a cradle and rocked the baby. Normally he would stay sleeping way off in the stalactite cave of Isara River, but on occasion he would venture out and take on the form of the suspension bridge. There he would check on the people coming and going to the village. Occasionally he would find a stranger from the world beyond and make a sacrificial offering of that person.

This person called Nazuna-san—they say she's my great-great-grandmother, but this is the first I've ever heard of her. My grandfather Masahito never mentioned a thing to me about a baby whom the villagers had feared and who had been rescued and brought up there. What sort of taboo could have kept my grandfather from telling me of it?

Masahiko remembered something. That time in the car, on the way to the mental institution. His grandfather's words had been called out in a low, sorrow-stricken voice. So *that* must have been what he was talking about.

"Masahiko! The string of the *biwa* has snapped. It's over now. It's no use. Just shove me in."

He must have been thinking of what happened during the war in Okinawa. Every time they passed a car on the expressway he had called out in a low voice.

"There goes one! Blasting away," he'd muttered. And the thundering, rumbling sound of the cars and trucks on the highway came swirling around in his head.

"Go on Japan, blow yourself to bits. Blow yourself up. Go on, and blast yourself away. It's okay, just go ahead. The string of the *biwa* of Moonshadow Bridge . . ."

He clearly recalled those orders his grandfather had called out.

"The enemy ships are filling the sea off Shinagawa. The capital's been completely surrounded!"

Suddenly Masahiko's eyes filled with tears. Now he understood the meaning of the enemy his grandfather had been talking about. And that one string that had never been sounded—it signified all that had held his grandfather connected to the world that had been taken from him.

"Won't you look after the *biwa?*"

One hot summer day when his mother was away from the house Masahiko had been watching his grandfather, who seemed to be in an unusually carefree mood as he tended his collection of potted trees. Watching him, Masahiko got the urge to try and tune the old *biwa.* He brought it out to the porch and tried plucking on it, in the same way one would play on a guitar. His grandfather stood up and turned around.

"That's not a bad sound."

With his pruning shears still in his left hand his grandfather squinted his eyes.

"Oh come on, it's no good."

"Beginners can't expect great sounds at the start."

"It's the air here. It ruins the condition of the strings."

He had spoken half in joke. The sound he'd made could hardly be called musical.

"You think so too?"

Judging from the serious response, Masahiko got the feeling that his grandfather had taken his vague feelings to heart.

"Well you're probably right. It's partly because I don't know how to finger it, but also somehow the noises of the city twine around the strings like dust."

"Right. I feel it in the pores of my skin even. It's hard to breathe. It's no good."

"Would it help if I tried changing the strings?"

"You could try changing them, but the quality of the strings these days has really gone down. It's the silk strings of silkworms. Both the silkworms and the mulberry leaves, they don't grow well any more."

As his grandfather was speaking the thin string that Masahiko had been touching suddenly broke and fell without even a sound.

"Ah, it's broken."

". . . broken, is it? Well it's been there for so long no wonder it's snapped now. I wouldn't worry about it. They have them at the music stores."

"I'm sorry about it, Grandfather."

"That's all right. It was time to change it. Better to play it with new strings. If the player calls out to the string and speaks to it while playing, the string will start to sing. The string is waiting to sing."

"Sure, that's what a really great player might say. But how can a beginner expect something like that—speaking with the string?"

"You have to try it, with that spirit."

"Well in any case, that's a nice way to put it; the string is waiting to sing."

"Those aren't my words. A master back in the old days used to say that."

"When you say the 'old days,' you mean the days in Amazoko?"

"Right. There was a great player who used to come over Moonshadow Bridge and stay in town for a month or so. That's the one who said it."

"Was it a man?"

"He was a blind man."

"A person who can't see must be able to exist in the midst of sound."

"I imagine a blind person's world of sound must be completely different from that of people who can see. That great player, when he crossed over Moonshadow Bridge and announced his greetings to the village, first he played the climax to the Tale of the Heike."

"Really? He must have been quite a player."

"Well in those days the level of not only the players, but also of the listeners too was high. Even though they didn't go to school they remembered and recited the Tale of the Heike."

"Was Amazoko that kind of village?"

"It certainly was. Most people could hear things very far away. Even though the sounds of that master player were gentle, people could hear it from far off. Why, for Mizumaro-san, people would drop their hoes and axes and come running to greet him. They said you had to be quick in going to make your greetings."

"You mean the villagers went to greet him?"

"Well, since he was blind they didn't want him to fall into the ravine, did they? And then too, going quickly also meant stopping work and getting to listen.

"Part of the attraction of the *biwa* is that it's accompanied by story telling.

"The stories were incredible. You couldn't tell whether it was the sound of the mountains or the sound of the winds that was speaking."

"Did you learn them from Mizumaro-san?"

Talking like this seemed to cause him pain. His grandfather's right hand was part of an artificial limb. His arm had been blown off from the elbow in the Okinawa battle.

"Well, you could say I learned them, but . . ."

His grandfather thrust his false arm in front of his body again and stared at it. Masahiko looked away. The material of the hand had been made to approximate the look of human skin, yet somehow it looked more garish than the skin of a real hand.

"If you touch those strings, my fingers will be moving together with them. The tips of my missing fingers will be touching the strings."

"Missing fingers—touching the strings?"

"That's what I said. My fingers will be touching them."

Masahiko looked carefully at the yellow skin of the artificial hand.

"I've liked the sound of strings from way back. Especially the *biwa*."

The grandfather broke into a faint but peaceful smile.

"I'm going to leave this *biwa* to you. You want to give it a try?"

These had been his words at the time.

Gradually he had started into the story of how at the time he had left the village, for the sake of being able to take a keepsake of his ancestors he had ordered a big mulberry tree cut down and had an expert *biwa* maker from Hakata build him an instrument from it. The maker told him that he'd never seen such fine wood for a *biwa* and that he probably would never see such wood again.

"The mulberry will be happy if you play it. It's the only thing left from Amazoko now."

His tone of voice changed and he turned around. His expression was hard to see in the back lighting.

So it seemed that this *biwa* was his only physical reminder left from Amazoko. The last thing his grandfather had spoken of was "the sound of the string." Hadn't old Chiyomatsu-san spoken of that sound of strings as the "pathway of dreams"?

The villagers all remembered well how Oai-san in her older days had delivered babies one after another. And in their dreams, it seemed, they still met from time to time. And the story of Nazuna had come down as a legend.

If his mother Machiko were to hear such tales, what would she think? No doubt they would represent to her just the sort of rural ignorance she disliked so much. In her wish to dissociate herself from this sort of world she had made a point of associating with people of "dignified standing." Her involvement in the fashionable Mission School class reunion had helped her to polish the social credentials on which she prided herself. She had fallen in love with Kiyohiko years ago when he was young, but even now she still thought of his countryside past and his grandfather as a drawback. She pointed with particular pride to her retired father's career in the diplomatic service. At one time he had been sent to investigate a rubber plantation in Malaysia. It was there, at her father's place during her university summer vacation, that they had met.

Even when his mother was entertaining guests Masahito had made no attempt to hide his rural dialect. At one such time Machiko had said to her women friends, "His dialect comes from the Kumaso, an ancient tribe in Kyushu. His lineage goes way back. As for myself, when I was young I traveled around the world with my father to foreign countries. When I first heard the coarse dialect of those natives I had trouble understanding what he was saying."

Masahiko had been in his second year of junior high school. He could remember how his ears flushed with blood. And even his mild-mannered father Kiyohiko hadn't been able to ignore such words from his wife. What Masahiko's mother had said at that time—things he couldn't talk about to anyone—had festered in his heart like poison. Words like "those natives"—whether they had been applied just to his grandfather's former hometown or to any other place—could only be considered insulting.

If his mother Machiko were to learn that his father's ancestry included people like Nazuna—a woman who had taken in a baby that had been brought to her by the guardian god of the village—a god who could take on the form of a snake—and if she had known that the family still had associations with the people from the village at the bottom of the lake, she would surely have shuddered in disgust.

Masahiko felt as if now, twenty-three years after his birth, he had become like Kappei the crab in Oshizu's dream—the dream she had told to the people at the crematory. The outer covering of his feelings was like the shell of a crab that had been split all the way from the bridge of its nose and eyes to the tips of its claws and then shed. He felt as if he were standing defenseless in the warm bed of a river, moving about with his body and soul exposed, softer even than when he was an infant, feeling his finger playing about in the water unconsciously.

Unexpectedly feeling as if he were about to break into tears, Masahiko opened his eyes wide and stared off into the darkness inquiringly. He'd been feeling that way since the night before.

He found himself awake, sitting up in his futon bedding. In waking, the cat that had been sleeping by his feet and now looked as if it had been pushed away stared blankly at Masahiko and then came up to the hem of the blanket and curled itself up. Probably it was one of the temple's cats. Even when it came close it seemed to check for danger before moving in. It was said that the day before, when the young wife came into the room with the vacuum cleaner, this cat had glanced at the nozzle and jumped up with a yell and then jumped again a full two yards to the side. Last night when she had spoken of how that cat didn't get along with her—and especially with the vacuum cleaner—it had sent the whole family into laughter.

Now he had already stayed two nights at the temple. He had a feeling he might be staying there a while longer. Last night after he returned from the cremation place the family at the temple had urged him repeatedly to stay with them.

"How fortunate your timing was. The guest room is empty now. Most of the wood for this room came from your family's mountains. We take good care of it and whenever we have a big funeral and priests come from distant temples to assist they always praise this room. It's done in a plain fashion, yet they always say that places built solidly in the old style make for better dreams.

"Until now no one from the old Silk Estate has stayed here and so now that you've come back at long last, everyone in the house is delighted."

Before the elder priest had finished speaking his wife, seated by his side and nodding as she listened, raised her head.

"You know, if no one lives in a house it soon goes to rot and ruin. It's strange, but it's true. And now, thanks to having a young person here, the room has become young again too."

Checking to see if her way of speaking had been appropriate or not, she glanced at her husband.

"Isn't that right? The guest room must be pleased at having a young person stay in it."

"And I've been giving it a good cleaning, as well."

The young wife added this from behind. Her voice had a smoothness that was completely changed from the way it had sounded the day before at the funeral. He had felt there was no reason to refuse their offer.

Such strange, unimaginable things were continuing to happen. He'd come to this town, along with his *biwa* and the old sleeping bag from his school mountain club days, just planning to take care of his grandfather's bones and then either find a cheap inn or, if it was still warm enough, to sleep out in the open.

Since his grandfather's death he'd been feeling an urge to get moving. He had been hoping to come up with something to bring his life and music together but he kept running up against a conflict that kept them apart. He'd tried his hand at music theory, but every time he tried that route it seemed it didn't lead to good music. It seemed that the sound he was really searching for would have to come from some other place.

Since his grandfather died, the colors he saw wherever he looked as he walked about the city—not only in the buildings but also in the advertisements and in people's clothes and even in the books in the bookshops—had seemed far too glaring. It was as if paintbrushes loaded with gaudy colors were waiting on the sides of the street, ready to paint everyone who passed by in a jumble of color.

Masahiko had the feeling that his eardrums must be especially weak. The way the sounds of the city just poured in through the pores of his body seemed to indicate that there was some problem with his ears. Once when the election-time trucks that blared out their amplified appeals in ear-splitting barrages came around he had even sought escape in an amusement park. Waiting under a trellis of wisteria until the assault from the loudspeakers passed he thought he heard, behind him, the clear tone of a young child. He turned around to look and saw three or four clumps of wisteria blossoms hanging down, but there was no person in sight. At the time, he'd thought it must have been a lone child singing, unaware that this world was falling apart. Even with my damaged ears—he'd thought—I heard it. Was it just an auditory hallucination? Even if that were so, it seemed that the rebirth of that voice was essential to the existence of people's songs.

Thinking about this as he rode the trains and gazed at the expressions in the eyes of the young people and heard them laughing raucously he felt, with a sense of anxiety, as if his eardrums were being pulled from his inner ear and trampled beneath people's shoes. When he heard the homogenized pronunciations of people of his generation it seemed as if they were creating reproductions of the people around them and talking to them in order to hide and protect their real selves from being destroyed. It seems I'm not the only one feeling this anxiety. It's as if, amidst all the virtual reality we're living in, and by treating everything as if it's part of a sort of pseudo-existence, we're trying to protect ourselves from being destroyed.

The other day I saw a girl who looked like she was hiding the same sort of things that I was. She was sitting in the train, across from me, with her eyes cast downward and her legs held together and she didn't look up even once. On her lap was a small bluish-colored handbag with an elephant embroidered on it. The train was swaying and each time the handbag started to slip down she grabbed the elephant and pulled it back up onto her lap. Since it was an elephant it looked as if it should be very heavy—yet the girl had slender arms that stuck out from her white short-sleeved blouse. For how many years had this girl been taking care of this elephant on her handbag? At night, did two people sleep inside that bag? If she had an unavoidable errand and had to take it out into the city it could pose a big problem. The city was filled with things that frightened elephants.

The girl showed no other response at all, other than caring for her elephant. Her facial color looked a bit greenish. Could she have been a tree spirit? In the old days this area was said to have been a part of the Musashino Plain, so could it be that the spirits of its ancient trees still rose up and wandered about amidst the darkness around the land beneath the elevated railways—and got onto the trains?

Not reacting even in the slightest to her surroundings, and appearing thoroughly buried within the deep cave of herself, she seemed far removed from the world of humans. But then, that couldn't have been so—what made me think a thing like that? Perhaps in that bag with the elephant she had a ticket to the concert of some bleached-hair singer. If she were in the light of the blue and pink lasers of a concert, probably she would have gotten up immediately and started dancing and running about. That elephant on her handbag must have been a pet that she took for walks. And while I was thinking about this she looked up, as if she'd been scared by something.

Masahiko was flustered. Perhaps she took me for some sort of kidnapper. And if I look deep enough into my soul can I really say I wasn't thinking such things? I must be really strange. She's just an ordinary girl with nothing special about her. Probably this girl, like everyone else, is making a copy of herself for her own protection and leading this copy around the city. They're sealing themselves off from the true selves they'd had from the oldest of times.

I turned my eyes away from the elephant, glanced down at her navy blue sneakers and then looked over at a businessman. It seemed as if I were being silently blamed by another being who was her true self. For just an instant our eyes met. Hers was the look of a wild beast surprised by something. She got up as if her whole body movement were expressing her surprise and then quickly she got off the train. I ended up riding three stations past my stop.

That morning the mood at the breakfast table had been worse than usual. It was the first week after his grandfather's death had passed and his father Kiyohiko was still taking time off from work.

"Grandfather's real wish was to return to his home in the country."

"That's not the impression I got."

Kiyohiko had answered his wife vaguely, opening the newspaper that he hadn't been able read owing to all the confusion of the week following the funeral.

"With all those country folks here, that was quite some local talk we were treated to." There really hadn't been many of Masahito's relatives present at the funeral, yet she had made a point of referring to them. Kiyohiko made no reply. There was just the dry sound of the turning of the pages of his newspaper.

"'Moonshadow Bridge, Moonshadow Bridge,'—that's what he said just before he died, according to the nurses. It was like a line from some play, it seems."

The sound of turning pages continued for a while.

"Was it really such a special place, as he claimed?"

"Well, I . . ."

"You've been there, haven't you?"

"I couldn't very well have been there, could I? It was flooded by the dam."

"So it's at the bottom of the dam? Well anyway, it doesn't matter much."

"Then don't ask about things that don't matter."

"When you talk that way you sound just like Grandfather."

Masahiko's father put down the newspaper and tried to light the cigarette lighter. It didn't catch and an empty sound hung in the air.

Whenever his mother Machiko said to Kiyohiko things like "those country people" or "you sound just like Grandfather," her comments always carried an extra edge of meaning. It might have been that Kiyohiko had been getting home from work late at night, or that her pride had been hurt at an alumnae group meeting, or such. Machiko would often say such things as, "Alumnae meetings are such a bother. I'm not going to any more of them."

The rest of the family would show no reaction. But when she said, "I'm not going any more" it really meant "I guess I'll go and see." When she got home, Machiko would bring up a classmate's name and without fail mention something like, "Her husband was posted overseas for a long time so she wears all sorts of different things. She had on a necklace that looked rather different from what most Japanese would wear."

This was the kind of thing Machiko would talk about at breakfast on Sundays. Kiyohiko would make a clatter with the butter tray and take a big slab of butter and spread it on his toast.

Machiko would say, "You know that's no good for your health, don't you?" and snatch up the butter dish without flinching.

"What do you think I ended up wearing?"

"I thought you said you were going to buy some fancy brand name thing for that meeting."

"I bought it, but didn't wear it."

"Well what was the problem this time?"

"I wore something my sister gave me. It was authentic, tailored in Paris."

"Is that something that people can readily tell—that it's genuine, tailored in Paris?"

"Certainly they know. They all have an eye for that kind of thing. These days you can see brand name clothes anywhere you go. They're all discounted. They have no value, it seems. My sister's was a Paris original, in a traditional style."

"Paris, Paris, for God's sake will you stop going on about Paris. We've had enough of that already. You're all just getting taken in by vanity."

"Well that's rather rude of you, isn't it? Right now I'm talking about the culture of fashion."

Masahiko's elder brother, looking disgusted, broke into the discussion.

"I'm going to have another cup of tea. I'll get it myself. Don't you think we could have a little higher level of discussion here? This is supposed to be our nice 'morning conversation time,' isn't it? Seems to me those ladies in their perfume are a big pain it the ass."

Masahiko, who hardly ever got involved in such conversations, added,

"If you want to know the truth, that sort of woman depresses me. Even over the telephone they reek of perfume."

"Masahiko! You and your abnormal sensitivities again—smelling perfume over the phone. I guess that must stem from your grandfather's blood."

Masahiko had been thinking he shouldn't get caught in the discussion, but now it was too late. Looking at his mother gave him a miserable feeling.

"Well now, isn't this a fine morning. Why is it that I have to be insulted by everyone? Do you have any idea just how humiliated I've been on account of your grandfather?"

These infrequent "morning discussions" had come to no good. Normally Kiyohiko was said to be quite proper in his manners, but now he made a loud noise in putting down the newspaper and then stood up, put on his jacket and went out. Machiko stood rooted at the spot, slowly clearing the breakfast things, and then after a while she spoke to the elder brother in an uneasy manner.

"I wonder where he's gone. The mourning notices—we have to write them you know. And your writing of Japanese characters is so poor. It's enough to drive me crazy."

"Why is it you have to speak so badly about Grandfather? You know Father doesn't want to hear it."

"But I've suffered so much humiliation. And from my own family too. I have to hear them talk about how that Grandfather was such a strange old man. And about how he was from the Kumaso tribe down south."

"Wouldn't it be better to speak of him as coming from the *Yamatai*, the original people of Japan?

"It certainly would not. Now just stop this foolishness."

Then Machiko spoke to Masahiko as if she were recovering her temper.

"He must be going to the Tetsusgakudo bookstore. He seems to like being there . . . Could you go and tell him that after he's finished with his walk I'd like to have him write some of the mourning notices that are still left?"

Her voice was tense. Masahiko thought to himself; in spite of being brought up as a so-called gentle, well-mannered child, here I am attacking my mother and saying things that shouldn't be said. She must have been hurt. With regret, he went out to look for his father, but he didn't apologize to his mother. At times like this he felt himself shunning her, even though she was his own mother.

Suddenly a cock crowed nearby.

Hey, don't surprise me like that, he said to himself. In the old days no doubt it would have been natural enough to hear a cock crowing at the break of dawn, but hearing a crow right here took him by surprise and nudged him back to the present. He glanced at his watch. It was just after five. Outside it was still dusk.

The humming and booming of the mornings in Tokyo with all the cars and trucks from near and far seemed like a lie. In all that noise could the voice of a cock be mixed in too? Perhaps there was one in a zoo. He laughed at the thought. No doubt a person from the countryside would find this amusing—a cock in a zoo.

He pushed at the sleeping cat with his hand. At the slightest touch, the cat bounded off. It was a medium-sized tomcat with short hair. Blinking its eyes and making a pretense of looking away, gradually it made its way back—after all, the blankets were warm.

Masahiko realized that he was uncertain about where it was he was drifting. Also he realized that the time was not so far off when he would have to move out of the house in Nakano. He had the uneasy feeling that everything he saw with his eyes, everything he heard, everything he touched with his hands and feet—it was all separated from living substance and he was just surviving by clinging to fleeting realities. The biggest cause of his uneasiness lay in the fact that he still had no work to support himself. What kind of work would be suitable for him? Totally dependent on the support of his parents, he couldn't really appreciate them either. If he got away from the house no doubt he'd come to understand them. He decided that as soon as he finished the business of taking care of his grandfather's bones he was going to look for a job.

It had been three days now since he had come here. It seemed as if it had been years. Am I changing into a new person? Or, more than myself changing, is it that the world is entering into me and changing? Or, rather, is it that I've come to a place where the world my grandfather taught me about and this world are being mixed together? From overcrowded Tokyo where the ties between people have been broken, if you just glance at the village of Amazoko, sealed off beneath the waters by a dam, it may seem that the village is an empty place. But couldn't it also be that the world of the unconscious within me is sleeping along with the drifting people of that village?

In this place a person can feel the beginnings of human consciousness, and how they grow, and how they are nurtured along with countless other lives by the waters that seep out from the depths of the earth into the folds of the deep mountains. The thought of an anatomical chart of the human body came to Masahiko. It had only been three days, and yet in walking about without riding on any vehicle, and in sitting down and looking around—if you were really aware of all the life that's teeming about the earth, what might you see? And what might you hear? He started to shiver. Even though it was southern Kyushu, in the mountain areas the mornings were cold. Once more Masahiko pushed off the cat.

4

WATER MIRROR

At breakfast the elder priest's wife asked her husband, "Have you heard the talk about the fire at Jimpei's place being caused by arson?"

Refilling a bowl of rice, the younger priest's wife stopped her hand and glanced at her husband.

The elder priest commented reprovingly, "So they're already making stories about that, are they? Better not listen to that sort of talk."

"Well I heard the women in the kitchen talking about it."

"Must have been that woman Osame. She's always full of hot air—blasting away like a trumpet."

The young wife bent her head forward and giggled.

"Arson, was it? Or an accident? Who's to know? There are times when it's better not to know."

The young priest looked up and surveyed his father's face. Then he resumed eating with his chopsticks as if nothing had happened.

"Jimpei's dead. His wife Oriki-san has gone crazy. And the horse stable was completely burned down to the ground. What happened to the horse?"

"I don't really know, but it seems nothing happened to it."

Chewing on some grated daikon and making crisp sounds, the young priest stayed out of the conversation.

"So it looks like one more from the old village is gone. Today's funeral—who's going to lead the service?"

"I hear a distant relative's coming. But he's not from Amazoko, so I doubt he'll have much feeling for it."

The head priest turned toward his son and spoke.

"You're ready?"

"Yes. The ashes should be here by now. Things should be mostly taken care of by noon."

The elder priest's wife still had something more to say.

"Have the police already . . ?"

"It's already finished. They say there's not going to be any further investigation."

"It seems his wife, Oriki-san, is in rather a bad way and she's gotten quite out of hand. I hear they had to take her to some mental hospital near the seaside. Apparently she made quite a scene about going."

"Under the circumstances I don't suppose anyone could have taken care of a person like that. I guess it couldn't be helped."

"I suppose so."

In saying this she glanced hesitantly at Masahiko.

"I suppose she must have been taken in by those dog spirits. The whole neighborhood is all worked up about it."

"Still going on about that sort of thing? How many years have you been here at this temple now? It goes against our doctrine."

"Well it may not go along with the doctrine, but the people in the village don't live by the doctrine. They say Oriki-san's been growling and crawling about on all fours. They say she's bitten people too."

"Oh come on, stop spreading that nonsense will you. It looks like you've been caught up in those delusions too. Dog spirits or gods, and in this day and age—it's a relic from the past century. And now it's gotten to you too."

"For me, doctrines have always been difficult. Actually the dog spirits seem closer to me."

The younger couple and Masahiko glanced at each other. They couldn't help smiling at the utterly languid tone of the elder wife in speaking of such grave matters.

"You know, we can find models for our life right in front of us. Isn't this a perfect example of the saying, one hundred sermons to no avail."

Again the younger couple laughed between themselves as the elder couple continued.

"There were quite a few rumors about Jimpei getting rich from that dam project."

"A speculator, a swindler even—there are always such people around."

"Yes, he certainly was a swindler."

She started to say this, but appearing to have concerns about Masahiko, she glanced up at her son. Then, perhaps deciding not to worry about it, she continued right away.

"Well, that Jimpei fellow, he came here and talked about it. 'When that dam comes in,' he said, 'this area's going to be a real hot spot for tourism. And when that happens the area around your temple is also going to be prime property, you know. They say all kinds of investment money from the big cities will pour in. And with that extra land of yours, you're in a great position to sell it off for putting up a hotel. And if a hotel comes in, it'll bring in plenty of high-class folks from the cities. But if there get to be too many who want to sell the prices will collapse, so now's the time to get into it. Why don't you just leave it to me . . .' That was the way he talked when he came here."

"I can imagine he'd talk of such things, and he must have done lots more. He was an odd sort of character for these parts." For some reason the old priest, who had been speaking calmly, suddenly laughed so much his body swayed forward.

"Putting up a disreputable hotel like that on the water's edge, it ruined the reputation of Amazoko. It looks like we've always had that kind of hotel."

"If it had been the old village there would have been no such building."

"As it turned out, even if he did get rich he ended up as ashes."

"Well, he was hardly a model citizen but he was one of the Amazoko people and now it looks like one more household is gone."

"It's not something we can talk about very openly, but it seems he took quite a fancy for Sayuri—I hear she was having trouble dealing with it."

The young priest cast an accusing glance at his mother for speaking in such a way.

Having finished eating, Masahiko was wondering when he should get up from the breakfast table. When the priest's wife's said that this was something that couldn't be talked about openly, he took it as a cue to get up from the table quietly.

The son, sipping his tea, scowled at his mother and then spoke in a voice tinged with the hint of a smile.

"You must excuse our family for such dull talk, Masahiko-san."

Rising part-way, the whole family busied itself with refilling the teapot and putting out oranges, trying to call their young guest back.

"Such boring talk, as usual."

It seemed like quite a frank breakfast discussion and so, deciding to sit down again, Masahiko spoke out decisively.

"There's something I need to think over. I want to go and take another look at that dam."

The elder priest's wife spoke in an understanding voice. "The dam . . . well yes, I suppose. That's where your old family place is, beneath the water now."

"Today Jimpei's funeral will be held here. I suppose if you were here you might feel a little uneasy so shall I go and get some rice balls for you to take with you in a *bento* lunch box?" The younger wife looked at her mother-in-law as she spoke. Actually, there was no *bento* shop nearby.

The elder wife added, facing her daughter-in-law and Masahiko, "The offerings of food for the funeral have already been taken care of and the women are all here and preparing rice balls. Just go ahead and take some. When you eat them you'll be making an offering for Jimpei."

As he climbed the mountain path Masahiko's feelings were quite different from when he first had first come. Walking among the fallen leaves, his entire body was bathed in the spirit of the mountains. When he stood still and listened carefully he felt himself being called to, from the treetops above to the ground beneath his feet, by the delicate presence of living things. He felt as if the pores of his skin were acting as finely tuned sense organs.

But then, the elder wife's casual talk about the dog spirits, and how they were connected with people dying and with mental hospitals—somehow it seemed rather odd. He found it interesting that she felt closer to the strange beliefs of the villagers than to the religious doctrines of her husband's temple. No doubt these feelings had come to him through staying for three days among these people of Amazoko who were so different from those back in the city. The rustling sounds from the woods made his heart beat strangely. It seemed that here in this village was the most ancient layer of a presence that still remained in the modern world.

I've been called back into the cycle of rebirth of the trees and plants of the ancient undisturbed village of Amazoko— such thoughts circled about in Masahiko's mind. The smells and feelings coming from the decaying leaves of the trees throughout the mountains suggested an ideal image of the abundance that lies in death. Were it not for that presence it seemed there could be no way to imagine the world of colors that appears when the mushrooms first lift their heads and the grasses and trees first sprout.

In tending his potted plants his grandfather had often muttered, "Unless you take care of them none of these different kinds of plants will put out even a shoot."

In general Masahiko had not been particularly attentive to his grandfather's words, but now, up in the mountains, those old sayings came back to his ears unbidden.

The water level at the dam, which hadn't changed from two days ago, reflected all the surrounding mountains. He soon recognized the spot where he had first met Ohina. The hut with the reed sides and the bamboo grass roof he had helped Ohina and her daughter Omomo build was still there. It made an unexpectedly welcome sight. He noticed the big persimmon tree on Utazaka Hill and remembered that it had marked the entrance to the old village. This landmark persimmon tree still remained, but the village of Amazoko it looked over had disappeared into the depths of the waters about the dam. Hadn't he been told that when traveling musicians and performers entered the village they played on their samisens and *biwa* as they walked along the roadway by Moonshadow Bridge and Utazaka Hill? If this were so then it seemed that all the songs of those times, along with all the people who had listened to them, must be sealed off in those waters too. Masahiko gazed into the depths of the stagnating green water. Here and there he could just barely make out the whittled-away shapes of the remaining stumps of trees. The people who had lived in the village before its flooding would have been able to tell just whose garden plot it had been over there, and whose deserted house it had been right here.

A hundred years ago the French researcher Pelliot un-
earthed from the deserts around Tonko the written scores for
some ancient Chinese flute music. It occurred to Masahiko
that if he could somehow raise the spirits of the ancient voices
of the songs from the village that lay in the waters he might be
able to create a similarly mysterious composition. Suddenly he
was reminded of the old word *yusai* that referred to a "sublime
ceremony." The sunken village and its lost songs seemed to
evoke the spirit of *yusai*. He wondered if he might be able to
put this spirit into music.

He wondered where the stalactite cave of the fabled Lord
Guardian of the village—the one who could take on the form
of a snake—might be. Could the old guardian still be living in
the depths of the waters? He squinted his eyes. Softly, the
grasses began to murmur. For a while the breezes reflected the
sounds of the banks about the dam, but passing into the distant fields of grass they gradually turned soft and quiet. As he
gazed at the mountains reflected in the water, it seemed as if
nothing had changed.

But then from behind the mountains Masahiko noticed the
distant Kyushu mountain range rising gradually on the water's
surface, reflected in the retina of his mind. Silently the distant
mountains, as if banded with numerous silver-colored pleats,
seemed to slide down, spread out, and cover the nearer mountains in the foreground. A colorless flame of water began to
flicker. Rising from the depths of the lake, a sound like the
drumming of the spirits of the earth became audible. It re-
sounded as if, according to some orderly set of rules, with
every beat it were urging on the stagnating dregs that lay at
the depths of the lake. But then great howls became audible,
rising from time to time from the cave at the bottom of the
lake. It seemed that it must all have been some sort of auditory
hallucination.

As the silver-colored mountains that had been sliding down onto the nearby lake began to work their way slowly back up into their original position, the alternating sounds of the drum beats and the howling from the bottom of the lake rose up from the taut surface of the water.

The words "birth of the first sounds" came into Masahiko's thoughts.

He wondered if it was right that he alone should be able to hear and see these things. He also had a sense that the strings of the *biwa*, on which he had been trying so hard during the past month to make sounds, had somehow become connected to the trees at the bottom of the lake. He felt as if these voices of the earth, in passing through his body, had released the passions of his emerging manhood. In the sky he saw Omomo swimming above him, her hair streaming in the wind and her body wrapped in that celadon-colored obi he'd seen in his dream. While thinking how it really should have been Sayuri, suddenly he heard a voice from behind.

"Masahiko-san, Masahiko-san."

Omomo was standing above him on a large rock by the shore. She was barefoot and dressed in a short indigo-colored kimono. For a while she said nothing.

"So, it looks like this is your first time to visit this world. What happened?"

"Well . . ."

"From behind it looked like you were a flame rising up from the water."

"I, well . . . just now . . ."

"You looked like you were going to be pulled into the water so I called out to you."

Being spoken to pulled him back to reality again. Hiking up the hem of her kimono, Omomo walked into the water and then, holding on to a stick from near the hut, wiped each leg.

"Sorry to bother you. Looks like you were thinking about something."

He must have looked odd standing there. He couldn't tell her about just having seen a vision of that obi and seeing Omomo and Sayuri on the surface of the water. If they had been with Ohina it would have been easier to talk, since she had taught him how to make the reed hut and had let him take part in the O-bon offerings. But now, suddenly, he didn't know which way to turn. Awkwardly, he stepped on the grass and sat down, leaning against a rock by the side of the hut.

"There are lots of things I'd like to learn. From you."

"Masahiko-san, you want to learn from me?"

"Yes, from you and from your mother."

"But why are you talking this way to me?"

Omomo spoke in a somewhat agitated tone of voice.

"I don't know what to make of this. I've never been spoken to so politely, so seriously like this."

She spoke in a hushed voice. Without thinking, Masahiko glanced sideways at her face. Omomo was sitting in a thicket of grass with her sandals off, drying her toenails with the hem of her indigo-blue kimono.

"Well, to tell the truth, I . . . just now, from the bottom of the lake . . . I heard sounds."

Omomo stopped wiping her feet and looked at Masahiko's face with great seriousness.

"That was the voice of the Lord Guardian of Amazoko, coming from the bottom of the lake."

"The Lord of Amazoko? You mean the one from Moonshadow Bridge?"

"Yes. Probably he was coming up from the depths of the stalactite cave." Omomo drew in her breath and then asked in a low voice, "And what sort of voice was it?" Her pupils glanced downward.

"How can I describe it . . ? Well, it was the voice . . . of the spirit of Amazoko."

Omomo took a branch of mugwort from beside her, snapped it off and glanced at its cut end.

"If it was the voice of a spirit . . . then I should have heard it too."

And then suddenly she assumed an attitude of reverence, knees properly together, and held out the mugwort to Masahiko.

"Smells good, doesn't it? It's a plant of the gods. It's a sacred plant that drives away bad spirits."

Flustered, Masahiko sat up straight and pressed his nose to the mugwort to smell it.

"Yes, it does smell good."

And then suddenly he asked, "That song you sang the other night. Could you sing it again? Would you sing it right here? I've been thinking of it all along. You must sing it for me again."

"The song from the other night? Ah . . ."

Omomo's expression showed her surprise. She opened her mouth as if to speak, but no words came out. Then she held out the mugwort bunch, smelled it, and waved it back and forth.

"This will ward off any bad spirits."

This woman's words and actions continued to surprise him. Shaking the grass, she urged him with a serious expression, "Why don't you try it yourself. It's the grass of the gods."

A bit uneasy, he tried the same motion with the grass.

"What sort of bad sprits?"

"The bad sprits of the dam, and of the mountain gods. There are still all sorts of them."

"All sorts of them, still? . . . So does that mean you think I brought some bad spirits with me too?"

"What?"

All of a sudden, Omomo, who had just been so formal, bent her head forward delicately, threw the bunch of mugwort toward the water and then broke out into laughter. She found it hard to stop.

"This is too much—you're bringing me to tears."

Omomo wiped her eyes with the blue edge of her sleeve, tossed her hair back over her neck, stood up, and then took the mugwort back from Masahiko.

"All right, I get it. Now I see. Maybe you did bring some bad spirits with you from Tokyo."

And then, with the motions of a Shinto priest bearing a sacred staff, she waved some mugwort over Masahiko's head.

"I thought something was strange. You're so different from us . . . maybe it's because of those bad spirits from Tokyo."

And in telling him it was all right she threw away the mugwort and sat down in her former spot. Masahiko felt much more at ease than before.

"There are lots of strange things I'm worried about."

"Well if you're worried about things, let me help get rid of them for you."

For the first time, Masahiko laughed.

"OK, then from now on I'll ask you to take care of them for me."

"All right, then why don't you become a member of the village."

"Become a member of the village? I thought I already was doing that."

"Well, you're not one yet."

"Then what am I supposed to do to become a part of the village? You have to tell me."

"You're still staying at the temple. You're still a guest there."

Masahiko was taken aback. Taking advantage of his great-great-grandfather's standing, he'd been staying at the temple as a guest. Even though the old village had been lost to the dam, the people from it considered him a guest from Tokyo.

"If this were the old days you'd have brought a couple bottles of *shochu* liquor with you."

"Well, I didn't know about that, but if that's all there is to it I can take care of that."

"I wouldn't say that's all there is to it. You're from the old Silk Estate, so there's that *biwa* . . ."

Instinctively, he looked at her face. Her eyes sparkling like rays of sun on water, Omomo returned Masahiko's glance.

"That *biwa*, it was made of the mulberry tree from the old estate, wasn't it? If you play on it the voices of Amazoko will come out again."

"Really? You think I should try? Well . . . if you say so."

"Everyone will be pleased. In the old days, right here on Utazaka Hill . . ."

Her voice wavering a bit, Omomo fell silent. From the far bank, what looked like a black wave of water birds was approaching; they may have been ducks. If people should come here to Utazaka Hill, would I play? What should I do? In Tokyo I dreamed of writing a piece of music for Japanese traditional instruments and doing a performance. I couldn't put on anything like the big concerts of the pop singers, but that's not what I'm aiming for anyhow. If only I could make a sound that the people and the grass and trees at the bottom of the water would listen to. But before that I need to listen again carefully to Ohina and Omomo's singing—that's what I've been wanting to ask them all along.

——What was that reverberation I heard, coming from the bottom of the lake and sounding like the beating of a drum stretched across the water, struck by the Lord of the stalactite cave? What was that sound? The hand of the spirit of the earth, living in the stalactite cave at the depths of the waters for tens of thousands of years, watching over the village from its birth to its last days—it must have regarded this manmade lake as a drum and struck it, beat by beat, sending echoes throughout the mountains all around. It's etched into my senses an idea for a composition that can't be expressed in Western music. Its sound will be built on Eastern musical tones but it will be based on the distinctive voices that are only in Amazoko. The plaintive voices of the spirits of its skies and land will be woven into it.

"Looks like you're thinking about something . . . Your face has that same look of a flame burning in water as it did a while back."

"Well, I'm thinking. About what I asked you."

"You mean that song from last night."

"You have to sing it for me."

"Well, I suppose I could, but . . ."

"And Ohina too. I want to ask her too. I know she seems so busy now, but could you ask her for me?"

"These past few days she's really been too busy. And me too."

"Well, with the two funerals and all I can imagine."

Omomo looked down a bit as she spoke.

"Actually it's been three—including your grandfather's."

Again, he had spoken thoughtlessly. He'd taken his meeting with them, when he scattered his grandfather's ashes, as coming about merely by chance. Certainly he had made the visit on O-bon to the site of the graves beneath the water and then he had happened to meet these two women. But then they had gone to all those efforts to carry out the ceremony for him. He felt ashamed of his behavior. In spite of my coming here intending to get away from the world of city people, who always just ask for things and expect to get things in return, in coming to this village haven't I acted as the worst one of all?

". . . Yes, you're right, there were three of them. I've . . . so many strange things have been happening to me. And you—your singing a song like that."

"Well, the song . . . the moon was beautiful and I felt as if Moonshadow Bridge had reappeared, and I felt like singing on the bridge . . ."

Masahiko felt as if he had already been at the edge of this village for a long time. Hearing the various stories about the villagers who were now dead made him recall parts of his grandfather's stories. It seemed that the meanings of his grandfather's words, along with the things he'd heard from the people in the village, had all become mixed together to create a new story in which the village at the bottom of the lake took form and created a hitherto unknown world.

He was becoming bound up with all the signs of life in the mountains and valleys, from the buds of the quince and magnolia to the faint gurgling sounds of running water. All these trees, grasses and flowers, whose names I hardly know—why have I never thought of their significance for the human world until now? I've just thought of these things as existing in picture books of plants. But now it seems that here is where the world begins. Even a lump of dirt—you can't look at it as something trivial. There isn't a single element that's not essential to the earth's make-up.

A bunch of red *manma* flowers formed a ruddy-colored patch that spread out about the base of the mugwort plants. What's led me on must have been my seeing the way grandfather cared for those pitiful potted plants of his; caring for the tiny buds of those andromeda trees that looked as small as the grains of sesame seeds. What would it look like if I went to the top of the mountain? From there the andromeda trees must look majestic—each one of them like a castle in a fairy tale. When the rays of the evening sun catch on the bunches of

their still-tight buds it must make an imposing sight. If I could
see tens of thousands of those buds in a mist of color, no matter if I saw them from just a small hill, surely I couldn't help
but take in the spirit of the mountains. Although Masahiko
knew hardly anything of the classics, a verse from the *Manyoshu*
came to mind.

> I would pluck the andromeda
> That blooms above the rocky shore
> But they say
> You are not here to see it

And come to think of it, could there be a more appropriate
person in whose hair to place a bunch of those sweet flowers
than the woman standing right in front of him? He wanted to
speak his thoughts to her but his words caught in his throat.
She seemed older than he. And today without lipstick she
looked so fresh and innocent.

"Look—over there."

Omomo pointed for him to look, taking his attention from
his thoughts.

"That's where the valley of vines used to be. In the old days
it used to be covered with *matatabi* silvervines."

In the direction she was pointing there were two mountains
with a stand of cedar trees in the pass between them. The
scene was reflected perfectly on the surface of the lake.

These past few days when the old women got together they
had been talking about how the valley used to be good for
gathering silvervines. Masahiko could imagine that these
plants must have some kind of fruit but he knew nothing
about silvervines. This talk, however, seemed to leave the matter of his request for the song dangling. What was it Omomo
was getting at? Falling silent he glanced at her face in profile.

Her eyes made him think of a bird about to take off.

"Since we've been taking time off for O-bon recently, today I'm going to have to go over there."

"Is there a road that goes all the way?"

"Yeah, there is."

An uncomfortable feeling came over him—here's someone with work to do—He realized he was just an idle traveler.

"It looks like you're busy—unlike me. But still, that song I asked you for . . . That was the first time I've ever heard such a song."

"It's a country song so that's not surprising since you're from Tokyo."

"What I meant was the voice. It was the first time I've heard such a voice."

Omomo's eyes blinked and narrowed, sparkling with a light like the scattering of water ripples. A flush of brilliant red spread from her neck to her chin.

"The voice? You mean my voice?"

"Yes, yours, and Ohina's too."

"Really? Her voice used to be even better. I can't sing like my mother."

"Well maybe so, but still I want to ask you both to sing for me."

"Well, I suppose I could sing, if you don't mind my voice, but . . ."

Omomo looked off in the direction of the dam.

"Today my mother will be coming up here after Jimpei's funeral is finished."

"Ah, Ohina-san."

"Right. After the funeral."

"Ah, that's right, today's his funeral."

He remembered how yesterday, when Omomo was carrying Sayuri's ashes, she trudged along through the wind and rain looking back along the pathway through the rice fields. But when Masahiko arrived at the temple following Kappei at the end of the procession, Omomo had already gone.

"You said you were going to gather some ingredients for one of your medicines, didn't you?"

"Yes, for *hyakumeikan*, our 'hundred lives' herbal tablets."

"But didn't Ohina-san hurt her leg?"

"Right, so I'll go with her."

"So you know how to make the medicine too?"

"I can make it, and I have to go out and sell it."

She spoke in a low voice as if talking to herself, but then she drew in her breath and her words became clear.

"The past three days I've been working nonstop with the transient world of the dead, so today I'm not going to sing."

Masahiko realized that she must have thought of him as incredibly childish. He, who couldn't even support himself, was acting as if he knew what life was all about in front of this country girl who lived such a difficult life. He could hardly expect to be accepted into the village. But even so, all that had happened—from the scattering of his grandfather's bones to the events involving Sayuri and Jimpei—it all involved strange ways of dying. Unlike himself, Omomo was a pure Amazoko person. It seemed that what she'd called the "transient world of the dead" was still working within her.

"Hey!"

Suddenly a loud voice sounded from behind. Turning around to look, Masahiko saw Kappei appearing from the shade of the andromeda tree and shortly after him Ohina, limping slightly as she walked.

"That was pretty quick wasn't it? Is the funeral already over?"

"Yeah, it went pretty quick today and they didn't need much help."

Ohina was panting and wiping her neck as she spoke.

"Mother's a bit slow, so I imagine you had to take care of her."

"Nah, I'm always amazed at Ohina's strength. Those old days are gone when no one could beat me climbing these hills."

"What's this nonsense? We both knocked ourselves out today. My feet are killing me. It was just too much. And especially with Kappei I overdid it."

"Hey—enough, all right? I'm no longer the guy they used to call 'Porcupine.' Since those two iron rods went through me I'm only half the man I used to be. I can't lift my feet so well any more."

The four sat down on the grass. Masahiko recalled the scene from the day before when Kappei had left the crematorium after everyone else and grasped at tufts of grass, trembling. Was that the sort of cry they call a "wailing lament"? It was just two days ago that morning that Masahiko had become involved with the people gathered around Sayuri's body when she was pulled up from the lake. At that time, and when he took part in her wake, and even during the funeral procession, Kappei had seemed imposing and openhearted. He wondered if Kappei was always this same sort of man. It seemed that whenever he spoke the older women picked up on it and immediately supported him in taking action. At the crematorium, after all the other people went off into the storm, it was Kappei who stayed on until the end to take care of things. He'd been left sitting on the grass, drenched in rain, exhausted and on the verge of collapse. He had held the last remains of Sayuri—just a handful covered in a small white cloth—tightly in his right hand. For Masahiko the scene would remain unforgettable.

Quietly he made room on his seat on the grass for Kappei and while nodding to him he noticed Kappei's feet. In place of yesterday's formal white *tabi* footwear he was wearing rough workman's *tabi*.

Looking uncomfortable as she sat, Ohina said, "These damn feet have been killing me since yesterday. Looks like I've done them in this time."

"I told you to take it easy today, so it figures they got worse."

"Well it looks like this unsettled state of things is going to continue past O-bon. And I have some orders for medicine."

Kappei spoke out.

"You're talking about medicine for other people, but what about yourself? You need to take care of your own feet before you get into that."

"OK, all right. Say, Omomo, do you have any matches on you?"

"What? Matches? Here, I've got some." As he spoke, Kappei pulled some matches from his pocket. "Thanks. That's good. Omomo, would you burn some mugwort for me?"

Omomo got up and soon started gathering mugwort. Almost simultaneously Kappei got up, collected some dead branches and started a fire by the shore of the lake. Then he began heating the fresh mugwort leaves. Dragging her legs along, Ohina pulled out a flat rock from inside the grass hut and motioned to Masahiko to come over. She asked him to carry it for her. It was the stone from the altar they'd set up for the offerings on the sixteenth night of O-bon. The fragrance from the roasting mugwort leaves drifted about.

"That should be about right now."

Saying this, Ohina placed the now-pliant mugwort leaves on the stone stand. Then Omomo picked up a small stone and beat the leaves rapidly. The mugwort again gave off a pungent fragrance. Kappei pulled out a hand towel and remarked, "OK, it's really hot now."

Omomo quickly rolled up a wad of the mugwort leaves in a hand towel and then wrapped it around her mother's knee and ankle. Breathing heavily, she grinned at Masahiko.

Ohina held out her bandaged knee carefully, as if to assess the effectiveness of the treatment.

"Unh. It feels a little better now. I think it's going to do the trick."

It seemed she had been speaking more to Masahiko than to Kappei. Seeing such layperson's medical treatment for the first time, Masahiko stared almost motionlessly at the proceedings being carried out on the grass.

"It's better than nothing. Once we get back we can put on some of our real medicine."

"Yeah, we can wrap it up again with the medicine, but for now this should be a lot better than nothing. Usually it starts from the back."

"You sell medicines, so you should be able to do your own health checks, right?" Kappei, with his voice returning to that familiar tone, teased Ohina. "If you can't cure your own troubles, how can you be giving out medicine to others?"

Crying out in pain as she extended her knee, Ohina turned toward Omomo.

"Ah, dammit. Looks like I've done it this time. It doesn't want to move."

"Well, didn't I tell you to take the day off today? No wonder it's gotten worse."

To Omomo's remark Kappei replied, "All right, enough. Let's just say this is not the sort of work to be doing on O-bon. When you work at a time like this it's no good."

"OK, but I had an order to fill."

"The people here know you can't work in unsettled times like this."

"Maybe so, but this is different. It's the season now."

"For what?"

"Snakes."

"Ah—for *mamushi*, the poison snakes. Then I'll go get some. I should be able to catch snakes like that."

"But they're most dangerous in the fall."

"I know how dangerous they get."

"But you have to catch them while they're still alive."

"Right—if they're dead when you catch them they're not as effective."

Kappei glanced at Masahiko.

"Well then my young gentleman, may I presume that you will be accompanying me in capturing some autumn *mamushi?*"

Flustered, Masahiko shook his hand in confusion. The other three broke into laughter.

"All right then Ohina-san, but not today. Just put it off for a day or two. To tell the truth, I don't really know how to catch them, and I've never caught them alive. But why don't we go along too—what d'you say, Masahiko?"

It was hard to reply. He'd heard hints about the work Ohina and Omomo did but he'd never heard it discussed directly. So they really caught live poison snakes for a living?

"Do you say some kind of incantation for the snakes, Ohina-san?"

"Sure I do. I put a charm on them. If you're too threatening there's no way you can catch them." Ohina replied gravely, gazing at the surface of the water.

"Maybe that's so. Ohina can look at them in a way that makes them get sleepy and coil up as they fall into a trance."

"It's not my eyes that does it. I sing them a lullaby."

"So it's lullabies you use, is it? Ha—that's great—a lullaby. And they drift off into dreams as Ohina sings to them. They just coil up and doze off into sleep."

"What's this you're talking about? Masahiko-san might take it as the truth."

"It *is* the truth. Look—I'll get her to put me to sleep too. This time it really is true."

For a moment there was silence. Ohina's frowning eyebrows looked like dried moss.

"I had a hunch that if I came up here I'd find Ohina-san and Omomo-chan. I figured I would."

"You know, I dreamed I met Kappei-san up here—right Omomo?"

"Unh. Last night she dreamed she saw Kappei coming here. He was carrying a streamer."

"A streamer?"

"It wasn't any ordinary flag. It was an obi made of bluish-colored embroidered satin. You remember it? The satin obi that was trailing behind Sayuri."

Masahiko looked at Kappei's face in silence. Could this be the same obi he'd seen in his own dream?

"Kappei—you've got to take that obi with you and carry it down from the lake up here. I asked you what you were doing taking care of the funeral all by yourself, but you said it wasn't a funeral. You said you had to take the obi to Oki no Miya and you were looking for the outlet of the waters. And you set up the silver-blue obi as a banner on Susukibara Plain."

Kappei's mouth fell open in astonishment as he tried to figure out what to make of Ohina's words. Then his eyes began to blink rapidly.

"When you set it up she appeared and walked down from Utazaka Hill through the waters, just as easy as can be. She was carrying a Shinto staff with folded white *gohei* papers and telling you, 'Kappei, this way, this way,' and she led you down the waterways that head off toward Oki no Miya. She went on ahead and showed you the way. On, and on, all the way down. She slipped past the mouth of the stalactite cave and in no time she arrived at the sea of Oki no Miya. Already the tide was rising."

His face dripping wet, Kappei spoke in a husky voice.

"And wasn't Sayuri-san there?"

"No, I couldn't see her."

". . . So Omomo-chan took me there in the dream?"

"I was worried about Kappei."

"Well . . . thanks."

In these people's world it seemed there were no distinctions between dreams and reality. And I dreamed of a water-colored obi too—that dream of the fire and the girl from somewhere. He was about to speak of it but the words didn't come out.

The obi was the one that had been brought up from the lake—the one wrapped around Sayuri's body. Ohina had received it with the elder priest's wife serving as a witness, and they had hung it on the *sal* tree by Ohina's house. At that time when Ohina asked her the wife had frowned at her.

"What do you think we should do with the obi that the person who died was wearing? Do you think it's right to just burn it? We can't just forget about it, can we?"

"Well, actually, Oai-sama talked about making Omomo the next successor."

"Successor to Sayuri?"

"Yes, Sayuri's successor. And in order to carry out the ceremony for the succession that obi is necessary. That piece of material has special meaning."

"Special? How's that?"

"Because they say that when Sayuri's mother died she was wearing that same material wrapped around her belly."

"Well if that's the case then I suppose it must have meaning. Look—this material, it's the finest quality."

"Oai-sama said Sayuri's mother might have come from the upper Mimigawa River."

"It seems the mother must have had some pretty strong reasons, and so with the baby in her womb she wrapped the precious material around her and left home. Oai-sama said she must have been from a good family, judging from her speech and the clothes she was wearing."

Seeing the way Ohina was so absorbed in her thoughts, the elder priest's wife realized that she wasn't likely to give up such ideas easily.

"Well it seems rather strange to me, but I suppose Sayuri-san and her mother have a special connection to your family, so you'll have to do what you think is best. It's not for me to tell you what to do."

With this sort of talk going on, Ohina had spoken briefly about how the obi had come to her and Omomo.

Would Omomo become the successor to Sayuri?

"Sayuri was such a beautiful dancer . . ."

From amidst the bushes, a bird called out in a plaintive voice.

"Omomo can't compete with Sayuri in looks, but she can still sing the sacred songs. Omomo, you shouldn't sing those popular songs so much. It's no good for your voice."

Omomo glanced at her mother but made no reply.

"We need to decide on the day for the conferring of the obi. We're not going to send out announcements to everyone. Kappei, I want you to be there."

Feeling drawn into it, Kappei nodded. Lowering her voice a bit, Ohina asked with a note of reserve, "Masahiko-san, do you think you could still be here at that time?"

"Well, I guess so."

Having spoken abruptly, his voice caught in his throat. Then he spoke again, more positively.

"Please let me be there."

Besides, he had just asked Omomo to sing. He wondered if Omomo and Ohina would both sing. Ohina's mentioning of

Omomo singing popular songs seemed to refer to her difficult character.

"A ceremony for the obi? So Omomo-chan is going to take over for Sayuri, is she?"

"Unless she takes over, the voices of Oki no Miya will disappear. After all, the village is under the water."

"Hmm . . . Amazoko is in my dreams."

"I'd like to invite the people who are the most closely related."

"The most related . . ?"

With his head bowed forward it looked as if it had become difficult for Kappei to speak.

"Your relationship is different, isn't it?"

Ohina's deep voice took on a husky tone, as if it were touching Kappei's bowed head.

"Yeah . . . my relation is rather different from that of most people . . . That night I heard a horse cry out."

Kappei picked one of the red *manma* flowers that were blooming in the space between his legs and placed it in the big palm of his hand. It looked to Masahiko like one of the little wildflowers he'd come across in Tetsugakudo Park, where his father liked to walk. But in contrast to the flowers and plants in the city, the flowers Kappei held in his palm were marked conspicuously with deep red colors. He opened and closed his palm around them as if looking after something of great importance. Ohina asked him again, "A horse?—You mean Jimpei's?"

"I suppose so. There's no one else in Amazoko who has a horse any more."

"Where'd you hear it?"

"Near the valley of vines."

"That's the place everyone's been saying Sayuri jumped off the cliff."

"I'd have to guess the same thing myself. It was just about the right time and the horse's voice was different from usual. It gave me an uneasy feeling."

"Were you alone when you heard it?"

"No, I was out with old Heisuke-san."

"Well . . . that's good. If it were just one person, there'd be more doubt about it. But what in the world were you doing out there at that time of night?"

"Well, it was a moonlight night during O-bon and he asked me to go along to pay respects to the graves at the bottom of the lake."

"What?"

With a deep sigh Ohina looked at Omomo and Masahiko, one by one.

"That was the same time when we were scattering Masahito's ashes here by Utazaka Hill."

Omomo, apparently thinking things over deeply, opened her mouth and spoke.

"If it had been in the daytime we'd have been able to see you, even on the far bank."

"Right. When we looked over there on the far shore we saw two or three lanterns flickering. That must've been you."

After a while, Kappei continued.

"And so I asked him, 'Did you hear that? Did you hear? It sounds like Jimpei's horse.' I said that, all right. But it was strange for a horse to be out there that night at the peak of O-bon. I thought it might be a spirit. Perhaps a spirit was imitating the sound of Jimpei's horse. I thought we should go back quickly and take a look. I was afraid it might mean that someone had just died. And then when we got to the embankment we saw the flames from Jimpei's house and heard people shouting. Actually, at that time I wasn't able to talk about it to the old man, but I could see Sayuri there, walking along the surface of the water."

"On the surface of the water? Sayuri?" Omomo asked in response.

"And it was no ghost. I could see the back of a girl with her obi hanging down, walking along just below me on the surface of the water. I saw it as clearly as in midday. And I could clearly see the color and pattern of her obi."

"You saw her from behind?"

"Right, from behind. I called out to the old man, 'Look! Look!—Over there.' And then in an instant it disappeared."

From this point, Kappei's voice suddenly changed.

"I . . . I was thinking of killing Jimpei."

The three cast their eyes on this man. The tip of the bunch of red *manma* flowers sticking out from his hand was shaking.

"I guess that, since I was just wasting time, Sayuri went ahead and set the fire and then took that horse she was so fond of. Not wanting to part with it, she must have gone with it to the top of the valley of vines."

No one asked the question of why she would have set the fire. Certainly Ohina and Omomo knew why they didn't want to discuss it.

"He thought she couldn't speak. That guy Jimpei . . . Ohina-san—I didn't want to go to his funeral."

Masahiko looked straight at Kappei's pained-looking face. Ohina nodded time after time, her eyes opening and shutting. Each time she moved her care-stained eyelids the black line of her eyelashes opened and closed like the lid of a pot, and each time they opened, tears streamed out. Omomo's eyes showed no resemblance to her mother's.

"Sayuri-san took things upon herself, and she finished them by herself."

Omomo stared at her mother and Kappei, and then gently drew her hand up to her nose and smelled it. Her fingertips were stained a tea-green color. It must have come from preparing and roasting the mugwort to get rid of the bad spirits. She repeated this motion two or three times. Masahiko thought that this too must have been done to drive off the bad spirits, but it wasn't something he felt like asking about. The parts of her fingers that hadn't been stained by the mugwort showed a fresh sheen. Looking at her face, he saw that her eyes had a sleepy look and he couldn't tell what they were focusing on. Rays of light swirled up from the surface of the water and played about Ohina's face and on Omomo's chest.

Probably the wind was blowing about in some distant place. How painful it must have been for Sayuri, who couldn't speak, to have to take care of all those things, all alone, all by herself. He thought about the whole train of events—her setting the fire that burned down the big house and stable of this newly rich family and killed its master and drove his wife insane and caused her to be sent to a mental institution—and how all this had driven Sayuri to throw away her own life. And now the person who was to become the successor to this shrine maiden, this woman with a mysterious background, was here. Would it be better if he escaped from them now? The idea occurred to him and played about in his mind. Yet on the night Sayuri died, the voices of Ohina and Omomo had seemed to Masahiko the very finest of human voices. They sounded as if they had sprung from the farthest reaches of the world, crept up among all kinds of things and emerged as limpid sounds. As he watched the whirlpools of light reflecting on Omomo's fingers, he knew in his heart that he had to do whatever he could to get them to sing that song one more time. Suddenly, he spoke.

"I, . . . I'm going to be at Omomo's ceremony for receiving the obi. You can be sure of that."

Twenty days passed, and Ohina stopped by the temple. She was still limping a bit. She repeated the invitation to be present at Utazaka Hill on the night of the autumn equinox to take part in "the aforementioned matter," and then she returned home. Before long the older priest's wife came in with a frown on her face.

"It seems you received an invitation from Ohina-san, didn't you?"

"Yes."

"Well, I must say, it seems Ohina and Omomo have been acting rather different from usual. That talk about succeeding to Sayuri-san's work. What's that all about?"

As he wondered how to reply, the woman continued to speak. "She even asked me to be there too, even though it's the autumn equinox, one of the most important days for the temple."

"Yes, but she said the ceremony would take place at night."

"Well, I might have some free time at night, but my husband—what would he say? He'd be very upset."

Which implied, as Masahiko interpreted it, that she was hinting that he too shouldn't go.

"Actually, I want to study Ohina's songs and I've asked her to sing for me, so I really would like to go."

"Songs? Ohina's? Well that's a rather unusual sort of research, isn't it?"

For a moment there was silence, but it seemed he might have persuaded her.

"Well if that's the case, it's true that Ohina has performed songs to call for the rains, but . . ."

As she nodded she looked back and forth between this young man who had been staying at the temple and his musical instrument. The whole family had been discussing this topic. He played well enough, but the pieces he chose were hard to appreciate. The younger wife and her mother in law took turns in listening to him as he tuned his *biwa*.

"That's a rather unusual sort of piece—it's one I'm not accustomed to hearing."

"Well, it's not finished yet."

Sensing they must have been disturbing him they withdrew from his room with tense smiles and looks of apology. Starting to feel uncomfortable under the pressure put on him by these two innocent women, he wondered how long he might be able to remain at the temple in good favor. Completely unaware of Masahiko's thoughts, the older wife quickly went on to ask him about the ceremony.

"So then, at this ceremony for the succession is Ohina-san going to sing?"

"Well, I'm not sure about it yet. But if she did sing and I weren't there . . . That's the start of my study."

He had stressed that he was going to carry out a study—and that, in fact, was no lie.

"Well I must say, I've never heard of such a ceremony until now; a ceremony for conferring an obi."

Entering the living room in the morning, the elderly priest offered an apology.

"I'm afraid these women here must have been bothering you. I tell them not to chatter, but we're just country folks here so they're curious. I try not to let them into your room too often."

Masahiko felt embarrassed.

"But these days it seems traditional Japanese music is going through some major changes—at least it does to our untrained ears. The *shakuhachi* and the *koto* as well. What we're familiar with is only the old style of music, you know. It seems to me that what you're playing is something that is, what should I say, far beyond that."

Sipping away leisurely at his tea, the elderly priest went on expressing his thoughts about Masahiko's music. Masahiko felt his face reddening. It seemed that some time ago when the younger priest had gone off to Hitoyoshi and Kumamoto he had tried to find the CDs of some Japanese musicians. In the process apparently he had listened to quite a lot of music. Then the younger wife spoke out, facing her husband.

"It seems Masahiko must represent the vanguard of modern music composition."

"The vanguard, you say? Well, you seem to be quite up on these things."

The young priest's teasing had been intended as a rebuke but it produced no effect.

"Think of the recent styles of calligraphy for instance. Even though most people can't read it, the artists get high recognition, don't they?"

"But that's different from my case—I'm just not good yet."

There was a burst of laughter at Masahiko's flustered reply, but from hearing the conversation at the breakfast table he realized that the crude, unrefined sounds of his *biwa* must not have suited the musical tastes of these people.

Apparently sensing it was a good time to speak out, the older priest's wife broke into the discussion, pointing at her husband.

"My husband, you know, he tells me I shouldn't be going to the obi ceremony for Omomo-chan."

As if caught off guard, the elder priest sat up straight and replied.

"My telling her not to go was not without reason, you know. In the first place, to go right in the middle of the equinox week would be inexcusable. The wife of a priest has all sorts of responsibilities toward the temple during this time."

"But it will be at night. The people will all have gone home by that time."

"Maybe so, but even at night someone might arrive from far off. It would be irresponsible."

"That time when Ohina sang the prayer songs for rain, I couldn't go. You told me that the duty of a priest's wife was to take care of the affairs of the temple and that I shouldn't be going off to such a thing as a ceremony to pray for rain. And so I didn't go. People talked about Sayuri's dancing, but I also heard that Ohina's singing was wonderful. They say that when the rains came, everyone there on the top of the mountain wiped away their tears. I was the only one that time who was left out and I felt bad about it."

"You, your interest shifts from one thing to another, like to that sort of thing, and you lack a sense of responsibility to your duties here at this temple. There would have been no point in your going up the mountain with all the others. At that time we welcomed everyone to the temple and we carried out prayers for the rain ceremony, didn't we? And you served *shochu*, didn't you?"

"Yes, that's so."

"So it's no good for you to be running off this time either. I don't know what all this business about an obi succession is about, but we will have people here for the *higan* dinner, according to the ways of this temple. During the equinox week it's your responsibility to be here in the temple."

"Yes, but Ohina-san is going to do something, isn't she? Probably she's going to sing. When there's something that needs doing, that woman gets a power from the divine."

"And so for that reason too we can have her sing right here in this temple."

"No, that wouldn't do. Even if she sang here at the temple, the song would be completely different from what it would be up on the mountain."

"Oh come on now. There are plenty of good songs in the Buddhist hymns of praise too. If you'd only put a little effort into practicing them once in a while."

"My voice isn't suitable for either the chants or the hymns of praise."

Karehito's eyes conveyed an embarrassed smile.

"In this obi ceremony—the obi will be Sayuri-san's. If it were a ceremony to celebrate a young girl then I'd understand, but I've never heard of anything like this before. How are they going to do it? I wonder who she's told about this."

The older priest's wife turned toward Masahiko. "I suppose the invitation for me was only a formality. Ohina-san must have known I'd be busy here at the temple with the *Higan* equinox duties. I guess she was really bringing the invitation just for you but she mentioned it to me just to avoid seeming impolite. So please, you go, and don't worry about what's going on here at the temple."

Karehito, the younger priest broke in. "She's right. These people tell stories about the old days of Amazoko Village. They can only go back there in their dreams. Actually I envy them, having a place they can return to in their dreams."

"What's this talk now? Since the old times this temple right here has been the place they can return to at any time. This temple has become the gate of return for the spirits of the people of this village."

"All right Father, perhaps that's true, but this temple may be too confining when you compare it to the world in their hearts."

"What do you mean—too confining? Why do you think we talk of the vast, the infinite, and the unbounded in Buddhism?"

"All right, we talk about those things. But still it seems confining. Sure we learn about the vast, the infinite, the unbounded, and all, but here we're living in the security of the temple, satisfied with ourselves and putting ourselves above the people who have to sweat to earn a living."

The elderly priest's face changed color.

"What are you talking about?"

"I've been thinking about this for a long time, you know. I was born here in this temple too. Don't you think we may have, unconsciously, become too puffed up about ourselves?"

"People are naturally endowed with dignity. That's the way I've taught you in bringing you up."

"All right, and I appreciate that. I agree with you there—about dignity, that is. For example, Ohina-san, whom we were talking about—what do you say about that power of hers? They say she makes a living off poison snakes and herbal medicines and such. She may look roughly dressed, and the other day she was limping along, but still it seems to me that her existence is somehow more profound."

"Ohina?—Why, we don't even know her lineage or family background."

"*Lineage?*—what do you think that is? Thanks to you, I suppose, by being born as the successor to this temple I'm considered to have some sort of good "lineage"—so-called. But what do I know of real human suffering? Sure, I've been to some other temples, and tried to follow the religious teachings, but there are plenty of things I'm ashamed of.

"Religion is supposed to help people deal with suffering, isn't it? Even though people who have been through all the pains of life are coming here, we at the temple, who don't know anything about such things, behave as if we were superior beings."

Masahiko could see that the elderly priest's wife was becoming quite agitated about the discussion. She looked at her husband and then at her son and then toward Masahiko as if asking for help.

"I do place importance on relationships with people associated with the temple, but I feel totally disgusted thinking that the temple people, including myself, are so insensitive. The people who come here to help with the cooking and weeding—it seems to me that they're living better lives."

"So what are you trying to do? Ruin this temple?"

The son remained silent for a while, gazing at his father and mother before he spoke. "Sure there are times I feel that way. But the believers here aren't going to ruin this place. Those people's hearts are far more infinite and unbounded than any theory or doctrine. Theirs is a true faith in the infinite and unbounded. The fact is, this temple has always been cared for by them, free of charge to us. They've given us their contributions and donated things. We have to be grateful for all this—don't you think Masahiko?" The young priest Karehito smiled, showing a row of white teeth. The elder priest seemed to wince at his son's words, and remained silent.

"Until recently I hadn't heard any of the stories about Oai-san being brought up as a baby by the Lord of Amazoko, who can change into a snake. It all sounds like, what should I say?—mythology—hearing the stories of Masahiko's great-great-grandmother picking up that old woman and raising her. But isn't this what lineage is about, Father? Lineage is about a person's depth as a human being, isn't it? It seems we, here at the temple, are just leading shallow lives. We're satisfied by getting superficial respect but we don't make efforts to get to know the hard lives these people lead."

"Don't try to tell me we don't know about that." And in saying this, the elder priest twitched his eyebrows and closed his eyes.

"All right—sure we may know the headings in the Buddhist encyclopedias and such, but if you take one day in the life of, say, Kappei-san, or even Omomo-chan, how can you imagine what sort of things they're going through in their world, both physically and spiritually? We're always sitting here high and mighty, taking their generosity, while they're out struggling just to make ends meet. Isn't that because we're cloaked in authority? It scares me to think that, living in a little hut like that, unless they can catch a poison snake alive they may not have anything to eat the next day. Yet she doesn't look debased by it and she's always cheerful. Don't you think so, Masahiko?"

As he nodded in reply, it seemed to Masahiko that the shaded eyes of this young priest, though older than he, held more appeal than usual.

"The Amazoko village that exists in their dreams, sealed off at the bottom of the lake—what I envy in its people who can go back there is that even though their world has been flooded, its essence remains firmly preserved and it's been entirely incorporated into their being. Their memories of the way things looked, and their meetings with people, and the sounds of creation they hear in the ears of their souls—this must be very different from what we know. In comparison, it seems we hardly have a grasp on the world at all. Our knowledge and consciousness seem vapid, empty."

"That's how I feel too. It's like I don't have a world I can hold on to. I don't really have any knowledge of the world at all."

"But Masahiko-san, your coming here has been very important to us and I'm grateful to you for it. Your special sound in playing the *biwa*—it's like your fingers are sort of groping along the strings—it reminds me of that old blind musician Mizumaro."

"Mizumaro-san? I remember my grandfather used to talk about him."

"What? Your grandfather told you about Mizumaro?"

The elderly priest's wife sighed, as if relieved that the conversation was finally calming down a bit.

"Well, my grandfather said a famous blind musician Mizumaro told him the *biwa*'s strings are always waiting to make sounds."

"Did he hear him in person?"

"Yes, and he said that whenever Mizumaro came over Moonshadow Bridge he played a greeting on the *biwa* and the villagers rushed out to greet him. It was while my grandfather was still young, but I hear Mizumaro-san would stay at his house for a month at a time and sometimes he went out around the town. The story became a legend."

The elderly priest broke into the conversation in a low voice, as if released from a proscription on speaking. "It's not just a story. I heard about it from my parents too. A generation back, people used to talk about how he used to come and play at the temple in the autumn during *Higan* —isn't that so?" He passed the conversation to his wife.

"Well yes, that's right. I heard about it many times right here in the tea room from the former priest's wife. She had a long life. Whenever the blind musician Mizumaro came, everyone would rush to the temple. I hear that they'd fill up the prayer hall and there'd be people seated outside on bamboo mats as well."

"I hear they even came from other villages too."

"Right. And when there wasn't enough of the ceremonial food to go around it was a big problem. The women had to heat up more rice, and with their wanting to listen to the *biwa* they might get distracted, so even the limited rice they'd prepared sometimes got burned in the pot. But even with charred rice, they'd make it into rice balls and everyone would eat it all and there'd be nothing left."

The wife continued on cheerfully, "He must have been quite some player, that Mizumaro. Since I came here when I got married I've never once seen the temple filled that way. It's hard to even imagine now. And it hasn't happened since I've been here either. And now Amazoko's been lost to the dam too."

In the midst of this pleasant family discussion Masahiko's mind turned to imagining. He wondered if he might write a piece of music that could recapture the feelings of those times with all those piles of charred rice balls. He could use the gongs and bells of the religious services as well.

Thanks to the generosity of his ancestors and kindness of the priest's family he'd been able to depend on the temple for food and shelter, but he wondered if the day would ever come when he could realize his dream. It was too much to speak of himself as being at the vanguard of the music world since, at least so far, sounds weren't flowing within him. The words of the young priest suggested that he might have sensed how Masahiko was feeling.

"Getting back to what we were talking about before, it seems that what you're trying to create with the sounds of your music is a pathway that might pull us back to that world beneath the water. But so far it seems you haven't found it. In Buddhism we often use the word *mumyô*, which means 'spiritual darkness.' It's in the depths of such darkness, more than in the brightness of light, that hints and signs begin to come to us, like water bubbling its way up. I don't know much about music, but when I listen, it's as if a spring also bubbles within me and brings premonitions of being taken into that world. I hope you won't hesitate to stay here and work as long as you need to bring these things out. It's certainly our great pleasure to have you with us."

5

SECRET SONG

On a day filled with the calling of shrikes, it felt as if the sky was deepening. Masahiko too noticed the hints of autumn in the light of the sun. As the shadows grew softer on the ground beneath the trees and grasses, one morning he noticed a small patch of brilliant crimson amid the grasses. Coming closer for a better look, he found it was the reddening leaves of a plant whose name he didn't know. The leaves were just over an inch long, similar in shape to soybean pods and turning shades of red.

Poking out here and there from the ground beside this plant were bunches of three or four pale green stems capped with tea-green crowns. Surprised to see such fresh sprouts coming up in autumn, he observed them each morning and saw the stems gaining height very quickly. Noticing that their green tips were turning reddish, he finally realized that these were actually flower buds. The stems stood out as solitary spikes until one morning they burst out into crowns of brilliant crimson flowers.

While he was bent over looking at them, the elder priest's wife called out from the porch.

"They always amaze me. Even if I've forgotten them, the *higan* lilies always come into bloom just at this time and help me prepare for the *higan* ceremonies at the autumn equinox. At the peak of the season the pathway to the crematory is all lit up with them."

In his college days in the mountain climbing club Masahiko had had a passing interest in alpine plants, but now in coming here he realized that the villagers read the changes of the seasons through the plants and that these occasions served as important turning points in their lives. Looking at the world afresh through their eyes he could see how the mountains about him had taken on a completely different aspect—as if from deep within the earth a workshop of the seasons had brought about all these changes.

The wife, apparently annoyed at the cat entering Masahiko's room, busied herself with chasing it away. She seemed relieved to have it out of sight for the day. Masahiko could tell her mood from her tone of voice.

"You know, we got some nice *Castella* cake from Nagasaki. I'll leave some here for you."

Turning around and lowering her head she went on expressing her thoughts.

"If you don't eat it soon that cat will start licking it. That's its bad character."

He thought it strange that she'd seemed unable to just tell him not to let the cat in.

Off in the kitchen, the women who had come to help were busily engaged in washing vegetables and chatting. It looked like the preparations for the *higan* festival were getting under way.

That afternoon, Ohina brought in some wild *matsutake* and *shimeji* mushrooms, as well as liquors made from silvervine and wild strawberries. Although she said it was for the *higan* offerings, it seemed she did it more in asking for memorial prayers for Sayuri, who had no relatives. As if just in passing, she looked into Masahiko's room and called out a greeting in a low voice, saying she'd be waiting for him at the "appointed event" for Omomo.

That evening when Masahiko was called into the living room, Ohina's offerings were placed right in the front and the elder priest was in good spirits.

"Well, well, these certainly are magnificent first products of the season. Such good full aromas. Masahiko-san, you can't get these kinds of things in the city, you know. And when it comes to finding things like these, no one can beat that woman."

"That's certainly the truth—why the mushrooms just send their smells straight to that woman. She always gets the best pickings of *matsutake*."

Her tone of voice lowering as she spoke, the elder priest's wife picked up the mushrooms, leaving some decaying leaves stuck to her fingertips. As the family handled the mushrooms they considered the various ways they might cook them. Finally they decided that roasting them on a grill would be best and so they prepared to make a fire under the big hibachi grill.

"It feels like we're getting ready to do the first tea ceremony of the year."

Tucking up the sleeves of his robes, Karehito called out to his wife.

"I'll take care of getting the straw and getting the fire going, but would you wipe off the hibachi for me?"

Masahiko too was asked to join in.

"Shall we do the cooking out there in the garden? I'd really prefer using this year's straw, but with the rain and wind recently most of the rice has been knocked down and we're late in getting straw. This here is last year's."

Saying this, he pulled out some straw bundles from the back of the shed, carried them to the garden and began lighting a fire.

"What's the difference between last year's straw and this year's?"

"Well, their smells and colors are different."

But this explanation hardly allowed Masahiko to distinguish them on his own.

"For cooking on a hearth or a hibachi, straw gives you the best ashes. The fire lasts better too."

He lit a fire, but it seemed to take a surprisingly long time to burn a bundle of straw down to coals. It burned and burned, yet still it took a long time to build up a small amount of ash. A bundle would catch on fire in a burst of flames and then become a blackened bunch of fibers. Finally the flames reached the embers of the bundle without going out and turned them into white coals. Seeing straw burning like this for the first time, it struck Masahiko that this changing of plants into ashes gave him a feeling of cleanness.

Masahiko thought back on the greenish stalks that had been thrashed about so much by the wind and rains in the rice fields on the way back from Sayuri's funeral. If he held a stalk of the rice in his hand it seemed such an abundance of growth. If he burned it, it seemed to change into such a small thing.

"Let's hold off on the old straw. This will give us a good base. Let's add some ashes from the new straw on top now."

Masahiko could readily understand the excitement in getting out the hibachi, but it wasn't until he saw the colors of the coals from the new straw that he understood the young priest's words, said in joking, about a "first tea ceremony of the year." The pungent fragrance that rose from the *matsutake* mushrooms roasting directly over the fire put the whole temple household in festive spirits.

Ohina's wild mountain liquor also helped put Masahiko's body—unaccustomed as it was to the powers of alcohol—in a blissful state, leaving his spirits floating about in pleasant inebriation.

"This is some fine liquor we've got here. They tell us we're not allowed to take fine liquor through the mountain gate of a temple, but doesn't the liquor get sweeter when it passes through the gate? Isn't that right Karehito—no, I mean Masahiko-san?"

As he spoke, the elder priest's face showed signs of his drinking. His wife was starting to get annoyed at the proceedings.

"There you go talking about the same old things again. Can't you move on to something else?"

"Now what d'you mean?—why, these are the highest sorts of matters we're discussing, and certainly the young people ought to know about these things too—isn't that right, Masahito?"

Of late, on a number of occasions the elderly priest had mixed up the names Masahiko and Masahito. His wife apologized.

"I'm sorry. He knew your grandfather. He often mixes up the two of you."

Masahiko felt perched on the borders of illusion.

"You can call me Masahito too. Masahito used to say the liquor from the mulberries of the old estate was sweet too."

"Oh, so you know about that too. The mulberry liquor was sweet . . . Well . . ."

Ignoring her husband, whose body was now swaying back and forth, she asked Masahiko,

"I suppose you'll be going to see Omomo on that day?"

"I'll be going. It's on the night of the *higan* festival."

Masahiko replied without hesitation and the elder priest caught his words.

"Omomo? Why, that girl has a wild character, I tell you."

"Oh hold your tongue, will you? She's going to be succeeding to Sayuri's responsibilities."

"So what's all this business about a succession? I'm telling you, you shouldn't go."

"How can you talk like that now? This whole feast we're having here—the *matsutake*, the liquor, and all—Ohina brought all these things to us."

"Oh, so this is Ohina's liquor, is it? Well, no wonder it packs such a punch." Karehito shook with laughter.

When Ohina had finished paying her respects to Amida Buddha on the day of the equinox she set off into the mountains before anyone else. Seeing her off, Karehito pulled out a flashlight from the sleeves of his black robe.

"I just changed the batteries. The moon will probably be out, but in the mountains it gets pretty dark under foot so you'd better do your climbing while it's still light."

His wife brought out a heavy handbag wrapped in a cloth.

"This is for everyone up on the mountain. It's a little something to eat when you're making your devotions."

"Actually, I'd like to go up there myself and see what's going on. It seems something new is going to happen."

In saying this, Karehito moved closer to Masahiko and continued in a low voice, as if whispering.

"To tell the truth, I heard Ohina's prayer songs that time of the drought—though I didn't let my parents know. When my father found out he turned pale. I'm afraid our chanting the sutras won't compete with it."

Every time he walked along the paths Masahiko found himself immersed in the fragrances of the mountains. He felt himself harmonizing with everything around him. The temple was filled with the activities of Buddhism and so when the reciting of the sutras began he would strap his *biwa* on his back and head for the banks of the lake by the dam. He didn't want to disturb the sutra recitations, and also he wanted to hear his own sounds purely. On the top of the mountain, however, he felt a painful awareness of the gap that remained between the powerful kinds of sounds he imagined in his thoughts and the actual sounds that came out when he plucked with the plectrum on the strings of the *biwa*. He realized that the strings were still not singing with their own voices.

Sometimes as he walked along the mountain paths he met people from the village. Some would call out greetings by making a gesture of playing an imaginary *biwa* and asking him, "How's the practicing going?" It made him feel self-conscious. Thinking over such things he arrived at his usual spot.

He looked around, seeking hints of the events to come that night. The roof and walls of the grass hut—the same one he'd helped the two women build that first day according to their instructions—had been fixed up. As the days had passed its thatched roof and reed walls had dried out and so now they had been completely replaced. It was clear that Ohina and Omomo had been preparing things for the events to take place that night. "At that place we were before," was all that Ohina had said.

He came to a stop. A fragrant smell floated in the air. Looking closely at the space between the walls and roof he noticed a faint, hazy smoke drifting about. He guessed Ohina or Omomo must be inside. It was unlikely that any one else would have repaired the hut and been inside at this time. The door of the hut was closed. He reversed his steps and backed away quietly. It seemed that this area in front of him was not a space he should intrude upon.

Judging from the burning incense he supposed they must be saying prayers. He decided to conceal himself in a thicket not too far away where he could keep the hut in sight. The colors of small flower petals danced about before his eyes. The thicket was filled with bush clover. The colors of the flowers were considerably brighter than those that grew around the temple. They grew in bunches here and there, composed of branches and flowers that were remarkably longer and larger, and whose energies were delicately entwined. Creeping forward and looking at the small flowers scattered about, Masahiko felt strangely as if he'd been changed into a fox. The sun had already begun to settle into the tops of the mountains. The sky was tinged with the first shades of autumn madders. Faint ripples colored by the sky spread across the surface of the water around the dam, gradually changing to a golden hue as if they held flames within. He focused his eyes on what lay below the water's surface. The shadows of fish flitted about like the scattering of willow leaves. While watching these fish shadows Masahiko saw a clear reflection in the water of his dream from the night he spent in the grass hut.

He saw an old tree silently going up in flames. At first there was an old house burning somewhere off in the countryside, but that scene shifted into the background and a tree with blackened leaves dancing about above the flames came into focus. The sight of the burning tree conveyed a deep solemnity. Then, by the side of the tree, a young girl appeared. Her back was turned toward him. In his dream it had seemed to Masahiko that the girl and the tree engulfed in flames were thoroughly bound together. An elderly man approached and as his white-haired topknot was blown about by the fire he spoke repeatedly to the girl and pulled her by the hand. The girl resisted strongly and before long broke away, turning around as she went. Then she slipped beneath a flame-colored stand of trees and disappeared into the river plain amidst the faint light of the water, surrounded in darkness. As she was moving away from the burning tree a silverish, celadon-blue obi hung down from her back.

He would never forget his impressions of that obi—it seemed to him that it was identical to the one that had risen from the water while wrapped around Sayuri's body. And now he'd heard that Omomo was going to wear this same one tonight. These thoughts made his heart beat restlessly. And on that day she'd risen from the bottom of the lake through the weeds and algae when the sun went behind the clouds the wet obi had given off a faint light. And even to Masahiko, who knew nothing at all about fabric, the sight had suggested that the obi must somehow have a special significance and history behind it. Somehow he had also come to understand the apprehensive feelings of the head priest's wife regarding the obi.

He had no way of knowing whether the obi of the girl in his dream and the one Sayuri had been wearing were truly the same or not. Certainly there was something poignant about the thought of people returning in dreams to a village that had sunken to the bottom of a lake. Nevertheless, he felt unable to tell Ohina and Omomo or the family at the temple about his strange dream. In the depths of that turbid water around the dam that single aged tree was burning silently. Who could that girl he'd seen from behind have been?

Could it be that my dream too has been sealed off at the bottom of the lake? If he spoke about this sort of thing to Kappei, no doubt Kappei would pat him on the back and say, "Well that just goes to show that you're one of us Amazoko folks after all, doesn't it." And so he felt he couldn't talk about this to Kappei either.

Something white passed by at the extremities of his vision. Shifting his gaze he realized that it was Omomo, standing on the shore not very far from him. She had a pure white cloth wrapped about her breasts, leaving her shoulders exposed. She was about to enter the water. Masahiko watched the reflected figure of her body. The thickets of bush clover provided sufficient cover to keep him hidden from sight. Ohina, standing by the banks of the lake, was gracefully putting on a white robe. Neither of the women was aware of Masahiko's approach.

Even though he felt he shouldn't be watching, the expressions on the faces of the two women were visible amidst the rows of thin stems and small flowers. It made a striking scene. The faces of both Omomo and Ohina were entirely different from those of any women he'd ever seen before. Catching a glimpse of the expression on the women opening their eyes slowly, Masahiko felt a shock that struck him directly in the middle of his forehead. Or perhaps it would be more accurate to say that the impression struck him gradually, over time and afterwards.

The expression he saw on the two women possessed a modesty he had never before encountered on a human face. With her long hair trailing down behind, Omomo's face appeared a bit gaunt but it looked like a face that, after having lived in this world, had found its way to a place of exalted spirits. She looked serious, but opened her eyes halfway, as if in a dream, and swayed slightly as she stood for a while in the water. Then she advanced until the water reached her knees. Masahiko stood perfectly still, imagining she must be performing a Shinto *misogi* purification rite.

Then Omomo released her arms, which had been folded over her breasts and, with a somewhat languorous expression, raised them above her shoulders. It all seemed like part of a very slow dance. Her long hair that had been combed in back now trailed down in front of her face. Then she bent over and, as if brushing the water with her fingertips, began washing her hair. Captivated, Masahiko watched the young woman wash her hair in the water of the lake. Omomo looked utterly different from the country girl dressed in a red T-shirt he'd seen in this same place on the sixteenth day of O-bon.

In the distance by the edge of the lake three white cranes were dancing about. Omomo rinsed her hair carefully, repeating the motions over and over again. When she was finished she held up her wet hair in one hand and turned toward her mother. She covered her body in a dry white cloth that Ohina handed her and then slipped off the wet white cloth beneath to let it fall into the water. Ohina moved around behind her daughter, brought out a wooden comb and began combing her hair.

Ohina looked like a lady in waiting. Her face expressed both sadness and grief, yet it differed so completely from what was typical of the times that it gave the impression the women were taking part in an ancient ceremony. It seemed to Masahiko that Ohina, standing in the evening on the bank of the lake, might be an intermediary for the gods.

Masahiko felt as if he had slipped back into the times of long ago and that his thoughts, which had been so bound up, had unraveled and expanded. Thinking about it later, he imagined that this might have been brought on by seeing Ohina with the wooden comb in her mouth. Certainly she had been carrying out a ritual, and the comb may have been a ceremonial object that signaled its beginning.

Standing in the water behind her daughter after finishing the combing, with one hand Ohina grasped Omomo's hair and with the other she placed the comb in her mouth. The comb was shaped like a three-day moon. Then, for some reason, slowly she turned toward Masahiko's direction. Since he was well hidden behind the clumps of bush clover there was no reason to suspect he could be seen, yet for a moment he was startled. Although Masahiko imagined he was out of Ohina's line of sight, and although the expression on her face holding the comb in her mouth seemed serene and gentle, somehow it created a sense of apprehension. Soon Ohina turned back in the direction of her daughter. Then she pulled a small towel from the front of her kimono, unfolded it and began drying Omomo's wet hair, continuing until she was satisfied that it was mostly dry.

In watching Ohina's actions he had wondered why she was carrying a string of long grasses hanging from the obi at her waist. But when she finished drying Omomo's hair and put the towel back into the front of her kimono she pulled the long grasses from her obi and set them in the water to soak. Then she gathered up the grasses with both hands, twined them around Omomo's head and after checking for size she tied them together from behind as if making a headband.

Even though he was watching the space between the white robes of Ohina and Omomo from a distance he could see that Omomo's hair had dried considerably and it was now waving softly. Ohina took the comb she had been holding in her mouth and, urging her daughter along, passed it to Omomo over her shoulder. Omomo nodded slightly and held the wooden comb above her head. She looked at it for a moment, and then with her other hand she groped about for the grass hair band. When she located it she gazed into the water. Masahiko could tell that she was looking at herself in the mirror of the water. As her head moved slightly, the colors of the water played upon the thin grass hair band she was holding back with her finger. The women were exchanging some brief words but he couldn't make them out.

Omomo's graceful arm moved slowly and, for added effect, she placed the wooden comb in the crown of her hair, entwined with the band of grasses. Then with her other arm she took the hair that was trailing down along her back and pulled it around to her front. She combed out her hair as if to finish the work her mother had been doing for her. In watching Omomo holding her hair and twisting her body as she combed herself, Masahiko was interested in the way Ohina's body also took on a similar motion, bending back slightly and moving both of her hands. It seemed there was an invisible mirror between the two women that was projecting—from the regions beyond—the image of a woman from a distant age as she would see herself in the future.

Again the two women spoke. Omomo held the comb in her mouth in the manner her mother had done and then she took the white cloth wrapped about her breasts, lifted it to the height of her shoulders, and turned about, facing his way. Her face bore a firm, quiet expression. She looked like a person resolving faintly into sight, appearing from a distant inaccessible time. Masahiko felt a strange feeling, difficult to describe, welling up inside. A pungent smell—redolent of what seemed like the scent of mosses and plants from the bottom of the lake—penetrated his body.

It appeared that the hair washing ceremony had come to an end. Ohina walked ahead and they climbed the embankment above the shore of the lake. For a while the two women gazed over the lake at the darkening sky. They both brought their palms together formally and, as if trying to confirm something, joined in a long prayer. Then slowly they walked to the grass hut and went inside.

Masahiko had been riveted in place amidst the stand of bush clover. Never before had he seen a woman take such care in combing and caring for her hair. Perhaps he'd seen such a wooden comb in an old photo in some magazine, but this was certainly the first time he had ever seen a woman actually holding one in her hands and using it. He had often seen his mother Machiko at her mirror working on her hair with an electric dryer and comb. But he had never even imagined such a sight as this—of a woman by a lakeside washing her long hair and combing it with an old wooden comb. In Tokyo he had often seen women with long hair, but never had he seen such an impressive comb or hair.

Masahiko had come up to the Amazoko dam hoping to hear Ohina sing, and with thoughts of creating a musical composition

259

for Japanese instruments. The thought of being able to hear singing at the ceremony for Omomo's succession to Sayuri's role had inspired him to come, but he hadn't imagined being able to witness the Shinto purification rite of hair washing. He realized that the matter of the hair told of a complex riddle of its own. Omomo's hair swayed back and forth about the back of her white robe as Ohina handled it carefully. It seemed as if women had been taking care of their hair like that for ages. Masahiko was practically numbed by the swirl of incomprehensible thoughts eddying about within his head, yet the feeling it left him with was by no means unpleasant.

A wooden comb had been passed back and forth between the toughened hands of the older woman and the rounded hands of the younger one, almost like the shuttle of a loom. Omomo's long hair looked like the threads of a loom. It was as if the very source of all that was Amazoko was being woven together by hand. The movements of the women's hands reminded him also of hands plucking on a koto. He had no doubt that for these two women a string had already begun to sound. It was a sound from a distant world—but could it be that this same sound had also begun to reverberate within himself as well? Such were the thoughts and emotions that swept through Masahiko's body and mind.

He felt as if the branches of bush clover, fully laden with flowers, were swaying back and forth in front of him. Sensing the presence of something he turned around and found Kappei standing behind him. Kappei spoke in a somewhat hushed voice.

"You're early, aren't you?"

Then he pointed to the hut.

"They must be here already."

Nodding in assent to his own words Kappei came closer, taking care how he stepped on the grass, and then he sat down beside Masahiko.

"What about Chiyomatsu and Oshizu; are they here too?"
Masahiko shook his head.

"I guess the two of us got here pretty early."

Masahiko must have looked somewhat different from usual. Kappei scrutinized the young man's face carefully. Falling into silence he took out a cigarette and lit a match. Masahiko had started jotting down in a notebook some musical ideas that were simmering in his imagination, but when he heard the sound of Kappei's hard dragging on the cigarette he quickly shut the notebook. In writing, the fidgeting motion of his hands seemed to express a sense of restless longing.

Compared to the wooden comb that Ohina and Omomo held in their hands, here in this place his pen seemed shabby. He understood this also from the way Kappei had sighed. With moistened eyes, Kappei looked at the young man with deep affection. Even so, Masahiko felt a sense of reserve toward this older man. It made him hesitate to speak and he couldn't help feeling ashamed. Even if he hadn't been writing music Masahiko felt he was still just a schoolboy, whereas Kappei knew so much more about the things of the real world. Even apart from the fact that he had fallen over the edge at the dam construction site, Kappei's life had in no way been an ordinary one. For Masahiko, who had for the most part led a pampered life, it was hard to imagine the life of such a person—someone who had lost his father in a flooded river and gone to work at the age of fourteen or fifteen as a construction laborer to support his mother and grandmother. And so this person might on occasion stagger about at the edge of the world. And even when telling of that time he got skewered by the iron rod this bearded fellow had said it happened because of the beauty of the moon.

On the night of the wake Kappei had muttered, "Sayuri-san, you too were so beautiful in the O-bon moon."

Perhaps beautiful moonlit nights were dangerous for this man. He was sitting on the grass with his legs crossed. When he finished his cigarette he placed his hands on his thighs and tugged restlessly on his trousers. Apparently feeling something needed to be said, Kappei opened his mouth to speak first.

"You smell that incense?"

And he did in fact notice a fresh smell of incense.

"Ah . . . just a while ago . . ." Attempting to say something about the hair washing ceremony, the words stuck in Masahiko's throat.

"A while ago—what about it?"

"Well, a while back the two of them came out from the hut and were standing there in prayer."

"Then I guess they must have started already."

The two men listened and watched carefully. From within the grass hut a low, chanting sort of voice became audible. It was a gentle, quiet sound, similar to that of the rustling of grass. Without stirring, the men listened to what was taking place.

Hearing the sound of footsteps on the fallen leaves, they turned around and saw a group of the older people coming through the bushes. Among them were Chiyomatsu, Oshizu, and the elderly men and women Masahiko had seen at the wake and the cremation ceremony. They seemed to be whispering something among themselves, but when Kappei stood up and signaled to them the expressions on their faces changed immediately. They came to attention and proceeded into the grassy area with measured steps, in the manner of entering a place for a sacred ceremony.

Watching the way they walked as they filed in, Masahiko was struck by a thought: That's the way Noh players walk as they cross the bridge that leads to the main stage. The steps of the Noh have been passed down from old times and they must be derived from the ways of walking through the grasses in the fields and mountains. The thought sent a quiver along his back. Thinking of the dead bodies that used to be set out in the mountains and fields, it seemed the steps of the Noh dance must reflect the spirits of the dead. And even the sprits of the dead—perhaps when they come back to this world they too have to tiptoe carefully through the grasses and bush clover, as if stepping over currents of flowing water. The steps of the old people in the countryside are tempered by their passing over the bridge of the unpredictable course of human life. This is what shapes the way they walk. And in turn this has been transformed into the embodiment of art.

As the shadows crept deeper into the folds of the mountains and darkened the waters, the landscape took on a new aspect. The leaves on the tree branches stirred up waves of light that rippled through the encroaching darkness. The elders gazed intently at the grass hut and then lined up along the edge of the lake. Facing the water, they joined reverently in prayer, swathed in the fading tones of the madder hues in the sky. Struck with emotion, Masahiko looked beyond them and tried to imagine what they must be seeing of the old village through the eyes of their spirits. Then he tried to draw up an image of the old household of his ancestors, the Silk Estate, and of the Isara River that flowed close by.

"In my dreams what I see is always only Amazoko."

The soft sounds of the villagers' voices were like the bubbling of water from a spring. One by one, their wrinkled faces passed by Masahiko's eyes, filling him with a sense of beauty and kindness. He had the feeling that, had he looked at Kappei, his eyes would have filled with tears.

Fortunately, the bearded man was standing together with the elders, their heads all inclined toward the bottom of the lake. He felt glad he had put away his notebook a while back. If he were to take it out now it would also seem out of place.

When the prayer was finished the door of the grass hut opened almost immediately. Ohina, the first to emerge, made a polite greeting.

"I want to express my deep appreciation to all of you for making the effort to come up here. It is difficult to make such a request, but your coming here is what Oai-sama fervently wished for. Truly, I am grateful to you all."

With these words Ohina ended her remarks and then, with all the elders silent, she looked back and nodded two or three times in confirmation.

"Omomo."

At Ohina's call Omomo emerged from the hut. Everyone's eyes strained in looking. Her white robe gathered the lingering rays of light from the lake and sky. A sense of wildness radiated from her entire body as she stood with her eyes cast downward. The band of blue-tinted material wrapped about her forehead made her appear even more striking. It seemed that the band of grass she was wearing about her forehead a while back must have been intended to ward off bad spirits. Beneath the opening of her loose robe she wore a thin obi. It was made of the same material as the band tied about her forehead.

Two of the older women remarked at the same time in low voices, "She looks just like a princess from the age of the gods."

"I ask your kind favor."

And with these words, Omomo bowed deeply to the elders who had come this evening as witnesses. Her freshly washed hair streamed down over her shoulders and across her breasts.

Masahiko gazed at her figure intently. Never having been alone with her, he had never had a chance to look at it carefully. Also, the image of Omomo that stood out from the hair-washing rite he'd come upon by chance was one of her being among elderly people. His eyes caught on the obi tied at her back. Could this be the same one he had seen in his dream? It was a shame he couldn't have taken a photograph of the obi in his dream so he could compare it, but it seemed that the obi tied around her back was the same as the one on the young girl beneath the flaming tree. Quickly, however, Masahiko pushed this thought aside. This was no time to be sifting through the back reaches of his dreams.

Ohina closed her eyes and continued her greeting. But more than a greeting, her words sounded like those of an incantation.

"I would like you all to realize that this is the obi that Sayuri-san used to wear. It is the same obi that—through whatever history it has passed—Sayuri's mother wore wrapped about her when she came here. All of you from Amazoko, you know the story about the weeping cherry, the one at the bottom of Utazaka Hill."

All the elders closed their eyes too and nodded their heads a number of times.

"Since the old times the cherry tree of Amazoko has looked after people in their last days. The woman who wore this obi made her way here from the Mimigawa River to this tree, and this is where she left Sayuri. Oai-sama, who delivered the babies of the village, brought up Sayuri and trained her as a shrine maiden who could pray for rain in times of drought. Worrying about the droughts to come after she was gone, Oai-sama asked Chiyomatsu-san and Oshizu-san to look after the waterways of Amazoko. But, as you know, the river of Amazoko was trapped by the dam along with the village, leaving us so distressed.

"Now we return to Amazoko in our dreams so we can take care of the waterways and the droughts. In order to prevent the Amazoko we see in our dreams from dying out, Omomo has received this obi and she is going to carry out the duties of looking after our waters. Chiyomatsu-san has seen this clearly in his dreams, and Oshizu-san, Gensuke-san, and Osayo-san have heard the announcement from his dreams and they are witnesses.

"Omomo can't perform Sayuri's dances, but she can sing the sacred songs. May the dreams of the people of Amazoko accompany her. Drawing on our connections to the sources of life, we ask that the wishes of this night may come to pass."

Ohina stared intently at the surface of the water. Chiyomatsu opened his eyes and took a step forward. Then he took a deep breath and followed up on her greetings.

"Tonight we have an exceptionally fine moon.

"I'm someone who hardly ever remembers dreams, but in one that I do remember I saw Amazoko on a moonlit night. Omomo was standing at the edge of the Isara River, facing the moon and singing. She was singing of how the rice plants were all soaked in water and how sad it was that they had all withered and died. It was an unusually beautiful song. So tonight I've come here with the hope that I might once again be able to hear her sing that song. In the old days it was said that deep in the mountains far, far beyond these mountains, there's an enormous lake that no one has ever seen. No one has ever seen that lake in the womb of the mountains. It seems that our souls were born in the depths of that lake. And it also seems the name of our village Amazoko had its origins there."

Omomo's body was swaying back and forth gently. She was holding a rather long set of light red prayer beads hanging from her hands. Two older women nodded to each other as if exclaiming "Ah!" since this string of beads—beads that Sayuri had used when she recited her prayers—was the very same string of coral beads that had come from Oki no Miya. Omomo fingered the beads, holding them to her breast as she chanted, and then she turned toward the elders to greet them. Ohina, standing at the back of the room, signaled to Kappei with her eyes. Then she pointed to the entrance of the straw hut. Kappei nodded as if he understood what was going on. He went to the entrance holding a carpet and spread it at the feet of the elders. Then he smoothed out the carpet with his big hands as if looking for sharp stones or twigs. Finally, he signaled silently to the elders to sit there.

"How comfortable," the elders commented politely. They sat down quietly and once again gave their attention to Omomo and Ohina in their white robes. Just then the wind gusted and Omomo's hair swayed to the side. With the sky not yet yielding its last rays of light, the tips of her long hair fluttered gently, as if expressing a sign of the coming twilight.

The first voice sounded.

On hearing it, the thought came to Masahiko of those *sal* trees faintly lit up amidst the mountain dew. He had seen those trees for the first time in this mountainous land. Their trunks were smooth and golden, with flecks of red. Omomo's song conveyed the impression of those trees murmuring, off in the distant mist.

> In the moonrise
> Of the autumn equinox
> From Oki no Miya
> Already your servant
> Has come
> Already your servant
> Has come

Omomo looked out with half-opened eyes. With the prayer beads hanging from the opening of one sleeve she raised them slowly to her breast in a just-barely perceptible movement. Her manner was entirely different from the flashy movements of the singers on TV. Her voice and the motions of her body were like the spirit of a tree, or of an object answering to a faint, distant wind.

The elders sat up straight to welcome the arrival of the servants of Oki no Miya.

Here at the
Meeting place
At the base
Of heaven
Welcome the new moon
Over the mountains
Come flowers
And pampas grass

The blue shell princess
From Oki no Miya

The god of the mountains
The master of the cave under heaven
The lord of the oceans

If you pass
Down the road
Of a thousand leagues
A thousand grasses
And vines too
Shall turn red
And become
Beautiful woven silk
Let us take
One stem of the
Thousand-year pampas grass
And make an offering

Oshizu and Chiyomatsu's eyes moistened as if they had already entered the darkening surface of the water. Thinking back on the story Chiyomatsu had just told about the lake in the womb of the mountains, Masahiko tried to hold onto the fragments of his grandfather's words. Yes, he used to speak of a lake of a "divine wedding." Masahiko remembered his mother's voice, sounding casual to his ears, after she had put Masahito into the mental hospital.

"The nurses talk about him, you know. They say Grandfather often talks to himself. And he goes on about some sort of 'honeymoon lake.' I suppose his memories of his youth must have been quite happy. It seems the nurses hear him talk about how his old days were good—but then he says we ruined his life and pushed him into the hospital. As he got older your grandfather often talked about that honeymoon lake. He must have spent some pretty romantic days there, don't you think? That lake, I wonder—which one do you suppose it was he went to?"

Kiyohiko, his father, had answered in his usual expressionless voice, "I didn't hear anything about it, but it doesn't matter, does it? It didn't hurt anyone, did it?"

"But I . . ." Machiko started to speak, but cut herself short with an unnatural-sounding laugh. Masahiko remembered the conversation well.

Masahiko now understood what his grandfather Masahito had really meant by his words. Omomo had sung of "one stalk of the thousand-year pampas grasses"; and in fact there really was a place called "Susuki Bara," meaning the "plain of pampas grass."

"Perhaps," Grandfather had said, "it was the remains of the mouth of a volcano. There was a plain called 'Susuki Bara.' The old folks used to say that below it was Amazoko Lake, where the goddess of Oki no Miya and the Lord of the Mountains met. It was the lake of the divine wedding."

His grandfather had told him these stories. The Isara and Tamama Rivers flowed into the ocean, and where they met amidst the currents of the sea was Oki no Miya. The old people said that twice a year, at the spring and autumn equinoxes, the goddess of the ocean palace and the god of the mountains met and exchanged places. In the village of Amazoko the people sent off the mountain god and received the goddess from Oki no Miya. The two gods came from the oceans and the mountains riding on dragon gods. According to his grandfather, Amazoko was the meeting place for the gods.

While Masahiko was listening to Omomo's song, the words of his grandfather, with their musical cadences, fell into context. So that was what it was about, he thought. His grandfather must have been trying to convey the spiritual world of his lost village to his weak grandson whose ears had become damaged. Thinking of it now, Grandfather must have been so overcome by his sorrow that he was unable to move either forward or backward. He had restrained himself with the strength of a man of the countryside. And yet, in the end, the words had just broken out.

"Go blow yourselves up, Japanese islands! Just go blow yourselves to bits!"

His inner world had already been destroyed. In the car as he was being taken to the mental hospital he had been completely surrounded by other cars—going forward, going left, going right and coming up from behind.

"We're in the midst of an army of enemy tanks. We can't escape. All we can do is go on like this!"

The voice that Masahiko would never forget had been the old man's cry of desperation. The inner cosmos in which he had been brought up, where people had lived in a world of myth, now lay destroyed at the bottom of the lake and he remained a lone survivor wandering in an unknown megalopolis. He must have come to think of himself as some sort of unripe rice plant that had been mowed down. He had seen it while being led away by a family that regarded him as just a demented old man. The Japanese islands had turned into a giant conveyor belt carrying slabs of concrete, all covered with trembling swarms of vehicles.

He must have imagined he was about to be devoured by the ever-increasing horde of cars that so resembled a pack of rice weevils. But it was his grandfather's very last words following that outburst that had sent Masahiko back carrying the urn of cremated bones to the lake that now covered the old village.

"The string of the *biwa* of Moonshadow Bridge . . ."

And now that string, urged on by Omomo's voice, had begun to stir within Masahiko's body like a small spring of water bubbling up into the mist.

Then in a low voice Ohina began to sing, taking over for Omomo. It felt as if the grasses and trees all about were waving gently in the wind.

Yaa
Hôre Yaa
The five-colored clouds
Are in the shadow of the moon
Dimly visible
In the mirror of the water

The sound brought something back to mind. It was the night he first met Ohina, after they had scattered the ashes and she had sung. How he longed to hear that song again. Then Ohina took a string of black beads into her hands.

CHAPTER 5

Yaa
Hôre Yaa
The waters' destination
Hold fast to the light
Of the distant world
In the darkness

Yaa
Hôre Yaa
Staying
Just one night
The feeling doesn't end
It is also in
The shadows on the water

When he had heard the song the time before without understanding the meaning of its words he had simply thought it interesting to discover that such songs existed, but now he realized that this song told of the wedding of the gods.

A half moon was rising over the water, its light reflected on the surface. Omomo started to sway back and forth and the tone of her song changed to a clear rising pitch. Masahiko felt he was hearing the sound descending from the heavens.

Ho-o—

Ho-o—

Ho-o—

Repeating the call three times, she passed along the edge of the lake in front of the people and then returned.

Masahiko was unable to see her expression. He could tell that
Kappei was breathing with great care. As the final "Ho-o—"
slowly faded away it made him think of birds vanishing into
a starry sky.

Ohina's voice swept low over the grasses behind her like the
traces of a breeze and trailed off into the spaces between the
trees. For a few moments there was silence. Then, in an unusual voice that sounded like the striking of a plectrum, once
again she sang the sounds, "Ho-o— Ho-o—," as if they were descending from the heavens.

The thought came to him—this is the moment where a vanishing mountain people's spirit is transformed into art. And
then, as if gathering together all her voices and breathing them
into the sky, she began a powerful new verse—weaving it into
a tapestry of sound.

White heron
White heron
Night singing bird
Let the flowers fall
The name of the princess
Whose bed lies in the water
Is the Blue Shell Princess
Of the Palace of the Ocean
The name of the mountain god
Is *Amazoko-no-unabara-no-mikoto*

This one night's stay
Amidst the thousand-year pampas grasses
Amidst the shadow of the moon
A stalk of grass
Sways and becomes
Countless flowers

Since ancient times
In Amazoko
The water of the lake
In the womb of the mountain
With its fragrant smell
When night comes
Keeps the dragons
Attending
The Blue Shell Princess
Pulling her long, shining
Blue hair
Till she becomes
The goddess of the mountains

The Isara River
Shows the way
Flow on
For the bounty
Of the oceans and the mountains

The landscape Masahiko's grandfather had tried to describe to him now began to appear. The lake that lay in the womb of Amazoko Mountain was where the wedding of the gods took place. The villagers paid their respects and offered songs so that the night of the divine wedding would come to pass successfully. On the eve of the autumn equinox the gods returned peacefully to spend the night together at the unseen lake. If on the following morning there was a faint whitish tint in the Isara River, even when there had been no rain, this showed that the wedding of the gods had taken place happily. And all along the river, in the mountains and in the fields, the land became moistened. And for another year fecundity would spread throughout the land, from the mountains to the distant sea. And at the depths of the ocean the plants and all the fishes too would thrive. Amazoko was the dwelling place of the gods who enriched the mountains and the seas.

In his childhood Masahiko had thought of these tales of a far-off forgotten mountain village as merely the fragments of memories of an old man who had been separated from his hometown. In those days the only one who had been there to really listen to his grandfather's stories was the big old gingko tree. Now he had come to realize that in order to see into the world that had been hidden in his grandfather's mind it wasn't necessary to resort to ideas from ethnology or recently fashionable ecological theories about saving the earth. All that was needed was to share in the feelings of these elders right here; these people who continued to return to Amazoko in their dreams.

Masahiko felt something in Ohina and Omomo's voices awakening emotions that had been slumbering in the deepest reaches of his heart. It was as if the strings that had been reverberating within him were at last sounding together. In Ohina and Omomo's singing he could hear the kind of sounds he'd been searching for—sounds like the verses of the *imayou* songs of the distant past. He could hear a composition that had not yet been performed for the outside world; one written for *hichiriki, shakuhachi, sasara, koto, otsutsumi* drums, and other stringed and percussion instruments. It was a piece that started singing all by itself; at times bursting out with a heavily layered feeling of life, and in some verses filled with the presence of an autumn evening in the fields and mountains, faintly reverberating with the soft sounds of insect voices calling to a distant world.

For the first time he could feel himself walking down Utazaka, passing by the weeping cherry tree and placing his hands on the mulberry trees of the old Silk Estate. He looked up at the sky, sharply framed by the ridgeline of the mountains.

Nearby was a large well, set off by a mossy stone wall with fern leaves waving about, growing from its cracks. The villagers called it the "Ikawa" well—but could it be that this well gave birth to the wind also? In its dark water the face of a person was reflected. The face of neither Ohina nor Omomo, it had faint, carefree-looking eyebrows and its eyes, which seemed partly cast downward, looked long, narrow and dim. Its slightly grinning expression was inscrutable. Could this be the face of his great-great-grandmother Nazuna who had taken in and raised the child left by the Lord of the cave? It was said that she had lived to over a hundred years in age; but would she appear with a face like this? He felt himself trembling.

His grandfather had slipped away from the world of such things and for a while he had tried to become a person of the city. Compared to the villagers he had been somewhat more cultured. Also, through the generations in which they had used the name Mikihiko, the family had owned enough mountain land to build a temple. And even if his grandfather's estate had been ruined, still he had established a home in Tokyo and had sent his son to college and on to a position with a trading firm, enabling him to make a decent living. Why then, had he become so strange?

The things in his speech and behavior that people called strange were limited to his military experience and to things connected with the village of Amazoko. Perhaps if the difference between two people's experiences is too extreme, one may become fearful of the things he or she can't understand about the other and end up saying the person is demented or mentally ill.

Masahiko felt the warm hand of his grandfather—the hand he had lost in the war in Okinawa—being placed upon his shoulder.

The words, "My lost fingers . . . they're playing the biwa," sounded in his ears.

The leaves of the mulberry trees shone with a fresh light and then became immersed in the thin fog. Why was it that Masahiko, who would have been supposed to be ignorant about plants, knew the shape and form of mulberry leaves, and of their delicate, slender branches that swayed and reached toward the sky? He found it fascinating to think how the strings of his biwa had come from the insect-chewed leaves of a mulberry and its body from the trunk of a mulberry. His own *biwa* might not be quite like one in the *Shoso-in* Museum, but to him the beauty of its shape was unrivalled. He couldn't help wondering what history lay behind the making of his *biwa*, with its exotic shape.

He recalled hearing the talk of his friends at school, leaning on one elbow and blowing smoke from their cigarettes as they spoke, casually spouting off things like, "The modern era is an age when meaning has become completely deconstructed." He wondered what kind of feelings about the realities of life lay hidden behind those words. They seemed pale and insubstantial.

But here in the village of Amazoko, he saw people living in pace with the growing of the trees, the flowing of the waters, and the waxing and waning of the moon. Here he couldn't say that existence was meaningless. Even just thinking of a *biwa*, couldn't a person discover within its form a profound world of order? The villagers see and understand such meaning and bring it together. They look on existence as being one image of the world placed in the midst of the entire creation; one in which all animals and all people, themselves included, have to play their roles. They can't help but give it meaning.

CHAPTER 5

He had understood this just from one moment of seeing the fresh light shining from the leaves of the mulberry trees. In this place, wasn't meaning being reborn moment-by-moment, like the plants growing on the bottom of the lake? At least, he thought, it's this way for me, and for people like Ohina, Omomo, Kappei, and the elders, and the villagers who return to Amazoko in their dreams.

He felt as if he had been entrusted with the responsibility of carrying out the last will of this dying mountain region. He felt himself trembling, as if he had been allowed to slip through a gate into a secret region.

Clearly Masahiko was traveling together with the villagers who were returning to their homeland in their dreams. Meaning was connected without bounds. And the mulberry orchard sparkled beneath the fog of Amazoko, appearing even more finely engraved than the fine lines on the intricate paintings of Balinese artists. The voice of his grandfather was floating about through the mist and calling out, "the string of the *biwa* of Moonshadow Bridge." The people guiding Masahiko had appeared, one after another.

From the time he saw the face of that woman from the old days floating in the depths of the waters that flowed from the well, a change had taken place in his imagination regarding the kind of music he hoped to compose. Although he didn't want to become completely immersed in his feelings, he couldn't help seeing his own self sinking beneath the mirror of the water. And it seemed there was yet one more of his selves, there on the bank of the stream.

A net had been cast directly on his sense organs. No doubt it was the richly colored voices of Ohina and Omomo that had brought this about. The net had dredged up hidden strata from the deepest layers of his soul and in one swoop it had raised them up and set them free in the skies above the old village that lay submerged at the bottom of the lake. At the time he became aware of himself walking down Utazaka Hill there had been a finger softly pushing from behind on his back. Perhaps it had been Omomo's finger. He remembered this when he reached the cherry tree. He sensed the flowing of the Isara River. There were gentle sounds of flowing water.

Masahiko was starting to grapple with the sounds that were constantly bubbling up. Composed of the voices from the leaves and branches of all the various trees, they drew in all the senses of his body. It was too much. Who, he wondered, could be making such sounds? It felt as if his breath was being taken away. The sound was like that of falling leaves. Although the leaves in this sea of trees had already fallen, and thirty years had already passed since the completion of the dam, it was as if the sounds of hundreds of generations of trees in this sea had gone unheard. Was this what he was hearing now, all at once? Perhaps it was the wooden comb and Omomo's hair at her purification rite that had called out these sounds.

In the deepening fog, it sometimes seemed to Masahiko that he was hearing the heartbeat of the world of living things that he had listened to before his birth. It also sounded like water flowing endlessly over falls. The sound was the same as smell, and color, and light. Sometimes he wished the sound would let up. Then he noticed Kappei, looking at him in the moonlight. Clearly Kappei was worried about something.

The layer of soil and rocks beneath the trees took on a slippery, clay-like consistency and he felt himself being enveloped in it. He wondered; am I being cast into the urn of Lake Amazoko and sent back home through the water? It was as if he was encountering the transparency of his own being for the first time. From time to time he let out a rush of breath. He could hear the voices of Ohina and Omomo. It was as if a bamboo breathing tube had been inserted for the ones who had been buried inside the urn.

Then the voices of the trees gathered together and changed into the thundering sound of a waterfall. He was swept into midst of a whirlpool. The sights around him spun about at supersonic speed. Masahiko felt as if all the things of the city that he had been drawing out of himself, along with all his new half-formed ideas, were being cast into the waterfall and his latent consciousness of both the village and himself were being merged together.

A small bright red flower appeared, its outline showing amidst the light shining through the trees. Quickly both sound and sight were stilled. The song was coming to an end. The white robes vanished. Perhaps it was because they had entered the grass hut? Nearby he heard a pleasant-sounding voice. It was Kappei. "Looks like it's about time for the pomegranates to bloom."

"I s'pose you're right," added Chiyomatsu. "The water's getting thicker. The pomegranate blossoms are beautiful around this time of year."

The muddied currents of the river were roiled and moving along at a good speed. Along the banks of the river the tree branches were hanging and swaying gently along the surface of the water.

"Seems when Kappei's father died it was about when the pomegranates were in bloom, wasn't it?"

It was Oshizu speaking. He couldn't make out her expression.

"Right near the spot on the river we used to use for washing clothes, that's where Kappei's family's house and the prayer hall Oai-sama built for Sayuri used to be."

Masahiko thought he could hear a bell sounding faintly through the fog. It sounded like a fire alarm.

"I saw Kappei when he was just a kid, running along the pathway through a rice field in the rain."

Since Chiyomatsu was telling him about these things, Masahiko took great interest in how the waking dreams of the group were steeped in countless layers of experience, gained over the long passage of reality. He wondered if he was watching the workings of dreams in which each person was not merely a single being but a part of the greater body of a community.

Suddenly he recalled something he had entirely forgotten. His grandfather had told him a story. When he was in the hospital after returning as a survivor from the war in Okinawa he had heard this story from a knowledgeable man he met there. It was about how a group of people in a town in Tosa had been haunted by a badger. It had actually happened and it had caused a panic, such that when the officials of the feudal government heard about it they had treated it seriously and dispatched officers to investigate. It was written down in the records.

"They say that back at the end of the Edo Period there was an eight hundred year-old badger that haunted many of the villages, and neither the village head men nor the priests from the Buddhist temples or the Shinto shrines could deal with it. During the daytime people would tend their fields, but when a warm wind blew in from the east they jumped about and acted completely unlike human beings, right in front of the officers. And they say that in the old days the badger was seen in Amazoko as well."

Masahiko had still been in junior high school at the time he heard the story and since it was rare for his normally taciturn grandfather to get so excited in talking about something it had stimulated the boy to imagine the village of Amazoko that had been submerged by the dam, without ever having seen it directly. He had imagined the village as being way off in the mountains and cut off from the modern age, but he hadn't been able to pass it off as representing a foolish, ignorant world. It had been strange to hear of people in the village being possessed—not just by foxes, but by badgers as well—and of their jumping about, but he understood that his grandfather had an indescribable intimacy with the old village he had left. He hadn't taken the story as a superstition-bound tale of ignorant people living somewhere off in the distant countryside. There were all kinds of spirits to be found in human history and he was comparing them with what existed among modern people, focusing particularly on the spirit embedded in the oldest layers of that history, and trying to read the hidden meaning that lay within it.

If Oshizu and Chiyomatsu, and perhaps the old priest had lived just a little earlier in time it wouldn't have been out of the ordinary for them to have been possessed by a spirit. If one compared these people who returned in their dreams to a sunken village with the people living in cities who, caught up in the march of civilization, have become so cut off from such things and no longer have a place of return, didn't it seem that the ones who returned in dreams were at least a little consoled, and perhaps better off? And yet these people's returns didn't seem to take such a long time. Such were the fragments of thoughts whirling about within Masahiko's head.

In the voices of Kappei and Chiyomatsu, Masahiko could hear tones of classical elegance and grace. These voices had become the sounds upon which he hoped to base his musical composition "Mountain Mists." Since coming here he had found that the sounds of the local dialect—that "Kumaso language" his mother had so ridiculed—had become pleasing to his ear, and this realization was far from unwelcome.

And tonight, in a world bewitched by things far more mysterious even than foxes and badgers, Masahiko from Tokyo had joined these people by the banks of the dam where Ohina and Omomo had sung the sacred songs. Hadn't the elders given their complete attention and dignity as they slipped their feet over the freshly prepared reed flooring and proceeded along what looked like the bridge of passage of a Noh stage? After receiving Ohina's invocation they had listened to Omomo's sacred song, and as their spirits were carried to the depths of the waters all of them had become part of Masahiko's poetic drama.

Even when they weren't performing such ceremonies, weren't these people continually enacting a living myth in which they were reviving their submerged village? No doubt the former village of the now-sunken Amazoko remained at the roots of their spiritual lives; lives kept alive by drinking from the waters of a spring that no longer existed in the reflected world above in which they were living. It now struck Masahiko that in their "reflected" lives they had constructed a sort of provisional residence in a world apart from their village below.

From the darkened stand of trees behind them shone the light of a flashlight. Someone was moving toward them. The men and women all strained their eyes in trying to see who it could be. Kappei took out a flashlight. He called out as he shone it at the person's feet.

"Here. Over here."

He used few words, so as not to make too much noise, and the other person seemed to have understood. This other person called out.

"Me. It's me."

"Karehito-san."

The people whispered together. Until hearing the voice they hadn't been able to tell who it was. The young priest bent forward, pressed his palms together, and whispered. "Have you finished already? Is there still more to come?"

Kappei whispered in reply. "I think there's still more."

"Since it's *higan* it was hard to get away, but finally I made it."

Breathing hard, the priest wiped his neck and chest. Silently, the elders pressed their hands together and bowed their heads respectfully in greeting.

Kappei stood as he waited for Karehito to catch his breath. Then he raised one hand lightly, leaned forward, and moved toward the grass hut.

In the space between the hut and where the people were seated there was a rock large enough for three people to sit on. Masahiko remembered that rock. Kappei was walking with his flashlight fixed on the ground, but when he got to the rock he groped along the top of it carefully with his hand. Then with slow steps he returned to his former place. It was clear that on this night Kappei was carrying out some sort of duty. Rather than his usual navy blue and red jacket, he was wearing a black robe. It reminded Masahiko of the black-robed stage workers at the traditional theater. It seemed that the elders took this as natural.

As soon as Kappei sat down, faint lights appeared from amidst the thatched grass hut, giving it the appearance of a wicker cage with fireflies inside. Captivated by the sight, everyone straightened up and strained their eyes to see. The only sound was the faint call of a nearby insect. It was so silent it seemed the insects on the far bank of the lake might even be heard. The lights from the grass hut were fainter even than those of fireflies in a cage; so much so that even the scattered light from the stars and the waxing moon sky was brighter than them. Had the two people in the hut perhaps even been changed into fireflies? Creating such an impression, the grass hut stood as if breathing.

The night sky appeared to be spread out even more broadly than the sky of daytime, making the grass hut with its barely-visible light appear even smaller. With not a single other light all around, the scene also looked as if it could be a nest of phosphorescent creatures at the depths of the ocean. Again Masahiko felt a sense of Chiyomatsu's words about the "thick" quality of the water.

In fact the mountain mist was rolling in again. The grass hut, which emitted a faint light, could be seen as signaling the whereabouts of the spirit of mountains that was now submerged under the water. In the mist the door of the hut opened. Ohina emerged holding a large burning candle. Then Omomo appeared holding a similar candle, encircled by the long white sleeves of her white robe. The wavering of the candle flames made visible the drifting of the fog.

"Looks like it's going to be a damp one tonight."

Oshizu, breathing heavily, pulled her quilted coat more tightly about her. She had brought it along knowing it was likely to be misty and damp up in the mountains. In the silence everyone nodded animatedly at the old woman so that she, with her weak eyes, could see them. Shining through the mist, the lights from the candle flames and white robes passed back and forth in front of their eyes and then moved beyond.

Trying to catch a glimpse of the blue obi he'd seen in his dream, Masahiko kept his eyes fixed like a hawk on Omomo's waist.

6

DELICATE FLOWERS

Aheavy fog rolled in from the stand of andromeda trees, wrapping itself about the people on the bank and spreading across the surface of the lake. The sounds of Ohina's softly uttered chanting filled the air.

> *O goddess of waters, goddess of wisdom, Benzaiten, goddess of the moon, we beseech thee. We pray for the sounds of your* biwa. *Let not the waters at the depths of this dam go stagnant. Let not these waters perish. Let not the spirits of the people run dry, and bring to us good dreams.*

A sound like the throaty whistling of a bird could be heard. It must have been from the breathing of Oshizu, making her way through the fog.

With Oshizu backing up Ohina's chant—*Goddess of waters, goddess of wisdom, Benzaiten, goddess of the moon*—and as they became mixed with tiny droplets of mist, the voices sounded like a *shômyô* invocation.

But—he had forgotten what his grandfather had taught him when he was playing the *biwa*. Benzaiten was the goddess of the waters. And she was also the goddess of wisdom who had power over fate. What was more, she was the one who had dominion over soft and delicate sounds. In spite of the fact that Masahiko had hardly listened very carefully to his grandfather's words, the words of Ohina's prayer now brought them back.

Masahiko was being drawn farther and farther into a world that pulsed and vibrated with feelings so different from those to which he was normally accustomed. He wished he could recapture that inexpressibly beautiful rapture he had felt back when he unexpectedly came upon the well near his family's old house, back before Karehito had appeared. At that time he had wondered if it was his great-great-grandmother Nazuna's face he had seen reflected at the bottom of the well, but now he also wondered if that unearthly, smiling face might have been Benzaiten. He chided himself for this strange short-circuiting of his thoughts. Yet in becoming absorbed in Ohina's chanted *shômyô* invocation he found he was pushing himself back, once again, to the place beside the well.

Around the dam was a new road that had been carved into the face of the mountain. At first sight the cut in the land had been disturbing, and yet now, with its far ends buried in the fog, he could see it as a moving part of the earth's crust and could feel the vibrations of the earth's skin conveyed through the wide outskirts of the Mt. Aso volcanic plain.

According to a geological record he had consulted back in the temple, the local area was composed of the same rock and fossil materials as those of the Sambo Mountains in Kochi Prefecture. The geology of the Sambo Mountain belt contained the remains of an ancient lagoon that lay at the top of a volcanic island formed of limestone. In it had been found the fossils of sea urchins, of a kind of clam called "megarodons," and of foraminifers dating from the end of the Triassic Period, approximately two hundred million years ago. The volcanic island had been formed somewhere near the earth's equator, but it had gradually migrated up to the southern region of Kumamoto Prefecture. According to the book, this had been determined by measurements of the earth's magnetic field. And so it seemed that this area contained some of the oldest geological strata in Japan. Sometime between the Jurassic and the Cretaceous Period this volcanic island which had been drifting amidst the oceans, and which contained a lagoon within it, had become attached to the ancient land of Japan.

If all this was so, then the stories believed in by the old people of the mountain villages—tales that told of how, not so far off, along the border with Miyazaki Prefecture above the headwaters of the Midorikawa and Kumagawa Rivers, there had been a lake set in the womb of the mountains—they could not be dismissed as the absurd dreams and delusions of country folk.

The vestiges of such dreams could be seen in the cuts of the mountainsides. In the cross sections of the earth's crust one could see small parts of the workings of the entire universe—of the wild energies in which the earth had been churned up and released amidst surges of basalt and conglomerate. Wrapped into the skin of the earth were countless trees and briars that had been stroked by the palms of winds and rains, and which had been covering the mountains since time immemorial. What sort of bewitching beings, Masahiko wondered, must be out there playing about in the far reaches of the mountains.

The sounds starting to be released within him were trying to establish relations with the moistures that had been slowly seeping out from the earth since the distant geological past. And so he realized that if, for example, there is enough moisture to make the thread of just a single insect, then the string that is the self will not be severed.

When was it, I wonder, that my ears began to get so damaged? Was it that they lost their sense of tuning and became closed off or, rather, have they been left wide open? He could reach no decision. He could no longer bear listening to the sounds of the city. In particular, he could not stand the women's voices. It sounded as if their voices were escaping from their bodies through the tops of their heads—as if detaching themselves from the lips that had owned them and seeking an independent existence on their own.

There was a time when Masahiko had looked on rather coolly when his grandfather, with that frightened look in his eyes, had seemed to be searching for a refuge amidst the scattered leaves at the base of the ginkgo tree. But now he could better appreciate his grandfather's feelings. Like his grandfather, he too had come to react to the din of city sounds with feelings of trepidation. What was more, he found that he had been losing his ability to distinguish between good sounds and bad ones in his mind and body, and that he couldn't adjust his hearing. It was as if, like a rapidly multiplying virus, both the voices of people and the sounds of things were undergoing nuclear fission. But now, thanks to hearing the voices of Ohina and Omomo, he was starting a healing process. It seems, he thought, I'm being healed by the soft moisture of the mountain mists that constantly flows from morning to night. If my ears become healed, what sorts of sounds might I be able to hear?

Masahiko was like an insect wrapped inside the thin covering of a semi-transparent cocoon, groping its way toward a corner of the heavens. His body felt as if it were being encouraged and led on by a regular drum-like heartbeat sounding from the depths of the earth. Urged along by the vibrations springing from the earth's primordial bedrock, he had the feeling that he was standing by himself. It wasn't a feeling of isolation, for he felt surrounded by the spirits of the water, the grasses, and the trees. And didn't these signs extend all the way to a meditative moon? Because of these things, he was now able to hear the sacred song welling up from the mists.

That sound of waterfalls I heard before—what was that about? Could it have been a premonition, or an announcement that my ears have been restored to hearing? He felt as if his insensitive eardrums had awakened to the hidden mysteries of the world. Certainly he had been hearing voices calling out from a distant world.

He wasn't sure if he could call what he'd been hearing "music." The rhythms the mountains exhale through the mists from the depths of the earth's thick strata are waiting for the unfailing dawning of day while the trees and plants preserve their forms and are dyed exquisitely in a multitude of shades of green. And in the flash of the first rays of the dawn light, all the colors of the trees are woven together. Color, like *kotodama*, the spirit of language, is born of such things as the union between the morning light and the grasses, trees, fields and mountains. And among those who can be present in this moment, there is joy. The people of Amazoko are characters in an epic poem extending back to the reaches of ancient times.

The smell of water grew fainter. Masahiko felt a power—as if someone were pulling him toward the sky on a thread he was holding onto with his teeth. From amidst the flowing mountain mists the thread grew thinner and thinner as he rose up. The back of his neck was trembling and, just when it seemed the thread was about to break, another thread the color of a rainbow came close to him and he merged with it. The thread must have been the limpid voices of Ohina and Omomo. High up in the sky a slender moon shone brightly, with a string attached to its bottom edge. Who, he wondered, would pluck that string? And as he watched, another thread appeared—a second string.

It seemed it must have been a string of the legendary musician Mizumaro. This famed player had been given the name *Benzaiten Myo-on Suijin*, meaning Benzaiten, the god of mysterious water sounds. Perhaps he had given himself the name Mizumaro because it too contained the word for water. And then, soon after—the light of a third string appeared. It must have been the Isara River. And then he heard a tremendous sound—a fourth string! Strung between the sky and the earth and resonating, it was the thickest of all. This string was a sigh that had emerged millions of years ago when the rocks were released near the equator from a volcanic island that held within it a lagoon.

He felt the sounds were drawing out and expelling the bad spirits that had been accumulating deep within himself.

There's no way that I, by myself, can pluck those four strings strung from the moon over Amazoko. I'm nothing more than a tiny silkworm wrapped in a translucent cocoon, keeping my heart low and listening with my neck lifted up.

The candles reflecting against the sleeves of the two white-robed women flickered faintly from time to time. They looked like the coming and going of spirits on the surface of the waters. Then the women placed the candles on the rock that Kappei had so carefully cleared off with his hands. Suddenly, Masahiko's body felt a chill. Could it be floating?

The light of the moon grew stronger. It was hard to make out the faces of the people.

Kappei turned his head. "After all, I . . ."

The tone of his voice was husky. Masahiko thought of asking him, "After all, you . . .what?" but he didn't feel like speaking out.

"I think I'm going to build a double-arched bridge."

In a voice that also sounded husky, Karehito inquired cautiously, "Where?"

"By the remains of the old Moonshadow Bridge."

Omomo began to sing again. She was seated on the rock with the candles. The mist was growing thinner. Her obi took on the darkened colors of the water.

Combing my hair
By the mirror of the lake
Strings of my heart
Flowers of the autumn equinox
I come to receive
The crimson color

Myo-on Benten Suijin
Water spirit of mysterious sounds
I come to paint
Your lips
With crimson

I remember hearing that!—Masahiko thought to himself. With the sounds of his grandfather's muttering voice lingering in the depths of his ears, Omomo's singing grew even clearer.

He recalled his grandfather's words. Little Benten-sama, she was there by the banks of Mirror Lake. She was the goddess of all the women. And on the twenty-third night of the moon, the women all gathered at our old place and drank the seven-colored liquor made from the fruits of the trees of the mountains. At the ceremony of waiting for the moonrise they drank and offered prayers to Benten-sama. And they painted their lips crimson. They received their crimson lip coloring in a shell from your great-grandmother. Her name was Nazuna and she was revered by all the women, but by the time she passed the age of one hundred her body was so small.

Combing my hair
By the mirror of the lake
Strings of my heart
Flowers of the autumn equinox
I come to receive
The crimson color

That was back in the old days, way off in the mountains, so the women didn't just carry around lip coloring the way they do nowadays with lipstick. And just before moonrise on the twenty-third night, the women-folk would pass around the mountain peach liquor and everyone broke out in smiles and laughter. And at those times little old Nazuna-sama had all the young girls of sixteen and seventeen sit down and she passed out little bronze mirrors. I watched them do it twice during my childhood, but the only time I really remember was the time Oai first colored her lips red.

I always thought she was my older sister, who cherished me and grew up with me. It was later that Oai told me that she was my grandmother's foundling. She had been abandoned by the bridge, but instead of being eaten by the wild mountain dogs she was found by Grandmother, treated with care, and sent to a midwives' school, thanks to which she could make a living. That time on the night of the moonrise ceremony, when she first had her lips colored by Grandmother, Oai didn't yet know that she was an orphan.

"This year the time has come for my Oai to have her lips colored. So this being your first time, you must have some wish to make, don't you?" And then, beaming, Grandma Nazuna passed the shell with the red coloring to Oai, who put her lips forward a bit. It was a sight I rarely had a chance to see. I watched from behind the women in silence.

The ring finger is called the rouge finger, and it was Grandma's finger that applied the rouge to my sister's lips, her lips, colored, were like the quince coming into bloom. Though she was my own sister, I felt as though I were witnessing something rare. All the women sighed and smiled. I began to feel excited.

Myo-on Benten Suijin
Water spirit of mysterious sounds
I come to paint
Your lips
With crimson

"All right then, let's go to Benten-sama. Let's get started."

And in saying this the women hurried to clean up, quickly shutting the doors and windows in a manner different from usual. At moonrise on the twenty-third night, as the night wore on, the owls were hooting off in the mountains where all the trees and grasses were asleep. The women received the red lip coloring from Grandma and then went to the pond and offered some of the crimson coloring, putting it on Benten-sama's lips. They made wishes, and—it must have been on the twenty-third night of the month. It must have been sometime after the rainy season, before the Tanabata festival.

The sight of both young and old people laughing as they walked off into the night along the dark bushy path was—as I think of it now—like that of a collection of old dolls missing some arms and legs, walking along on their way. It was really quite a sight. When I tried to follow I was chased back, since young children weren't allowed to follow.

When they arrived at the banks of the pond they made their wishes and took turns putting some of the red coloring on the lips of the stone face. Then they took some of the same coloring and put it on their own lips.

Usually when the women went out with the men to the mountains and did work like carrying loads of firewood, or cutting things with their scythes, or chasing wild boars, it was out of the question to color their lips. But when they made their wishes to Benten-sama, even the oldest women applied a little of the crimson coloring to their lips. Then they sang and danced by the pond. Those nights made the men kind of apprehensive, so they'd sit off by themselves drinking *shochu* liquor and go back home rather early.

What did the women wish for?—Well, the old men told me about that. The women were told not to tell the men anything about what they wished for, so they said nothing about it. If they spoke about it they'd receive Benten-sama's punishment. The women drank the seven-colored liquor and sang by themselves. Yes, I guess it must have made the men feel pretty apprehensive.

In the back of Masahiko's eyelids the color of Sayuri's lips—something he really didn't want to recall—was superimposed on Benten-sama's mouth. The image reflected dimly and then receded from sight. For some reason he felt a bit relieved. Even when he tried to drive it out of his consciousness he hadn't been able to forget the sight of Sayuri's dead body being taken out of the water. His first meeting with Ohina and Omomo by the banks of the dam had also made a strong impression on him, but with the passing of days the image of Sayuri's body being pulled out of the water at daybreak had remained firmly fixed within.

When the image of that small, crimson-colored stone mouth of the moss-covered Benten-sama floated into his vision, suddenly he felt released from the spell of the dead body. He wondered what the thoughts of Sayuri, and of Ohina and Omomo who had been so close to her, would be. As he thought about this night when the conferring of a successor to Sayuri was taking place, Masahiko realized that the emotions of Ohina and her daughter must be far deeper than anything he could possibly imagine.

The singing continued. Omomo began to wave a large flower-patterned fan in front of her face. Along the night shore the white robes of Ohina and Omomo and the flames of the candles moved slightly. Her fan became a focus point in the drifting fog.

Dawn is breaking faintly
Myo-on Benten Daibosatsu
Preserve the secrets of our prayers
For you we scatter flowers

Ah—the waters of autumn
Reflect the light of the heavens
The one who has already
Sunk into the waters
Has been changed
Into a celestial maiden
And returned to Oki no Miya

Floating on the waves
The delicate flowers
Floating on the waves
The delicate flowers

As she sang the last verse, Omomo opened the fan in front of her face, creating the effect of a bird just about to take flight. Slowly she turned about once, and then once again. He couldn't catch her expression, but from her slightly opened eyes—eyes like goby fish eyes—Masahiko thought he could see a blue light radiating outward and piercing through the fan.

The band of fabric wrapped about her forehead and tied in back now trailed across her white robe, along with her long flowing hair. He could tell that the band was of the same fabric as the obi that was wrapped about her waist. He could hardly believe that this was the same country girl wearing a T-shirt he'd met when he first arrived. With her white robe sheathing the movements of her body, when she sang the words "delicate flowers" it seemed he was hearing the singing of the very figure of Omomo's body itself.

The celestial maiden whose return to Oki no Miya she had sung about must have been Sayuri. Had Sayuri been a *hitogata* human sacrifice? Did the dam support itself by swallowing up humans as sacrifices?

The song came to an end. Ohina took another candle in place of the one that was going out. And then, holding a string of prayer beads, with her eyes cast downward she attempted to say something.

Ohina's voice was muffled. "Here at the bottom of the water, the Mirror of Ikawa well by the Silk Estate . . . Look—see how fine the day is, the sun is shining on the sea of trees of old Amazoko. See how the waves of light catch on the wind-swept tips of the branches of the mulberries and oaks."

Hushed sounds of amazement rose up amidst the group. The fog thinned and the light of the moon shone on the sea of trees beneath the waters. It was as if Ohina were seeing the village at midday.

"It's time for our noon rest. Look—not only the monkeys and boars, but even the cicadas have stopped chattering. Everyone who works in the mountains and fields is dreaming in the shade of the trees. And look over there by the old *agariya*—there's a nice striped snake running along the stone pathway of Flying Stone Ginza."

Once again, everyone nodded beneath the slender moon. The *agariya* was the section of the village Oshizu was from. All the houses on the narrow lots of the hillsides were built upon generations of stone foundations. The *agariya* was near "Flying Stone Pass" and built on the highest stone walls of all. It was the pride of the village. Just beyond its stone walls, on the steeper slopes was a forest filled with monkeys, boars, crabs, and all sorts of other creatures that would sometimes come down and pass along the pathway known as "Flying Stone Ginza." When intruders who didn't know the lay of the land would sneak in to the village tying to cause trouble, once they reached the base of the *agariya* a sudden gust of wind, known as the *matsubori kaze*, would pelt them with stones. And so that was how the name "Flying Stone" came about. The *matsubori* was a gust of wind that originated in this area. It was a wind not found in the flat places of the earth. Even with the *matsubori* blowing all about, the stone foundation walls of the *agariya* held firm and never collapsed. Back in the times when the village had been very isolated this place had been a stronghold for the people of Amazoko.

Oshizu pulled up her quilted collar and shivered a bit as she stuck her chin into it.

"Oshizu-san—the black cat of the *agariya*, it just flew over from the stone wall. It jumped over to the trunk of the first oak and it's climbing up."

"Ah, our black cat. When it flies over to the first oak, that signals the time the gods are passing through." Speaking like this in a low voice, Oshizu pressed her shaking hands together prayerfully, as if she sensed the presence of a spirit. Everyone in the village, even the children, knew the story. On the first and last days of the autumn equinox the gods from the mountains and the oceans traveled along the veins of the waterways to meet, passing beneath the stone walls of the *agariya*. The black cat had a long tail, and when it flew down from the high stone walls to the first oak by the grassy pathway it foretold the coming of the passage of the gods.

The black cat would settle on the lowest branch and listen for the gods' procession. Its eyes flashed a bluish-colored light that served a warning to any children or people from other villages who might cross the path unaware of the visiting of the gods. There were many stories told by people from other places of having escaped danger thanks to the warnings of the black cat. It was said that if one were to unwittingly cross the path during the time of the procession of the gods, that person was certain to be bitten by a poisonous snake and become cursed. Generations of black cats had carried out the function of serving the advance notice. When the kittens of a black cat were born, if they weren't needed by the household they would be taken to the *agariya*, where they were cared for.

At Oshizu's mention of "our black cat," everyone recalled the image of that landscape. Ohina picked up the thread of the discussion.

"Today the mirror of Ikawa well has cleared, so we can see the Amazoko of old.

"It seems Sayuri-san and Oai-sama have brought this back to us. And now, with the long-awaited return from far away of the successor to the Silk Estate, at last our dreams are settling into place and we're coming together again. The whole village is appearing to us again.

"It was in the morning . . . As the sun rose above the *agariya* amidst the shadows I could see the neck of a horse, and Masahito-sama holding the reins.

"Masahito-sama was sent off to school and he couldn't get back to the village very often. But in any case, I supposed he was going to be called into the army.

"Usually he didn't get up so early and he wouldn't be seen about the *agariya* at that time, so I thought, ah—he's already been called up. One by one the young men were being taken from the village, so I assumed it was only a matter of time until Masahito too would be called.

"I wondered why he was up before the morning dew had cleared and was leaving the village from Flying Stone Corners. It was nothing special for a person like me to be out in the morning dew cutting grass, but it was unusual for Masahito-sama to be out at that hour. He didn't have to work in the mountains and the fields, but I guess he liked horses.

"I also wondered what he was up to setting off on a horse without any baggage. I thought maybe he was doing some early morning training in the mountains. I was in the thicket below the *agariya* cutting vines to make a bit for the horse so I took off the towel wrapped around my head and waved a greeting with it.

"'What brings you out here heading off into the mountains so early?'

"Masahito was staring off into space somewhere and he was surprised. He stopped the horse but didn't reply quickly. Then he stroked the side of his horse and replied,

"'Oh, you're cutting reeds. Thanks.'

"And then, gazing at my bundle of reeds and looking down, he added,

"'I'll be off to the army before I've learned how to work in the fields and mountains like everyone else.'

"'All the men are being taken and almost the only one left in Amazoko is you, Masahito, since you're going to school. But your family has these mountains where you can get materials like the pine oil that's used for airplane fuel, and the flax used for parachutes. If you supplied those things you could get an exemption from the army, couldn't you?'

"'But Ohina, that wouldn't mean anything to the army. Pine oil isn't much use in a war. Wouldn't it be better to just leave the pine trees as they are?'

"After saying this, Masahito loaded onto his horse the bundle I'd left by the side of the road. And then, with a smile, he said,

"'If I die, I imagine I'll come back here to Amazoko and I'll be watching over everyone from above. When I become a spirit I'll be able to see the village from every angle and direction. I'll come down from the sky to the Flying Stone wall in a flash, with the rays of the morning sunlight. Or I'll come in singing along Utazaka Hill.'

"I don't know what I answered. I thought then that Masahito might well be the last villager taken as a soldier. Even the schoolteachers and priests had been taken, so only old people and children were left. Only Chiyomatsu-san wasn't taken since, whether out of bad luck or good, he'd injured the tendons in his ankle. That's right, isn't it, Chiyomatsu-san?"

"Yes, that's a fact." Old Chiyomatsu, perhaps half asleep, murmured automatically, and gave a slow nod.

Ohina resumed her story. "'I'll come down from the sky to the Flying Stone wall in a flash, with the rays of the morning sunlight. Or I'll come in singing, along Utazaka Hill.'"

"I really thought Masahito didn't want to go off as a soldier.

"'What d'you think Ohina; when I become a spirit, where do you think I'll return from?'

"I was on the verge of tears but since I thought it would set people off making rumors if I cried, I made myself speak in a normal voice,

"'Well, when the time comes you'll be coming down Utazaka Hill carrying a *biwa*, like old Mizumaro-san. We'll all come running to greet you.'

"Masahito replied laughing,

"'A spirit carrying a *biwa*—well that's good to hear. And everyone will come out to greet me. What d'you say Katsura—if I return from the mountains I'll be riding on you. But I guess it'd be better to come in from Utazaka—right?'

"Katsura was the horse's name, and the latter half of what Masahito said was addressed mainly to the animal. And so he rode off, pulling the bundle of reeds over the sides of the horse. I called out after him, standing with my sickle in hand.

"'When you go off I'll be there with everyone, carrying a samisen.' But as I spoke, my voice choked up."

Oshizu, Chiyomatsu, and Kappei all turned their heads together and exclaimed in a voice that sounded as if it came from the depths of the water, "Ah—the traveling samisen player."

Masahiko felt a tightness gather in his chest. How, he wondered, would he ever be able to express this voice through sound?

"Masahito's eyes darkened and then he said, 'Ah, the traveling samisen of Utazaka.' He remained sitting up straight as he said this. And then without saying more he glanced backward from atop the horse and headed off down the hillside."

"My older brother, when he went off down that hillside, he too glanced back as he was leaving." Chiyomatsu said this as if suddenly remembering something.

Then, in a tearful voice, Oshizu spoke. "Both my brothers went off down that slope too. People came out from all over the village and sent them off to the music of the traveling samisen. I'm grateful for it."

Kappei, who seemed almost hypnotized by the elders' talk, muttered, almost in a groan, "My father made it through . . . and he even returned for a while . . . but then he died in the river."

"Once they left Utazaka, none of them came back."

When Chiyomatsu said this everyone nodded and sighed. Nearby, a pale white frond of pampas grass was swaying gently back and forth.

"Ohina-san, won't you sing us that old song—we haven't heard it for so long. Sing it for us once more."

And other people joined in pleading,
"Yes, Ohina-san, won't you sing it for us?"
For a while there was silence.

The shoreline had grown a bit more distinct than before and the hum of insects sounded more clearly. The flame of the candle beneath Ohina's chin flickered. It seemed the grass hut behind her had expanded in size. It looked like Omomo was inside, but no one could see what she was doing.

"Look—The firefly hut. It has the light of the old days."

Oshizu stood up and started walking unsteadily, pointing toward the grass hut. Suddenly Kappei started to get up, but right away he sat down again. Oshizu's shadow fell in front of Masahiko. Then he noticed that she had a white towel tied about her head. It may have been just to keep her from getting wet in the fog, but it made him recall what he'd heard about Sayuri's foster mother Oai—about the way she always wore a towel wrapped about her head.

"We had lots of fireflies around our house too. It wasn't such a great house, but when it was surrounded by fireflies it was like—well it was like the house of a lord. It was the highest one on the *agariya*."

"This was the birthplace of the fireflies too . . . *Hoo— Hoo—*."

And in saying this, with her back hunched over, Oshizu reached out with one hand and groped her way toward the grass-colored light coming from the hut. She looked like an old doll walking through unknown mountains at night. Passing near Ohina she spoke with gestures like those of a doll.

"I remember that day well. We had only one horse in the village. I was listening and I thought I could hear the sounds of the horse's hooves at Masahito's return. The horse was named Katsura. It was a mare, a bright glistening one too."

"Yes, she sure did shine. I used to take care of that horse and I always rubbed her down beautifully. When I was cutting reeds I chose the best grass. Masahito's father used to joke, 'Why, that horse is so expensive it's worth three humans.'"

From time to time the fog appeared to be lifting, yet in the sky above dark clouds started moving in.

Above the lake it quickly turned dark, but to Ohina and the people of Amazoko it looked as if a sea of dark green trees at noontime was spreading out. To Masahiko, who was in an extreme state of awareness, it seemed as if beginnings and endings were becoming merged together. And that, in fact, was what was slowly unfolding before his eyes. He realized: one person's story has started carrying me along to a past I've been completely unaware of. And as Ohina was telling her story, Chiyomatsu and Oshizu assumed their roles, like in the creation of a genesis tale.

There's such an incredible past here, yet it's remained so unknown. I've been completely unaware of it. If it weren't for Grandfather I'd know absolutely nothing of this little mountain village in southern Kyushu. And I'd never have thought of things like a village being sunk by a dam. If I hadn't met Ohina and Omomo I'd never have been thinking about the stories of a village called Amazoko, sealed off beneath the water. They're all little stories, and yet . . . Such were Masahiko's thoughts. But weren't such stories the original forms of undiscovered classics?

In the beginning there were springs and rivulets. There were winds and rains. There were people and there was spirit. Voices came and went. And with them came songs, so they might call to the souls that existed with them.

Meeting these two women and hearing their songs has shaken loose the spirit within me. These women have freely offered their songs to the spirits of the ancestors at the bottom of the lake and to their world. Certainly their songs reached the distant places beneath the water. And they even reached beyond the time-space continuum to me, who came here knowing nothing at all about these things. From here on I have to continue thinking of them.

Although I heard that song on the night of O-bon, and at the same close range by the waterfront as they did, that doesn't necessarily mean it reached my heart. At that time there was a huge gap between those women and myself; not only in regard to time, but also in regard to the relation between time and space. The closer I was, the farther the distance was between us. No doubt Ohina and Omomo must have been aware of that long before I was. As for Ohina, since that time she realized her mistake in taking me for my grandfather she must have gone back to her place. But what sort of place is it where these two women live?

Though she was a woman, Ohina was renowned as a catcher of poisonous snakes and for making and selling the medicine known as "Oai's hundred lives tablets." Her daughter had built a tiny cottage with only a single window—hardly more than a big box—on the banks of the lower Isara River, just above the flood line. It was rumored that when her mother was out, Omomo entertained men who came from various places. One time the younger priest had firmly stopped his mother from whispering things in Masahiko's ears about that house.

"It seems you're on quite familiar terms with those two women. But you know, it would be better for you if you remained more distant from them," was the way she had put it.

Masahiko hadn't asked her reasons for saying this. He supposed it must have had something to do with the family's lineage being in question. Both mother and daughter, in part because of their exquisite voices, seemed to possess spiritual powers, and so they carried out various duties for the village in times of trouble, such as praying for rain. They appeared to be held in awe by the villagers, yet in daily life a subtle distance was kept from them such that they seemed somewhat removed. Probably the two women were aware of this themselves, so they maintained a suitable distance and preserved their position within the village.

From time to time flashes of silent lightning dashed from the sky and were absorbed into the lake and ridgeline of the distant mountains. Here in the valley this had become a familiar sight in the night sky. Kappei had imagined that this night would certainly bring a shower of lightning. Since Sayuri's death he had often seen lightning.

Here and there the night sky was rent, and then it soon was brought together again leaving no trace. Kappei's grandmother had once told him,

"Lightning is a sign of the dragon gods wandering through the sky. The gods of the skies tell them, 'Don't fight, don't fight!' and wrap them up in their sleeves. When autumn comes, the dragon gods send off flashes of light all over the place, so the gods of the skies have to keep their eyes on them."

——"I don't quite understand, but perhaps there's a world of a different dimension contained within lightning. But then, what the devil is a different dimension anyway? What's gotten me thinking like this? It's not like me. I guess this kid from Tokyo has been getting to me. I suppose I'd better watch out or I'll fall off a cliff again . . .

"I wanted to take Sayuri to see the lower reaches of the Mimigawa River. According to Ohina, when her mother gave birth to Sayuri she was wearing a beautiful piece of silk fabric, the color of light blue water, tied about her belly. What sort of town, and what kind of family did she come from? Wearing such beautiful old silk, she couldn't have come from an ordinary family. And why did she end up beneath the weeping cherry of Amazoko? These are the kind of things Oai-sama, who brought up Sayuri, used to talk about. I used to have daydreams when Sayuri was alive, but since she died those dreams have stopped. Sayuri went off in those flashes of lightning . . ." Kappei thought it was fortunate that the night had hidden his face from the others.

That piece of glossy silk with figures of dragons and flowers had been wrapped about Sayuri's waist as an obi when she was pulled out of the water. At the time of the autopsy, at the request of the police, Kappei, along with the other men, had unwound it right on the spot. Her dead body, whose hand he had never even touched while she was alive, had already turned completely stiff, right up to the ears, even though it rocked back and forth every time they moved it. Kappei felt as if his emotions had been frozen and only his arms and legs were moving about meaninglessly. The wet old fabric had been thickly padded and it was extremely difficult to undo. Ohina had helped, her eyes filled with tears and her mouth shut tightly. The men kept silent and picked flowers to cover Sayuri's face, following the sparsely worded requests of the women. But then, whose new towel was it that had been placed over her face?

At the time of the final washing of her body in the yard of the temple one of the women had remarked in a quavering voice as she worked at loosening the knot of the obi with her fingers, "From the time she was born to when she died she never spoke, not even once."

Even though the temple had a large tub room it was rather cramped for washing and preparing a body. And also, the head priest's wife had made the comment, "Even though this is a temple, if you bring in the dead body of a woman who's died in an accident, the place will become unclean. It will leave a bad feeling with the visiting priests who come." And so they had set up a temporary washing area beneath the *sal* tree.

Outside the washing area which was set off by a circle of
hanging straw mats, many of the men had lit sticks of incense.
From time to time they caught some of the conversation going
on within.

"She never married, though I think there was one guy she
really liked."

"You mean you don't know about that? Well . . . it certainly
looked as if she liked . . ."

"Now, no more of the loose talk." Oshizu's voice had
sounded a stern rebuke. On occasions like this she was always
present, taking control. "That's enough of that."

". . . She was Kappei's guardian spirit. He called her his
"Benten-sama."

"That's right—Benten-sama. Well, after all, she cured him
when he had that terrible injury, didn't she?"

"Everyone thought he was beyond help."

"With a wound like that, just a human's power couldn't have
healed it."

"What a precious woman. She never had any children of her
own, but she saved other people. And now she's gone."

"She managed to be born here under the cherry tree, and
yet now her lineage has ended."

The intertwined voices had slipped out from the interior of
the reed mat enclosure. Kappei had no recollection of his
thoughts, sitting on a rock in the garden holding a plate of salt
and incense sticks for the women, until he was called for after
the work of preparing the body was completed.

"Say there Kappei, what is it then? She's all set to become a
Buddha now. Why don't you get things started by saying a
prayer for her. She's a fine Benten-sama now."

Oshizu's voice had snapped him back to attention. There
was still some salt left on the plate. It seemed that each time
the women went into the enclosure they took in salt. The body
had been particularly difficult to prepare. Sayuri was dressed

in new funeral wear with white cloth wrapped about her legs from her knees on down. It seemed the women had colored her lips. The disordered state she had been in when she was lifted from the water had been completely transformed and she had become a peaceful Buddha.

"Thank you, Sayuri-san."

After saying this there had been nothing more he could say. There were preparations to make in order for the procession of the coffin to take place. Tasks were assigned for the work of carrying it to the place for cremation. It had not been a time for sifting through his emotions.

The year before last, during the record-breaking drought when the water in the dam dried up, the remains of the old Amazoko had become visible. Kappei had gone down to take a look, choosing a time when none of the old women were around watching. A miasma had crept about the remains of the village that had become a mudflat. The remains of the houses in the lowlands lay covered with mud and, as he looked past the edges of the old tea fields, it seemed that a whitish, brown-colored scum was oozing along sluggishly. On the dry riverbed were countless leaves plastered everywhere, like an ogre's toys.

The big old ginkgo tree that stood watch over the graveyard had been covered in congealed sludge and nothing could be seen of the imposing figure that had once sent golden leaves dancing about through the village. And as for the horse chestnut tree by the base of the Moonshadow Bridge, after being submerged for such a long time under the pressure of the water and then suddenly exposed to the extremes of the drought, it looked as if it had been dried out and pasted on the barren shore.

How could he express such a sight? It was almost as if an enormous snake's den—one that had not yet been dissolved by the pressure of the water—had been exposed. This was the wretched bottom of the dam of the watershed that had once provided the water for the villages, fields, and farms all along it. He wondered; if he came to see it at night, might it even radiate a phosphorescent glow? It was horrible to see how the village had changed into such a state. Kappei felt it had been disgraced. Where had the beautiful sights of that river valley gone? Even the raging flooded river that had carried off his father had looked more beautiful than what he saw in front of him.

Worrying that his feet were about to be sucked into the mud, Kappei had trudged along slowly.

It's flooding! It's going to be washed away! It's flooding! The sluiceway is giving way! ——

During the drought he had been able to see for the first time the extent of the desecration of the village of Amazoko that now lay at the bottom of the dam.

At the time his father died in the Isara River Kappei had just been a child and his remaining family, which consisted of just his mother, his grandmother and himself, had been in no position to stand up and oppose the dam. It wasn't that there hadn't been any people who opposed it, but with his family having lost its breadwinner they were in urgent need of the compensation money. He often heard his mother and grandmother talk about how they should try to go to the meetings as often as possible and how they should work together with the majority. Even though he was still a child, when he went along he was counted in with the number of those present. And that was why, in his childhood, Kappei had attended the meetings.

"You have to tell them to let you join the majority—you hear me?"

His ailing grandmother had raised her head from her pillow to tell him this, and his mother had explained with pensive eyes,

"They say that if we don't get you included with the majority group our share of the compensation money will be cut. You have to take the place of your father now."

He could clearly remember taking part in the meetings, feeling he was sitting there in place of his father. But as to how much the compensation money had been, or whether it had been fair, he had no idea.

In the "modernization" that the late Jimpei had talked so much about, there had been no feeling at all for the idea of purifying old things. In time, the villagers had come to understand this. And little by little they also came to understand what it meant to have the village where they had spent their lives be covered over by water. At the time the weeping cherry was cut down, the sawdust that spewed from the cut looked like the hemorrhaging of blood. Kappei too had been there watching when it was done. It was the first time he had ever seen an electric power saw. When they were building the sluiceway for the dam the construction company man had said that the cherry tree was in the way and they couldn't continue the project unless it was cut down. It seemed that the presence of the great tree had forced the construction chief to address the villagers.

That old weeping cherry had become rooted in the thoughts of all the people of the village. Word that it was going to be cut down spread through the resettlement village below the dam within the span of one night. At the time, Kappei's grandmother had been picking mugwort around the newly erected resettlement housing, dragging herself along as she went. The young wife from next door had come over and called out to her,

"Say, have you heard they're going to cut down the cherry tree of Utazaka? Don't you think we should go for a cherry viewing?"

"What? Cut down—the cherry?"

His grandmother had spoken the words very slowly, and then her face went pale.

"We've all gotten our compensation money, moved out, and turned our backs on it—so now it looks like we we're going to have to face our regrets."

"Cut it down? Are you sure?"

"That's what I hear. They brought in a big electric saw for it."

"That tree—it's the lifeblood of Amazoko."

Suddenly the neighbor woman's voice became choked with tears and she clung to the old grandmother who was smaller than she.

"It's our lifeblood. It's the life of Amazoko . . . And they're going to cut it down? Tomorrow?"

"As long as that cherry's been standing there for us I've felt things would be all right."

"That's the truth. I never imagined something like this happening."

At the time, Kappei had been surprised to see his grandmother—who since the previous year had been stooping over badly as she walked—suddenly stand up straight and then grab firmly onto his wrist.

"We have to go. You too, we're going cherry watching."

And in saying this she had stopped suddenly and gazed intently at his face.

"We've laid up a stock of home-brewed liquor back in the woods—you know where it is, don't you? Go fetch us a bottle, and take care you don't break it."

Having said this, she adjusted the towel wrapped around her head and moved forward quickly. Feeling possessed with authority, Kappei quickly picked up a bottle of liquor and ran with it all the way back to Utazaka. Viewed from the distance, the scene looked like a snowstorm of falling petals. People were gathering and bowing to each other silently and then sitting down under the cherry tree and looking up at the scattering blossoms. They looked around the nearby construction shack wondering where this rumored "electric saw" might be, but they couldn't find it.

A number of people had brought straw mats to sit on, and soon the entire group began to drink the liquor, but their words were few. His grandmother gestured to him with her hand, saying,

"Today you're a man. So here, take a drink of this in place of your father."

And so he found himself in the unexpected situation of holding out his cup to receive a drink of the liquor. A few times before, off in the woods, he had tried sneaking a drink to see how it tasted, but this was the first time he had been invited to drink, taking the place of his father. In the expressions on the faces of the men sitting around him, he saw no objections to his drinking.

As instructed, he took just one drink, but for the first time he really felt the power of alcohol—a feeling he still remembered clearly. He stood up a bit shakily and said, as if reciting the lines of a speech he'd been taught,

"You know, the longer we look at these blossoms, the more beautiful they get."

"Here, here—listen to him talking now. Looks like that liquor's going to good use on him."

Nor could he forget the tears he had seen in the faces, wrinkled with laughter, of the adults who were cheering him on. At that time he was still quite an imp. He'd chased after petals, jumped across the narrow stream that fed into the Isara River and gone to look at the spring. He'd felt an urge to drink its water. In the village there were two good springs that flowed with especially sweet water. There was the Ikawa spring, here beneath the cherry tree, and the other one at the Silk Estate.

Since early childhood he had often heard stories of how, in the old days, many of the wayfarers who traveled to the cherry tree came to drink the water beneath it before they died.—But if that cherry tree is cut down, where will those people go?—Such had been his thoughts as he stared into the well, holding the dipper in his hand. Petals were floating on the water surface of the well. And a person's face was reflected amidst them. It was Sayuri. He felt his breath had stopped. Sayuri was the child of one of those people who had fallen by the cherry tree.

It was from this time that Kappei's special relationship with the woman who would become his Benten-sama had been established. When he scooped up some water and held it out for her she lowered her head and smiled the most beautiful slight smile. The droplet that ran down her small chin seemed to him the most sacred of things. He realized she was unable to speak. The words of his grandmother had sounded in his ears.

"Her being unable to speak must be the expression of God. No one must ever hurt that child. Anyone who does will be punished."

Kappei had taken her words to heart and vowed to keep an eye on her and protect her, should anyone try to cause her harm.

It was on a clear, bright morning that the cherry tree was cut down. The electric saw turned out to be entirely different from what Kappei had imagined.

Everything related to that big saw, starting with its sound, was different from what he had known when the old local tree cutters went about their work so carefully.

Someone had yelled out, "Hey you!—Get out of here!" The person grabbed him by the collar and shoved him away. At the same time, the howl of the saw started. It had a heartless metallic sound that echoed throughout the valley. To Kappei, it seemed that everything had been amputated then—and everyone agreed that blood had flowed. The sawdust that flew out from the tree was drenched in the color of fresh blood. In the midst of these sounds and sights that made him feel that the colors of his world were being drained away, he had noticed Oai-sama standing there, grasping Sayuri's shoulder. The cherry tree was in full blossom and it toppled over slowly, rolling over and exposing what looked like a freshly severed head. It was the body of a fallen giant.

His grandmother had hobbled over to the tree on her knees. She reached out her hands to touch its open wound and sobbed as she stroked it.

"Forgive us. Forgive us. You were sacrificed for our lives . . . We were poor and couldn't buy you back. If we could buy up everything in Amazoko we'd buy you back." The other old women had staggered over to the tree too and sat around it, placing its blood-stained sawdust in their palms and weeping as they rubbed it in their fingers.

"Forgive us. Forgive us. Forgive us for what we have done."

Even through his child's eyes, the sight had been overwhelming.

A large flash of lightning struck from up in the sky. It seemed to Masahiko that Kappei was muttering something over and over. His voice had the sound of bubbles rising from the depths of the lake. Since the shower of lightning had started, the mood of the old people had changed. It was not only Kappei. Chiyomatsu, as if speaking in a dream, asked, "Ohina-san, won't you sing that old song of Moonshadow Bridge for us?"

Masahiko recalled something—the words Omomo had spoken to her mother that first night he met her.

"If you can't get to Amazoko, then call it up. Call it up from the depths of the water."

It seemed clear to him now that Omomo and her mother were trying to do just that. Withdrawing to the reed hut and gathering everyone together were all done to call up the spirit of Amazoko.

Still seated on the rock, Ohina began singing in a low voice. The lights had been put out.

Flowers of the moon
Scattering, scattering
People crossing
Over the bridge
The ringing of the bell
That is life
Sounds the connecting
Of the fates of life
And death

The voice sounded as if it were striking out along a pathway through fields in a distant land. Suddenly, Masahiko was transported to a world that seemed completely different from this world. He felt he had become one of many tiny lights on a bridge of vines, set amidst the scattering of the petals of the moon. He felt himself crossing over the bridge, passing over a valley a thousand fathoms deep, wrapped in its darkness.

Where am I am going? Certainly I, along with these people, am crossing over a moonlit bridge of vines, and Ohina and Omomo have called up the village of Amazoko from the bottom of the lake. As he glanced at the expressions of the elders, not always sure whether their eyes were open or shut, Masahiko saw a vision of the "petals of the moon" falling above the lake.

Kappei had worked his way into people's dreams, starting from their memories of his earliest childhood.

He hadn't actually talked about it with other people, but on spring nights the weeping cherry of Utazaka became like a water globe filled with petals whirling about in the midst of the lake around the dam, and it seemed that even now it was scattering petals in the villagers' hearts. The sight of that cherry tree and the sound of the electric saw had become joined within Kappei. There had also been an old song the men used to sing about cutting down trees, but that too had been killed off. Any time the subject of the cherry tree came up, the old woodcutters would fall silent. After the village was flooded and the people moved down below the dam they didn't stop getting together. They'd bring out *sake* and they'd sing, but the old mountain men would glance about with a vacant look in their eyes and their singing lacked the spirit it had once possessed.

Even now, when Kappei heard the sound of an electric saw it made him shudder. That time he had fallen from the dam at the construction site and was skewered by that long iron construction rod all the way from his rear end to his neck, he had felt the burning heat of that saw running through his entire body as it cut away. And still his body ached, especially in winter and summer. Again and again he had slipped in and out of consciousness and groaned and screamed, "Kill me! Kill me!" over and over again. The scene of that cherry tree appeared over and over again in his hallucinations, and as he drifted about on the border between life and death he had probably been possessed by associations linked to the sounds of that saw. The droplet that ran down young Sayuri's chin appeared to him as a coolness in his dreams, and the words "Could you get me some water?" sometimes slipped from his mouth.

No one had believed he would ever make it out of the hospital alive. Sayuri was called in by Oai-sama and, unexpectedly, in the dark courtyard of the hospital she had performed a dance of prayer for his recovery. The patients in the hospital gathered around and listened in silence to the sounds of her bell, but they all understood that a mute shrine maiden had come to pay him a visit, and this became a regular topic of conversation.

"Old Kappei there must have taken a pretty good look at her too. That was like the dance of an angel."

The patients never tired of talking about her with sighs. The most amazed of all had been Kappei, who found himself opening his eyes on the world again.

"I have to get better. I have to show her I can do it."

Kappei was convinced that Sayuri's wordless dancing had been more effective than any drugs or the treatment of any famous doctor. As soon as he was released from the hospital he went to express his gratitude. Gesturing with his hands he explained,

"Before I was carried to the hospital they cut off a steel rod that was stuck in me from my rear end all the way to the side of my neck."

Oai-sama had gasped as she listened, as if her own body were being skewered by the iron rod.

"I was on anesthetics and my body was as good as dead. But I guess somehow I still had some consciousness left. I could see as if I were looking down on my own body from somewhere up above. I became that weeping cherry tree. I could hear the ripping sounds of that electric saw, and sparks were flying. When they started operating on me I was half dead, and when the iron rod was cut out I felt my body becoming that weeping cherry tree.

"The saw snarled and groaned. Sparks scattered. And then I was aware of the petals of the cherry whirling about.

"Sayuri still had her hair bobbed and she was watching over me intently. Her face looked sad as she watched me—looking like a skewered pig about to be barbecued. I told myself, 'Come on, you're a man, you've got to die beautifully, like the cherry tree falling. I kept thinking—compared to that cherry tree I must look a mess, but I have to die beautifully. My life's at stake here.' And yet with that rod stuck in me, no matter how hard I tried, I couldn't die beautifully. I felt so ashamed.

"When I think about it now I wonder what I was living for then, just hovering there at the last moment. It fills me with regret . . . *Such a damned fool—that's what I've been!* . . . It's not that I was clinging to life, but I felt so bad about dying like that. Back then I couldn't appreciate the feelings of the cherry tree, or of the old women. It's such a shame, such a damned shame. While I was alive, I couldn't accomplish my function. That's what makes me so sad.

"And before it was cut, while its new blossoms were falling, I heard the voice of the cherry; 'Come over here and sit down. Come sit and bring a *sake* cup. I'm going to let you drink some of Amazoko's seven-colored liquor, so take your cup and drink.' I was shocked—but that was the first time my soul flew up and came into me. It came from around that cherry tree, and it felt as if it came to me directly.

"There was no one else around the cherry tree. When I took a glance around it looked as if, by the big roots of the tree, there was a plain wooden stand and on it had been placed a white *sake* bottle and a white *sake* cup.

"Then I remembered the words of my grandmother. Back then I always used to be up to some sort of trouble. One time my grandmother held both of my hands and looked hard into my face and said,

"'You know, you're the only grandchild I have, but it seems your soul must have been stolen by some bad spirit. Now how are you going to get it back?'

"She said it with such a sad face. And even after being spoken to by her like that, I just acted like nothing had happened and went on doing the same old things. But looking back on this after she died, I felt her words had remained here and there, like patches placed over my body, on my shoulders and back, and where her hands had touched me. And at that time, just when I was about to die, that soul my grandmother had told me about jumped into my body through those patches. My soul came out from that cherry tree.

"It was during that time when I was hovering on the edge of life and death that I first realized my grandmother had probably been saying a prayer for me back on the night before the cherry tree was cut down; that night when she let me—not even ten years old then—drink some of the seven-colored liquor. I realized that she'd been saying a prayer to the cherry tree, praying that I'd recover my soul.

"My soul flew right to me. It flew to me like a packet of light. And I myself became light. It was, how can I say it, something new, something I could actually see. It wasn't only my own life I could see, but it was like I was seeing in one flash the workings of things that stretched all the way back from ancient times to the present world. I wondered—how did I come into this life as such a fool? It made me ashamed. I felt completely embarrassed.

"I raised my *sake* cup as I had been told to do by the voice from the tree. A liquor made of the fruits of mountain trees had already been poured into the whitish cup. I drank from it and took it as a sacred liquor that signified that my soul was being brought to me. Sadness and happiness came to me all at once in a flash of dazzling light, that first time my soul came to me.

"There was no one else there besides the cherry tree and me. I wondered, Where am I? Is this Amazoko? The word 'Amazoko' means 'bottom of heaven.' It's a place directly connected with the heaven up there. So then I realized; *that's* it—the cherry was a tree that connected the heavens and the earth. And even for the wayfarers who died beneath it, it provided their final drink of water before they took their last breaths.

"So in other words, that was a function of Amazoko village.

"I have to tell you what I saw when I was there at the boundary between life and death, so let me continue up to that point—when I saw Sayuri-san's face. My face must have looked different from usual to her. She was gazing at me and her face had such a sad expression; like that of a Buddha. She focused on my face for a moment and then looked down.

"I wondered if she could hear a single word—or if she could hear nothing at all. Since she couldn't speak, all she could do was give a faint smile, like a Buddha. But come to think of it, who did Sayuri-san and Oai-sama have to talk with about their innermost feelings? Perhaps since Ohina and Omomo were also from households without men, these two families could open their hearts to each other. Although Sayuri couldn't speak, that didn't mean she didn't think about the things in her heart. When she prayed for other people, for the animals and for the *inugami* dog spirits, wasn't she also praying for herself? I know a little about the Mimigawa River—the place they say her mother may have come from. It looks like a dragon tramped up and down that river, splashing through it with its head up. It's a deep river that cuts through a deep valley. If I could have shown Sayuri-san the color of that river, wouldn't it have reflected something into her spirit? Since she couldn't speak, she must have understood her existence in this world as one of spirit. And since her birth took place under the weeping cherry, surely she must have received her spirit from that tree before I did.

"By the Mimigawa River in a village on the outskirts of Hyuga once I saw a night performance of Kagura, with sacred Shinto singing and dancing. It was like going back to a former world and I wanted to show it to Sayuri. From the time I heard that her mother came from the area around that village, I was convinced that Sayuri's style of dancing came from that re-

gion. Why is it that I—the one who was told I was going to die—
was returned to the world of the living, while Sayuri was the
one who died? And then on top of that she drowned and was
exposed to the public. That girl who sleepwalked, she said a lot
about Sayuri leading a horse along the embankment on the
night of the fire. Something must have happened to Sayuri
that obsessed her, and because of it she must have set fire to
Jimpei's house. Even though I'd gotten my soul back from the
cherry tree, at the critical moment I didn't have the wits or
ability to help her. . . ."

Except for Masahiko, who had never seen the original place,
everyone there had actually seen the old village of Amazoko
when it was about to be flooded. Everything was flooded, all together—all the flowering clover, the Chinese milk vetch, and
the countless little violets that lay along the ridges and borders
of the fields. For a short while, even submerged in the water,
the scene had looked like living vegetation. What surprised
everyone most of all was seeing the amazing variety of insects—
beings that normally went unnoticed—floating about in a mass,
covering the surface of the water. All sorts of creatures were
drifting about—numerous kinds of ants, both large and small,
along with fantastic-looking tiny light green butterflies in the
process of breaking out of their cocoons, with their thinner-
than-paper wings torn apart. Okera bugs and salamanders were
swimming about. Even tiny baby birds that looked like they'd
just been hatched were floating in the water in their nests.

After hesitating at first, most of the people had gone out to
witness the flooding of their village. Kappei's grandmother too
had said,

"I'll have to tell about it when I get to heaven."

With a hand towel tied about her head in the manner of the
younger women, she had started down Utazaka Hill and was

watching what was going on when a construction worker
called out,

"Say there lady—the water's coming up to where you are.
You better move higher, it's too dangerous there."

Slowly, bit by bit, the water inched its way up. When it
reached the field on the slope where they had hastily dug up
the last of the potatoes, the water became a turbid red color
and bubbles rose and floated about.

"Oh no, look—those baby birds in that nest over there."

Three tiny chicks with mottled downy covering and wide-
open mouths were faintly chirping away in their nest. Nearby,
a little snake was swimming in the direction of the nest. For a
moment, it rose onto the top of a clump of earth—that's what
its intention must have been. Then suddenly, from amidst a
group of birds circling in the sky, a strange piercing voice was
heard as one of the birds swooped straight down and grabbed
the snake. The people gasped as they watched it happen. It
was a bird slightly larger than a crow. Someone called out,

"Look—a *mugitsuki* bird."

It must have still had a nest in the elm tree by Gongen's
Shrine.

The elders had milled about nervously on this suddenly created shoreline. Kappei's grandmother went out to the elm,
which looked like it was going to be covered by the water, and
as she clung to its wide trunk she squinted her eyes and whispered to her grandson—who for once was behaving himself,

"I want you to remember this well—all these insects here are
among the ten thousand beings. What's going to become of
them now, with no place to go?"

Then she bent over in the shade of the reeds, folded her
hands and recited the Namu Amida Butsu prayer. The phrase
"ten thousand beings" had sounded unfamiliar to Kappei. The
words had an unusually clear sound, and the phrase stayed in

his ears. A year ago at the time of the drought when he had gone to look at the recently exposed remains of the village he had found a small toppled stone pagoda inscribed with the words "Memorial for the Departed Souls of the Ten Thousand Beings." When he saw it, he recalled his grandmother's words. That was the first time he had really understood the meaning of the idea of worship.

On the day they let the water in, Jimpei had gone to watch the proceedings, wearing a vest. His being somewhat more formally attired than usual was likely owing to the pride he took in being a member of the dam promotion group. He'd declared,

"Well, a lot of things have certainly turned out well. I know some folks here were pretty attached to these things but, well, that's why Amazoko fell behind the times."

Not surprisingly, his words seemed to make many of those around him uneasy. His face turned solemn and he clasped his hands together.

"With an old country place like this it's, well, I guess it's only natural to feel something for it still, but now that it's all done and taken care of, we've, we've taken a step forward. Isn't that so, Chiyomatsu-san?"

With his voice raised to full pitch, he clapped the shoulders of the slightly built Chiyomatsu, who was standing by his side. Chiyomatsu didn't say anything. He just stared at the surface of the water, covered with insects, all struggling and floundering about. The people must have been recalling times such as those during the heat spells when the crops had been hard hit by insects and they had performed ceremonies to drive them away. Chiyomatsu remembered all the experiences he'd gone through there using his body, in cooperation with the others. They watched their fields, paddies, pathways and houses all being taken under by the water, right before their eyes. Yet all they could do was stare vacantly in a daze.

Along with the insects, who seemed to be crying out from hell, they felt as if they too were being exterminated, even before they knew what was happening.

The lack of response to Jimpei's words had indicated that the others shared Chiyomatsu's thoughts. They all had enjoyed the passing of the seasons there—with all the festivals, and the making of wines and liquors from the different fruits and grains, and the weaving of baskets from vines and bamboo, and the making of charcoal, and the burning of the fields for raising good shiitake mushrooms. The villagers had managed to get by with just a little extra income from outside, such as from trimming trees and weeding for the forestry department. And even without that, the village had been able to get along self-sufficiently.

Kappei thought of them as a people who relied on the mountains and rivers for their living. It had been that way since the oldest times. They hadn't owned the mountains, but that was the way it had been with them.

All of a sudden Kappei felt a pain in his chest. Sayuri, who was brought up by Oai-sama, had been well aware of these things. In the season when the rice plants came into blossom she had gone to the edge of the rice fields where she loved to bend over and draw the flowers to her nose to smell them. Suddenly, Kappei was moved to speak out;

"Even if I have to blow up the dam, I'm going to rebuild Moonshadow Bridge with stone, with a double-arch, and get the water flowing through it."

It seemed he was completely serious about what he said. Chiyomatsu blinked his eyes open and then, turning toward the dark surface of the lake, he replied in a low voice as if he were whispering a secret.

"Let's do it. It'll be something good to take with us to the next world."

Black clouds appeared, obscuring the moon from time to time. The surface of the water was dark.

Oshizu began to speak. "The moon looks like it's glowing orange tonight."

"You know, I've been smelling the scent of sunlight for some time now. It's the smell of grass in the sun."

"Yes, it's been a long time since I've smelled sunlit grass."

"It's like the old terraced fields. It hasn't changed since the old days."

"That's right—the terraced fields. Chiyomatsu-san, you have a great nose. You've always been able to smell the rain and crows, and even with your eyes shut you can always sniff things out."

"Well, in the old days my eyes were sharp as anyone's, but these days it's only my nose. Why, I can't even make out the rocks at my feet these days."

The elders broke into laughter.

"The sun's so bright on the old stone walls—such gorgeous sunshine."

People breathed peacefully, exhaling in small breaths.

They said the reason the moon was glowing orange was because the sun had struck on the terraced fields beneath the water. The elders had been transported by the songs of Ohina and Omomo and they were smelling the scents of the grasses and stone walls that used to lie along the old terraced fields near where the stands of pampas grass now covered the banks of the dam.

Masahiko took a leaf of mugwort that had been touching his hand and tried chewing on it. It had a bitter, astringent taste. From behind, Omomo approached with her hand extended.

"Here, I'll give you this as a remembrance of this night."

He realized that it was a wooden comb. Earlier in the day, before the sun had gone down, Omomo had washed her long hair in the lake when no one was around and Ohina had combed it out carefully. Was this the same comb? The comb still held the warmth of Omomo's hands and smelled faintly of the oil from her hair. It seemed like the smell of sunlight.

"Look—the *higan* lilies. They're the hairpins of the mountains."

At Oshizu's urging they all looked up, and here and there, amidst the fields on the hillsides, the *higan* lilies were glowing brilliantly, emblazoned against the sky. The times of the distant past had merged comfortably with the village that lay in front of their eyes. Even though the village was at the bottom of the lake, it did not seem strange to imagine they were walking along the narrow pathways through the terraced fields under the midday sun. At the top of the hillside on the far bank was Flying Stone Pass, and they could see the highest house of all, the *agariya*. That was the house of Oshizu.

Its walls were a model of hand-built construction, made by gathering rocks from the mountainsides and carefully placing them together to form a thick fortification against the winds. The cracks between their tightly packed stones were filled with various kinds of ferns and ivy, making it an imposing-looking wall. There was a tree standing in front of the enclosure. Already he could tell it was a *yusu*. The first time he met Ohina she had asked him about it.

"That shining *yusu* tree at the bottom of Utazaka Hill, it marks the beginning of Amazoko."

He looked as if he were waiting for a password. That tree also marked Oshizu's house. Was he seeing this landscape in the present, or seeing it through these people's dreams? Perhaps the mulberry wood comb he was holding in his hand could tell. Touching the wooden comb made him feel as if he were recalling the touch of a woman's hair. It was the feeling of a hand picking up red *yusu* leaves and placing them in a woman's hair. The memory of the nape of Nazuna's neck, reflected in the spring, came back to him.

Even if he had not actually experienced things, it was possible to know them through dreams. When he raised his eyes, the solidly constructed terraced fields came into his vision. His grandfather Masahito had never tired of telling him about these fields.

"Humans' livelihood and the work of their hands. They come together with the earth and from time to time they produce great works of art. The Pyramids too were good, but here in the farming villages we have our stone-walled fields."

It didn't seem those walls had been built in two or three hundred years. The first field had been made by just one person, gathering stones one by one and piling them on each other. He wondered what crops had been sown on that field. Probably the people had put down the simple grain crops that filled their bellies. He'd heard that in the old days they used to grow buckwheat, soba, millet, various kinds of barnyard grasses, and wild millet. A grain of wild millet is only one tenth the size of a grain of rice. It's what birds eat. Thinking of how his ancestors had fed themselves on what they could grow on these mountain slopes moved him almost to tears.

What had this mountain been like originally? People had cut down trees and dug out their roots. They scurried about like ants, leveling and preparing the ground. Ten levels, then fifty levels, and then more. Gradually the number of terraced fields had increased and the village also had started to take shape.

The mosaic-like constructions of stones that his grandfather had called works of art were now reaching toward the skies. When the winds blew, as they streamed, whistled and howled through the countless spaces between the stones, their sounds differed from day to day. The village was wrapped in soft autumn sunlight—from the sun-exposed mountainsides to the stone-reinforced terraced fields, to the houses that lay scattered about the lowlands.

As he breathed a deep sigh, Masahiko whispered to himself that sunlight too can be reborn.

Omomo passed the comb to him and returned to the grass hut where it seemed she must have been praying for something.

Before the landscape changed, he had to run down the hillside. Perhaps right now at the Ikawa well by the Silk Estate Nazuna was holding a baby. He went down through the fields enclosed by rows of low tea bushes, passing through their narrow pathways where every time he brushed against the densely growing little tea leaves they released a fresh scent. But no matter how he ran through the small and large fields, it was like a maze, and he couldn't reach the well.

He was annoyed at getting so tangled up in the fields, knowing he wouldn't have gotten lost if he had planted the fields himself. It was all part of a carefully prepared dream, so unless he got through quickly night would fall about the dam and the smell of sunshine would disappear. Nor was there any telling whether the grass hut that Ohina and Omomo had used would still be there tomorrow. And also Omomo's words, "as a remembrance," hung in his thoughts. And Ohina and Omomo had also said, "these days it's been getting harder to find enough materials to make our medicine."

The thought occurred to him that perhaps the wooden comb was something that had been passed down from Nazuna. Perhaps Nazuna had used it as a charm to call to the place where the Master lived in the womb of the mountains.

People said that the Master had made himself into a cradle, that he had taken in that baby near the base of Moonshadow Bridge, and that Nazuna had brought the baby up. People said that Nazuna did not have the usual nature of humans. And didn't Ohina, Omomo and Sayuri also give the same impression?

The light and water
Of Kodenbara fields
The birds calling at night
Make the flowers fall
And the name of the princess
Confined in bed
Is Oki No Miya
The Blue Shell Princess

As he was listening, Masahiko felt as if warm hands were softly touching his back and his blood was starting to circulate. Feeling his entire body coming alive, he was plunged into thought.

My family's household has been broken up and destroyed, but my family itself has always been connected to water, hasn't it? Sayuri served the god of water and just before she died, when she set the fire to Jimpei's house that burned him to death, even if she had her own motives, couldn't it also have been because she, as an incarnation of the water, was driven to do it by the tortured spirits of the waters? She had never spoken a single human word.

That girl in the fire, whom I saw in my dream—she must have had some connection to Nazuna or Sayuri. Her obi must have been woven by the women from thread that was dyed in the muddy lake. The women had gathered at the Silk Estate to do things like washing clothes, cooking, and spinning silk thread—but had this been a group that was connected to the veins of the water?

The baby brought up by Nazuna had never married, but she had helped deliver the babies of all the women, and she had raised Sayuri, who had carried out the prayers that were essential for the rains. The men had kept their distance from these women's gatherings, saying with a laugh that they were "frightening affairs."

CHAPTER 6

When night came the women had gone to the pond by the grove of oleaster trees and reddened the lips of the old stone statue of Benten-sama, and even the aged Oai-sama had put a little of the red coloring on her own lips and gazed into the mirror of the water. And then they had drunk together the seven-colored liquor made of mountain fruits and clapped their hands and danced through the night without returning home. And from what Masahiko had heard of how the men were not allowed in during those times, it made him feel a bit apprehensive too. The women had many things they kept secret from the men, and they obviously looked forward to such times.

"This is our role," is what Omomo had said in the grass hut the first time they met.

At her side, Ohina had added, "It's not something to reason about. It's just a woman's role, performing the rites for the water gods."

Masahiko reflected on how, on this night, the various procedures for the "succession of Sayuri's role" had been carried out. Probably men's roles had been different.

Omomo emerged from the hut and started walking back and forth along the lakeside.

Yaa
Hôre Yaa
Staying even
Just one night
The feeling doesn't end
It remains in
The shadows
On the water

The white sleeves of her robe billowed and flapped in the wind. The elders sang along with Omomo's words as if chanting a prayer to the Buddha.

"Oki no Miya, Oki no Miya."

Just how far away from this mountain village was Oki no Miya? Omomo's song sounded as if it were sung not to any person, but launched above the earth's surface on a voyage to a distant place.

Oshizu called out in a wheezy voice, as if speaking to herself, "Let's go together—all of us."

"Our guides have been arriving for some time now."

Old Chiyomatsu turned toward the water, extended a hand, and opened it for them to see. It seemed there was something in his palm, but Masahiko couldn't make it out clearly.

"It's an insect, and it's brought the announcements."

The others whispered,

"An insect?"

"Yes, an insect."

It was a bit larger than a firefly and was crawling about in Chiyomatsu's palm in the dim moonlight.

Perhaps feeling reluctant to call out to the group whose members looked as if they were dreaming, he directed his words to Masahiko only.

"Guides often come to the temple as well."

It seemed the elders had heard him. In a voice that arrived from the bottom of the waters, Oshizu said to them, "It's the insect that shows us the road to take through the mountains."

"When the sun goes down and you start to lose the way, this insect flies about and stops—flies and stops. And for children too, when it flies about and gives them directions they're able to follow it and return to their houses without fear."

"But I've heard there are also times when it doesn't lead you back home. Some people say it's led them to the lake in Amazoko Mountain."

"That must have been Chiyomatsu's great-grandfather, wasn't it?"

"That's right. It was when my great-grandfather was still a kid."

"Right, we're listening, we're listening. They went looking for him all through the village, ringing a bell, and it caused a big stir. After three days he turned up around Uge-san's place, carrying a bunch of fruit from the andromeda tree, didn't he?"

"Well I've heard the story plenty of times too. It seems he crawled his way through Uge's cave. Normally, it's frightening just to get near that cave, but with something to guide him, I guess he was able to sneak through. A white-tailed monkey came along and stood in front of him and asked, 'Hey there, are you going?' And he led him along, so I heard."

"A white-tailed monkey!"

Although the elders had heard the story any number of times, when it came to the climax they all let out a sigh.

"That white-tailed monkey was really an amazing one. Some of the old timers actually saw it alive, up until about twenty years or so ago."

"That was quite some feat for him to make it back alive from Uge's cave."

"Well, ever since he was a kid he had a good spirit. He did his best to help others and he lived to a good old age. He knew the mountains well and knew where the tall hemlock trees were, and where the monkeys hid their wine, and where Matsutake Mountain was. My father told me all about it. He also knew about the mountain gods, and whenever he ate in the mountains or slept there he never failed to offer the proper greetings to them. If you didn't, he said, your life would be in danger."

"So he must have gone to the white monkey and asked to be guided, is that what you're saying?"

"That's what they always said in our family. And they told us that the insects too had souls. They were beautiful if you looked at them in the daytime."

"That's right, and when folks came to the cherry tree and died there they were guided across Moonshadow Bridge, weren't they?"

"Sure they were. At the front entrance to the village there was Utazaka and at the back there was Moonshadow Bridge, leading off into the mountains. The ones who came in through the back way often came for reasons they didn't talk about, isn't that so?"

"Sure it is. And there are many of those folks buried down there at the bottom of that dam."

"They were led here by little bugs, something like fireflies."

"And the water we drink comes from the lives of people like them."

For a while there was silence and everyone stared at the dark, mirrored surface of the lake. Then Chiyomatsu called out to the insect in the palm of his hand.

"Hey there, it looks like you're a survivor from Amazoko."

Two women, trying to look into his palm, spoke by turns in low voices.

"Whose soul do you suppose it's brought us?"

"I wonder if it's a soul without a destination."

It seemed that their memories—their thoughts of this face and that face—were floating about. Once again, a thick cover of clouds started to hide the moon.

"Ah . . . the smell of sunshine has faded. It's getting chilly."

Chiyomatsu glanced about, saying "there," and "there," as he placed the little insect in the dark grass. Masahiko noticed that a different stream of air had blown in from beneath the clouds.

"It's been a good night."

"It sure has. Good songs. And such voices. Thanks to them we've had a good dream."

Oshizu spoke in an animated voice.

"It's been a good dream all right. Just now I crossed Moon-shadow Bridge and went up to the lake in the womb of Amazoko Mountain. I heard Omomo-chan's singing all the way as I went."

"And what did the lake look like? Was it blue?"

"It had a semi-transparent greenish color. And it had lots of red coral that had sunk down into it. Come to think of it, the coral on Sayuri's family altar for the gods may have come from the same place. That was Oki no Miya, and it sure moved me."

"What?—Oki no Miya is in the womb of Amazoko Mountain? If that's so, that's where the waters of life spring from."

"So that's the sort of dream you had, was it? But you know, that time when my great-grandfather came back from Uge-san's cave they say he was holding a small piece of red coral. His parents were amazed. They said it must have been one of the mountain god's treasures and he'd be cursed for stealing it. They told him to return it right away. 'If you go through Uge-san's cave,' they said, 'you might not make it back alive. But Benten-sama of the Mirrored Lake is a relative of the goddess princess of Oki no Miya. If you send a message to Benten-sama and ask her, she'll return it for you.'"

"So Chiyomatsu, that must be why the women in your family took such care with the ceremonies on the twenty-third night."

"Well, I guess you could say our family was pretty careful about the ceremonies for the river and the moon. It was something that was left to us by our ancestors. They say the village of Amazoko had a special role. It carried out the rites that looked after the whole water system."

Kappei was snoring away where he was seated.

"Kappei. Kappei! It's getting time to head back down. Are you still dreaming? Come on, it's time to wake up. Wake up now."

Oshizu took off the short coat she'd been wearing and gave Kappei a shake as she draped it over his shoulders. The coat was well padded with cotton and still had a slight body warmth left in it. She wrapped it gently around his shoulders.

As if in a daze, he mumbled, ". . . Mimigawa."

Above the lake, the gentlest of air currents, like the brushing of a mulberry wood comb, began whispering softly.

ABOUT THE AUTHOR

ABOUT THE AUTHOR

Ishimure Michiko[1] has often been called the "Rachel Carson of Japan." Her best-selling documentary novel, *Paradise in the Sea of Sorrow: Our Minamata Disease* (1969), helped alert the world to the dangers of industrial pollution. Her writing has been praised for the beauty of its literary style as well as its important role in starting the environmental movement in Japan. Ishimure has published over forty volumes of writing in a wide range of genres including novels, historical and documentary fiction, poetry, autobiographical memoirs, children's books, essay collections, and a *Noh* drama. Her work is noted for its characteristic mythopoetic imagination, rooted in a powerful incorporation of local stories, dialects, and customs. Ishimure has continued to work as an activist on behalf of the victims of environmental disease and in related efforts to preserve local culture, community, and environment in the face of rapid modernization. She has been awarded literary prizes internationally and in her own country, including the prestigious Asahi Prize in 2002.

ABOUT THE TRANSLATOR

Bruce Allen is an Associate Professor in the Department of Foreign Languages, Juntendo University, Japan. Originally from Boston, he has lived in Japan for the past twenty-five years. His writing and translation has focused on American and Japanese environmental literature, particularly the work of Ishimure Michiko.

NOTE

1. The author's name is written in the Japanese order, with surname first, followed by the given name.